A Return Ticket

TOM DUKE

I'd like to thank my family for their patience, support and (in the face of all logic) constructive suggestions while I created this flight of fancy. I'd also like to extend my thanks to my fellow passengers who, without exception, endured my elbows while I typed on numerous long haul flights. Finally I'd like to thank Andrew Meehan for a great photograph used on the cover.

One

Jack Stevens was tired and feeling like he had a cold coming on. Fucking air travel. It always happened. A long-haul flight packed in economy next to some other middle-aged wage slave, whose career had also not yet delivered a business class seat and whose hands were probably coated in virus-infested nasal mucus. The result was some severe jet lag and a heavy cold imported from a random place, Frankfurt or Salt Lake City or wherever the neighbour was from. The jet lag would peak after two days with only inadequate packages of sleep, but the cold would wait until he had just started to recover, four days usually, before jumping in with both snotty feet.

And that is where Jack found himself. He had arrived in Sydney three days ago and actually had got some sleep last night. Well, five hours constituted a good night at this stage of the jet lag, he thought to himself, doing the maths to work out how long it was between 10pm and 3am.

Tomorrow the cold would be in full swing but he would still need to work. Not that he would get in trouble if he called in sick, but it would delay the install by at least the day he was out of action. In fact, maybe even more since the odds were better than even on Rick doing something stupid that would then take Jack another day to unpick.

So tomorrow, Thursday, would be a day where he would alternate between typing and blowing his nose. Type, blow, type, blow. Repeat. He would need a huge supply of tissues, he thought to himself. Truly massive, in fact. What was worse than trying to wipe away snot with a tissue that was already completely saturated and was falling apart? He could already imagine the look of undisguised repulsion that Cynthia would give him, as he fumbled for another unit of crumbling essence-of-contagion from his pocket. Cynthia was not a woman any man wanted to look bad in front of, but he didn't really have a choice.

"Another beer?" the trendy barman asked him, mouth smiling but eyes untouched by it. Jack had been staring blankly at the face of his phone. He knew he was only doing so in an unsuccessful bid to look less sad and lonely to the other inhabitants of the bar. Even given this honesty about yourself, it's hard to publicly embrace the fact that you have no friends.

"Absolutely," he replied, trying to inject some animation into his voice. Who was he kidding? The barman knew exactly what he was and so did all the other people in the bar.

"I'll take that for you," said the kid, who can't have been more than twenty, putting a new beer in a tall glass in front of him and heading off with the old glass and empty plate.

Jack was sitting at the bar in his hotel, getting some food, killing some time and taking on some amber anaesthetic to try and promote sleep. The hotel was a non-descript three star affair but was at least reasonably central. Rick had headed to bed thirty minutes before, claiming he didn't feel great. No doubt engaged in the same jet lag and foreign-virus process that Jack found himself in. Cynthia had declined to come out at all saying she felt "tired". And since they were the only two people Jack knew in this city, he was on his own.

Jack was a technician. A programmer. He worked for McArthur Security Ltd, who made and installed office security systems. McArthur was based in a little town called Fleet in England and whenever Jack was away from there, which was often, he missed it. Not that Fleet was anything special. Jack had no illusions about that. Many places he visited were nicer. Warmer, friendlier, much, much more scenic (not a lot of scenery you wanted to see near Fleet). Sydney, for example, Jack thought to himself. What a stunning city. Bathed in sunshine, with blue harbour and glass skyscrapers all glinting in the Southern sun. Beautiful, bronzed people strolling the streets laughing and looking like they were part of some projected lifestyle advert for washing powder or tampons.

But despite all this, it couldn't compete with his smallish, three-bedroom house just outside Fleet. Family is what counts, Jack knew. It's all that really counts. Jane and the three girls. That is why he would get up and type and blow tomorrow. Why he would do everything he could to get the install done by the numbers and get home on schedule in ten days. Why he would do the same in a few weeks' time to keep the family secure and the mortgage paid.

He looked round the bar. It was pretty well empty. The only other customers, two men in business casual, sat engaged in a conversation they didn't look like they were enjoying. One in particular looked uncomfortable, with big sweat stains on his pale blue shirt. It was quite hot in here, Jack realised. Normally these places were air-conditioned to simulate Greenland, but Jack was also sweating and even the young barman had a damp shine on his otherwise glossy exterior.

Jack blew his nose on the napkin that had been placed under his beer.

He took a big swig and mimed writing to the barman who didn't notice. The young guy was staring at the floor fiddling with the leather surfer bracelet he wore and looking morose. Jack had to wave his hand and eventually even come up with an embarrassed "Umm, excuse me," to attract his attention.

"I'm sorry, I wonder could I…"

"Oh, yeah. Sorry mate. Wasn't paying attention. To tell the truth I'm, well…" he trailed off, obviously deciding against sharing whatever he had been going to say, gave another smile which didn't touch his eyes, and turned to the cash register.

God these on-site jobs were terrible, Jack reflected. This hotel was about as lively as a morgue this evening. He was due to be in Sydney for two weeks, installing a new security system in a government office. It was a great contract for McArthur, Jack knew, but that didn't make it fun.

"This has got to go smoothly, Jack. It's vital. That's why I'm sending you,' Matt McArthur had said. It was bullshit, of course, but he always said it. They were all vital. Jack certainly couldn't remember Matt, who owned and ran McArthur Security, ever saying "This one's not important, Jack. Fuck it up if you like, I really don't care".

No. What he got, what he *always* got, was the pep talk. That said, Jack had seen the projected revenue from the new contract with the branch of the Australian government that dealt in agriculture supplements and it was certainly going to boost things at McArthur and allow them to take on a few extra staff.

"I've chosen Rick to go along with you." Matt was always keen to stress that decisions were his, even when they weren't. The actual reason was that Dave Corby, twice as competent as Rick, was on holiday.

"Rick's coming on well, so it should go OK. He did a good job in Edinburgh last month. And Cynthia is coming of course. She will deal with the customer so that you guys can focus on getting it in and tested. It's pretty well the McArthur A-Team." Jesus! Jack couldn't see the three of them donning welding gear and turning a minibus into an armoured tank to take out the bad guys. C-Team more like. The A-Team didn't work at McArthur.

"Timing is important on this one," Matt had said, another standard part of the pep talk. "I've asked Cynthia to really focus on the schedule. She'll be working really closely with the customer and with you two guys to make sure it happens on time."

Jack mentally translated this last statement even as Matt was still talking. In Jack's mind, Matt said something more along the lines of "Cynthia will be standing behind you drumming her fingers and asking how it is going every 90 seconds. She will also go out to lunch and allow the customer manager to flirt and dream before returning to ask you how it's going. You, of course Jack, will not be going out for lunch but Rick's real function is to go and get you a sandwich so you don't need to leave your desk. Rick will also run errands for Cynthia. She will then eventually take all the credit and I will give a small speech on your return to the workforce about what a success she made of it."

Not that Jack blamed Cynthia, whom he had nothing against. He well knew, in fact tribesmen in the Kalahari knew, that Matt was desperate to get into Cynthia's pants. Those same tribesmen also knew something Matt himself could not see. There was no danger.

He was three inches shorter and at least five stone heavier than the object of his desire and his mid-range Lexus and MD title would not make up for that. Matt's long-suffering wife, a small but friendly woman named Elinor who Jack actually rather liked, probably also knew both facts.

No, Cynthia understood that her power lay in Matt's hope, rather than his fulfilment. She was ambitious, of course, and reasonably competent, Jack was prepared to concede, and so she used the tools available to her. *Does she have share options?* Jack had wondered to himself, as Matt continued to pep. Matt kept promising them to Jack, but they had yet to materialise.

And so here he was. Stuck in a beautiful city with Rick, who he didn't really want to talk to, and Cynthia, who didn't really want to talk to Jack, spending ten hours a day debugging the door locks and security tags in a huge government building.

Jack finished his beer and decided that it was time to be in his bed. He really didn't feel too good. This cold was going to be a bad one, by the feel of his sinuses. He felt a little bit dizzy as well or maybe that was the beer. He'd only had two but they do say that your tolerance decreases as you get older.

Jack said goodnight to the barman, who muttered a response, fiddling with his wristband again.

Up until this part of his life, Jack had led an ordinary existence. And as part of that normal life he had had countless conversations. Chats, discussions, arguments and jokes shared with his fellow human beings. In that long, long line of verbal interactions that had made up Jack's ordinary life, the terse exchange with the barman seemed unremarkable. And it was unremarkable in almost all ways, except one. What made it special was that it was the end, the terminator, the full stop. It was the last in that normal life.

Two

On arriving in his room Jack didn't waste much time. He was unaware of the line he had just crossed and so simply got ready for bed. He stripped off and eyed himself critically in the mirror.

He was medium-height, strongly built, what people described as stocky. It gave him a physical presence that made him seem taller. That presence, as well as his tendency to few words, was what caused Jane to refer to him as 'the strong silent type'.

Jack, like so many desk pilots, found it hard to keep in the shape he had been as a younger man and now, approaching forty, he was definitely thickening a little at the middle. It could be worse, he thought to himself. His sandy coloured hair was still thick above his squarish face and the small amount of grey was hardly noticeable.

He, perhaps, wasn't looking his best right now though, he had to concede. His eyes were red, rimmed with substantial luggage below them and there was a drip on the end of his nose.

He gulped down a glass of water, refilled the glass, grabbed his phone and crawled into bed. He typed out a text to Jane saying he was heading for bed and that he loved her. He didn't think much about it as he pressed send, but his mind would, in the months to come, worry at that text message countless times. Like a tongue feeling a broken tooth, it would be with him. Did she get it?

He was, of course, oblivious to the significance. Would she be awake now? Doing the time difference calculation seemed too much like hard work, so he switched his phone to flight mode so that nobody could call him in the night (he was thinking of Matt – could almost hear his voice saying "Oh sorry, Jack. I forgot what time it was there. But now you're on I wonder if…") and checked the alarm was still set for 7am. The phone was new and he still didn't totally trust it. Thirty seconds later he was asleep.

When he woke he was drenched in sweat. His head was pounding and his mouth felt like a colony of rodents had been nesting in it. The room was pitch dark, but looking at his watch didn't seem worth the effort.

Water was a priority but, going for the glass he had left by the bed, he knocked it over.

"Fuck." It hadn't broken but water had presumably gone everywhere. Still in bed he felt around on the floor. The carpet was wet but he found the glass and heaved himself out of bed. His head started to spin wildly and before he knew it, he had crashed into the wall and dropped the glass. This time the sound was clear. It had smashed.

Jack stayed still, leaning against the wall and trying to regain some equilibrium. Slowly his balance returned, but his head was pounding worse than ever. Jesus, work was going to be a struggle in the morning.

He gingerly stepped back, hoping to avoid stepping on any of the glass. He felt that he should really switch a light on, but he couldn't remember where the switches were and the thought of bright light was not appealing. He slowly felt his way to the bathroom, where the light switch had a tiny glowing LED that cast just enough light for him to find the other glass without switching on the main light.

He filled it with the warm water that came out of the cold tap (or was the other one the cold tap? Jack couldn't really remember, or bring himself to care) and drank the contents twice. He then emptied his bladder, refilled the glass a third time and headed back to bed.

Once he was lying down again he realised that it was probably a good idea to turn the aircon down a few degrees. But that would involve getting out of bed again, which seemed problematic given the thumping in his head, and also the control was over near the smashed glass.

Too hard. He slept again.

When he woke again he knew something was wrong. With his eyes still shut he realised two things. He didn't have a clue where he was and he had the worst hangover of his life. And given that he had played rugby at university, it wasn't as if he didn't have extensive experience in that particular field, but this was surely the worst ever.

Eyes still shut, he tried to think back to what he remembered. Nothing came back to him, so he gingerly opened his eyes. What was that noise?

The room was dark but there was some light filtering through a gap in the curtains, making a small white sliver on the ceiling. He recognised the hotel room and the alarm noise his phone was making simultaneously. He didn't immediately reach for it. What the hell had happened last night? He must have had a crazy night out to feel this way. What had he done?

His mind seemed to be working on stand-by power, because it took him quite a while to realise that no, he hadn't been out drinking. That meant he must be ill.

Jack managed to reach his phone and shut the noise off. He also managed a few sips of water, although he spilt more than he drank. At least he didn't break the glass.

By now he was able to think clearly enough to realise that he was not going to work. No way. That meant he should phone someone, Cynthia he supposed, and tell her he wasn't going to make it. The thought of actually speaking to someone was daunting and he was not sure he would manage an intelligible croak. With relief it occurred to him that it was too early anyway. He could phone later.

Soon after that thought, he was asleep again.

The weekend before he left for Australia was much like any other in the Stevens' household. Rose, who was approaching ten, had gymnastics on Saturday morning. She had gymnastics almost every day these days. Jack and Jane had discussed many times whether it was a good idea to let her get drawn into the world of highly competitive sport at such a young age. Their friends were never slow to offer an opinion on the subject, but these opinions varied so wildly it was hard to draw anything from the wisdom of that particular crowd.

Some were strongly against. "You two should limit her involvement because she'll miss out on her childhood. You mark my words she'll end up disappointed. They *all* do. There'll always be someone better and she'll regret spending so much time in the gym when she should have been with her friends."

On the other side "It's *so* exciting. You *must* do everything you can to make sure she has the best possible chance. She'll never forgive you if you don't make sure she reaches her full potential."

Luckily, Jane and Jack were in agreement on how to deal with it. While Rose wanted to go to gymnastics then they would take her. They would provide what she needed, within reason, and be supportive, but they would not drive it themselves. Nor was there any need to. Jack found it slightly intimidating that his nine-year-old daughter could be so motivated and so competitive. He himself had enjoyed sport as a younger man and been quite good at it. But he had never had the competitive drive that some of his team-mates displayed and which took some of them forward into the world of club rugby, and which now his daughter displayed. The twins, Daisy and Sophie, were now seven and so alike that only family members could tell them apart. Their teacher had asked that they dress differently so that she knew which was which and so Daisy had special permission to wear a big daisy badge on the front of her red school sweatshirt. The girls were eager to please, but had admitted that they had, on more than one occasion, swapped the badge on to Sophie in the playground and gone through the day role-reversed. There was no malice in it, no test to cheat on or advantage to be gained. They had giggled as they recounted it over supper one evening.

"And Mrs Featherstone never even knew! She kept saying 'Daisy do this, Daisy do that'," Sophie told them with glee. "And I kept doing what she said and she didn't know and neither did anyone on my reading table." Neither Jack nor Jane had been cross with the girls, although Jane had produced a half-hearted "You really shouldn't do that again, girls. If you do I'll have to stick the badge to your forehead, so it's there forever." The girls giggled again. They knew Jane's cross voice and that certainly wasn't it.

On the Saturday before leaving for Sydney, Jack had made the twins come with him to drop Rose at the gym, and then on to do some chores. Rose was ready to leave fifteen minutes early but they were still a bit late because the twins wouldn't turn the TV off . When they did, it seemed to take them forever to match shoes with feet and unite all eight items. Rose gave him a very grown-up peck on the cheek before getting out of the car and he then headed to Homebase. He needed to buy some tap washers, so that he could stop that tap dripping.

"It's driving me mad," Jane had told him that morning, "and so if you want to come back from Australia to a sane wife, you have to sort it out today."

"That's all I am to you, someone to do DIY and bring home the bacon," Jack had said, not meaning a word of it.

"Quite right," Jane had replied, quick as a flash. "Are you trying to tell me you have other uses?"

"Not in front of the children," Jack said, even though there were no children in the room, and they had both chuckled contentedly.

So the day was spent in domestic bliss, despite the feeling of doom that Jack always felt before he went away. It was similar to the feeling he got when the end of a good holiday was looming, only without the holiday. Jane seemed to handle it better, but then she was only going to be separated from one quarter of her immediate family, Jack himself, whereas for him it was a hundred percent separation.

The day seemed to skip by, and before he knew it he was checking that he had his phone and passport as the taxi drew up outside on Sunday morning. It was early, but Jane had come down in her dressing gown.

"Have a good trip. I hope it goes well. Come home safely." The words she always spoke, in the same matter of fact way.

"I will. I love you," he had replied, before jumping in the taxi to Heathrow and a 24-hour flight via Singapore to Sydney.

When Jack next became fully aware, things had changed again. His headache had miraculously reduced and he knew where he was almost immediately. The light through the gap in the curtains was brighter, so it was obviously full daylight. He did have a case of bed-spins and his eyes hurt to move, but on the whole he thought he felt a bit better.

It was when he decided to reach for the phone to text Cynthia and say he was ill that he got the shock. His body just plain did not respond. He sent the signals but it was as if he was crushed under a massive weight. He could feel his limbs, but he couldn't move them.

Oh God, he wondered, am I paralysed? Do I have locked-in syndrome? His whole life his body had been doing his bidding and so this paralysis struck him with a fierce and cold fear.

He summoned all his will and directed his arm to move. The fear was excruciating, worse than any pain. Tears welled in his eyes when he moved his arm. It felt like it weighed a hundred kilos, but it moved. Exerting himself like he was lifting weights, he rolled over and got hold of his phone, but a massive wave of nausea swept over him and he lay for minute or two panting and clutching the phone to his chest, as the room seemed to swoop about him.

The nausea receded a little as the rollercoaster came to a slightly less wild piece of track. He got the phone off flight mode and waited for it to acquire the network. The screen was so bright in the dark room he had to screw his eyes up against the glare. No signal. Fucking thing. Why did technology always let you down when you really needed it to work?

Jack realised that he also had a raging thirst. Moving like he was a hundred, he managed to swap phone for full water glass, locating it by the glare of the phone screen. He got a few sips but coughed a lot up and spilt a lot too. He just had to drink, but there was no way he could walk in the dark. He fumbled clumsily for the light switch but, when he clicked it, nothing happened. Double fuck. In a moment of clarity he recognised that the LED on the TV was also off. That meant the power was out.

It took him what seemed an age to crawl into the bathroom, clutching the empty glass. He kept needing to stop and lie still to let the nausea subside a little. The effort involved was just ridiculous, but eventually he hoisted himself up to actually stand and fill the glass. Even in the darkness he could tell that it was just a trickle of water coming out of the tap. Obviously the pumps needed power. He was going to need water so he got back down on the floor, shut the plug on the bath and turned the tap on. He lay back down and waited for it to fill.

He was woken by the cold water on his face, which was pressed against the tiles of the bathroom floor. The bath was overflowing in the dark. He got the tap turned off, although the T-shirt and boxers he was wearing were now soaked. He drank another glass of water filled from the brimming bath and crawled back into the bedroom. There was more light in here but that just showed him that the bed was high up. He needed to rest before he got on the bed and phoned Cynthia and so he lay still.

The next time he became aware, he knew time had passed. There was still some light coming in through the window. What time was it? He had no idea and moving to look at his watch seemed too hard. He became aware of a strong smell in his nostrils. Vomit. Oh God, he'd been sick on the carpet. And not just vomit. He'd soiled himself as well. *Fucking hell,* he thought to himself, *this is serious. I need help. I need a doctor.*

If anything, movement was even worse than before. He got his phone down off the table, but lay retching in his own filth for a minute before he could look at it. Still no signal. Must be related to the power cut. More effort and more retching and he propped himself up to get the hotel phone. No dial tone. All he managed was to lie back down and roll over away from the worst of the mess he had made before he let himself slip away again.

Looking back, Jack could not have said how many times he woke up, crawled across the soaking floor of the bathroom, drank from the brimming bath using the glass, which was on the floor, and crawled back out on to the carpet. Several times he found his bladder full, and he just emptied it where he lay. He was sick a few times as well, waking up in a pool of vomit. The effort to move was enormous, but the thirst a powerful imperative. The levels of light seemed to vary as well; sometimes very dark, sometimes twilight in the room.

Each time he woke he looked at the TV and the bathroom light switch for the pinpoint of the LED. Nothing. How long would this power cut last and why didn't anybody come looking for him? His phone was on the floor by the bed, he thought, although he couldn't see it in the gloom. Far too far away, anyway.

Was he afraid that he might die? That was a question he would wonder about when he would look back on those hellish hours in the Sydney Harbour Marriott. Just because he couldn't remember being afraid, doesn't mean he hadn't been at the time. Does it?

Jack felt that he had a strong will to live. Especially since becoming a father. He wanted to take part in the girls' milestones. Be there when they passed exams, got a driving licence, a job, married. He wanted to dandle his grandchildren on his knee as much as the next man.

But that was not what he remembered. His memory was of suffering, but a strange calm and acceptance. He ceased to care that he was plastered in disgusting substances that his body had expelled and ceased worrying about what would happen. His mind seemed to turn off those higher functions. When he was awake, all he did was focus on getting a drink of water from the bath and whatever bodily function was pressing. The only higher piece of analysis he managed was to check the TV light for power. Somehow the power was why nobody had come to help him and so it became his focus and talisman. When the LED glowed again he would be alright.

Eventually he woke and the effort to move didn't induce quite the same gut-wrenching nausea. He was still absurdly weak, but the crushing weight that had pinned him down seemed a little reduced.

He crawled across to the window, actually crawled rather than simply dragging his prone body, and twitched the curtain back a little.

Blinding sunshine lanced through the gap, dazzling him brutally. He crawled back round the bed and found his phone near several unspeakably disgusting stains on the green carpet. It wouldn't switch on. The battery must be flat. Sitting on the floor he clicked the light switch a few times but nothing happened. The phone still emitted no dial tone.

Fuck it. He was going to have to go out and get some help. The light from the gap he had created was bright enough to see the state he was in. His red T-shirt and blue boxer shorts were heavily stained with vomit and worse. His skin was also smeared. Even at the time, he recognised that what was happening to him was far more important than a bit of embarrassment and that the urge to clean himself up before finding help was irrational.

But despite that knowledge, he did not want anybody to see him like this. He struggled slowly out of the clothes. Would the shower work? It would involve standing up so instead he crawled into the bathroom, let some water out of the bath plug so that it wasn't so full and slithered over the edge and into the cold water. It made him gasp, but felt wonderful. It was pretty dark in the bathroom but he could see enough to rub at the worst smearings. After a few minutes he started to get cold, but his limbs felt a bit stronger and so he sat on the edge of the bath and levered himself up on to his feet, steadying himself on the sink counter.

He felt disproportionately pleased with this achievement. Partly because it showed he was recovering and partly because it meant he didn't have to crawl through the filth on the floor.

He shuffled out into the bedroom and to his suitcase, still on the stand and not yet unpacked. He managed to find a clean T-shirt and a pair of jeans. He was cold now from the bath, so he took them across to the bed, which was miraculously stain-free, and snuggled naked under the wonderfully clean and warm duvet.

Waking this time was altogether different. Jack felt like he was actually waking up, rather than just regaining consciousness. He rolled over to assess how he felt and the answer was he felt weak, but much more normal. Not nauseous and the room didn't spin.

He swung his legs out of bed and surveyed the ruined carpet. He'd certainly kick up a fuss if the hotel tried to charge him – it was their power outage that had trapped him in the room for…how long?

He looked at his watch. 10.30. Must be in the morning, because daylight was flooding through the gap in the curtains. He'd kind of expected it to be evening because he felt he had missed most of Thursday but realistically this meant it had been longer than he thought and it must now be Friday morning. He'd missed a day of work and was going to miss today as well and so the whole trip was going to be extended by two days. Great. He tried to text Jane but his phone was flat and wouldn't switch on and the TV had no red eye and so he wasn't going to be able to charge it.

He got up but rather shockingly his knees buckled and he found himself kneeling in something his body had earlier expelled.

"Crap." He spotted the accuracy of this observation only after the word was out of his mouth.

Gingerly rising, and feeling shaky, Jack made his way through to the bathroom. He tried to walk on clean bits of carpet but it wasn't easy. There wasn't much that he hadn't re-coloured.

Nothing came out of the bathroom taps, so he dipped a flannel in the murky water in the bath (there'd be no drinking that now), wiped down his knees and then opened the bath plug.

Next he got himself dressed. Slowly, because he still felt pretty shaky, but eventually he was wearing jeans and a T-shirt with his feet shoved into trainers he'd packed in the hope of getting time for a gym visit.

Time to go and find out what the hell was happening in this powered-down hotel.

Three

As he opened the door, it occurred to Jack that he didn't have his key card. So instead of heading out he stood in the doorway. He could just stop someone in the corridor and ask them to get some help.

After a minute he lost patience.

"Hello," he tried to shout, but even to him it sounded like a raspy croak. He tried a few more times.

"Hello. Hello. I need some help. Can someone help me, please." Silence.

Keeping the door open with his foot, he looked up and down the long corridor. One way it was pitch dark, but the other had some light coming round a corner where there must be a window.

"Help me. I need help. Please. Somebody." His voice was getting stronger but the results were no better.

"Help me. Please. Fuck." The last word was under his breath rather than shouted down the corridor. It was true that not many guests stayed in their rooms during the day. Especially in a hotel like the Marriott, which was aimed squarely at people like Jack, Rick and Cynthia – business travellers. So either these rooms were empty or the doors had pretty good soundproofing. Probably the former.

It was also quite hot in the corridor. No aircon, so no wonder the guests hadn't stuck around.

He retrieved his keycard from his suit trousers, which were hanging in the cupboard, but holding the plastic card in his hand gave him another thought. Would the locks even work with no power? Did they have batteries or were they on the mains? Although Jack knew about locks he didn't know about hotel locks. McArthur didn't do hotels.

Jack reckoned that they probably ran off mains power and that meant the hotel was deserted. You couldn't stay in a hotel if you couldn't open the door to your room. No wonder there was nobody answering his rather pathetic shout.

He retrieved his wallet and also a pair of clean socks in a ball. He used the socks to wedge the door slightly open. He didn't want it to be too obvious, his laptop was, after all, still in there, but he didn't want to lock himself out either.

Satisfied he headed for the stairwell that he had noticed by the lifts, which was the area lit by the window.

The stairwell presented another problem. It was pitch dark with the only light coming through the door that Jack opened to get in there. He couldn't work out how to wedge the door open. In the end he crossed quickly to the railing while the door was shutting, leaving him holding the metal banister in utter blackness.

"Shouldn't there be some kind of emergency lighting?" he said aloud to the dark. It took him a while to feel his way down from the 6th floor. Ground was zero, so that meant six floors – twelve flights of stairs – holding the warm metal railing and feeling for the next step. He deliberately didn't count steps in each flight, in case it made him lose count of the flights. After twelve, he let go of the railing and felt for the door. It was where he expected and he emerged into dim light. Round the corner and he was in the lobby.

It was deserted. Not a soul. Nobody behind the reception desk, which meant he was right. No power meant no guests. The hotel had been evacuated. Presumably someone had come round and banged on the door while he was out for the count, but he had been too ill to hear.

"Hello, is anybody here?" he called as loudly as he could. Not that loud, to be honest.

"Earth to Marriott staff. Come in Marriott staff. Are you there, Marriott staff?" Insulting, but there was an undercurrent of anger starting now. They had left him festering in pool of his own output and buggered off to God-knows-where. Surely they would leave someone here to mind the place.

"Is. There. Anybody. Fucking. Here?" No answer.

He crossed to the reception desk, went behind the counter and picked up the phone. It was dead. He pressed the cradle switch a few times, but no sound came out of the handset.

"Bollocks." He wanted to hear Jane's voice, even if it was sleepy and complaining that he had woken her up in the middle of the night, but the world seemed determined that he wouldn't achieve that aim.

There was a sofa by the wall in the dim lobby and Jack sat on it. He was sweating and perhaps a little freaked out by the lack of response.

Well, he had no choice now. Go outside and find out what was going on. But as he sat there his stomach rumbled and he realised he hadn't eaten for two days. He headed for the restaurant.

His reasoning was that if they were going to leave him, a paying hotel guest, then he deserved a bit of light looting. In to the kitchen, but it was pitch dark with no windows. How was he going to find anything in here?

Instead he went down to the lobby and into the bar. Also totally deserted, but under the bar were fridges that were stocked with various bottled drinks. He grabbed a bottle of Lucozade and drank it all. The fizz hurt but it tasted *so* good. He left the bottle on the bar, took another and, sipping at it, headed to the main doors on to the street.

Up until this point the crisis had, in Jack's mind, been about him. He had been horribly ill for a day and he had been left alone in the hotel. He had not been fed or looked after as you expect when you travel on company expenses. As soon as he opened the swing door to the little semi-circular driveway that the hotel boasted, he stopped thinking about himself and realised that something big was happening.

The silence was palpable. You would expect silence in a deserted hotel, but no city street sounded like this. There was a very gentle rustling from the trees that were on Pitt Street, but that was literally all. The driveway itself had no cars in it, which was unusual on its own, but Jack took the few steps onto the actual street and looked up and down it in astonishment.

There was no sound, no movement. Jack's head swivelled again and again to look each way as he shuffled out into the middle of the road. His eyes hunted for movement but, aside from the gentle swaying of the trees there was nothing. It looked normal, cars were parked in the shady street in an orderly way, but none were moving.

"What the fuck has happened?" His voice sounded strange in his ears - the only human sound.

What could have happened? The city had clearly been evacuated. Would they do that for a power cut? No, Jack didn't think so. In fact it was probably the other way round. They had turned off the power because nobody was here. But why? Sydney was a major city, a humming centre of commerce and human activity.

It would have to be some hazard to the population and a few popped into Jack's mind. A hurricane warning? Well, the gentle breeze ruffling the trees didn't seem too threatening and even that would not cause total abandonment, surely. No this was some kind of unheard of threat. It had to be a terrorist thing. A threat of a nuclear bomb, perhaps. Was he about to be smashed to atoms by an atomic fire-ball, like Sarah Connor in The Terminator? Jesus.

Or some kind of biological threat? Was he even now breathing deadly, engineered spores that would multiply in his lungs and leave him choking on the pavement? Well, if he was then it had already happened, so there was nothing to be done.

Jack walked down towards the harbour, walking in the middle of the street and fighting the urge to move on to the pavement. Past a big office building on his right, silent behind reflective glass. Shops on his left all shut up. Metal shutters over some, some just silent glass fronts. A jeweller, a souvenir shop, money changers, all totally silent. The jaunty flags on their posts swayed a little and the leaves rustled. There was even the odd tweeting of some antipodean bird. But nothing else.

Jack peered up side streets as he passed. Same story. Down at the end of the street was an open area with a Starbucks on one side and a pub on the other, both silent. Jack dropped the bottle he had now finished into a litter bin. No point in making a mess.

Suddenly the corner of Jack's eye was caught by movement down a side street. He looked intently, but the street seemed still again. He was sure he had seen something move. And there it was again. A ginger cat making its way quietly along the street, close against the building. It spotted Jack and stopped, eyeing him curiously. Then it set off again, approached the junction with Pitt Street and turned south, back towards the Marriott. It didn't spare Jack another glance. He debated going after it, but what was the point. Even if it did let him catch it he could hardly interrogate the animal on what was going on. No, he would have to find that out for himself.

Moving on, he spotted a payphone on the corner. He crossed to it and cursed as he felt in his trouser pocket for change but came up with only British money. He picked up the handset and held it to his ear, but heard nothing. The little LCD screen was blank. Once again he pushed the cradle switch, more in hope than expectation, but got no response. The power must be out at the exchange. A kind of pressure to speak to someone, ideally Jane but any human voice would be welcome, was building inside Jack. He found himself jiggling the switch on the cradle with far more force than it needed, and had to consciously stop himself from slamming the dead receiver back into its mounting. He took a deep breath.

"Get it together, Stevens," he muttered to himself.

Up ahead was a raised causeway, some kind of expressway, Jack supposed. He couldn't see on to the road it held but the lack of sound told the tale. He walked underneath the causeway and stood looking at the harbour. It was beautiful, with the sun sparkling on the water. Purple blossoms moved in the park and the famous bridge and opera house rose proudly on either side of Circular Quay. But it was utterly deserted. Wide expanses of walkway that were usually teeming with tourists seemed vast in their absence. An enormous cruise ship loomed on the Quay, but overlooked no people.

Jack swore under his breath. How big an area had been evacuated? He couldn't see movement on the other side but would he be able to from here? Certainly no boats moved on the piece of harbour he could see.

"Right, get yourself moving, Stevens," he told himself. He had to make a plan. But what were his options? Broadly, they were stay put or get moving, he supposed. Staying put would involve finding something to eat and sitting in the sun. But Jack's mind worried at the reason for the evacuation. The people would only have left because of some extreme danger and logic told him that he was now in that danger. So moving it was. But first he needed to eat something.

He retraced his steps and looked around. The Starbucks might be an option, so he walked over to it and surveyed the front. It had a glass door that he tried. Locked.

Could he break in? Nobody could blame him, he decided, so he put his foot on one side of the door, gripped the handle on the other and pulled as hard as he could, which was not that hard. The door, which was only secured at the bottom, gave way much more easily than he had expected and Jack staggered back.

OK then. Inside it was dim but Jack headed behind the counter and surveyed the selection of food. He chose a blueberry muffin and, ripping it to pieces with his hands, he stuffed it unceremoniously into his mouth. And another, orange flavoured this time. They were sticky and a bit stale, but tasted fantastic. One more blueberry and he was slowing down. That should keep him going. He turned to the sink and water came out of the tap. Great. He washed his hands and face so they weren't sticky.

There was a green phone hanging on the wall next to the shiny metal coffee machine, but when Jack picked up the handset it was just another lifeless piece of plastic. He pressed some buttons, just in case. Was it 999 or 911 here in Australia? Or something different? Jack had no idea, but dialling both numbers gave the same results he'd already achieved. There, however a white dish on the counter, which was a quarter full of small change that customers had left as a tip. Jack emptied it out and picked up all the silver coins, pocketing them and sweeping the rest back into the dish. He may as well add robbery to the looting he had already done. He then grabbed a bottle of juice out of the dark fridge and headed back on the street. His first ever burglary had gone well.

The food had made him feel a lot better; the sugar from the muffins was kicking in quickly. The shaky feeling he had had was receding.

He still didn't feel strong, but he could walk.

He walked back to the payphone and picked it up. Although it was still dead he fed some coins into the slot. They fell straight through into the reject tray with a metallic clatter. He tried again with the same result. Despite the machine's inability to retain his stolen money, he dialled 999 followed by 911. He dialled his home phone number with the UK country code on the front. Nothing. He dialled Jane's mobile number.

Jack knew that he wasn't being rational here, but couldn't really help himself. He had to speak to someone and this pressure was starting to override his logic processes. He had to let Jane know what was going on – that he was stuck in an evacuated city on his own. But the phone remained a lifeless piece of plastic, as his rational mind knew it would, since the exchange to which it was connected had no ability to push the coded batches of electrons, that he so desperately needed, down the wires.

After the second pointless attempt to dial Jane's mobile he lost the battle to feign calmness and slammed the receiver back on the cradle, emitting a wordless groan. He rubbed his face, fingers rasping over stubble, shutting out the world for a moment and trying to marshal his thoughts. Nothing was working here. His only option was to head out of the evacuated zone and find people and a connection to the outside world.

But which way, he asked himself. And what did he need? Jack didn't know this area very well, since he'd only been in Sydney a few days and they had just got a taxi to the office each morning. So what he needed was a map, or even better a GPS, and he knew where there just might be one.

Now, what room had Rick been in? Seventh floor. 721 or 731 Jack thought back to their conversation in the bar last night. No, two nights ago he reminded himself. Could he force the door? He reckoned he could, so back in through the lobby of the Harbour Marriott, into the dark stairwell and then counting flights in the blackness. Fourteen flights took a while and Jack was panting and sweating hard by the time he reached the seventh floor, with just a hint of the dizziness and nausea returning.

The door from the stairwell opened - he had wondered if it might not - and he took a few moments to recover before he found himself in front of room 721 in the dim corridor.

He mustered his energy and delivered a good solid kick. No result initially, but the third did it and the door sprang open with a crash.

It was bright inside with the curtains open but the room was empty. Not made up, obviously a guest had stayed, but they had left. There were no personal effects and in particular Rick's black rucksack was not there. Clearly there had been time in the evacuation to pack up luggage and take it.

"Fuck." Again his voice sounded loud. It was the only word he seemed to be using recently.

The fact that there were no signs of panic in the room, the bed roughly made and a towel hung up on the peg, made Jack wonder about something. He crossed to the window and looked at his watch. It was now approaching midday, but it was the date he was looking at. The 14th. Was that Friday? He had flown out here on Sunday 7th of November and so that made the 14th... a Sunday?

That can't be right, he told himself, but he was sure he had left home on the 7th. He even remembered discussing with Mary, the receptionist in McArthur, whether he should fly on Saturday 6th and have a day to recover. Mary had looked amazed that anybody would pass up a weekend in Sydney, but Jack would rather spend the Saturday at home.

So if today was Sunday, that meant he had spent *three days* locked up in his room. Jesus, he had been even worse than he had thought. No wonder he hadn't heard anybody knocking.

Was it worth checking room 731? Probably not, but he was here now so he may as well smash in that door as well.

He was getting better at it. Two kicks this time. 731 was dark, but the smell hit him immediately. Not unlike the smell in his own room, he recognised. He crossed the room, opened the curtains and surveyed the room.

It turned out that room 731 was indeed Rick's room, and not 721. Jack could tell this from that fact that Rick was still in it, lying sprawled on the bed and was quite obviously dead.

Four

That he was dead, Jack had no doubt. He had never seen a corpse before, but Rick's stillness and wide, staring eyes were enough to tell him that he had seen one now.

Dressed in only a pair of stained boxer shorts, the body was sprawled on its back and there was vomit on pretty well everything in range.

Jack approached slowly and wondered what he should do. In the end he reached out and felt Rick's neck with one finger, looking for a pulse. More because he had seen people on TV do that, rather than in any genuine expectation that Rick's heart was still beating.

The flesh was not cold, which gave him a shock, but then the room itself was quite hot, so that was presumably why. Not cold but it felt rubbery, like this was actually a life-size model of Rick, rather than the corpse of the man himself. Rubbery and, well, dead.

Jack swallowed, feeling suddenly nauseated by the smell and sight of Rick's messy end. He hastily retreated to the corridor to think about what he should do. What about Cynthia? Her room was on the 9th floor.

Jack only knew this because on the second night they had all had dinner together and, after the meal, Cynthia had coolly declined

Rick's invitation for a drink and Jack, not wanting to sit and talk about work with Rick, had also said he wanted to get some sleep. So the three of them had ridden up in the same lift and Jack had noticed which button Cynthia's long finger had pressed.

Back to the stairwell and another four dark flights upwards before Jack was on the right floor. Where to start? Jack, being a logical person, went to the end of the corridor and started at 901.

First kick this time. The room was totally empty and made up. Ready for a new guest who certainly would not be arriving today, Jack reflected. So. On to 902.

"Oh God!" The smell told him the story before he even saw the large, fat, naked man who was dead on the floor of the bathroom. Jack didn't feel *his* neck. He didn't want to step in the congealing mess that covered the small bathroom's floor.

903 was empty, but 904 contained an elderly couple who had died together on the bed. The man's liver-spotted hand rested on his wife's scrawny arm. Their heads were turned towards each other. Jack felt tears prick his eyes as this scene pierced him. He heard his own breathing catch. *Don't lose it*, he told himself.

Out in the corridor he tried to compose himself. His brain couldn't process what he had seen, couldn't put reason to it. Jack thought of himself as a logical individual, always analysing and trying to understand the world around him, but in the horror of what he was seeing this faculty was totally overwhelmed. He didn't know what this meant and was unable to consider implications.

He sobbed out loud, tried to stop but was incapable of holding back more.

With tears still streaming down his face he went on to the next room. And the next. And the next.

He found Cynthia in room 933. The worst of the sobbing had subsided, but he still needed to wipe his eyes as he stared down at her. In the thirty three rooms he had been into, he had found maybe five or six that were empty. The rest had been occupied by corpses. Mostly alone, nearly all with some level of vomit, or worse, permeating the room with a nauseating smell. All stone dead.

Cynthia was one of the tidier bodies. She had been sick over the side of her bed, but she lay on her side on un-soiled sheets. She was naked, her slim body curled as if in pain, but her face looked calm. Jack wiped his eyes. There had been enough discussion amongst the young men at McArthur on what Cynthia would look like naked, but now, looking at her small but slightly drooping breasts and rounded curves, Jack almost dropped to his knees with the weight of what he was seeing. In the end all he did was cover her still form with the bed sheet and retreat to the corridor. Once out of the room he sank to the floor and cried again.

An hour later Jack was striding south along Pitt Street in the sun and, although he couldn't yet say he was feeling better, he could say that he was, at least, starting to function.

He still couldn't quite decide who it was he had been crying for on the floor of the ninth floor corridor. Was he sad for Cynthia, Rick and the touching old couple, or was he sad for himself because he was alone in an evacuated city, thousands of miles from his home? Probably a bit of each.

In the end, he had started thinking enough to realise that his original plan was still the best one. He now knew why the city had been evacuated, but he still needed to find his way back to civilisation. He pictured road-blocks and troops in Hazmat suits forcing him to the ground to be taken into quarantine. ("Sir, get down on the ground with your hands behind your head. Eagle Two this is checkpoint five. We've got another one.").

He had gone back down to Rick's room and retrieved the item he originally came for, which was a global Garmin unit, which had, allegedly, maps for the whole world. Rick had been proud of this device and, while Jack had his doubts about the accuracy of its maps for Mongolia or Brazil, he had already seen it working perfectly well in Sydney.

The battery was charged and, on impulse, Jack had also retrieved the car charger cable and windscreen mount that were in Rick's laptop bag with the Garmin.

He had then gone down to his own room, emptied his own laptop rucksack of work paraphernalia and replaced them with clothes and toiletries. He didn't need his McArthur laptop, but he did need his phone and he took its charger as well. Top priority was going to be getting in touch with Jane.

He had then headed back down the stairwell and left the Harbour Marriott and its gruesome stock of dead bodies behind. He started to walk south along Pitt Street, away from the harbour. He spotted another payphone and crossed the street to check whether it was alive. It was not, but Jack reasoned that at some point he might cross a boundary to a different exchange that might be powered; and so each time he passed one of the frequent booths, he lifted the handset, listened briefly and almost defiantly left the lifeless object dangling on its metallic cable.

His plan, such as it had formed so far, was to walk until he came to wherever the perimeter had been set up.

"So how far is it?" he asked himself out loud. He had no way of knowing, but he reckoned that it was unlikely to be less than five miles. In fact, giving it a bit more thought, it was likely to be quite a bit more than that, since with an epidemic as severe as this they would have had to be careful. It could be as much as fifty or a hundred miles.

Which he was certainly not going to walk this afternoon. So he had to find a vehicle. He also kept an eye open for other survivors. Even thinking the word moved Jack to a different place in his mind. He was now a survivor. And there must be others, so he should look out for them. Maybe he was late to this particular party. Had all the others already made this trek?

Jack understood very well how bell curves worked, but where was he compared to the mean time to yomp out of Sydney? Was he one of the first to recover, with the buildings he walked past peopled with other survivors still too weak to get moving? On that thought, should he have kept searching the Harbour Marriott for survivors? A wave of guilt swept over him. He had searched half of one floor and given up. At the time, after a crushing succession of dead bodies, he had reasoned that, extrapolating from what he had found, he would simply smash in a few hundred doors and find a few hundred corpses, minus the empty rooms.

He stopped walking and half turned.

If he went back would he find people? He had no way of judging. He didn't know the survival rate of this plague and he didn't know the average recovery rate. Maybe nobody other than him had survived in the Harbour Marriott. Or maybe they had but had already left. Or maybe they had and were still lying in their rooms.

He had been walking for about fifteen minutes.

"I have to go back." This talking to himself was becoming a bit of a habit.

But first he needed to eat. By chance he had stopped next to a City Convenience Store – Open 24 Hours, it said, but it was closed now. He had a go at forcing the door, but it felt extremely solid, so he walked around the side and looked through the window. He didn't fancy kicking that in, the plate glass would be deadly. So he walked twenty yards up the street and wheeled a large green wheely bin down to the window. Although the bin was empty, it was with some difficulty that he hoisted it up on to his shoulder and heaved it through the window.

The result was a shockingly loud crash, which echoed around the street. As the chimes of falling glass died away, Jack looked around to see if the noise had brought anybody running, but no. Pitt Street was silent once again.

The inside of the shop was dim and warm, but he made a meal of a couple of malt loaves, which he simply ripped into chunks and ate. When he had finished he went behind the counter and had a good hunt around, but didn't find what he was looking for. Car keys (or maybe van keys) were what he really needed. Jack didn't rate his chances of hot-wiring a modern car and so if he didn't find keys he had no transport.

Well, wheels would have to wait. With his stomach full, a half litre bottle of Mountain Dew in his hand and another two in his rucksack, he set off back towards the harbour. He was resolved to search the whole hotel. If he found someone alive, he would take them with him, whatever it took, to the edge of the evacuated zone. If he didn't, well, he couldn't search the whole city, so he would stop when he had finished the Harbour Marriott.

Two and a half hours later Jack was sitting in one of the chairs in the hotel lobby, drinking another of those bottles of Mountain Dew. He was shattered, emotionally and physically.

He had got back to the hotel with a clear idea that he was doing the right thing. He knew he would find it hard to live with himself if he just ran to save his own skin, because that was less effort. So he had tackled the familiar dark staircase with a sense of purpose. He had headed up to the top floor and starting kicking in doors.

About 200 doors later, that sense of purpose had well and truly evaporated. Both his ankles were aching and his reserves had all but run out. As he progressed through his gruesome, self-appointed task he had kept count of the corpses. It seemed only right to know how many people had died and the answer was 197. Before today Jack had never seen a dead body and now he had seen 197 of them. *So far*, he reminded himself. And only one solitary living human in the hotel. Himself.

He was limping as he made his way back down the last few flights and into the dim lobby, collapsing into one of the chairs there. It was now approaching four o'clock, his watch told him. And although his body was telling him it wanted him to stay in the chair, the thought of staying where he was sent a chill to his core, despite the heat. A five minute rest and then he would have to get moving.

As he rested, he started to think about transport. This epidemic, if that is what it was, seemed to have decimated the biggest city in Australia and so it seemed less and less likely that the border of the evacuated zone was anywhere near the centre of Sydney. It could be hundreds of miles away. Certainly, a lot further than he could walk in what remained of the afternoon. He needed a vehicle.

Jack wasn't worried about the ethics of taking a car (as the incident with the City Convenience Store window had already demonstrated) but the practicalities were tougher. He needed keys.

As he mulled this over, the answer that came to him was obvious, and he immediately realised that he should have thought of it before. He headed back into the stairwell and up to the first guest room floor. After 20 minutes he had four sets of car keys, whose owners would not mind them being used. He had searched in trouser pockets, coat pockets and hand-bags and had left keys that looked personal, taking only hire car keys. His reasoning was that it was less likely that anybody would drive their own car to Sydney and stay in a hotel.

He made his way back downstairs once again, out into the street and then walked around the hotel until he found what he had hoped was there. In a small lane behind the Marriott was the entrance to the underground car park. And even better, it was open.

He entered the dark interior, which echoed to his footfalls. It was not large and was crowded with parked cars. Jack started pressing buttons.

The third set paid dividends. A grey Toyota Corolla answered his call with a flash of its hazard lights and the click of unlocking doors.

"Fantastic". Jack settled into the Toyota's interior. It all seemed so totally normal. The horror upstairs in the Marriott seemed immediately distant as he started the engine and adjusted the seat and mirrors. It was only after he had done this that it occurred to him that people driving behind him were unlikely to be an issue.

He started the engine, plugged in the satnav and mounted it on the window. He would like to charge his phone, but he only had a mains charger so there was nothing he could do about that.

"So where to?" he asked himself. He spent a few minutes scrolling around the maps on the satnav and eventually settled on Canberra as a destination. He hoped he wouldn't have to drive that far, but the Australian capital seemed like a sensible choice.

Jack eased the Toyota out of the cramped garage and set off.

Five

Driving down the empty road was almost more surreal than walking along it had been. Traffic lights were dark and Jack barrelled through junctions with hardly a glance to left and right. The first couple of times he couldn't help a lift of his foot and a small internal clench, but this past very quickly.

The GPS had yet to acquire a satellite lock but here, in the urban canyon of downtown Sydney, that wasn't a surprise.

Jack stopped at the City Convenience Store and did some more 'shopping'. He carried two carrier bags loaded mostly with junk food (this didn't seem the time to be worrying about his weight) and loaded them into the back of the Toyota that he had parked, or perhaps abandoned was a better term, right outside the door, which he had opened from the inside with ease.

He spent a few minutes scanning through the radio frequencies for, well, anything, but came up with nothing. This was, he admitted to himself, a bad sign. It was hard to see how silent radio bands could mean anything other than an enormous evacuated zone. Maybe he had a long drive ahead of him.

So, in the late afternoon sun, he found himself cruising through silent streets with only the sound of the Toyota in his ears.

He just about crashed the car when a voice suddenly spoke up.

"In one hundred metres, turn left on to Eddy Avenue." The Garmin lady had obviously acquired enough satellites to know where she was. It was a surprisingly emotional experience to hear a voice, after so much silence. Tears pricked his eyes again. He wiped them away and obeyed his only companion, veering through multiple lanes because he felt that at the moment a car crash would be a welcome interaction.

He was now out in the suburbs and had opted for ground level streets rather than the freeway that Ms Garmin wanted him to take. The streets were still and silent. The only movement he had seen so far were several cats and even a dog with a collar, making its way somewhere in a purposeful way. Jack wasn't tempted to stop for the pets and was running through some mental calculations. The Garmin was telling him he had more than 250 km to drive to get to Canberra and it estimated it would take him about three hours. The Toyota had just under half a tank of fuel. Jack actually had no idea how far he really needed to drive, but Canberra was the target he had set, so he should probably make a plan to get there. If he drove slowly he might just make it on that tank, but by the time he got there it would be dark. He didn't see how he could easily refill with fuel, given that there was no power, so the Toyota was throw away.

In fact, whatever speed he drove it would be dark when he got there, so he decided that he would push on, but stop in a town along the way to change vehicles – assuming he hadn't reached the edge of the evacuated zone before that.

At that point he came across his first seemingly abandoned car. Up until that moment the roads had been clear and the only cars had been neatly parked, but here was a large silver BMW four-wheel drive crashed into one of the parked cars at the side of the road. Jack drew up a few yards short and sat in the car for a few moments, just having a look at the scene. The BMW had hit the parked car head-on and, judging by the damage, it had hit it pretty hard. There were also short skid marks leading to the scene of the accident, which indicated that the driver had only seen the imminent crash just before impact, and the scene was liberally decorated with broken glass to which both cars had contributed. Jack could see that the driver's side door on the far side was open, but nobody was visible and nothing was moving.

He got out, approached the crash, and what he found was not pretty. There were two children in the back of the crashed car. The closer one, a boy with fair curly hair and an angelic face, was still a toddler, no older than two, and strapped in a car seat. The other child, presumably his sister, was a girl who must have been about five or six with dark straight hair and pretty pink dress. *About the same age as the twins*, Jack thought. She was flopped against the far door, lolling in her seat belt.

The stillness, as Jack peered through the unbroken window, was total. He looked for signs of breathing, but there was nothing. The rear door opened easily and he stepped back as several flies took off from the two children. One crawled out of the little boy's mouth as Jack watched. He forced himself to feel the boy's neck and almost snatched his hand away from the lifeless corpse and the rubbery feel of the dead flesh. The lack of pulse was not a surprise.

Jack walked around the back of the car intending to check the girl, but the first thing he found was the driver of the car. She was sprawled on the ground next to the BMW and looked no more alive than her children. She had probably been beautiful before this had happened to her, but her corpse was repellent in a way that nothing Jack had ever seen on a screen had been. She lay on her back with her blonde hair spread around her head. The eyes were staring blankly at the sky and her face was bruised and puffy. Her legs had several large grazes, which were revealed by her short skirt riding up over her thighs, and were crawling with flies.

Jack couldn't bring himself to check if the mother was alive, but he did open the rear door of the car. The girl fell out but was stopped from hitting the floor by the seat belt that was still around her. Jack did feel the little girl's neck that was as obviously lifeless as her brother's. He looked around, fighting the nausea that surged in his gullet.

After a few moments to compose himself by taking a few deep breaths and looking at the horizon, Jack walked decisively up to the front door of the house overlooking the scene of the crash. The front door was not locked and, moving like an automaton, Jack walked straight in and looked for copses. He found three. A man, skinny and naked, in a bedroom. An obese woman and a toddler on the floor of the bathroom. Jack didn't touch them, just walked straight out and on to the house next door.

This one was locked, but the door moved on the third kick and opened fully on the fourth. Four corpses. A good-looking couple in their forties and their two teenage daughters. All of them were undignified and messy in death. There was a bright pink phone next to the bed of one of the dead teenagers. Jack picked it up. The battery was flat. He replaced it and went to find the kitchen. He found two iPhones placed on an otherwise clear island in the large kitchen. The first was dead but the second switched on. It asked for a code but Jack pressed the "Emergency Call" button, despite the "No Signal" message at the top of the screen. Neither of the three digit emergency numbers he was trying worked. Pocketing the phone he moved on. There was a phone in the hall. Dead.

He checked three more houses and every single one contained dead people. Dead families, in fact. He also found three more phones with enough battery to switch on, but none had a signal. He kept them all.

He listened briefly to each house phone he saw, pressing a few buttons before walking away. He did all this without pausing or even thinking much, but after the fifth house he walked back to the Toyota, still parked near the crashed BMW, dumped his stolen phones on to the passenger seat, started the engine and headed straight for the freeway.

So for the next hour he just drove. He saw two more separately crashed cars on the freeway as he left Sydney, both had seemingly collided with stationary barriers, presumably as the drivers either lost consciousness or died at the wheel. Jack didn't stop at either crash site.

As the miles unrolled beneath his wheels, Jack's sense of unreality was gradually replaced by a different, more aggressive, feeling. His speed started to edge up from the 110 he had been doing until he was doing over 140 kph and then on up to nearly 160. He started to veer on purpose across the road, starting to test the limits of grip and stability of the Corolla. He couldn't even tell if he was having fun, or if this was simply an ebbing of his self-preservation instinct in some strange backlash to what he had witnessed that day. He deliberately drifted two wheels off the side of the road and then fought the wheel as the Toyota bucked and rumbled, before veering back on to the blacktop. Then the same on the other side of the road.

He backed off the speed a little, until he was doing a mere 100 kph and then bounced across the wide, flat central reservation, smashing a few small scrubby bushes, before arriving on the other carriageway with a cloud of dust spreading behind him.

Jack was just about to do the same thing back on to his original carriageway, when something large and brown bounded off the verge, on a collision course with the car. He wrenched the wheel to one side and the tyres screeched as he shot past a sizable kangaroo that had stopped in the middle of the carriageway. The car fishtailed wildly and, despite Jack's frantic efforts to regain control, went into a long skid, and finally came to a halt facing back the way he had come. Jack watched the kangaroo through a cloud of tyre smoke, as it hopped nonchalantly off the road, picked up some speed and bounded athletically across the other carriageway and into the wood beyond.

"Jesus Christ," said Jack, letting out a big breath as the car rolled forward.

"When it is safe to do so, make a U-turn and continue west on Hume Highway," suggested the Garmin lady.

He got the car turned around, but took it out of gear and got out. He sat on the bonnet and let the shakes subside.

"What the fuck were you thinking?" he berated himself. He certainly didn't want to wreck the car here, since it didn't seem like there was a whole lot of help to be had. He retrieved his stock of stolen phones and tried them all again with no success. There was still no signal on any of them. He replaced them and went back to sit on the bonnet for a few more minutes.

Once he felt a bit calmer he got back behind the wheel and got moving again, keeping the speed down. He crossed back to the left-hand carriageway, using an actual junction this time, so that he could he see the signs. He knew he was approaching somewhere called Goulburn, and it seemed as good a place as any to stop and find another vehicle. He was now down to less than a quarter of a tank and, just as he didn't want to crash, he didn't want to run out of petrol either. He doubted he had the strength for a long walk in this alien, deserted landscape, and it might be quite a while before the AA, or whatever they had in Australia, turned up.

Ten minutes later he was taking the exit to Goulburn, which swung left and then back right and up over the main highway. He took it at speed, glancing up and down Hume Highway as he crossed the fly-over. And as he sped off the bridge and into the trees something caught his eye off to the left, down on the highway. It took him a second to process what he thought he might have seen before he slammed the brakes on and, from the 110 kph he was doing, brought the Toyota to an abrupt halt.

"Were those headlights?" he asked himself, as he got the car into reverse and backed down the road. It seemed to take forever to cover the thinking-plus-stopping distance in reverse and by the time he had a clear view of the carriageway, the car he had spotted had already passed beneath the flyover. He could see its red taillights retreating fast up the carriageway.

Jack looked around desperately. How were you meant to get down on to that road? There didn't seem to be any obvious way, and so he executed a three-point turn, which had at least five points, on the narrow bridge and gunned the Toyota back the way he had come.

He sped back down the off-ramp and re-joined the main highway. The carriageways were slightly separated and so he couldn't see the other vehicle, which was being law-abiding on the left-hand carriageway. Suddenly a junction loomed and he wrenched the wheel over to send the Toyota screeching through the gap in the central reservation. Once on the east-bound carriageway, he put his foot to the floor and tore off in pursuit.

It took him less than a mile before he saw the car again and not much further before he was coming up behind it. He eased off the accelerator and flashed his lights, which had been off so far. The car ahead, a large four-wheel drive, noticeably wobbled as the driver noticed him and they both slowed in unison. He came to a halt about 20 yards behind the vehicle, a red Volvo four wheel drive, shut off the engine and climbed out of the Toyota. He peered at the other car, suddenly hesitant.

There was a pause of about 30 seconds, in which he could see movement in the car, before the driver's door opened and woman got out and stood beside the car, squinting at him and holding up her hand to block the setting sun, which was shining in her eyes. She was dressed in shorts, walking boots and a white, long sleeved T-shirt, and looked small next to the large car.

"Don't…" she cleared her throat. "Don't come any closer." Her voice sounded clearly in the silence. Australian accent.

Jack, still processing what she had said, started forward.

"You have no idea…" the words died in his throat as he watched her pull a shotgun from where she had stowed it in the car and point it in his direction.

"I said, don't come any fucking closer," she repeated. Jack processed it this time and stopped walking. He was ten yards away and suddenly the evening felt cold as he faced the twin barrels of the shotgun.

"I. Um. What are you doing?" he managed to get out. He had no idea what was going on. There was another long pause.

"I'm just protecting myself," she eventually said. Yet another pause.

"What from?" he finally managed to ask.

"Look, I don't know you, and I don't wish you any harm. But there's nobody here and nothing to stop you doing whatever you want." Pause.

"Like what?" Jack asked her. He didn't really have a handle on this conversation and was trying to work out what was going on. She considered this for a few seconds before replying.

"You know, steal my stuff or, like, rape me or something." This time there was a very long pause before Jack replied.

"Well, that all sounds nice. But if it's OK with you can we do the stealing and the raping later? If you're not in too much of a hurry? For now could we just, you know, talk?" This was followed by the longest pause yet, as Jack watched her think about what he had said.

The barrel of the shotgun drooped a little and she sniffed. Then it drooped further and she gave a small whimper and then, as the shotgun pointed at the ground, her face crumpled and she covered it with one hand and sobbed.

He hesitated a few more moments while she cried, before covering the ten yards, and, without even bothering to take the shotgun out of her one hand he took her in his arms. She buried her face in his chest and sobbed, while tears streamed down his own face in silence.

Six

It was a couple of hours later that Jack got the full story, since they had exchanged only brief introductions and the sketchiest of details on the road. Jack had released the stranger after a minute or two and stepped back to give her some space. She had wiped her eyes on her sleeve and put the shotgun back in the car, before turning to him and holding out her hand to shake.

"I'm Xanthe. Xanthe McDonald," she had said, her voice still a little wobbly. "I'm sorry about that."

Jack wasn't sure if she was apologising for crying on his shirt or for threatening him with the shotgun. He had shaken her hand.

"Jack Stevens," he'd told her. "Where are you heading for?"

"Sydney. There's got to be people there."

"I'm afraid I don't think there are. I've just come from there and I didn't see anybody. Alive, that is." This last statement had sat between them awkwardly for a few seconds. Xanthe just stared at Jack like she didn't believe what he was saying.

"That can't be right. Sydney is, um, gone too? How can that be?"

"There isn't any power and, well, no sign of anything. Where have you come from?"

"Melbourne. It's the same there. You're the first person I've seen alive for two days."

"Fuck. That's, um, not good." There had been a long silence while they both considered what this meant.

"Well, it'll be dark quite soon," Jack eventually broke the silence. "Why don't we head into Goulburn and find something to eat and talk about what we should do? I promise there'll be no stealing or, um, raping."

Xanthe had not managed a smile at this.

"Do you want to follow me?" he had asked, but she was not keen on that.

"Why don't we go in the same car? It'd be easier." It seemed that she had made a decision to trust him. At least to the point of allowing him in the same car.

"OK. Yours looks better. How much fuel is in it?"

"About half a tank, I think. It's not mine. I stole it." She announced.

"Well, I stole that one as well and it has less than a quarter of a tank, so let's go in yours. Hold on." Jack had retrieved his rucksack, the GPS and the stolen phones from the Toyota and, at Xanthe's suggestion, got in the driving seat of the big Volvo.

An hour or so later they were sitting with food on a plate in front of each of them, lit by candlelight.

The house was a small two-bedroom bungalow (Australians mostly lived on a single floor, Jack noted) in Goulburn on a nondescript road. The thing that had marked it out as suitable for their purpose was that there was no car on the driveway and also no garage where a car could be hidden.

"No car might mean no dead bodies," Xanthe had pointed out. In fact this one was the second one they tried. The first had also had no car but did have the dead bodies. The second was empty and so fitted the bill perfectly. Having kicked in enough doors that day, Jack put a plant pot through the window that was fitted in the back door and reached through to unlock it. The bungalow appeared to belong to a single man, judging by the decoration and pictures (he appeared in most of them). Maybe that slightly overweight woman he was pictured with in several frames, and once on the fridge, was his girlfriend. Perhaps he was at his plump girlfriend's house, since he wasn't at home.

After a quick tour of the house and a now ritual check of the phone (Xanthe had watched him with a blank expression as he tested the useless instrument) they had rifled through drawers and cupboards until they found candles and matches, although Xanthe already had some matches in her bag. They had also come up with some pasta and a sauce to put on the top of it. There was even a four pack of beers in the fridge. The gas hob still worked, and so they had cooked up a meal as the sun set and now sat at the small kitchen table. Jack had dumped all the looted phones on the table and, as he ate, he checked each one again for signal, but there was none. The almost unbearable pressure to speak to Jane had subsided somewhat, although it was definitely still high on his agenda. Although he was desperate to let her know what was going on, and aware that she must be frantic with worry, he was not so totally alone as he had been a few hours before.

Since setting off in the Volvo, any talk had been focused on the business in hand - finding somewhere to stay - because it was clear that they were going to stay the night in this little town. But now that they had sat down together, the obvious questions loomed.

"So," started Jack. "What happened to you? If you tell me what happened in Melbourne, then I'll tell you what I can about Sydney."

"Well," Xanthe began slowly, "I suppose the best place to start is on Wednesday evening, when I got back from work. I…"

"Sorry to interrupt, but what is it you do?"

"I'm a nurse. I work at the Royal in A & E."

"Sorry. I'll try not to interrupt." She looked at him for a moment, face serious, before carrying on. She spoke quite slowly, her voice flat and surprisingly devoid of emotion, but her face betrayed the effort she had to make to hold herself together, as she re-lived the last few days of her life.

"So, anyway. I got home on Wednesday evening and was meant to be going out with Steve. He's my boyfriend." She paused a second. "Was.

"But when I got home I wasn't feeling great. I felt like I was coming down with a cold, so I decided not to go out. I phoned Steve - we don't live together - and he said he wasn't feeling too good either, so we decided to stay at home. Him at his and me at mine. I watched a bit of TV and got an early night."

As she spoke, Jack took the opportunity to have a good look at Xanthe in the candlelight. His first impression by the car had been right. She was definitely a few inches below average height, but looked like she did a lot of exercise. She was about thirty, had shoulder length, blondish hair and was definitely what you would describe as pretty, but perhaps not beautiful. Her face was serious as she spoke, but she had smile marks by her eyes, although he hadn't seen a lot of smiling this evening.

"The next morning I woke up feeling pretty grim. I sent a text to Elaine, my boss, telling her I couldn't come in. We're good friends. I didn't get a reply but didn't think much about it. My nose was runny and I had a headache, so I stayed in bed. I woke again about midday and noticed that the power was out. Didn't think much about that either. I just went back to bed and read my book from the light through the window. By evening there was still no power and no phone signal either. I was starting to feel a bit better but was getting a bit freaked out. It's weird how we have all got so used to being connected all the time. A few hours without my phone or access to Facebook was freaking me out.

"So I walked round to Steve's. He only lives about ten minutes walk from me, but even on that walk it was weird. It was *so* quiet. I only saw one or two cars and nobody out walking.

"Anyway, when I got there I could see that Steve really wasn't well. He had a really high temperature and a terrible headache. I gave him some ibuprofen and made him drink lots of water. But a couple of hours later I was getting really worried. He'd vomited and was starting to become delirious. Obviously the power hadn't come back on, so I got him into the car and headed to the Royal.

"The drive was weird. Beyond weird. That was when I realised that something really serious was happening. There were no streetlights and no other cars *at all*. It took about half the time it usually would to get to work, but when I got there it was a nightmare.

"I suppose I knew it was going to be, even before I arrived. I already knew that something big and terrible was happening and that that was always going to mean that the hospital was bad. And it was. Really bad." She stopped for a few seconds. Her gaze fixed, seeing whatever had met her at the hospital that night. Jack watched her, the candlelight reflecting in her eyes, but he stayed silent.

"It was absolutely mobbed. People were lying on the pavement outside because there was no room inside. The lights were on because of the emergency generators, which seemed like a blessing, but I suppose didn't really turn out to be one.

"Quite a lot of people weren't conscious, or at least were pretty well out of it. All the ones who were still lucid begged me for help. And I mean *all* of them. Calling out 'Help me. Please help me.' It was awful. I left Steve in the car went inside, where it was even worse. People just lying everywhere. Vomit, urine and diarrhoea on the floor. God, it was terrible."

She paused for a few moments but Jack left the silence unbroken. Xanthe clearly needed to say this and this was as much therapy as an exchange of information. She rubbed her face with one small tanned hand, before tucking her hair behind her ear and continuing, her eyes fixed on the scene in her mind, not looking at Jack at all.

"I recognised some doctors and nurses who worked there. Mostly they were self medicating. Or had been. They had IVs stuck in their arms. I even had a conversation with one of them, who told me he thought it was an infection and that I should inject him with antibiotics. Well, I did that, and I got Steve on an IV and injected him with antibiotics.

"Then I got a whole big bag of that same antibiotic that the doctor had told me to use and I went round injecting as many people as I could. To start with I was doing it properly but pretty quickly I realised I was going to have to go faster. And people had started dying. Some of the people I came to inject were already dead. So I just started using the same syringe and needle for maybe ten people at a go. I also stuck IVs into people who looked like they were bit better.

"Everywhere I went people were begging for help, and I stuck a needle into them saying 'This'll help.' But it didn't. I was totally alone. I was only person active in the whole fucking hospital. Occasionally someone would stagger around and I would think 'Thank God, someone to help me,' but it wasn't. Just some ill person trying to get a drink or something.

"I worked the whole night without stopping. I kept going outside to see how Steve was. He was unconscious pretty well the whole night. He had vomited in his car. I felt so helpless. When he died, which must have been about seven in the morning, I had a bit of a break down. I cried for about twenty minutes, just lying on the tarmac next to the car.

"I think I was crying for myself and all the other people in the hospital as well as for Steve. Steve and I had been together for two years and, to be honest, I was thinking about splitting up with him. I think he was thinking the same thing, but neither of us had quite plucked up the courage. Don't get me wrong, I really liked him, but I was starting to realise that he wasn't the one for me. And I think I wasn't his one either.

"Once I got it together I started to work again. I probably knew it was hopeless. More than half the people were dead by then, and it was obvious that the antibiotics weren't helping, so I started trying other things. I tried things like antivirals, adrenaline, Aranesp, Zofran and quite a few other things. I went for high doses, because I was desperate to save someone."

She paused again and sniffed once, looking down at the wooden table. Once again Jack remained silent and she glanced up at him, but didn't return his attempt at an encouraging smile, before carrying on.

"I definitely killed some people – well – speeded up their death, I suppose. But nobody got any better. A few hours later I was walking around the hospital looking for anybody left alive and by about two in the afternoon it was getting hard to find people. By four I realised that I hadn't found anybody alive for at least half an hour. At that point I knew I had to leave. I was absolutely shattered and had no idea what to do. So I simply left. I took an ambulance and drove it around for a while. I had an idea that I would be able to find and help people, but I didn't see anybody. After about an hour I almost crashed when I half fell asleep.

"So I drove the ambulance back to my own house and just went to bed. It seems pathetic now. The whole city was dying and I just went to bed. But I was *so* tired and I didn't really know what to do, so I just slept."

Xanthe paused and looked at Jack. She hadn't really looked at him throughout this whole monologue and Jack got the feeling that she wasn't really talking to him at all. Just talking. And maybe getting it all straight in her own head. He waited for her to continue and, after a minute or so, during which she stared dry-eyed off into the middle distance again, she did.

"I didn't wake until early the next morning. I got up and walked out of the front door and just listened. The city was silent. I could hear a dog barking, but nothing else. I went next door. The house wasn't locked but Jim and Margaret Williams and their baby, Melinda, were all dead. Margaret was on the floor next to Melinda's cot. It was awful. They're a lovely family and I know that because I babysit for them sometimes. It was almost worse seeing them than it had been at the hospital. I've seen lots of people die at the Royal, but seeing the Williams', in their own house was absolutely unbearable.

"After I pulled myself together I went into a few more houses and it was the same. The cars were parked outside, as if they had just come home as usual, but inside they were all dead. One thing I noticed was that almost everybody was there. I mean in each house everybody who lived there was inside. Like everybody felt a bit ill and so went home and then it got worse and they died in their houses. At the same time. Which doesn't make any sense. What kind of illness hits everybody at the same time?

"Anyway. I went back to my house and packed some things and then I went back to the Williams' house. I found Margaret's keys easily, in her handbag but I had to go into their bedroom, where Jim was, and go through his pockets to find his keys. I felt like I needed to be quiet in case I woke him up.

"Seeing his keys reminded me that he owned a shotgun. He once showed it to me and I remembered that the key to the gun safe was on the same ring as his house and car keys. So I got the gun out of the safe, and a box of shells, and took them with me.

"I checked Jim's and Margaret's cars and Jim's was full of fuel, so I just took it. I drove all day to Canberra. The only time I stopped was when Jim's car was getting near empty. I drove into a small town and found a house with a couple of cars in the driveway. I went into the house, which wasn't locked and then I simply took the car that had the fullest tank. I drove on to Canberra and got there in the late afternoon.

"It was exactly like Melbourne. Totally silent. I drove around a bit. I even got out and wandered around the National Library. The fountain wasn't working. Obviously. In the end I did like we did this evening and found a house that had no cars and spent last night there. I didn't really know what to do with myself, but eventually I just went to sleep in some stranger's bed.

"This morning I slept in until late. I suppose I must have been tired. I went to the hospital, the Calvary, in Canberra to see if anybody was alive there. No one was. I stole some food from a shop in the hospital. Then I decided I needed a car, but instead of just picking one, I found myself going from house to house, just in case someone was still alive.

"Eventually I realised I was wasting my time and so I found a car that was full of fuel, the Volvo, and started out towards Sydney. I'm heading for my parents house, but I suppose I know that they are dead. You've told me that."

After this last statement they both sat in silence for another minute or two. Silent pauses in the conversation seemed to be a feature of their short relationship to date, Jack reflected. Still, he had no idea how to respond to this harrowing narration of Xanthe's last few days, and was also rather embarrassed at his "Oh, they're all dead in Sydney" statement that he had made on the road. Perhaps he could have been more harsh and abrupt, but it was hard to see how. Eventually Xanthe, who had been staring into the candle flame, broke the silence.

"I really am sorry about what happened when we met," she began, fixing her eyes on his as she spoke. "I felt so vulnerable, as I was wandering around on my own. Normally we have so many things in place to keep us safe. You know, things like police and neighbours and alarms and mobile phones and all that stuff. I had been thinking about how there was really nobody to help me and, I suppose, just feeling sorry for myself, when suddenly you came speeding up behind me and all I could think was 'there's no safety net, I have to look after myself' and then, before I knew it, I was pointing the gun at you.

"You seem like a nice guy, and are certainly a good listener." He got a small smile as she said this, the first he had seen. "I'm... Well, I'm glad I'm not on my own now," she finished.

Seven

Xanthe opened her eyes and took a few moments to work out what they were seeing. The sun was slanting through a crack between the thin curtains and making a bright sliver on the pale wall, illuminating a stripe of a rather boring print of desert sand dunes.

She had been having a dream in which she and her sister were being chased by something feared but unknown, although it turned out to be an enormous road-train, which almost ran them over, and she woke with her heart pounding. The feeling that something was very wrong persisted after her eyes were open, and it took her a few moments to establish full consciousness and realise that, in fact, it was even worse than her dream. Amelia was, in all likelihood, dead already, and she was alone in a strange and deserted town with an English stranger and no plan.

She lay there for a few more minutes, partly just to delay the beginning of the day, and partly because she could hear Jack moving around and wanted to be sure he was out of the single bathroom before she got up and washed.

The night before she had talked herself to a standstill, before asking Jack what had happened to him and hearing his tale. After that they had headed for bed and Xanthe, who had already established ownership of the spare bedroom, had simply swept the clutter off the bed and fallen into it. That left Jack to sleep in the owner's bedroom and she had seen him hunting for clean bedclothes before she firmly shut her bedroom door. There was no lock and so she had moved a chair in front of the door. It probably wouldn't keep anybody out but it would at least wake her up if the door was opened.

He was an odd one, Jack, there was no denying it. He was certainly a good listener, Xanthe couldn't fault him on that score, but there was something different about him to most of the men she knew. He had listened with a focus and concentration that she found unnerving and the only way she could tell her story was to mostly ignore him. His own account of his last few days had been so controlled and analysed it had seemed like a machine's version of the story rather than a living person's.

Still, she was glad she had met someone and was no longer alone and had told him as much. She made that statement out loud partly because it was true, but it was also partly, she recognised, a cynical move to manipulate Jack. Any protective feelings she could invoke in his calculating mind were probably a good thing. Although he was a geek, he was still a man, after all, and that feeling of exposure and vulnerability had only partially subsided.

She heard footsteps moving down the hall towards the other end of the house, which meant that Jack was out of the bathroom. She rolled out of bed, retrieved her wash kit from her bag, moved the chair and opened the door quietly. The hall appeared to be deserted and so she padded quietly across to the bathroom to pee and to wash. God, she hated cold showers, but it was probably marginally better than being dirty.

After the shortest shower she had ever taken, she dressed and headed for the kitchen. She'd chosen a singlet, although only after a bit of internal debate. Was it a bad idea to show too much skin? In the end she went with the singlet but put on no make-up. She didn't want Jack to think she was making an effort for him.

She joined him in the kitchen and noticed that his glance in her direction was slightly longer than perhaps was needed. He was frying eggs and bacon on the hob, which, she had to admit, smelled good. They both said good morning in what seemed like a slightly stilted way, a bit like two people who had had a drunken one-night stand but didn't really know each other at all, Xanthe thought. She decided that maybe getting this relationship on a more even keel was in order.

"You must be desperate to let your wife know you're alright."

Jack looked up at her and she pointed at his hand. "Your wedding ring. I don't know if lucky is a word either of us can use at the moment, but you must be relieved that she doesn't live here." He frowned at this statement, taking a few moments to frame a response. As he thought about it, she took another look at him. He was not a bad looking man, she reflected, although not bursting with charm. He had shaved this morning and the lack of stubble suited him better in her opinion. It made him look younger. He looked strong, she thought, and there was no point in fooling herself that she was no match for him physically. She needed to keep him on her side.

"Yes, of course. It's hard to know what anybody outside Australia could have heard, but it can't be good. I have to find a way of letting her know that I'm OK. I think these eggs are reasonably fresh. Would you like a couple fried?"

"Absolutely, thanks. So how are you going to get in touch? Is there a way? Can we find a radio or something?"

"I've been thinking about that. These things are useless. Too short range," Jack indicated the collection of mobile phones on the table. He hadn't said where they all came from but it was pretty obvious that he'd taken them from dead bodies. However she was hardly in a position to be critical of that. "So we need something that can reach further. I'm not really sure what the range on a big radio set is, but it seems to me that that's a pretty specialist bit of gear. I think what we need is a satellite phone."

"OK. Where would we get one?" That computer in his head was obviously still processing away.

"And that's the difficulty. I'm not really sure," Jack admitted. "I don't think it's the kind of thing you can buy in shops, which means we've got to locate someone who would need a thing like that, and I can't really see a way of doing that. Maybe if we drove a long way into the Outback, then farms out there might have that kind of thing. What do you think?"

"Maybe," Xanthe spoke slowly, thinking. His mention of a satellite phone had rung a distant bell. "But perhaps there's an easier way. I have a friend who was at nursing college with me and she works for the RFDS. They might carry satellite phones." In fact, now that she thought about it, Xanthe had heard her friend Emma mention exactly this piece of equipment when they met in Sydney for a night out the year before.

"RFDS?"

"The Flying Doctor Service. They go to lots of places in the back of beyond and need a reliable way of keeping in touch with base."

"The flying doctors? I thought that was just a TV show?"

"No way!" Xanthe was slightly affronted by this suggestion. Foreigners sometimes have an odd view of Australia, she reflected. "It's real. Emma, my friend, works in Sydney and flies out of Bankstown Airport. It's only a few hours from here."

"Fantastic!" Almost for the first time she could see an emotion play behind his features. He obviously was desperate to speak to his wife and this surge of hope showed that perhaps he wasn't such a robot after all. So that took care of his agenda, but she had one of her own that needed to be taken care of.

"Today I'd like to go to my parents' house. I know there's not much hope, but I have to see it. I think we should..." she was suddenly uncertain of how to say it. "I think we should stick together. If that's OK with you, Jack?" Jesus! That sounded pathetic. But Jack answered straight away.

"Absolutely! Of course. I've done quite enough blundering around on my own. I definitely need a native guide." That was a nice response and she smiled at him, getting a rather self-conscious twitch of his lips in return.

"So should we just head straight there? To Sydney? We should go to the airport first because it's on the way to... to Mum and Dad's." Now that she was thinking of heading back to Sydney the enormity of what was going on was starting to re-assert itself. Was she going to see Mum and Dad's dead bodies today? She forced herself not to think about it but instead to think about what Jack was saying.

"Well. Two things occur to me before we leave," he answered, looking down at the pan of eggs he was frying. "Firstly we're going to need a different car at some point. The Volvo hasn't got enough fuel to get us to Sydney. And secondly I think we should tool up a bit." She gave him questioning look. "Not like that," he nodded at the shotgun, which she had propped in one corner. "But, you know, tools. To help us break into places. I've already smashed a few windows and kicked in some doors. Some kind of pry bar would make that process easier, and maybe some bolt cutters, so we need a hardware store or similar. Here. Get a plate. The eggs and bacon are ready."

So an hour later they found themselves outside a Magnet Mart Home Warehouse, having cruised around until they spotted it. The only signs of life had, as before, been the occasional cat, although they had also come across a single crashed car. On a normal day this would have been horrendous, but compared to what Xanthe had seen in the last forty eight hours it was relatively mild. Although both Xanthe and Jack had inspected the scene, there was no need to touch anything. The middle-aged woman was clearly dead in the driver's seat. Xanthe had seen a lot of dead people in her life, but she had never got totally hardened to it, and it seemed more immediate, sharper, here in the sunlight.

They were now wondering how to break into the Magnet Mart. The irony of this, along with the demonstration of Jack's point about needing tools, wasn't lost on either of them. There were no windows, but the sliding door was handily made of glass and so succumbed to the attentions of Jack and a length of 2-by-4 from a stack next to the shop.

"Wow. It's weird to see places like this in the dark. Oops. Sorry,' said Xanthe as she bumped into him from behind. The enormous shop seemed unnaturally dark after the bright street outside.

"No problem. We need to find torches let's split up."

"No way, mate. This place is way too creepy. I'm coming with you."
Xanthe knew this sounded a bit girlish but the shop *was* creepy. She was regretting all those zombie movies Steve had made her watch.

Once they found torches in the dim interior, it was a little better, but it still took them a while to get what they needed. But eventually Jack had assembled what looked like a pretty extensive burglary kit, although stealth wasn't really on the agenda, as a large lump hammer and chisel formed part of the kit. It was all shoved into a sturdy bag with handles, that they had found in the garden section. Jack also went back to where they had found the torches and threw four of the large units into the bag.

"Right, next I think some food for the journey," Jack suggested, heaving the break-in kit onto the back seat of the Volvo.

"You're just keen to use your new tools to break into something."

Xanthe told him. She tried to keep her voice light in denial of this situation, although she wasn't sure that she'd succeeded. The attempt at banter struck an off-note in their sombre mood.

"You say it like it's a bad thing," he replied, deadpan.

They hadn't seen a supermarket in Goulburn, although presumably there was one, but without Google maps it was lost to them. They had, however, passed a corner shop that looked like it sold what they were looking for and Jack said he had noted roughly where it was. His processor was obviously fully online this morning.

When they found it, he efficiently set to work on the steel shutters, and his new kit worked well, the bolt-cutters making short work of the padlock. They stocked up on what they needed.

"What sort of car do you want to drive to Sydney in?" Jack asked her as they headed out of the town centre in a random direction.

"I don't care. Let's just find something quickly and get going."

"So what, in your medical opinion, do you think this illness is? Any idea?"

They were about half way to Sydney and had been driving, for the most part, in silence. The silence could only be described as brooding, rather than companionable, and so Xanthe was actually quite glad that Jack had broken it. She glanced across at him but his eyes were on the road as he drove.

"I've been thinking about it and I really have no idea. It's not any normal kind of illness. Something totally different." she replied.

"What makes you say that?"

"Well," she continued, "it's the timing. You must have noticed how everybody, including you and me, got ill at almost exactly the same time."

"Yes, I had wondered about that," Jack admitted.

"Well, it's more than just a bit odd. It means that it wasn't any normal virus or infection, since those things work by sick people infecting people who are not yet ill."

"Yes, but don't some things have an incubation period when you are infectious, but not yet ill?" Jack suggested. Xanthe had considered that exact option from every angle, but just couldn't make it fit what had happened.

"Sure. But even then you still need to catch it and incubate it for a time before you can infect other people, even if you don't show symptoms until much later."

"So if it isn't a virus or infection what is it? Radiation poisoning from sunspots or something?"

"Well, I've thought about that too," Xanthe said slowly. "But it doesn't really fit. It works from a timing perspective but the symptoms are wrong. I'm not an expert on radiation poisoning but we did have one lesson on it when I was training. I think there are symptoms that the people in the hospital didn't show and also symptoms they did show which don't seem right."

"Like what? I thought the symptoms of radiation poisoning were nausea and vomiting, which you said was exactly what they had? What I had for that matter."

"Yes, they did have those, and in the later stages the symptoms were similar, but then lots of fatal things have those symptoms. The headache too.

"But at the outset it looked like a cold for everybody, and I don't think that is consistent with severe radiation dosage. Also I can't explain how I didn't really get ill at all, just a few sniffles. You sound like you got pretty ill, but I really didn't, and I just don't understand that. I don't think I was anywhere shielded during Wednesday. Do you think you were?"

"Well, no. I don't think so," said Jack, visibly casting his mind back. "I spent the day with the other people in the office and they died. I was with Rick and Cynthia nearly the whole day and they didn't survive like I did. I've wondered how close I came to dying. I lost two whole days that I can't really remember at all."

"And that's another thing that's weird. You were incredibly ill but you seem to have made a full recovery. If you had received a near fatal dose of radiation I don't think you would have recovered so quickly or probably not at all."

"So if it's not a transmitted infection or radiation sickness, then what?"

"I really have no idea," admitted Xanthe. "It seems to me like an infection that was triggered by something external. So something we were all carrying that was activated by something, a sunspot or something. But I'm just guessing, I'm only a nurse and I think this stuff would be outside most doctors' experience." It was frustrating to have so little idea of what had caused this, especially when, as Jack pointed out, this was an area in which she was supposed to have expertise.

"I'm sure we'll find out eventually,' Jack predicted.

There was a long pause during which, once again, Xanthe's mind went back to those hellish hours in the hospital.

"The thing I can't stop thinking is that if I had just found the right drug I could have saved hundreds, maybe thousands of people. I can give an injection pretty damn fast and so if I had found the thing that helped, I could have run round giving it to everybody. If I'd done that there wouldn't be just two of us."

"Maybe that's true. But maybe there was no drug. Maybe those people were going to die whatever you did. There's no point in torturing yourself over it. You did your best."

"I know that. But I can't help it."

Jack had shown Xanthe how to work the Garmin that he was so attached to, and the reliable lady directed them to Bankstown without incident. It was a large airfield, although airport was probably rather a grand term for it. There were many buildings lining the roads, divided by sunlit, deserted lawns.

It took them twenty minutes to locate the Flying Doctor office, which was a single story brick building with a large sign pointing them to reception.

The door was unlocked and they entered a spacious carpeted area with some slightly threadbare seats spread around the wall and a blue vinyl counter at one end.

The access gate was open in the counter and Jack stepped through, with Xanthe following. She was wary of what they might find on the other side, but there was just an unoccupied office chair. Jack was scanning the area behind the counter but it didn't look to Xanthe like they would find what they were looking for here. It all seemed to be official looking forms and stationery at the reception station.

However it was a different story through the door behind the counter. A large man dressed in stained chinos and a once-white shirt was sprawled on the floor in the small hallway, which had several other doors off it. Neither Xanthe nor Jack said anything as they stepped round the corpse. The first door was to a kitchen, which they didn't waste time in, but the second led to a storeroom that held a variety of equipment. Most of it was medical (Xanthe identified several varieties of trauma packs as well as two defibrillators), however in one corner Jack found a row of three small black bags with shoulder straps, that looked to Xanthe like they might contain cameras.

Opening the first one showed that he had found what he was looking for, his face lighting up. Xanthe took some satisfaction that her instinct that Flying Doctors would carry satellite phones was correct. The bag contained a power charger, what looked like a large mobile phone with the word "Iridium" on the front and a user manual which said "9505A – Satellite Phone" on the cover.

Jack peered at the phone with a noticeable tremor in his hand. They exchanged glances before he shoved the phone and manual back into the bag and the two of them wordlessly retraced their steps, past the body in the hall and out into the sunshine.

"You have a look at that while I see if I can make this work," Jack pushed the manual at Xanthe while grasping the phone itself. Although this was pretty rude, she was prepared to cut him some slack given that he was about to make contact with the outside world. The phone had a large aerial which swung round and extended out. Xanthe watched Jack get it into position and turn the phone on. As he did so he strode away from the building on to the lawn, presumably to get a clear view of the sky, and Xanthe had to almost run to keep up with him, trying to peer at the little screen as it came to life.

She watched him dial a long number, presumably his home number, and hold the phone to his ear. He held it there for what seemed like a long time, before peering at the screen again. Xanthe couldn't see what it said, but his face was clenched in a grimace that almost looked like pain. He didn't speak, but instead dialled again, she didn't know if it was the same number or a different one, and once again Jack held the phone to his ear.

This time when he took it away Xanthe asked, "What does it say?"

"It doesn't say anything, but this light is flashing yellow." Jack's voice was unsteady. "What's the emergency number in Australia?"

"Triple zero."

He dialled the three digits, but once again had no luck.

"Still flashing yellow. Find out what that means," he ordered, flapping his hand at the manual that she had forgotten she was holding. She opened it up and starting examining the contents while he dialled again.

"Apparently it means 'Service Temporarily Unavailable'," she told him, as she found the relevant bit. His mouth was pinched tight and his face was flushed as he tried again. And again.

They kept trying for twenty more minutes, including removing the SIM card, replacing it, rebooting the phone and everything else they could think of, but none of it worked. The service remained temporarily unavailable. In fact he kept going long after she would have given up. The phone clearly didn't want to work for them, so they should just put it away and try later. But Jack persisted and she did not dare suggest that he stop.

Eventually however he was forced to admit defeat, which he did by handing her the phone and slumping to the ground, almost as if the strength to stand had left his legs.

"But how can that be?" Xanthe asked, examining the device. "These things are up in space, right? They should still work." Jack didn't answer and she glanced down at him. He was staring into the distance, clearly doing his best not to cry, and Xanthe felt her heart squeezed by his pain. She sat down next to him but kept her attention on the phone to give him some space to recover. Jack had handled her tears well last night and she wanted to do the same for him, which probably meant letting him try and keep his dignity in one piece. She had a fair bit of experience with tears and the general consensus among nurses was to pretend that men didn't cry.

After a couple of minutes she glanced across. He was looking more composed, although still staring into the distance as he marshalled his disappointment.

"Jesus, Jack. What do you think is going on?" she asked, her voice softer.

He cleared his throat before replying in a voice that was mostly under control. "I suppose the issue is at the ground side. The satellite has to talk to a dish here on the ground and that dish must be out of action. It must be here in Australia, since that's what the satellite is over, and it's defunct. The same as with the mobile phone base stations, I suppose. That's, um, disappointing."

Xanthe gave him a look, which showed that she understood his pain, but said no more. He responded with the ghost of a smile that showed his gratitude. They sat in silence for a couple more minutes.

Xanthe had learned one thing, anyway. She had thought Jack a cold fish up until now, since he had displayed little emotion about their dire situation. But she now knew there were plenty of emotions boiling under that surface but he kept them well buttoned down. *Good to know*, she thought to herself.

After a couple of minutes he broke the silence. "OK, let's get moving. We can take two of these," he nodded at the useless device, "with us and try them periodically in case the system comes back on line."

"It's just up here on the left." They were approaching Xanthe's parents' house, which was in Baulkham Hills, a leafy suburb on the north side of Sydney. There had been no need to plug in the GPS, since Xanthe directed Jack along the familiar route. It was less than two months since she had last been back here, she reflected, although she had flown rather than wasted a day driving. That day Dad had picked her up from the airport and she'd enjoyed a long weekend at home. Mostly catching up with school friends, she realised now looking back. She'd hardly spent any time with Mum and Dad. Just thinking about it made her eyes sting. Jack was driving the stolen Honda and didn't notice a thing, although even he must have sensed how tense she was.

On their route through Sydney they had passed three more crashed cars and two apparently abandoned in the middle of the road, but Jack had, by silent, mutual assent, manoeuvred round these without stopping. Apart from her issuing occasional directions at deserted junctions they drove in silence, each lost in their own thoughts. No doubt he was still brooding about the disappointment with the satellite phone, but Xanthe's mind was taken up with what she knew she was going to find at home.

The largish bungalow was set back from the road, mostly hidden by the surrounding trees. As they pulled up outside, Xanthe made no move to get out of the car, but instead stared at the entrance and the grey Toyota that was parked in the driveway. They sat in silence for a few moments as she tried to steel herself. The car was obviously not a good sign."Shall I wait here?" Jack eventually asked? She didn't look at him but replied in a small voice.

"No. You may as well come in." Jack followed her up to the front door.

The neat front garden looked so normal that Xanthe found it hard to shake the feeling of unreality, mixed in with her dread. Were they really about to witness a scene of gruesome death? She'd walked up this path thousands of times, and everything was so *the same.*

The only thought that Xanthe's mind kept jumping to was about genetics. She didn't want to hope but just couldn't help herself. She had, in some way, been virtually immune to whatever plague had decimated Australia and so it was possible that whatever made her different was an inherited trait. If that was the case then maybe it wasn't a foregone conclusion that both Mum and Dad would be dead. Although if it was some special genetic trait, then it seemed that this must have come from only one of them and so the other was likely to be dead. God, how could she deal with this? *Be tough, Xanthe,* she told herself.

She didn't ring or knock but tried the front door, which was not locked.

"They only lock it if they are going out," she muttered, more to herself then to Jack. She paused in the hall, and Jack remained on the threshold. There was a bad smell coming from inside the house.

"Mum? Dad?" she called.

There was an immediate answering noise through the closed kitchen door straight ahead of Xanthe. No decipherable words, but a kind of croak. Xanthe felt even more adrenaline pumping into her blood stream. She snatched the door open and rushed through into the kitchen, dimly aware of Jack following more slowly.

The large kitchen with its scrubbed wooden table in the centre, looked the same as it always did. The smell was strong in here, but it was immediately obvious that there was nobody in the room. It was Rufus, and he was alive. Xanthe crossed the room in a few quick strides and knelt down next to the little dog, which was sprawled next to the back door. He raised his head and tried another bark, although the result was barely audible. She picked him up and cradled him in her arms. Jack approached, a frown creasing his forehead.

"Roofy. Don't worry, I'm here now," she said softly, and then "Jack, can you get him some water and then some food. In the cupboard there." She jerked her head at the closed door to the kitchen cupboard and held the dog out to Jack. Its fur was matted with filth, which was also spread liberally on the floor, but Jack took the dog and held the animal gently.

"No problem."

Xanthe stroked the little old dog for a moment before nodding to Jack and heading out of the door.

"Come on my friend," Xanthe heard Jack's English accent behind her as she walked quietly down the hall. "Let's get you some water first."

She stood outside Mum and Dad's room for a few moments, taking a couple of breaths. The fact that Rufus was in that state was a clear message. She was almost certain she knew what she was going to find. Almost.

She opened the door and stepped over the threshold. The smell was worse in here, but all she could do was stand, rooted to the spot and stare at the scene.

Her parents were indeed both dead. Dad was sprawled on his side on the floor naked next to the bed. His small pot-belly, the subject of so many family jokes, hung down and his skin seemed slack and slightly too large for his frame. His legs and arms looked skinny and his mouth was wide open. His genitals hung in plain view, shrivelled and pathetic looking.

Mum was no more dignified. She lay on her back in her underwear. Flesh sagged all over her body and her open eyes stared at the ceiling. Her mouth was also open and with her open eyes it made her look as if she was about to shout at the top of her lungs.

Xanthe knew that she should arrange them in a more dignified way. Perhaps cover them. But despite years of training as a nurse all she could do was retreat back into the hall.

She could feel a fierce almost uncontrollable panic building up inside her, making her want to scream. She had to be tough. Not go to pieces. She should go and help Rufus.

She went back to the kitchen where Jack was kneeling next to Rufus, who was eating a bowl of food that Jack had put next to him. The Englishman looked up at her as she entered. She found herself meeting his questioning gaze, but all she could muster was a shake of her head. He stood, crossed the kitchen and stood in front of her for moment as the tears started to force their way out of Xanthe's eyes, before folding her into his arms. For the second time in the twenty-four hours they had known each other she buried her head in his shirt and cried.

Eight

"God. Sorry," Xanthe sniffed, a few minutes later, wiping her eyes with some kitchen roll.

"Nothing to be sorry about," Jack replied mildly.

"I tried to, you know, prepare myself. But when I actually saw them I just couldn't…" she squeezed her eyes shut and attempted to compose herself. He was quiet as she took a few shaky breaths.

She crossed to the table and sat in one of the chairs, her chair, the one she had always sat in at family meals. Jack moved round the table and sat as well. Mum's chair. She looked down at Rufus, who was lapping at the water that Jack had put out for him.

"Would you like me to bury them?" Jack asked. This question caught Xanthe by surprise. She hadn't given any thought to what they would do with the bodies. But now she thought about it, it was the right thing to do. They couldn't bury everybody but a proper dignified grave for Mum and Dad was what she wanted.

"Would you?" Xanthe was aware that her surprise was clear in her voice.

"Of course. I'd want that, if they were my parents." *But it's not your parents, it's mine,* she thought to herself, but simply nodded and blew her nose.

"Thanks. That'd be really kind," she said, when she had finished. He was only trying to be nice. It wasn't his fault that his family were elsewhere.

"Well, the day is getting on and so I'd better get digging. Does your Dad have a shovel?"

"Yes, in the garage. I'll show you."

She rose and went to the back door but stopped on the way to kneel and stroke Rufus, who had finished the food and half of the water and was lying still.

"Hi there Roofy. Feeling better, boy. It's good to see you. Back in a minute." The dog's tail twitched feebly which was an improvement.

"His name is Roofy?"

"Short for Rufus. He's a border terrier. You're a good dog, aren't you Roofy," was answered with another tail twitch.

She stood and picked the garage key off the hook by the back door and unlocked the door using the key that was always in the lock. Both actions felt so familiar, her body having carried out those precise movements a thousand times. Still running on muscle memory she opened the door and then she stepped out on to the veranda. Jack followed her along the wooden decking to the garage door, which she also unlocked and opened, before flicking the light switch. The light, of course, stayed off, causing her to glance upward in momentary surprise, and feeling slightly foolish.

"It should be here somewhere," she said, indicating the back wall of the garage, which was stacked with various garden implements. Dad was never very tidy with his tools and Mum hardly ever came in here, but there was enough late afternoon light coming through the door to identify the spade. There was also a pair of stout gardening gloves that Jack picked up and examined briefly, taking them with him.

"So. Show me where you think would be a good place."

"I think down at the end here," Xanthe led him down the garden, to the area she thought of as belonging to Amelia and her. It was screened by bushes, which were a lot taller than they had been when she and her sister used to come down here and sit behind the bushes in the evening and talk. If ever they had something to say that they didn't want to be overheard this is where they used to come. The sun was low now, lighting the trees but no longer touching the grass.

"This is the best place, I think," she gestured to the patch of lawn.

"Right. This is a nice spot. I'll get to work. I think it'll take quite while so why don't you... I mean, there's no need for you to stay and watch."

"OK. I'll come back in a while and see how you're getting on," and she left him to it.

Back in the house she checked on Rufus first. He raised his head when she came in, shutting the back door behind her. His fur was matted and he had made quite a mess on the kitchen floor. She'd deal with him in a while. In the meantime she opened all the doors to let air circulate and dispel the smell of dog-shit that Rufus had created.

"I'll be back in a while, Roofy," and she gave his head a stroke before stepping into the hall.

She didn't want Jack to see Mum and Dad like that, so she determined that she would sort them out before he finished digging the grave. How long did a grave take to dig anyway? Quite a while, she guessed.

She retrieved two sheets from the airing cupboard and Mum's sewing kit from the cupboard in the sitting room. She stood for a few moments in the hall, before opening the door once again and facing the task ahead. She tried to be swift and practical. They were just bodies now, she told herself. Mum and Dad were gone and these remnants contained nothing of them.

However telling herself these things didn't really help. Tears streamed down her face as she rolled the two bodies, both seeming smaller in death than they had in life, into the sheets. It seemed to take a long time to sew the sheets roughly closed, hiding her parents for ever.

Once this was done she stripped the bed and took the stained bedclothes out of the front door into front garden. It did occur to her, even as she dumped them into the grey wheely-bin that stood next to the car, that nobody was going to collect this rubbish in the near future. However she had no idea what else to do with the sheets and blankets, so she dumped them and followed them with her singlet. She stood for a moment in her shorts and bra and surveyed the deserted street, before retrieving her bag from the stolen Honda. She fished out another white singlet and pulled it on while still standing on the pavement before taking the bag back inside.

There was quite a bit of cleaning to be done, especially in the kitchen where Rufus had been incarcerated, but first she thought she might check on Jack's progress. She filled a big glass of lukewarm water from the tap and took it down the garden towards the rhythmic sound of the spade biting into the earth.

Jack was standing in the hole, the grave, which was only a little over a foot deep, and Xanthe struggled to hide her dismay. She thought he might be nearly finished.

"Wow, that looks like hard work." She commented. Jack's shirt was sticking to him from the sweat, which he was also blinking out of his eyes. He straightened, climbed out of the hole and accepted the water gratefully, draining it in two long pulls.

"You know, it's actually good to take some exercise. It'll take quite a while but I'm happy to do it." He wiped his mouth.

Seeing him there, soaked in sweat in the fading evening light, she suddenly felt a surprising pang of gratitude towards this strange man. He hardly knew her and yet here he was labouring to bury a pair of people he had never met. And he was doing it to try and make her feel better. He was even pretending to enjoy it so that she wouldn't feel guilty about making him do it.

She looked across at him and he returned her look, no smile on either of them.

"Do you think there's a lamp of some sort?" he eventually asked. God, he was certainly one for practical matters. Although maybe, she reflected, that was a good thing, given the circumstances. "In another hour it'll be getting quite dark and I won't be finished by then."

"Perhaps you should finish it off tomorrow," Xanthe felt compelled to make this suggestion, although she didn't want to sleep in the house with her dead parents.

"Not at all. If there's some kind of lamp, or maybe even one of the torches in the car, I'll keep at it until it's done."

"OK. I'll go and see what I can find."

Xanthe spent half an hour cleaning up inside, mopping the kitchen floor and making beds before tending to Rufus, who seemed to be regaining strength remarkably quickly. She then retrieved a torch from the car and went back into the garage. After a few minutes searching through the bric-a-brac on the shelves, almost none of which Mum and Dad had had any use for, she found a box containing camping gear. Inside was a battery powered camping lamp with flat batteries. She remembered being dragged on camping trips when she and Amelia were teenagers. They'd moaned, as all teenagers do, but the memories were precious now. She had used this very lamp to check the ground for red-backs and snakes before dropping her trousers and peeing in the dark undergrowth. She knew where Dad kept his battery store and so the lamp was soon up and running, although she switched it off after testing it.

She filled a jug with water this time and placed it, the lamp and a glass on a tray, which she carried down the garden. Jack had removed his shirt and was working steadily in the gloom, the grave now waist deep. He didn't see her immediately and so she watched him working for a few moments. He was, she judged, in his mid thirties, maybe even forty, definitely older than her thirty-one years, but obviously kept himself in shape. He wasn't skinny, but not really overweight. Solid looking. He was digging methodically, not rushing, but not pausing either.

She approached the grave and he caught the movement, turned, straightened and then clambered out, not hurrying.

Xanthe put the tray down on the grass and picked up the gloves.

"You need a break. I'm going to do some." Jack didn't protest, or in fact offer any comment, as she donned the too-big gloves and jumped down into the dark hole. There was just about enough light to see what she was doing, and so she got to work.

She worked hard, determined to move as much earth as she could, and actually Jack was right. It *was* good to take some exercise. He watched her in silence from beside the grave as she worked. Was he checking her out? No, more likely assessing her digging technique, she decided. She dug as long as she could, but eventually stood up straight, stretching her back.

"OK. That's enough." She straightened, pulled off the gloves and wiped some of the sweat off her face with the hem of her singlet. "I think I'll leave it to the expert."

Jack offered his hand to help her out of the hole and Xanthe accepted, managing a smile, which he returned.

It was quite some time later that the two of them were finally sitting on the veranda, sipping a warm beer and digesting the large meal they had just eaten. The lamp was turned off because it was attracting insects and so they sat in the pale light from half a moon and talked about what they were going to do.

The grave had taken Jack three hours in total, which had given Xanthe a good opportunity to clean and tidy, wash Rufus and get the barbie lit and ready. All using the light of one of the torches they had taken that morning. She had even washed (by hand) the clothes she had been wearing yesterday and hung them up to dry in her room so she would have some cleanish clothes in the morning.

"Do you want to, um, bury your parents now, or wait until morning?" he had asked her, after crossing the garden holding the lamp aloft. He was smeared in mud and looked tired. She'd like to let him have a rest, but was keen to finish the job.

"Would you mind doing it now? It might be better to get it done."

"Do you want me to...?"

"I think it's a two person job. Let's do it together." She couldn't ask him to do *that* on his own.

And so she had led Jack though the kitchen, all eerily lit by the camping lamp in his hand, into the main part of the house, and through the door to her parents' bedroom.

She noticed how relieved Jack looked when he saw the two bodies lying next to each other wrapped in her mother's ironed, white sheets. Obviously he was happier digging the grave than dealing with the corpses.

Between the two of them they had half carried and half dragged the shrouded corpses through the house, into the garden and to the edge of the grave, which was now a bottomless black hole in the moonlit lawn. It was awkward trying to lower the bodies into the grave and the second one, it was Dad, fell out of her grasp and landed heavily on top of Mum's wrapped shape.

Xanthe had immediately jumped down into the hole, which was deeper than she was tall, and carefully arranged the bodies to lie beside one another. Jack had then helped her out of the grave and they had stood for a few moments in a silence which Xanthe had finally broken.

"I'm not really sure what to say. I'm not religious and neither were they. But I feel we should say something."

"I'm not either, but I agree. Why don't you tell me, and the world in general, who they were, what they were like and what you will most remember about them?"

And so Xanthe did just that. Haltingly at first, but then more fluently, she spoke about her parents who were now lying in the dark hole in their own lawn. She talked about how happy her childhood had been and how selfless her parents were throughout her life, always putting their children first. She talked about how their thoughts and values were always with her. As she spoke she slipped from referring to them in the third person, to talking to the couple directly. Even as she spoke a cynical part of her knew that this emotional claptrap meant nothing, and was just for her benefit. But it felt good to let it out. She had spent so little time with them over the last few years, just fleeting visits snatched from her busy life, that she wanted to tell them how she felt. Even if they couldn't hear.

"And so, even though this unbelievable disaster has happened here, I will always remember you. I have survived, for whatever reason, and so your memory will still exist. I'll miss you, but I'll try and smile when I think about you and not be sad, because I know that that is what you would want."

Tears had spilled again as she spoke, but she didn't know, or even really care, if Jack could see. Her voice had remained strong and she thought it was fitting. They stood in silence after she had finished, with Xanthe thinking about how she had crossed the line that most people eventually crossed. Parents alive. Parents dead. Did it hurt this much for everybody?

Eventually she consciously shook herself out of her self-pity and turned to the present. Jack had remained silent throughout, which was not unusual for him. She was enormously grateful for what he had done here tonight. He'd given a dignified ending to her Mum and

Dad and she didn't really know how show her appreciation.

After a few moments' thought she turned to him and put her hand lightly on his arm.

"Jack, thanks for helping me with this. I really appreciate it," and she reached up and gave him a light kiss on his cheek, before releasing his arm, turning away and pulling the shovel out of the ground.

"Right," her voice was almost normal, there was just a hairline crack in it, "let's get this finished."

"I'll do this," he held out his hand for the shovel. "Why don't you cook us some supper on that barbeque you've got burning?"

Xanthe hadn't protested and had let Jack fill in the hole. She didn't want to watch the soil covering those beloved, shrouded forms. Despite this, as she walked back to the house, her imagination supplied images of the loose earth falling on the couple where they lay. In her mind she saw them, more clearly perhaps than she could have in the dark hole and failing light, gradually being covered up until only a sheet-wrapped toe or nose protruded, to be itself covered by the falling rain of soil.

Luckily it took Jack a while to fill in the grave and so by the time he approached the veranda, carrying the lamp out of the darkness, she had a firm hold of herself. She had also shut her parents' bedroom door and had no intention of opening it again.

"God, you're filthy," Xanthe told him, not unkindly as he stepped up on to veranda. "There's still water in the tank so why don't you go and have a shower. It'll be cold, but better than nothing."

By the time he emerged, Xanthe had decided that the food in the freezer was probably still safe, although it wouldn't be in another forty-eight hours, and so there were burgers sizzling gently on the barbeque.

"How are your hands?" Xanthe asked him, sitting down next to him and handing him a warm beer. "That piece of digging I did made my mine sore, even wearing the gloves. Have you got blisters?"

"A couple. Nothing too serious."

"Let's have a look." Xanthe switched the lamp back on and held it up in front of him. He offered his hands for her inspection. There were a couple of blisters, one or two of which had burst and must have stung in the shower.

"Right. We need to make sure those don't get infected. Wait here." Xanthe took the lamp and strode back into the dark interior of the house. She went to the medicine cabinet her mother kept in the bathroom and selected what she needed.

She was back outside a minute later with a small bottle of disinfectant, some wipes and a couple of plasters. Jack meekly held out his hands and she cleaned the raw skin on his hands and dabbed on disinfectant before applying the plasters. Once she had finished, she got up and flipped the burgers, which were nearly ready. Jack didn't speak as she assembled their meal, such as it was, but thanked her as she handed him a plate with two burgers in buns and some chopped peppers which she had briefly roasted. They ate in silence for a few minutes, but as Xanthe neared the end of her food, she decided it was time to talk about what they were going to do.

"So, what now?" Xanthe asked. Up to this point, apart from the conversation about the illness itself, the two of them had largely avoided the whole topic of what was going on, focusing instead on short-term practicalities. But Xanthe recognised that they couldn't carry on in this state of semi-denial in which they had, by mutual consent, taken refuge.

"Well. Two thoughts have occurred to me and neither are overly cheery, but you're right we have to talk about what we do next."

"Obviously I've been thinking about it too," Xanthe replied. "What are your thoughts?"

"The first thing is kind of obvious," Jack spoke slowly, measuring his words carefully. "This epidemic has obviously wiped out a massive proportion of the Australian population. We can't tell how far it has spread but it's possible that it is the whole country and even beyond. If it can hit Melbourne, Sydney and all the towns in between on the same day, then I think we have to assume that there is nowhere we can drive to for help. It's quite possible that places like Darwin or perhaps Perth escaped, or were less badly hit, but I don't think we should just jump in the car and start looking for help. We'd just be guessing."

"Well, I kind of agree," Xanthe replied. "I agree on the scale of this thing, but I was thinking that we don't really have anything better to do. We may have no idea where we're going but we might as well go and look. I'm not sure I can bear just sitting around waiting to get rescued. If it has hit other countries then who knows how long that will take."

"I agree that rescue might take quite some time," Jack replied, "but I think there is something else that we could be doing."

"What do you mean?"

"How many people have survived do you think?" Jack asked and then let Xanthe think about it. She took a couple of moments to give this question some proper thought. Obviously she didn't know, and he knew that, so why was he asking? Having been extremely gallant this evening he was back in computer-mode again now.

"Do you mean in the whole of Australia? Obviously I have no way of knowing the extent of the illness. There's no way we can know which cities have been affected. That's what we're talking about."

"No, I don't mean which cities have been affected. I mean in the areas that *have* been affected. How many people in Sydney, Melbourne, Canberra and the rest of the affected area. What do you think the survival rate was?"

"Oh. Well we haven't seen anyone else. But then I suppose if it was a small number we might not have."

"That's my thinking," Jack continued. "We can't be the only two people. We ran into each other by complete chance, but there have to be other people. Even if the survival rate is one in a million, we're not the only ones. What's the population of New South Wales and Victoria?"

"I'm not sure. I think Sydney is maybe about three or four million and Melbourne about the same. I don't know about New South Wales and Victoria."

"Me neither. But if we assume that half the populations of both states are in the cities then that gives a population of more than 10 million in those states alone. And there are other cities, like Adelaide and Brisbane. If we've survived then there must be other people and I think we should try and find them. We've been lucky to run into each other but imagine facing this on your own."

"I see what you mean," and she did. Although he was putting this point across like a logical conclusion that his analytical mind had reached, underneath it was a concern for lost and lonely survivors. It rather humbled her that while she had been thinking about how she could get herself rescued, he had been considering the possibility of rescuing other people. He was, without doubt, a strange mix of thinking and feeling. She remembered his disappointment at the airfield earlier in the day. "But what about your wife? Surely you want to let her know that you have survived?" Jack didn't answer immediately, and she wondered if she'd said the wrong thing.

"Of course I do. But I'm not convinced that charging off across country is going to be the quickest way. Sydney is a massive city and I think it's the first place that a rescue operation will go. But after a plague like this that won't be soon. The whole infected area, however big that is, will be quarantined. I think basing ourselves in Sydney is the best way for me to make sure I take the first opportunity to get word out to Jane. We can keep trying the satellite phone, but in the meantime I'm going to focus on what's going on here." And that made sense to her. He was trying to push his family to the back of his mind and focus on immediate concerns. It was a self-protection mechanism that she understood well.

"So what should we do, do you think?" she asked him.

"I've been giving some thought," he continued, "to how we can find survivors and, if you agree, I think I have a plan."

Nine

The arrival of morning the following day once again saw them up and out reasonably early. Over a breakfast of slightly stale toast (happily the gas cooker was powered by a LPG cylinder in the garden) with marmalade and honey, Xanthe informed Jack that her sister lived in Sydney and so she wanted to go and see the house and 'make sure they are dead'.

"You know what I mean," she finished, realising what she'd said only after the words were out of her mouth.

Xanthe had slept surprisingly well in her old room, but the morning had brought with it a sinking feeling as she thought back over what she had found in the house the day before. The image of her parents sprawled in death was still vivid and she knew it would be with her forever. She could never un-see that, however much she wanted to. She lay in bed for a few minutes after waking, trying unsuccessfully not to think about it, before she forced herself out of that temporary haven. Distracting herself with action might help, she reasoned.

She'd put Jack in Amelia's room, and he emerged still looking rather grimy, since he was wearing the same clothes he'd had on yesterday, although she had heard him having a cold shower as she lay in bed.

Before they set off Jack walked into the garden with the satellite phone. Xanthe didn't follow him, but tidied away their simple breakfast while he tried to establish contact with the outside world. He was at it a few minutes, and she was starting to wonder if perhaps the gadget was working today when he opened the back door and put the phone down on the table. One look at his face was enough to tell her that it still wasn't working, without the shake of his head that was the sum total he had to say on the subject.

So the two had once again set off after making Rufus comfortable in the garage. The little dog seemed stronger this morning but still didn't seem to have a lot of energy and so Xanthe chose to leave him at the house. Jack offered no opinion on the subject and Xanthe did not ask for one. Rufus was probably the only member of her family who was still alive and so she was going to make sure she looked after him.

They took her parents' car, a Toyota Corolla, although rather less new and shiny than the one in which Jack had chased her down on the highway the day before.

The day was sunny and, although it was still quite early, it looked like being a hot one, with tiny fluffy clouds drifting across the blue sky and the sun shining down just as if nothing had changed.

"Amelia and Xanthe. Typical Australian names are they?" Xanthe was driving since she knew the way and Jack was looking at her from the passenger seat.

"Don't start. You have no idea the grief the two of us had to take growing up with those names. Mum and Dad never did really explain to us why they'd chosen them other than that they thought unusual names would help us become 'individuals'. Has it worked, d'you think?"

"Definitely." The banter sounded hollow to Xanthe. Maybe to Jack as well since he didn't make any other comment.

It only took them twenty minutes to get to her sister's house, which was another bungalow, but rather smaller than home, and in a rather less leafy and rather more urban district of the Sydney suburbs. Jack's head swivelled as he scanned their surroundings. What was he looking for? Signs of survivors? Xanthe still found driving the familiar but deserted streets eerie. Like all the people had just vanished, although she knew full well they had all returned home to nurse their suspected cold and then died there.

"Shall I come in?" Jack asked her as Xanthe parked the car on the street outside the slightly faded bungalow her sister lived in with her husband.

"You may as well. I promise not to cry on you again." She didn't mean this as a joke and he didn't smile in response. He obviously knew the effort she was making to keep control.

And she managed to remain true to her word. The front door was locked, but there was no need to use the break-in kit that Jack had brought with him. He stepped back and administered a solid kick to the door. It survived the first but not the second, and Xanthe led the way straight to the bedroom, not even bothering to call out, as she had little expectation of finding anyone alive. The smell told her that.

The bedroom door was open and they stopped on the threshold and looked at the scene inside. After a few seconds of contemplating the scene, Jack asked, "Would you like to bury them?" But Xanthe did not answer his question.

"It's funny, I wasn't close to Amelia and I never really liked Simon, but it's still not easy to see them like this."

The dead pair were both on the bed. There was less mess than some dying people had produced and the two were actually cuddled together in an embrace that couldn't help but touch the heart of the observer.

"I never thought he was right for Amelia. He was so brash and full of himself and she was so timid and quiet. He totally dominated her and I never thought that that was healthy. Maybe I shouldn't have judged their relationship so harshly."

Jack didn't say anything as she thought back to the last time she had shared a meal with these two. Simon had lectured Xanthe on how to move her career forward, a subject that he was totally unqualified to talk about, being an accountant himself. He'd almost ignored Amelia, who had fetched and carried the whole evening. Only when the plates had been cleared had she had a chance to talk to Amelia with Simon not in the room, but her sister had little to say about her life other than that she was 'happy'. Xanthe remembered how she had glanced repeatedly at the kitchen door, obviously expecting Simon to walk in any moment.

Eventually Xanthe did get round to the question that Jack had asked. "I can't ask you to dig another grave. It took you hours yesterday." This was, she thought, a very kind offer. While she would very much like to bury the two of them she really didn't feel she could ask Jack to bury two more strangers. She knew that he would do it if she asked, which was, she supposed, a measure of the trust she already had in the Englishman.

"I think it would be the right thing to do," he answered, "and I may have a way to making it a bit quicker."

Fifteen minutes later they were ransacking a Portacabin for keys. Jack had spotted the construction site on the way to Amelia's house, so obviously all that looking around was not just idle curiosity. He'd thought beyond the finding of Xanthe's relatives and applied his mind to the problem of grave digging before they had even left home this morning, she realised. He had also remembered exactly where it was and had driven them there without error.

The door and windows of the Portacabin were quite heavily fortified, but Jack and his break-in kit was equal to the task. Now he was looking for the keys to the large yellow JCB that was parked outside, while Xanthe stood in the doorway and watched him. He pulled the small crowbar out of the break-in bag and forced the top drawer of the scuffed wooden desk with one efficient wrench. He lifted a set of keys that dangled from a dirty paper tag.

"Bingo. Want to drive?"

"No. I'll take Mum and Dad's car, thanks very much."

"OK. I'll follow you. Don't go too fast," Jack requested.

"Do you actually know how to drive that thing?"

"Not really. I did drive one, years ago on a farm, but I can't really remember. I'm sure I can work it out though." He gave her a slightly lopsided smile, but Xanthe wasn't in a smiling mood and simply headed back to the car.

Xanthe stood and watched while he climbed up into the cab and started to examine the controls. He spent a minute doing that and then started the machine up with roar that was rather shocking in the silent city. He then had a couple of false starts, including stalling it once before he was in motion. He gave her a thumbs up and Xanthe couldn't help smiling to herself as she walked back to Mum and Dad's car. Boys do love their toys.

She drove slowly, keeping the JCB in the rear view mirror as Jack bounced along at thirty kph behind her.

It took rather longer than it had on the way there, but it wasn't too long before he was positioning the JCB, ready to dig a grave on the front lawn of Amelia and Simon's bungalow.

The hole itself progressed quickly and so Xanthe went and dealt with the bodies, once again rolling them in clean sheets. Rather than sewing she used safety pins to keep them fastened. By the time she went back outside Jack was backing the digger away from the deep, but not very neat, hole that he had produced. They then embarked on the task of dragging them to the grave.

Xanthe reflected how even a task like this could become routine, however strange that seemed. By the time they were dragging the fourth family-member corpse out of the house in less than twenty-four hours the process was becoming horribly routine. Xanthe desperately tried to focus on the practicalities of the task in hand and not think about what was really going on here. She could feel the tears welling up again, but she was determined not to break down. *Deal with it*, she told herself. *It's happened. Just deal with it.*

After they got the two bodies into the grave, they stood for a few seconds in silence. Jack obviously didn't know what to say since he said nothing. So Xanthe broke the silence.

"I'm not going to say anything over the grave. You may as well get on with filling it up." She turned away immediately but knew that there had been an audible quiver in her voice. Well, who could blame her? In two days she had buried her whole family.

Jack climbed back up into the JCB, started it up again and set about filling in the hole, which, with mechanical aid, was once again a quick process, while Xanthe stood by and watched from a distance.

"OK. We should make a list of the stuff we need," Jack said, walking behind the counter of the café they had just broken in to. It was dim, of course, but Mr Practical had brought a torch with him from the break-in kit.

"Well, first I think you could do with some new clothes, those ones have seen better days,' Xanthe suggested, as she pulled two cans of coke from the chiller cabinet (not chilled, of course) and found two glasses. His clothes and trainers were all ingrained with dirt from digging the night before. *Grave dirt*, Xanthe thought to herself.

Xanthe went back outside into the sun and sat down at one of the tables. She closed her eyes while she waited for Jack to emerge. She had to try and put this behind her, for the moment at least. She and Jack were still alone in a completely empty city and she had to focus on what needed to be done right now. There would be time to grieve properly later. But it was *hard*.

Jack emerged from the shop with a pen and paper, evidently what he had been looking for. The breeze ruffled the nearby trees gently, but it was hot in the sun and so Jack put the umbrella at their table properly up, so that he and Xanthe were in the shade.

"I came here a few times with Amelia. Seems weird now. Like it's not the same place." Xanthe remembered the day, several years ago now. Amelia had told her that day that she and Simon were trying for a baby. Thank God they'd been unsuccessful, Xanthe thought to herself. She didn't know if she was capable of burying a tiny niece or nephew.

"Everything is different now." Jack spoke the words in a matter-of-fact tone of voice, as if he was telling her the time, or what he had eaten for breakfast.

"You're right. Everything *is* different now." Xanthe placed much more emphasis on these four words than Jack had. He looked across at her, before sitting back and taking a sip of his coke.

"I think all we can do now is look for survivors and try and make ourselves as comfortable as we can while we wait to be rescued," was Jack's suggestion, his tone not sounding too sure.

"And how long do you think that will be? A day? A week? A year? We have no idea, do we?" Xanthe was struggling to get her mood under control. She knew it wasn't fair shouting at Jack. None of this was his fault.

"No, of course not," Jack kept his voice calm and neutral. "It's totally possible, likely even, that some kind of quarantine will be applied and so it might be some time before somebody arrives. I don't know how long any more than you do. But I was thinking about this last night," he continued, "and it seems that we need to fix a planning horizon."

"A planning horizon? What the hell does that mean?"

"Well, you know, a length of time we'll plan for. Say a week to start with. We'll plan for a week and then if nobody has arrived in a week, we can set another one, maybe a bit longer."

"And how does that help us?"

"It doesn't get us rescued any quicker, but it does mean that we know what we're doing. Right now, I mean. We're gathering what we need to last one week."

"And then if nobody comes before the end of the week?" Xanthe wanted to know, aware that her challenging tone was totally unfair.

"Then we'll set another horizon. Say two weeks. Obviously if people arrive at any point during the stint then that's fine. Nothing lost."

Xanthe thought about it for a few moments. She took a deep breath, and suddenly her aggressive mood collapsed. She could feel tears not far behind her eyes and she regretted giving Jack a hard time. Where the hell would she be if she hadn't run into him? He watched while she took another deep breath, a little shaky perhaps and then forced herself to engage her mind in the conversation.

"So you're suggesting we now gather what we need for one week?"

"Exactly. What we need to live and also what we need to help us find survivors."

"What day is it today," she asked.

"Umm," he had to think for moment, "Tuesday."

"OK," Xanthe said. "I'll go with your 'planning horizon'. Let's make the list to last us until next Tuesday. Once we've made the list maybe we should split up to get things more quickly."

"It would be quicker, but I don't think we should. We should stay together. We have no way of contacting each other or finding each other if something happens. We're not in a rush." Even as she had made the statement about splitting up her insides had clenched at the thought of wandering round Sydney on her own and so relief flooded through her at his disagreement.

"That makes sense and I think I..." she trailed off, looking at him. Jesus! She'd been about to tell him that she felt safer with him around. She'd known this man for less than a day and seriously needed to get her emotions under control. "Well, yes, you're right. OK. Let's start with 'Clothes for Jack'," she said, suddenly business like, and tapped the paper on the table in front of him.

By mid-afternoon they were both exhausted, although now dressed in new clothes and with a car boot full of tinned food and other supplies. Shopping with no credit limit had certainly been a new experience for Xanthe who had never had a great deal of money back in the 'real world', thanks to her modest nurse's salary. She had 'bought' mostly practical clothing, fighting the temptation to buy decorative things, although all really nice quality. She had a full set of wet weather gear, some great walking boots and some lovely fleeces, as well as the usual singlets, T-shirts, shorts and jeans. Fresh underwear was also in there, still in the packaging. All these were packed into a large hold-all from a shop that had supplied them both with luggage. It certainly was a strange experience to walk into large department store and just take whatever you wanted, even if finding it in the torchlight was not so easy.

Jack had also gone for practical gear and was, like Xanthe, dressed in shorts but wasn't really carrying the look off. His legs were extraordinarily pale, although his T-shirt did reveal some muscle beneath his pale skin.

Unopposed looting was more tiring than Xanthe would have imagined. Obviously the first problem had been where to find things. This was, to some degree, solved by acquiring a Yellow Pages from a nearby house and this book, together with Jack's Garmin GPS, was a way of tracking down things that they needed. But it was a time consuming process, despite Xanthe's local knowledge.

It had occurred to both of them that there was not any need to find new versions of any given item. Most items, other than clothing, would be just as good looted from a house as a shop. Theft from private individuals, now deceased, was no different from theft from a business whose the owners were also deceased, but unfortunately there was no book in which you could look up who owned the items you needed to steal. Because of this they had stuck to shops so far. They had also wrought a fair amount of destruction, since it was a lot easier to put the crowbar through a plate glass window than try and jimmy open the steel shutter over the door of a department store.

"It's hard not to think of it as theft. Even though it's not really stealing at all. It's more like we're parasites living off the carcass of society," Xanthe had declared dramatically, as they made their way along the dark, glass walled corridor of a shopping mall, lighting the windows, and the displays within, with their torches.

"We're starring in a zombie movie without the zombies. That we've seen so far," had been Jack's reply, as he aimed the torch and the manikins stared back with their blankly painted eyes.

When they decided they had had enough they set out for home. This time he asked Xanthe to set the address into the GPS so that he could be sure to find it even without Xanthe's guidance. It seemed that he never stopped calculating, thinking ahead. On the way, however, there was an incident that did give them both pause for thought.

They had agreed that they needed a more practical vehicle and eventually saw what they were looking for parked in the driveway of a cleanly painted white wooden house as they passed. It was a big Mitsubishi pick-up truck, bright red and new looking. The keys would be in the house and so they needed to get inside, but the front door looked pretty solid. Xanthe suggested they try the back, which they could get to by squeezing past the large pick-up, down a neat path, via a gate, which stood open, and into a carefully maintained garden. This proved to be a good choice, as the back door was mostly glass, which gave a good view of the large kitchen beyond. One casual swing of the crowbar and Jack was reaching in through the broken pane and unlocking the door.

As the door swung open a large brown dog exploded into the room, snarling and barking ferociously. Both Jack and Xanthe jumped back down the steps they had been standing on and retreated a few yards into the garden. The dog, perhaps some kind of retriever, Xanthe thought, continued to bark and advanced to the threshold. Jack hefted the crowbar, which he was clearly now thinking might now have another purpose, while Xanthe slightly embarrassed herself by almost involuntarily retreating behind him.

"You're a dog person, Xanthe. What do we do? Or should we just try another house?" The dog had now stopped barking and was growling menacingly.

"Back to the car I think," Xanthe replied and so the two of them edged back around the house. The dog barked again as they retreated, and even advanced out into the neat garden, but didn't follow them around the side of the white painted house.

"So. We'll just need to find another pick-up. Pity, that one looks good," said Jack, opening the driver's door. He obviously didn't fancy taking on the dog, which was clearly guarding its key-containing territory, even with the crowbar. They had the shotgun with them, of course, but Xanthe certainly wasn't going to let him do *that*.

"Not at all. We can take this one," was Xanthe's deliberately cryptic reply as she opened the boot of the car and rummaged around amongst the tinned groceries they had put there.

A moment later she had found both a tin of dog food, planned for Rufus, and a tin opener and was using the latter on the former.

"Will that work? It looks angry," Jack sounded dubious.

"Trust me," she said, and gave Jack a smile, which seemed to surprise him into silence.

Once she got the tin open, Xanthe led the way cautiously back around the house. The dog was still in the garden and immediately started barking and snarling on seeing the two of them. Jack still held the crowbar ready, but now he was behind her, and she had a different plan. She advanced on the dog a few steps, causing it to retreat a little, although it crouched low to the ground as it snarled. It was clearly readying itself to spring. Xanthe, however, started talking, hoping that her voice, which she kept as light as she could, might help to calm it. It was a pet, after all, and hadn't heard a human voice for a few days.

"Hello, boy. I bet you've been lonely for these last few days haven't you. Lonely and hungry, I bet. Well I've got something for you. Yes, I have. I've got something you'll just love…" and as she continued to witter on with mindless doggy-drivel she emptied the contents of the can out on to the path. The food lay on the floor and Xanthe stood over it, not retreating. If the dog wanted to eat then it would have to come to her.

The dog clearly smelled the wet dog-food and was distracted by it. Its nostrils flared and it advanced a step, continuing to bark, but the conviction behind the snarls was greatly reduced. Xanthe stayed right next to the food and kept up a stream of mindless but soothing chatter as the dog eyed the food and advanced another step. Xanthe extended her hand. "Come on you silly boy, it's delicious and I know you can smell it."

At that point the animal's guard dog instincts gave up the fight against canine greed and it quite suddenly stopped snarling and advanced meekly on the food and started hungrily eating it. Xanthe stroked and petted it while it ate.

"Good boy. Who's a good boy? That's better isn't it? That's much better, yes it is."

It took the dog surprisingly little time for it to finish the contents of the tin, right down to licking the flagstone clean, leaving only a wet patch on the path. Once done it continued to allow Xanthe to stroke it and even moved a little to get a bit closer to her.

"Impressive. You never said you were a qualified dog-whisperer," Jack commented drily.

"Well, he was just hungry. Although not as hungry as he would be if he hadn't eaten anything for most of a week," Xanthe said darkly. "If you want to think about what he's been drinking and eating in that time, I can only come up toilet water and human." Despite this gruesome statement she continued to stroke the dog. "Not that you can blame him, given the choices he had, trapped in the house. You or I might do the same." Jack didn't deny it, although he did eye the dog from a distance, despite its wagging tail and eager licking of Xanthe's hand.

"I'll go and look for the keys," he stated.

He was back in a couple of minutes with the keys, but he didn't comment on whether he had seen the former owners of the house or whether her theory on the animal's food source was correct.

Ten

In the end the house with the pick-up truck turned out to be a bit of a bonanza of looted material. Not only did they come away with the truck itself ("Called a 'ute' in Oz," Xanthe told Jack) but quite a few other things that Jack had put on the list while they sat in the cafe. After transferring their booty from earlier in the afternoon from the Toyota to the Mitsubishi they stood on the small, but neatly mown, front lawn and took stock. The dog was glued to Xanthe's heels and looking surprisingly sweet natured and appealing, for a man-eater.

"Are you OK to just leave your parents' car here?" Jack asked her. He was certainly being pretty solicitous, Xanthe thought to herself.

"I suppose. Cars aren't important now, are they. It just seems weird that we are just going to abandon something which a few days ago was valuable. I'm really struggling to adjust my thinking to Zombieland."

"Me too. But we're in a weird world now where the fuel in a car is more valuable than the car itself. I'm guessing that when this is over we'll look back on this whole time as a surreal experience. People will ask us 'what was it like?' and we'll say we just wandered around taking whatever we wanted."

"Yeah. Let's hope that happens."

"I tell you what. Why don't you drive the Toyota and I'll follow you in the big truck," Jack suggested. "That way we'll have one car that can carry a good load and one that doesn't burn so much petrol."

"Nah. I want to drive the big truck. You can drive the little car," Xanthe surprised herself with this, as if the old Xanthe, or perhaps normal would be a better word, suddenly made an appearance. She liked how it felt.

"What?" Jack looked initially taken aback, but then went for mock outrage. "What if someone sees me?" Xanthe found herself laughing for the first time for quite a while. It was a good come back and she enjoyed the joke. She'd been thinking that Jack was a serious individual with not much sense of humour, but maybe it hadn't been just him.

"But before we go I'm going to look in the garage," Jack indicated the big door set back from the house, behind the Mitsubishi, "and see if they have anything else useful. Anyone who has a truck like this has got to have some of these other things on the list."

And so it proved. They couldn't find the key to the garage door and, since it wasn't connected to the house, there was no other way in. But he was determined and ended up bending the corner of the metal door up until there was a gap big enough for crawling. Once in he released the door from the inside and opened it right up (or as far as the bent corner would allow) and they surveyed the hoard within.

The first things Xanthe saw were not on his list, but certainly caught her eye. Two shiny blue and apparently identical off-road motorbikes sat on a purpose-built trailer that occupied a good deal of the space, within.

"Can you ride one of these?" Xanthe asked him, putting her hand on the tank of one of the bikes, dog at her heels still.

"Well, I'm not a pro, but I can certainly get from A to be B on one. I owned a bike for a couple of years when I was younger and my brother in law has something similar to these things. He's really into it and I've had a couple of goes. You?"

"I had a boyfriend, before Steve, for a few years who had one. I went with him quite a few times and he taught me to ride. It was fun, but I mostly went just so we could do it together. After five years I caught him cheating with one of my friends and so that was a waste of time. All I ended up with was the ability to ride a motorbike. They're still together. Well. Not now, I suppose."

Jack looked like he didn't really know how to respond to this personal detail from her life and busied himself looking around the back of the garage. After a moment or two he held up a jerry can and a hose.

"This is what we need for refuelling the cars," he announced, looking disproportionately pleased with himself over finding such simple objects. He took them outside and dumped them into the ute.

Xanthe had also started rummaging around the various junk stacked in the garage. There was some camping equipment, which was well used, by the look of it. A couple of sleeping bags, a large blackened pot, a metal grill and a pair of metal tongs that were obviously used for cooking on an open fire. None of that was on the list and Mum and Dad had equivalent anyway. Right next to this, however was another jerry can, but this one was made of white plastic. A quick sniff told her that this one was water. Could be useful. She took it out to the ute.

The final big find was probably the best of all and seemed slightly out of keeping with the rest of the equipment. Whoever was living in this house (*did live*, Xanthe reminded herself) obviously liked to head out into the wilderness at the weekends and tear about on their shiny motorbikes. They liked to camp while they were there and why not, camping in the bush was an Australian tradition. But they must also have some equipment that needed power while they were camping, because underneath the sleeping bags was a bright red Honda generator.

"Fantastic," Jack announced when he found it. "They have a generator. I mean, *we* have a generator. I put it on the list and here it is. Luckily these people seem to have been preparing for the apocalypse. Either that or they were just keen bikers and campers. Maybe they have a cabinet of automatic weapons somewhere."

"Serious?"

Jack laughed. "No. They are just campers, why would they have guns? What are the laws on guns here anyway?" Xanthe had never been a big weapons fan. She'd dealt with a few gunshot wounds in A & E and that was enough to put you off the things.

"Well, you can own most types of guns as long as you have a licence. I'm not really sure. I've never tried to buy a gun. Why do you want guns?"

"I don't. I was just curious. I haven't scheduled shooting anything within my current planning horizon." She smiled at him. She was definitely feeling a bit better this afternoon, she realised. Did that make her a shallow person? Whatever.

They got the stuff loaded into the back of the Mitsubishi and were ready to leave. Jack started to shut the garage door, although Xanthe wasn't sure why, so she asked him "Aren't we taking the bikes?"

"What for?"

"I don't know. Seems a waste to just leave them here. And it might be a useful way to get around." Jack didn't argue and it didn't take long to hitch the trailer to the tow-ball on the back of the big truck, although Xanthe did wonder why he was connecting up the trailer lights. He was the only person who would see the back of this trailer and so getting arrested for not having proper brake lights really didn't seem an imminent danger, but old habits die hard, she knew.

"What about the dog?" Xanthe asked, bending down and petting the animal, who was nothing but friendly now. Jack held up his hands, palms outward. "We can't just leave him here," she said, finding her heart being softened by the enthusiastically wagging tail.

"Well. We can. Or we can take him with us. It's entirely up to you. Will he eat Rufus?"

"I don't think you will, will you boy. Will you eat Rufus?" Jack looked on, face neutral.

"We should take him. I'd feel bad leaving him here."

"Despite what he's done, or maybe done."

"Like I said, he did what he had to do. And it's not as if they were alive."

"What will you call him?"

"I don't know. Any ideas?" Xanthe asked him.

"Are you sure he's a boy dog?"

"His testicles say that he probably is."

"Oh. I didn't notice. How about Idi Amin. Didn't he used to eat people?"

"Did he? Anyway, that's not what we'll call him. I think we'll call you Alf. After my grandfather." Alf's tail wagged on.

"Alf it is. OK. Let's go. I'll follow you in the Toyota. Make sure Alf doesn't eat you."

Back at home they considered their next move. Jack had unhitched the bike trailer from the big Mitsubishi and left it in the road outside, but only after Xanthe had rather impressed herself by backing it into position first time. Whether or not this feat had impressed Jack she didn't know, since he didn't comment.

They were now drinking tea, which seemed like a minor miracle. The generator had started up first pull and was running, surprisingly quietly, in the garden. Xanthe had retrieved Dad's extension cable from the garage, which Jack had plugged in and unrolled into the kitchen. The kettle had then been connected and duly boiled, although it took a little longer than the mains would have achieved, delivering hot tea (powdered milk instead of fresh was the only down side) before Jack killed the generator and they sat in the ensuing silence on the garden chairs her parents kept near the back door.

"So, should we get straight on with your plan to find other survivors? It's only four o'clock," Xanthe wanted to know. She was tired but didn't want to be the one to block Jack's rescue mission. She was absent-mindedly stroking Rufus, who lay next to her, as they sat on the veranda at the back of the house.

On the drive over she had considered what would happen when the two dogs met and so had been prepared for the encounter. What had happened was the two had eyed each other suspiciously and then both had emitted low growls with their hackles rising. Xanthe had immediately delivered a fairly hefty slap to the side of Alf's head, which had caused Jack to look slightly shocked, but Xanthe had been matter of fact ("You have to show them whose in charge, and I mean me.") and sure enough the two dogs had relaxed and now seemed calm. Xanthe was conspicuously stroking Rufus and ignoring Alf. She knew that dogs were happy if there was a clear hierarchy established.

"We could, although it'll take quite a while and well, I feel like I've looted enough shops for one day. Now there's a sentence I've never said before." Xanthe smiled in response. She was happy with that verdict. If there were other survivors they could probably survive until tomorrow and she was weary, probably more from the emotional turmoil as any actual exertion. There also, she admitted to herself in the comfortable silence, a reluctance on her part to shake up their world again. She was becoming more comfortable with Jack and new people would undoubtedly bring new issues to worry about.

As things turned out the pair had not been nearly reluctant enough to execute on Jack's plan to round up survivors.

Xanthe sipped her tea in the quiet and thought about the day they had just spent. So utterly unlike any day she had ever experienced before. After a while she voiced some of her thoughts.

"It all seems so surreal. It's only been a couple of days but already I'm adjusting to, well, this way of living, I suppose. For the first day or two I kept, you know, almost reaching for my phone to text someone or something, but now I'm getting used to whatever *this* is. Just being in the moment, you know what I mean? There's no distractions, no people to communicate with, no TV or Facebook. No schedule of places I have to be and stuff I have to do."

"I know. It *is* weird." Jack agreed. There was a pause.

"You must be thinking about your wife and family a lot."

" Well. A bit. They will be worried or assume I'm dead, and that's not good. But like you said, I've just been thinking about the here-and-now really. There's nothing I can do right at the moment and so there's no point in worrying about it." He lapsed into silence with a frown on his face that had not been there before. She regretted bringing up the subject now. He was clearly trying not to think about it, just as she was trying not to think about the images of her dead family. Jack didn't keep reminding her about who they had buried. Eventually his frown smoothed out and he gave her a small, ironic smile.

"I hope Jane doesn't re-marry before I can tell her I'm alive," he said.

"That's a joke, right? God, I can never tell when you're joking. Bloody Poms."

"Yes, that's a joke. I hope. I'll touch my nose like this when I'm joking so it's clear for you, OK?" Xanthe stuck out her tongue in response.

"So if we're not looting and survivor-hunting, are we just going to sit and drink tea all afternoon? We brought beer, we could start in on that, " Xanthe suggested. Sitting drinking beer did sound appealing. Although there was definitely a danger that a couple might lead to quite a few and then that might in turn lead to way too many.

"That does sound good, but there's one or two things I might spend a bit of time on first."

"Like what?"

"How much fuel is in the big truck? Sorry, the ute," he asked.

"Just under half a tank, I think. Quite a bit."

"So I was thinking I might find out how easy it is to refill it from other cars. We're definitely going to need more than half a tank in the next week and I want to, you know, practice stealing petrol. There's also the water issue."

"What water issue?"

"Does this house have a cold water tank in roof?"

"Oh, I see what you mean," Xanthe replied. "Yes, I think it does."

"Well normally that will only supply some of the taps. Some will be directly off the mains. Either way, the mains water is going to stop working at some point. In fact it may already have done so, and we need to work out how we are going to get water once that happens."

"D'you think you could manage hot water? God, a hot shower or a bath would go down well, I can tell you."

"You want hot water. Jesus, what kind of girl are you?" he said, failing in his attempt to look outraged.

"One who wants to lie in a hot bath, mate."

Xanthe said she was going to stay in the house and "do a few things" while Jack set off with his fuel tools to try and steal petrol.

While he was gone she busied herself bringing all their loot into the house and started unpacking it. She first tidied her own new clothes into her room and then the food, which was mostly tins, into the larder in the kitchen. Once that was done she even took Jack's clothing into Amelia's room, which he was sleeping in and unpacked them into the chest of drawers and cupboards, which were otherwise pretty well empty.

It was therapeutic, getting everything sorted out, and she even caught herself humming at one point. Ridiculous to feel guilty about humming but it was hard not to.

When Jack returned smelling of gasoline, Xanthe had just finished cleaning out the fridge and had another task for him.

"Do you think we can get the fridge working? It would be great to be able to keep stuff cold."

"I don't see why not. We can run the generator as much as we like. The fuel's free, after all."

"Great. Would you mind…?"

"I'll sort it out," Jack assured her and so she left him to it.

It seemed like only moments later that she was in her room, examining the various fleeces she had acquired that day when his voice suddenly spoke from the doorway. It made her jump since she had had no idea he was there.

"Do you know how I get up to the water tank?" Xanthe's head whipped round and she put her hand on her chest, before smiling a slightly embarrassed smile.

"You made me jump. How long were you standing there?"

"Five seconds. Maybe less."

"Oh. The hatch is in the bathroom, but I've never been up there. Dad used to go up there sometimes, if something needed fixing." She led him to the bathroom and indicated a simple square hatch in the ceiling. Jack positioned the laundry basket underneath the hatch and clambered up as Xanthe stood, arms folded and watched him.

He lifted the hatch out of the way and stuck his head in the dim space beyond.

"You couldn't get me a torch, could you?"

"Sure. Back in a minute." By the time she was back in the bathroom

Jack had vanished into the dark rectangle in the ceiling.

"Here you go." She called, and climbed up onto the laundry basket herself. She was only just tall enough to poke her head through the hatch and look around, holding the torch up.

"Wow, I've never been up here. It's huge." It was so weird that all those years she had lived here, this massive space was just above her and she'd never seen it. Never really even considered its existence.

"It is. Pass me the torch and I'll check out the tank."

The tank itself was only a yard or two from the hatch and was a large black plastic mass, shrouded in dust. Jack lifted a square of plastic from the top and shone the torch down inside.

"The tank's full, so that's good," he commented before reaching out and pushing something, which caused water to audibly flow into the tank.

"And there's still water coming out of the mains, but I don't know how long that will last. Depends on how many people have left taps on and how many leaks the system has, I suppose."

"Maybe it'll last weeks. Way past your 'planning horizon', Mr Project Manager."

"Maybe. I've no idea. But I agree it's not fantastically urgent at the moment. Although when the mains supply stops flowing it'll become more urgent. In the meantime we can use as much water as we like. I doubt whatever we use will make any difference to how long it lasts."

"So what about that hot water I mentioned? Anything you can do about that? It's a week since I last had a hot shower."

"OK. I'll look at that now. Where's the hot water tank?"

"It's in the airing cupboard. Get down and I'll show you."

Jack didn't take long on that task either. He spent a few minutes in the garage with the camping lamp before emerging with a length of electrical cable with a plug on one end and stripped wires on the other. He also had Dad's toolbox. She held the torch for him as he stripped away the lagging from the front of the tank and got to work on a gizmo sticking out of the bottom of it. A couple of minutes later he stood back and told her that he was done and that they should try it. He plugged the cable into the extension lead that ran to the kitchen.

"OK. Give it an hour and there should be hot water."

Eleven

"That," Xanthe declared, "was fucking fantastic," as she collapsed on the chair next to Jack. She had just spent an hour having a hot bath, and the whole process of getting ready, lounging in the hot water and then dressing afterwards had been an unspeakable luxury. She had festooned the bathroom with candles that had provided a soft light in the steamy room as she soaked for a good long time. The water was piping hot and she had emerged pink as a lobster, having taken another step towards recovery. Amazing what luxuries they had all taken so much for granted before the sickness had snatched it all away.

After wiping down the mirror her survey of herself was, as ever, critical. She knew she had a good body, which she worked reasonably hard to keep trim, but she was just beginning to detect the first signs of aging. Her breasts were certainly not quite as pert as once they had been, as gravity began to edge the inevitable battle, and her previously flat stomach was just starting to bulge despite plenty of abs exercises. Oh well, it could be worse. She was also, of course, too short. She always had been and always would be. How she had longed for long limbs as a teenager, but she was more sanguine about it these days.

Short wasn't too bad, as long as she could stave off short and fat, which she had so far managed.

What did Jack make of her, she wondered, as she brushed her hair. He had not made a particularly favourable first impression on her, but that was starting to change. She'd thought him overly formal and, well, anal, on first meeting but now that she was able to read him a little better she knew there was more to him than she had first thought. He was certainly quite good looking, although he could do with a bit more time in the sun. *Perhaps better not to think about that*, she told herself. He was, after all, married and now was not a time to be creating complications. But it was certainly to her advantage that she had met him, and also in her interest that he like her enough to stick around. So she took a couple of minutes to apply a small amount of make-up before emerging on to the deck where he had the barbie burning.

"I can strongly recommend that. You should go. There's a shower, if you'd rather. How long does the water take to heat?" She was wearing jeans and a different singlet but had one of the looted fleeces draped around her shoulders. Jack had a good look before she turned the lamp off.

"Not sure, but I've been heating it while you were in the bath and so I think I'll do as you suggest. A hot shower does sound good. I think the barbecue's ready for cooking on, although we only have tinned food, so I suppose some kind of stew in a pot is all we can manage."

"Leave that to me. You go and have your shower."

Jack emerged a while later in clean clothes and looking, to Xanthe's eye, more relaxed.

They spent the evening after supper just sitting and chatting about life before the plague. Xanthe started quizzing him about life in England, but Jack looked a bit uncomfortable talking about home, although he did describe his family, the three girls in particular.

"It's weird. It all seems like another life now," he said, thoughtfully. "I miss them, of course, but it seems hard to imagine that I could just resume normal life at home."

"So if the helicopters arrive tomorrow," Xanthe asked, "would you just go back to your job like nothing had happened?"

"I suppose I would. What else would I do? A couple of interviews on CNN, I'm guessing and then back to the office on Monday morning. Maybe I could get a week off for mental trauma. Or maybe a year while I recover from PTSD, which I can already *definitely* feel the first twinges of. What about you?"

"Well, it's different for me. I'm Australian and the Australia that I know has been wiped out. Even if parts have survived the plague, the nation's been destroyed. It won't ever be the same again and so there's no life for me to go back to. I suppose I'll go and live somewhere else and work and stuff. Or maybe get involved in re-building, although how that would work I don't know. After the interviews on CNN, of course." She said all this quite matter-of-factly. It was something she'd been working out in her head over the last few days, including as she lay in the bath.

"I haven't given much thought to what happens after we're rescued, but it sounds like you have," Jack observed.

"Of course. My life's gone and so I've been thinking about what the future holds. But it's probably best not to think about it. I can't make any long-term plans and so I think I'll just live in the here-and-now. Focus on what we're doing day to day."

"I agree. I think we should both do that. It seems to me that this is like watching a film, you know? When you sit down to watch a movie it's like a two hour break in your normal life and you just immerse yourself in the plot and the characters and don't think about what else is going on in your life."

"Well," said Xanthe slowly, "if this is a movie then are we characters in the movie or are we just in the audience? Are you and me just two strangers who happen to be sitting next to each other in the cinema because all the other seats were taken?"

"No way. We're the main characters in the movie. There are people out there right now," Jack pointed out into the night, "who are tucking into pop corn and wondering how it will end."

"And how, Brad Pitt, will it end then?"

"Not sure yet, although I have to apologise that Brad Pitt wasn't available to play my part, so you'll have to make do with me. Sorry about that."

"You're right, that is disappointing. Oh well."

The next morning it was raining and windy, which meant that Jack's ill-fated plans to hunt for survivors had to be pushed back, since they weren't really compatible with rain.

"So what shall we do? What do we still need within your 'planning horizon' Mr Planner?" Xanthe asked Jack over breakfast after he had announced that the weather was going to delay his plans further. He was a bit damp having already done his morning test of the stolen satellite phone, although he had not looked overly disappointed as he returned to the kitchen shaking his wet head. Either he was doing a good job of managing his expectations or he was hiding his disappointment well.

"Not much actually, but I did have one thought. It's not really vital for the next week, but it seems like something that might not be feasible later. If there is a later. I don't mean that we're going to be, well, I mean…"

"Spit it out." God! Sometimes he did have trouble just saying what he wanted to say.

"Um, OK. I think we should find some chickens."

"Chickens?"

"Yes," continued Jack. "We could find a poultry farm and get some

111

chickens and bring them back here. The reason we need to do it now is that they'll be locked up and they'll all be dead if we leave it too long. They may already be dead but I think it's still worth a try. Think of it as a mission of mercy rather than resource scavenging."

After some breakfast and an inspection of the yellow pages they were on their way again in the Mitsubishi pick-up.

"Do you know anything about keeping chickens?" Xanthe wanted to know.

"Well, not really," Jack admitted. "But my aunt keeps them and it doesn't seem overly technical. They seem to eat most stuff and then they put themselves to bed at night. All you have to do is feed them and shut them up each night so that the fox doesn't eat them. Are there foxes here?"

"Actually yes. They were brought to Australia about a century ago. Deliberately, for hunting. Which seems unbelievable in this day and age, doesn't it? And now they've spread and are busy eating all the Australian wildlife. It's a big problem here."

"So we'll need to lock them up so we're not feeding the foxes, but other than that I think it shouldn't be too complex. They're only chickens."

Although 'only chickens' didn't seem so convincing an hour later when the two of them were walking through sheds in which the only noise was the buzz of flies. They'd found the poultry farm fairly easily but investigating it proved rather more harrowing. The farm consisted of a number of long sheds, set parallel to each other, and the only sign of movement were the various cats, which were circling the sheds eager for a way in. Jack and Xanthe found the door and let themselves in, while keeping the hungry cats on the outside.

The first building contained many thousands of tiny enclosures and each packed with five or six dead chickens. Nothing stirred in the enormous, dim shed except the flies and dust motes that danced in the shafts of sunlight coming through the two grimy windows that failed to sufficiently light the cavernous interior.

Everything that could be seen was crusted in filth and the flies crawled over the carcasses of the hens. They had been fed through some kind of conveyor system mounted on each row of cages but its inactivity was the obvious reason for the chickens' demise. Below the food conveyor was a gutter which was filled with eggs. The last crop from these poor animals. The sheer number of the dead birds in stacked ranks marching into the dimness of the shed left both of the survivors without words. They stood for minute just looking before Jack turned and let them both out, back into the daylight. The rain had stopped, but although it was still cloudy, it seemed painfully bright after the darkness inside.

"I think this has been a wasted trip," Jack reluctantly suggested. "Perhaps we should head home. The weather is improving, so let's go into the middle of Sydney.

"We should check the other sheds first," Xanthe suggested, a touch stubbornly. The sight of the ranked corpses of the battery hens had shocked her.

"You think they'll be any different?"

"Probably not. But we're here now."

The next two buildings were identical to the first, huge dimly lit racks of dead poultry, but the fourth was a wholly different experience. Even as they approached the building they could hear the noise emanating from inside. Jack opened the door and the two of them slipped through the gap and hurriedly shut it behind them, taking care that they weren't accompanied by any cats. Once inside the noise was loud and continuous, the combined squawking and clucking of thousands, maybe tens of thousands, of live chickens. These birds were not crushed into crates but instead packed into large enclosures maybe ten feet square that ran in two rows down the length of the shed. The light was dim, as with the other sheds but the whole place was alive with noise and movement, so sharply in contrast to the other silent sheds it was almost a physical shock.

"My God. Shall we just grab some and put them in the car?" Xanthe looked at Jack and practically had to shout.

"Let's go back outside and talk about it," Jack shouted back and they retreated back to the peace of the outside world.

"That's unbelievable. What's your plan, Chicken Man?"

"I'm afraid I haven't really thought this through. I suppose we should find some sort of container to transport them in. They've got to have crates or something similar here."

"And what will we do with them once we've got them home? Lock them in the garage? Won't they just shit everywhere?"

"They will, of course, but is that a big issue? We can just hose the place out every few days."

"We can while the water's still working," Xanthe pointed out.

"That's true," said Jack slowly. "Let me think about this for minute." There was a pause while Jack did just that. The noise and movement inside the chicken shed was slightly shocking and had rather disorientated both of them after so many days of quiet and stillness.

"You know what. You're right. I haven't thought this through at all. How about this? We make sure that the chickens have food and water now, but leave them here for a day or two and get things ready at home. We could build a chicken run for them in the garden."

"That sounds like a better plan. Right then, let's make sure they have food and water."

So Jack and Xanthe spent the next hour gathering all that they could for the chickens. Back inside the noisy shed they ascertained that the chickens were fed some kind of pellets from a hopper, powered by nothing more complicated than gravity, mounted on each enclosure. Water came down narrow troughs that ran the length of the shed, and since water still seemed to be flowing they left that.

"So how do they fill these hoppers? There's got to be a reasonably easy way," suggested Xanthe, and after a bit of searching they found it. The final shed didn't have chickens in it at all, alive or dead. Instead it housed various equipment and machinery, more like a rather dirty factory than a farm, and parked by the entrance was a large forklift truck, which supported a huge bag of chicken feed. The keys were in the truck and so getting it started and manoeuvred to the end of the 'live' shed was easy but here they were presented with a trickier problem. There was no obvious way to get the forklift in through the big double doors without admitting the half dozen cats that had gathered near the loudly running engine, obviously reasoning the same way.

"Do cats kill chickens?" Xanthe asked. "Or are they too big?"

"I don't know, but they certainly seem keen. And hungry. So I'm guessing they might."

"They do look like they rate their chances, don't they. Any ideas on how we keep them out?"

"Actually I have. Let's just let them into the other sheds. That should be sufficiently interesting to keep them busy while we get this in through the doors," Jack patted the side of the idling forklift.

And this was exactly how it worked out. They left the machine running by the building with the live birds, but as they walked over to the dead sheds the cats accompanied them. They obviously knew that the humans were their best bet of getting at all the chickens they could clearly smell. Jack threw open the door open to the first shed and stepped back. Xanthe thought that the cats would shoot straight in there, but actually they were a bit more circumspect and approached the door with caution. But approach and enter they did, and there must have been well over half a dozen.

Jack hurried back to the forklift.

"OK. Open the doors," he called, as he swung up into the driver's seat, and Xanthe rolled the door back to let him drive through.

They got the forklift inside without feline company and then set about filling the hoppers, which were all empty. This took a bit of practice and involved some spillage of chicken pellets, but there was enough in the bag to fill all the hoppers. The chickens in the pens went into a frenzy to get at the food as it filled the troughs, the noise level rose higher with each hopper filled.

"How long do you think that'll last?" Xanthe asked after they had filled the last hopper and shut off the forklift engine.

"No idea. Couple of days, maybe. It'll keep them alive for long enough for us to build a coop. I hope so anyway. I think the water will be more important, so let's hope that keeps flowing. The hens won't last long if it doesn't."

"Right then, what's on the menu next, boss? Shall we cluck off home again," Xanthe gave him a smile as they stepped out into the sunlight and closed the door behind them to seal in the chickens.

"Well, the weather looks to be clearing, so I suggest we stop off at home and pick up some things and then a little light looting before we head into town and find our fellow survivors."

"You really believe that there are more people out there? We've seen nothing that says there are."

"I don't know, Xanthe. Logic says there must be, but then logic also says that aliens should be here and we haven't seen them."

"Really?"

"Yeah. It's called the Fermi Paradox. It says that aliens must be out there because there's billions of stars and the universe is old. A combination of those things means that even if a vanishingly small percentage of stars have planets which develop intelligent life, which goes out and explores the universe, then they should have reached here by now. So where are they? Anyway, my point is that just because I think there should be people, doesn't mean there will be. But we have to have a look and, hey, we're not doing anything else. Even if we don't find anybody we can still enjoy the show. Let's get the doors of the other dead sheds open to keep the cats and foxes busy."

Xanthe didn't know quite what to make of this speech. There were lots of things going on in Jack's head behind the awkward silences and every now and then she'd get a brief glimpse of the activity. He sometimes made her a little uncomfortable, revealing that he had thought three steps further than she had managed, but then at other times he seemed strangely behind.

None of the men in her life had been what she would call brainy. In fact, in just about all relationships she'd had since she first kissed Jimmy Thatcher at school, she had been the clever half. She hadn't joined her fellow nurses in the pursuit of young doctors and so maybe she just wasn't that used to dealing with intelligent men.

It was most of the way through the afternoon before they arrived at the Sydney Botanic Gardens with the big Mitsubishi loaded with the items that Jack had declared they needed.

"So you think this is as central as it gets?" he asked Xanthe as they stopped outside a set of iron gates set in a warm sandstone wall, the skyscrapers of central Sydney close behind them.

"I guess so. It's as good as anywhere. Reckon you can get that gate open?"

This task actually needed a bit of work and so while he worked Xanthe climbed the gates despite the spikes on the top.

"You look like you've done that before," Jack commented, as she dropped lightly down on the far side.

"Not these particular gates, but others like them. Who hasn't?" She shrugged one bare shoulder and turned away, walking towards the sunlit lawn beyond the nearby trees. She stood looking out over the lawns and thought back to the last time she had been here. It was years before, while she was still at college and she and Daniel had come here. He'd wanted to hold hands and stroll about all lovey-dovey, but she'd spent the whole time trying to pluck up the courage to dump him. If she remembered correctly it had taken her few more days.

When the gates finally gave up the struggle against Jack's hacksaw, he drove the truck through and found Xanthe lying in the sun on a lawn, which had a sign saying 'Please walk on the grass'. Xanthe didn't think this extended to 'Please drive your ute on the grass' but times change.

"You made it then?" she didn't stir from where she lay, forearms behind her head. "How does this spot look to you?"

"This'll do nicely. I think those two trees should provide the wood we need and it's nice and open. I'll get to work."

"You're really going to cut down those trees? They're part of the Australian heritage. I might report you." She was joking, but her tone was more wistful than anything else. These gardens were a part of her country, and it seemed like a recognition that Australia no longer existed. She knew she was attaching far too much emotion to the cutting down of two trees, but what you feel is not always the same as what you think you should feel.

Despite her slightly sombre mood, the two of them worked hard for the next hour. Jack had brought a chainsaw with him (taken from the garden shed of the Normans, who lived two doors down from home) and he used it to fell the two small trees and cut them into carry sized logs, which they then gathered into two large piles.

"Right, now for the fireworks," Xanthe was a bit more enthusiastic about this part.

The back of the pick-up was stacked with fireworks that they had looted from a pyrotechnics wholesaler that afternoon. Each rocket –

and they had a lot of them – had it's own launch tube which needed to be stuck in the turf and they made two long rows of the skyward pointing missiles.

When they were finished, they sat for a few minutes, drank some bottled water and contemplated their handy work. The evening was glorious, with the cloud almost completely cleared away and the low sun peeping out from behind a skyscraper.

"Shall we run a sweepstake on how many people will be here once we've launched all of these?" Xanthe asked. She swept some hair back behind her ear, still wearing the gardening gloves she had been working in, and gave Jack a smile.

He suddenly looked doubtful, she noticed, as if he was having second thoughts. He gave her a long look, definitely taking in more than her face, but she didn't really resent the admiration.

"OK," he finally said. "I bet five. Let's get lighting."

Xanthe was quite right about Jack having sudden qualms. The following day he would bitterly regret dismissing his doubts so easily.

Twelve

"There's no point in sending too many up at once. I suggest we begin with a few and then start leaving a gap between each one. Say fifteen minutes."

"Why so long? If someone is close enough to see, then they'll head straight here and it won't take them that long, will it?" Xanthe wanted to know. She knew that Jack would have reasoned it out but just wanted him to state his thought processes.

"Well, it seems to me that there might be people who aren't that near and so might only be able to hear the bangs if they are outside. If we spread the rockets out over a long period then we maximise the chance of everybody in range hearing the noise. Also, if we make them regular we will be easier to find, since people will know that they can drive and then stop and look for the next rocket. It should make it easier to home in on us."

"OK. Sounds reasonable. Remember though, this is Australia and not England. We don't all cower from the weather behind double-glazing. Even if people are inside, chances are that they have windows open so they'll hear the bangs. How long before the first people arrive, d'you think?"

"There's no way of knowing how long. Or even if anybody will arrive. It could be anywhere from fifteen minutes to never. We'll just have to give it a shot."

"And how long do you think we should keep firing them off if nobody comes?" She may as well get his full plan out on the table.

"Well," Jack replied. "We've enough rockets to last until around midnight, if we fire off four or five to start with and then one every fifteen minutes after that. I think we should just do them all. It's not cold and we have sleeping bags and will soon have a fire, so there's no reason to stop."

"OK," Xanthe turned and opened the passenger door of the pick-up, climbed in and returned a moment later. She handed Jack the long firework lighter that they had taken from the warehouse they had raided. "You light the first one."

Jack lit the first rocket in the row and retreated back next to Xanthe and the Mitsubishi. It went off with a whoosh and exploded high above their heads, spreading green stars and leaving a visible cloud of smoke at the point of explosion. The stars weren't as bright as at night but the bang was impressive and surely audible from a good distance, especially with little background noise to muffle it.

"The smoke might help as a marker to find us," said Xanthe as she craned her neck to look at the dirty remnant of the explosion spreading slowly above their heads.

"Do you want to light the next one?" Jack asked her.

"OK. Now?"

"Let's give it a couple of minutes between each one at the start."

They lit four in a row, leaving about two minutes between each, although neither timed it accurately.

"Right," Jack looked at his watch. "It's quarter past six now, give or take. We'll light the next one at half past."

"Should we light the fire now, d'you think?"

"I think so," replied Jack eyeing up the wood piles. "Were you a girl scout? Do you even have girl scouts Down Under?"

"Girl guides, idiot. And yes, we do have them and, no, I wasn't one. But I've done enough camping though, so I can certainly get the fire going."

"Good. You do that. I'll take some of the wood off the pile. We don't want to burn it all in one go."

They busied themselves getting the fire going. Xanthe was pleased that her claims were borne out as the fire started to catch, although the can of petrol they'd brought had accelerated the process somewhat. As they worked Jack could see Xanthe doing the same thing he was – glancing up the hill towards the gates looking for arrivals – but after fifteen minutes they were still alone. The freshly cut logs were starting crackle and spit although the flames were still quite low and no real heat was being generated yet.

"Right, time to launch the next one," Jack offered Xanthe the lighter but she made a shooing gesture towards the row of rockets, so Jack went and lit the fuse on the next rocket in line. He retreated rapidly and stood next to Xanthe as they craned their heads and watched the burst of red sparks above. The fireworks were noticeably brighter in the fading dusk, but the smoke puff was still visible after the red stars had faded.

"Beautiful," Xanthe murmured quietly. The fireworks transported her back to when she'd stood and watched displays at times like New Year.

"They are," Jack agreed. "Like everything else now, they're the same and yet different."

"They're the same. We're different. Even when, or I suppose I should say if, we get rescued there's no going back. It's only a week but there's no going back for us, is there. Even if other parts of the world are OK it will be a different place after this." She gestured with one hand to indicate the Sydney skyline, although really meaning the whole of Australia.

"It's still possible that parts of Australia have survived, you know." Jack was making an effort to sound upbeat, which was sweet of him. "We only know that Melbourne, Sydney and Canberra and the areas between are affected. It may be that other areas or cities weren't as badly hit, or maybe even not at all. You said yourself that the effect was not like a normal infection, so we don't know the rules. Maybe Brisbane or Adelaide are still OK. And Perth is a long way from here."

"If Brisbane was OK don't you think people would be here by now," Xanthe pointed out. "And anyway, you were the one that said there was no point in gallivanting off to other places." Xanthe didn't want to argue and rather regretted this comment after she had said it. Jack had a trace of the defensive in his voice as he replied, although he was obviously trying to be gentle.

"Well, people might not be here because of quarantine, which would also perhaps be a reason we shouldn't go, since they might not let us out of the quarantine zone. Anyway, my point is we don't know what's happened outside what we've seen. We shouldn't jump to conclusions."

There was a long pause as they stood side by side and contemplated the sky, which now had the occasional star pricking its surface.

"Jack I know you're trying to cheer me up and I do appreciate it. All this isn't your fault. I'm grateful to you for, well, everything you've done for me. The graves, the hot bath and everything. I'm glad you're here."

And with that she took his hand and they stood in silence watching the stars multiply and listening to the fire crackle as it started to burn in earnest. She wanted to show him that she wasn't cross. In fact she wasn't quite sure what she wanted to show him, she realised, but it was nice to hold his hand as a wave of sadness washed over her. Tears trickled on to her cheeks that she didn't bother to wipe away. Jack diplomatically said nothing.

After a long, but Xanthe liked to think, companionable, silence he looked at his watch but he kept hold of Xanthe's hand as he did so as if he were unwilling to break the contact.

"Time for the next one," he said, with a touch of reluctance. She released her grip and sat on the grass, staring into the growing fire. She stroked Rufus who was never far from her, with her eyes fixed on the flames, but she didn't trust her voice to come out right. Jack went and lit the next rocket and got back to the fire just in time to sit and enjoy the shower of purple that exploded into the sky above them.

They'd been sitting in silence for about five more minutes when suddenly Alf jumped to his feet and barked. He ran away from the fire towards the south and barked into the night again. Xanthe also jumped up.

"He's heard something. They've got much better hearing than us." Then to Alf, "What is it boy? What have you heard?" Jack, who was not a doggy person, was probably wondering why she was asking this question of a mute animal, but he wisely said nothing.

Alf continued to bark intermittently and they moved away from the fire to reduce the noise of the burning logs, and in a break in Alf's barking they both suddenly turned to each other simultaneously.

"Did you hear that?" Xanthe exclaimed excitedly. "Did you? An engine."

"I did. Coming from there," Jack gestured to the southwest. And there it was again, this time unmistakable. The distant scream of a high-revving engine at full bore. It muted below audibility for a few seconds and then rose again, clear enough that they could hear the driver going up through the gears.

"Is that a motorbike, d'you think?" Xanthe asked.

"Sounds like it. And not hanging around either. Let's hope he doesn't crash before he gets here."

"Or she," Xanthe suggested primly.

"Or it." Jack probably meant this as a joke but Xanthe didn't find it that funny.

The bike, if that's what it was, was moving north and was now about due west of them, heading past them towards the city. They could hear the engine note clearly although could see nothing beyond the trees blocking any view in that direction. They heard the engine note start to drop and eventually, quite decisively, the driver went down through the gears until they couldn't hear it any more. Silence once again.

"Is it time for another rocket?" Xanthe asked, her tone meant to suggest that it was.

"Five more minutes," Jack replied, looking at his watch in the firelight.

"Just light it now. Why wait?"

"Well, if there are other people they might miss it." Jack suddenly didn't seem so keen to bring the biker to them, but Xanthe overrode him.

"Do it now. You can light another in five minutes as well if you like. We've got plenty." There was no arguing with that logic and so Jack sent another firework up into the night sky. The green stars had barely faded when the bike engine rose again. It wasn't quite as frenetic as it had been, the driver clearly negotiating some turns, but by the time Jack lit the next rocket it was not far away. The engine note was steady as the driver cruised the perimeter of the gardens looking for a way in. Although the silhouette of the skyscrapers was still visible, everything below the skyline was black now, outside the ring of firelight, with Sydney dark in a way it had not been for hundreds of years. Suddenly Xanthe gave a shout.

"There it is!" The loom of the headlights through the trees to the north. The glow brightened and moved until suddenly the beam from the single light shone direct on them as the bike turned through the gate Jack had opened, and cruised towards them across the grass. Xanthe could see nothing of the rider behind the dazzling headlight until the bike pulled into the ring of firelight and shut down.

The man who sat astride the machine was not remotely what Xanthe had expected. Somehow her mind's eye had seen the high-speed rider dressed in leather with a black helmet and tinted faceplate, but the reality could not have been further away from this image.

The man on the motorbike wore khaki shorts and trainers with no socks and a white singlet. There was no helmet on his head and his blond hair fell on to his shoulders as he looked at Xanthe and Jack, who looked back. The only noise was from the fire for a few seconds as they contemplated one another, before he smoothly dismounted the bike, set it on it's stand and walked up to the two of them.

"How're going? I'm Ben," and he stuck his hand out to Jack to shake and then to Xanthe. Jack said his own name as he shook the offered hand, and Xanthe could see that quite a bit of pressure was applied by the newcomer, although Jack managed to not wince. He then turned his attention to her and offered his hand to shake. Her own was lost in his broad grip, although he was gentle, and as he looked into her eyes she felt that strange flutter. He was certainly her type. God, he was anybody's type. Wide-shouldered, well-muscled, with tanned skin that positively glowed in the firelight. As he held her hand he smiled revealing even white teeth, his eyes locked on hers, and she felt the flutter again.

"Are you on your own," Jack asked him, but Ben waited a moment before releasing Xanthe's hand, breaking the eye contact and turning to Jack.

"No. There's two others with me. They're on their way." Ben's voice immediately gave him away as an Aussie. "How many of you are there?"

"Just us two," Xanthe replied. "You're the first person we've seen since it happened."

"Oh. Right." Xanthe watched Ben as he absorbed this information, but if the man was disappointed that this was not a rescue, he didn't show it.

He was a couple of inches shorter than Jack but must have weighed at least as much, maybe even a bit more, and it didn't look like much of his weight was fat. The muscles in his arms and shoulders made his tattoos – and he had several – flex and bulge as the muscles bunched. He was, Xanthe estimated, in his early thirties, so about her age and had a couple of day's stubble on his face, which was framed by a disordered shock of blond hair.

"So whose idea were the rockets?" Ben asked, looking between them.

"Mine," Jack answered. "We thought it would be a good idea to find out if there were other survivors."

"Oh. You're a pom. Might have known you guys would survive." Ben followed this statement, which was delivered without seeming malice, with a short laugh. "Good idea on the rockets though, matey. Here come the others now. So what are your stories?"

Xanthe could also hear the engine note, although not nearly so aggressive as Ben's driving had been.

"Well, shall we wait for the others and then we don't need to..." Jack trailed off. He sounded so formal next to Ben's relaxed drawl.

"Yeah, OK mate. Whatever." There was a bit of a pause in which the engine note died away and Jack muttered something about launching another rocket and did exactly that. Ben and Xanthe stood side by side watching him do it. They matched, Xanthe noticed, in their shorts, singlets and trainers.

"You beat them here by quite a way," Xanthe observed, nodding towards the restarted engine that was approaching.

"Yeah. Tim's a pretty cautious driver and that thing," Ben pointed his thumb over his shoulder at the bike, without turning his head, "is an absolute crotch rocket. I've always wanted one and now I've got one." Jack and Xanthe both looked towards the machine, which was a red Ducati, although Xanthe only knew that because it said Ducati on the tank.

"Shouldn't you wear a helmet?" Jack spoke, although the same thought had occurred to Xanthe.

"What for? There's no fuckers to tell me what to do now and no hospitals either, so I'd rather die than injure myself, for sure. Here they come."

And sure enough a pair of headlights had turned in through the gate and were heading their way. As with the Ducati, the space behind the headlights was impenetrable until they stopped on the edge of the firelight and the engine and headlights died. Even then Xanthe could only make out a low shape with the odd glint of firelight. Two doors opened and closed and two more people walked tentatively into the light.

The first thing that struck Xanthe was the contrast between the two of them. The driver of the car was tall and angular, his movement not fluid like Ben's, but transmitting his awkwardness clearly. He looked to be in his early twenties, or maybe even younger, and had acne. His hair was cut short over a narrow skull. The passenger was altogether different. She was also tall, not as tall as the boy she stood next to, but as tall as Jack was. His skinny arms poking out of his T-shirt looked even skinnier next to her chunky limbs and her movement made awkward not by shyness, but more by simply moving her bulk. She was also young, although it was harder to tell her age, and she had smooth skin over her round face and dark hair held neatly back in an Alice band.

"Hey guys. You made it, at last. Stop for a sandwich?" Ben called out.

"We went as fast as we could," the boy replied, his voice sounding defensive and thin compared to Ben's confident tones. Jack walked over to where the two had stopped.

"Hi. I'm Jack," he said as he shook hands with both. Xanthe joined him and did the same.

"Hi, I'm Melissa," the girl spoke up first, her little-girl voice sounded incongruous coming from someone who must weigh close to twice what Xanthe weighed.

"Tim," the boy offered, eyeing them both cautiously. "Is it just you two?"

"I'm afraid so," Xanthe replied. "Just us two. Although I suppose there are five of us now and maybe more will come." There was a pause as they all looked at each other and thought about that.

"Neat idea about the rockets. How many've you got?" Tim asked.

"Loads," Xanthe said. "Jack wants to keep launching until midnight and we've got enough."

"Cool. It would be good to gather people together," Tim commented.

"OK then," Ben joined the small group. "Now we've all shaken hands, said hello and all that shit, let's sit by the fire and swap stories. You guys were here first so why don't you start?"

Thirteen

Xanthe told her story first. She provided a lot less detail than the narrative she had given Jack that first night in Goulburn, but still found it fairly harrowing to retell the hours spent in the hospital. It all seemed like a bad dream now, which was probably a combination of the sleep deprivation she was suffering at the time and her mind defensively distancing itself from the horror. They sat in a semi-circle near the fire with Xanthe flanked on either side by Alf and Rufus, who lay contentedly with one of Xanthe's hands resting on each. Jack and Ben were either side of the dogs with Tim and Melissa sitting next to each other on the other side of Ben. Xanthe was conscious of Jack keeping an eye on his watch as she told her tale, which she found illogically irritating. Half way through he rose to light another firework, but Xanthe kept on talking and didn't wait. He'd heard her story before. During her whole narration Tim and Melissa were silent, but Ben interrupted a number of times, but with comments rather than questions.

"I thought about driving to Melbourne. Glad I didn't," was one such comment and was shortly followed by "You're a nurse. That's great." And later, on hearing Xanthe's account of meeting Jack on the road and the involvement of the shotgun, Ben interjected, "You got yourself tooled up? You go, girl!"

Xanthe explained that she and Jack were staying in her parents' house, omitting any mention of her parents themselves and conspicuously nobody asked, and finally gave a brief account of the last few days of looting, including their failed attempts at communication using the satellite phone.

"And today we went and fed some chickens," she finished up. "Jack reckoned that they might all die if we didn't find some soon and he was dead right. No pun intended. They were mostly dead but some were alive, so we gave them food to last a day or two. We're going to go back and get them when we've built a coop. If we haven't been, you know, rescued, by then."

At this last comment Ben gave rather a harsh laugh and then, when all eyes were on him, he added, "We're not going to be rescued, love. Or not any time soon anyway."

"What do you mean?" Xanthe asked him.

"Look. How long since it happened?" he asked, his eyes on Xanthe. After a pause it was Jack who answered.

"A week."

"A week, right," Ben continued without breaking eye contact with Xanthe. "And how many planes have you seen in the sky?" His Australian twang was blunt and matter of fact.

"None," Xanthe eventually answered.

"None. That's the same number I've seen. None. And that means that the whole of Australia is fucked and probably the whole world. If it was something that had just happened here don't you think the planes would be buzzing around the sky by now?" He immediately answered his own question, "Of course they would. If things were OK in other places they'd be a fucking aircraft carrier parked in the harbour by now, wouldn't there. Even if we were quarantined, the

Yanks would be sending planes to take pictures to put on Time magazine. No. No planes means no people. We're on our own my love. Just us." This last statement was spoken almost as a challenge as he held out his cupped hand palm up to indicate the little group sat by the fire, but he didn't look at Jack or turn his head to Tim and Melissa. Xanthe was the focus of his attention.

She looked down at Rufus, whose flank she was stroking, and was silent for a few seconds. Could that be true? Was Ben's analysis the right one? It felt as if the ground had shifted underneath her and she looked to Jack to try and restore order. She looked across to the Englishman and, in a small but controlled voice, asking, "D'you think that's true?"

"Of course it's true. Look around, love. They're not here," Ben answered with a another gesture to the whole of Sydney. "They'd be here if they were still alive." Xanthe looked round at him as he spoke, but it wasn't his opinion she was looking for. He'd already said what he thought and she didn't need a second iteration. When he'd finished she looked back at Jack and waited for his answer, and this time Ben also waited.

"Well. I don't think we know that." Jack spoke slowly. "I think Ben has a point about the planes. If this was a local thing, so just New South Wales and Victoria, say, then I agree there *probably* would be planes in the sky. But even then we can't be sure about that because we don't know the cause…"

"These two are from Brisbane," Ben interrupted, gesturing dismissively at Tim and Melissa. "So it's up North as well."

"But it's also possible," Jack continued, "that this is much wider and so Sydney is just one of many big cities and they haven't got round to us yet. Maybe the aircraft carriers are in Beijing and Hong Kong and, I don't know, Bangkok or Tokyo. Say, for example, that the plague was caused by some kind of radiation from space, then maybe it's one half of the world, the half facing the source, that got irradiated. If that were true then there probably wouldn't be planes here yet, and certainly not aircraft carriers.

"The bottom line is I don't think we know enough to be sure of anything, but it's probably better for us to assume that we're not getting rescued soon."

"You're just hoping that the Queen is still alive. Well let me tell you that just because you want it to be true, doesn't mean it is." Jack didn't answer Ben's statement, although Xanthe was slightly shocked at how Ben had dismissed Jack's comments. Her initial opinion had been a judgement that he was not the sharpest person she had ever met, and his statement about the Queen backed that first impression. After a few seconds Tim, who had been silent up until now, chipped in.

"I thought about that radiation thing as well and I think Jack has a point there. Obviously you noticed," he was looking at Jack and Xanthe as he spoke, "how everybody got sick at the same time and some kind of radiation seems the only explanation for that. That might mean that Jack is right and half the planet got a dose but half didn't."

"Doesn't space radiation go right through the planet without stopping?" Xanthe asked, seeming to remember some such fact from a long-passed physics lesson.

"Well there are kinds of radiation that do that," Tim answered, his voice more confident on this topic, "but the kinds that go right through the Earth interact so little with normal matter that they're incredibly unlikely to make people sick. If a particle goes right through you without stopping then it can't do you any harm. I'm not a real expert but I think that any radiation that could make everybody sick wouldn't go through the Earth, meaning that the Earth would have shielded half the world."

"Depending on how long the dose lasted," Jack pointed out.

"That's true," Tim agreed. "If the dose lasted more than twelve hours then the whole world would get some exposure, and if it was more than twenty four, i.e. a complete revolution of the planet, then everybody got a full dose. Even then it's possible that some areas, near the poles if the sun was the source, where the radiation was much less dense and so the survival rate could have been much higher." Ben's head swivelled like he was watching a tennis match during this exchange, but Xanthe noticed he wasn't so quick with his opinion on radiation from space.

"That's a good point about the poles. I hadn't thought of that," Jack sounded impressed by Tim's analysis.

"Well I'm just saying," Ben interjected, not sounding at all impressed, "that if rescue was on the way then they'd be here by now. I reckon we're on our own." He said this with an air of finality that did not invite reply. Jack looked at the Australian for a few moments, his face carefully blank but didn't pursue it any further. Xanthe could sense an edge between the two men already and hoped that it wasn't going to be a problem.

"Time for another rocket," Jack said getting to his feet and looking at his watch.

"We've got some food," added Xanthe, standing up beside him. "I'll get it." She headed across to the Mitsubishi, but before getting food she retrieved the long sleeved T-shirt she'd brought with her and put it on. It wasn't that cold yet but it was cooling off so it wasn't a strange thing to be doing, although the actual reason was that Ben's close attention was making her a little uncomfortable. One of the things that made Jack interesting was that he was difficult to read. Ben's thoughts, on the other hand, were not such a secret.

The spray of red light that Jack created above them provided some additional light. Xanthe, who was returning from the ute with several packets of snack food and some beer, got a better look at the car Tim and Melissa had arrived in. It was some kind of sports car, she thought maybe a Porsche, and its metallic paint gleamed in the firelight. It squatted low to the grass and the contrast between its high-technology sheen and the primitive flicker of the flames seemed sharp.

Jack re-joined the group as Xanthe was handing out sausage rolls (looted from a petrol station on their way to the Botanical Gardens that afternoon) and Tim was adding another couple of logs to the fire. Ben was sitting on the grass opening a bottle of beer from the slab that had also come from the petrol station.

They sat down in their former spots, Xanthe settling between the two dogs who hadn't moved. The others also obeyed that nonsensical instinct to go back to 'your place'.

"Right pommie. Your turn," Ben announced, nodding to Jack but also glancing at Xanthe who, was feeling a little bit more comfortable with the extra layer on.

"OK. I'm in Australia for my job. I was working here in Sydney and had been here three days. I was staying in a hotel by the harbour." Jack pointed towards downtown Sydney.

He gave a short account, even more factual and stripped of non-essential comments than the one he had originally given her when they met. There were few questions or interruptions, although Ben did respond to Jack's short statement that he had checked the hotel for survivors.

"You went into every single room?" Ben asked.

"Yes. Every one."

"And every room had a dead body in it?"

"Almost all, yes. Some were empty, but most had a corpse or two."

"How many rooms does a fancy hotel like that have?" Ben wanted to know.

Jack answered the question simply "A couple of hundred."

"And you didn't notice a pattern emerging after, say, the first hundred?" Ben sounded incredulous.

"I wanted to be sure that there were no people like me. You know, survivors."

"Jesus," was Ben's comment on this before waiting for Jack to continue. The difference in the two men's attitudes that this exchange revealed was not lost on Xanthe. Ben might be good looking, but questioning Jack's motives as he searched for survivors didn't show a great deal of inner beauty.

Jack briefly described his drive to Canberra before finishing with, "And then I bumped into Xanthe on the road. Luckily for me she didn't shoot me and you've heard the rest from her." The following silence was broken by Melissa who had hardly uttered a word since they had all met.

"You're married." Jack looked unsure if it was a question or a statement, but he nodded.

"Yes, I am."

"Got kids?" Melissa asked in her little-girl voice.

"Yes. Three girls."

"It must be terrible. Not knowing." Jack didn't answer Melissa's comment before she continued. "That's why you're thinking about the other side of the world, isn't it."

He paused before answering her. "It is," he said simply. "Anyway. It's your turn." He nodded towards Ben, Tim and Melissa.

"Well, my story's a bit different from you guys," Ben started without a glance towards the other two, although he did now appear to be talking to Jack as well, rather than exclusively to Xanthe, she was rather relieved to notice. He took a swig of beer before continuing.

"I'm from here, Sydney, and the first thing that's different is that I hardly got ill at all. I guess more like you Xanthe, but even less. I had a little bit of a headache on Wednesday afternoon but woke up on Thursday feeling fine. I got up and went to work but of course there was nobody on the streets and nobody at my work. There was no bus and so I had to walk. Took me ages but all the time the streets were just empty." Ben's manner was easy as he spoke, he was comfortable telling a story and his timing and tone were all natural.

"What is it you do? At work," Xanthe asked.

"Well, these days I don't do anything, love. But up until last week I worked in construction mostly. I've done a few things in my life, but recently I've been working for a big building firm here in Sydney." Xanthe reflected that this might, in part, explain Ben's impressive physique.

"So when I got there and nobody was around I went round to my mate Tomo's flat to see he how he was. He was there and not in a good way. I got some stuff for him, but there wasn't much I could do, so I left him for a while, and wandered around. It was unbelievable and spooky, as I suppose you know, on that first day. Wandering around the city with nobody there and all the shops shut. I did see the occasional car, people trying to get to hospital I suppose, but there weren't many. Just really spooky." He looked around at everybody in the group and Xanthe once again felt the force of his presence that had so struck her when they first met. He had charm when he chose to switch it on, no doubt.

"So anyway, I passed this car place that I go by every day on my way to work. You know, one of those places that sell crazy cars, Ferraris and things like that. It's all glass, so I walked up to the front door and tried it and guess what? It wasn't locked. I don't know why, but maybe the guy whose job it was to lock up had got ill and forgotten or something. The lights were all off since the power had already stopped, but the door was open, so I went in. I just wanted to look at the cars without someone breathing down my neck or kicking me out. I've always been keen on cars but someone like me couldn't normally get in there without some officious busy-body giving me hassle."

He paused and took another swig of beer, looking entirely comfortable as he told his story. What is it with men and cars, she wondered to herself. Status symbols don't mean anything now. Ben glanced briefly across at his two young companions before turning back to Xanthe and Jack and continuing.

"So I went in and was able to see and touch the cars in peace. They were *so* cool. I could get in them, none of them were locked and I sat behind the wheel of all of them. I knew something bad was happening in the city, that some kind of epidemic had made everybody ill except me, but I thought it was like a one day thing. That the next day everybody would be better and it would be back to man-handling steel beams for me.

"So I took one of the cars. I didn't mean to keep it. You can't hide or sell a Maserati, or at least the people I know couldn't handle that kind of wheels – way too hot. I just looked in one of the back offices and there was a metal box on the wall that wasn't locked either and it was full of keys. I took a bright red soft-top Maserati, a GranCabrio, and it was *so* beautiful. There was this sign next to it giving all the specs and stuff. It had a four forty horse V8 and I just opened up the back of the show room – the key was also in the box – and started up the Maserati and drove it out on to the street.

"Everything was quiet except for the roar of the engine and I had the streets to myself. No cops, no traffic. It was bloody great. I knew I'd never own a car like that and that this was my day in the sun. I just zoomed round the streets for an hour having an absolute blast. The Maserati was *sooo* sweet. Just bloody great."

He gave them a wide smile, showing his white teeth again in the firelight. There was no doubt that he looked like the picture of

Australian manhood; straight from a tourist board advert.

"Anyway. After an hour I went back to Tomo's flat, just to show him the car really. He was still there and wasn't well at all. Delirious - not with it at all. Messy too. I didn't know what to do so I got him water and stuff and made him as comfortable as I could, but I'm not a doctor or a nurse or anything so I had no clue. I thought about taking him to hospital in his car, I didn't want him throwing up in the Maserati, but I figured that it would be mobbed since everybody else was obviously ill as well, so I left him at home and went back to my place. I took the Maserati and parked it exactly back where it had been. I didn't want them to know it had been taken since they might, you know, run my prints.

"The car place was near my flat, so I went home, lit a candle, had a few stubbies, got bored and went to bed. Next day was the same. No one around. I walked up to the car place and this time I took a Ferrari California. It was grey and was just sex on wheels. Even faster than the Maserati and so sweet. It made a noise to die for. I went straight to Tomo's flat but he wouldn't buzz me in, so I kicked in the doors. The one on the street and to his flat. He was there but totally out of it. Unconscious or in a coma or whatever. So I carried him, not easy I can tell you, he was a big bloke, down the stairs of his flat and put him in his car and drove him to the hospital. Well, *you* know what it was like," Ben reached out and tapped Xanthe's knee with one finger. "It was a nightmare. Everybody in a terrible state, no doctors or nurses or anything like that. I didn't see a single person who wasn't either ill or dead.

"I'm not proud to say that I left Tomo there. The whole place freaked me out and I got worried that I might catch whatever it was. I didn't know what to do so I just bailed. Went back to Tomo's flat and got the Ferrari and just drove. Like a fucking maniac, I can tell you. I hadn't seen any other cars that day so I screeched around the streets, and even out into the 'burbs. I broke into a shop to get some food. Didn't see a soul. Not one person, although I did run over a cat that ran out in front of me. Nearly crashed the car but luckily didn't kill myself or total the Ferrari. Killed the cat, obviously." He certainly hadn't been too cut up about the animal's death though, Xanthe observed.

"Eventually I headed for home but I ran out of petrol about two miles from my flat so I had to walk the rest of the way. I think it was starting to dawn on me that this was not going to just go away. To start with I thought that it was like a holiday. Just a few days off while everyone but me did a bit of hurling, but walking home it started to dawn on me that it was, you know, bigger."

Ben gestured with both hands, one still holding the beer he was working on. His outstretched arms indicated something that he wanted them to know was *very big*. His hand brushed her shoulder as he let his arms drop back down.

"Next day I got up late and took another flash car, a hard top Italia, and went straight to the hospital. Tomo was where I had left him but deader. There were loads of dead bodies. A couple of people still breathing, but not all that many. There wasn't anything I could do for them – they were clearly going to croak too so I left them to it.

"At that point I decided that I needed a base to live at, and that my flat wasn't ideal. So I took the Italia and went to a house that I'd done some work on last year. I remember thinking at the time that it was a place you could hole up if you were mega-rich, 'cos it was more like a castle really. A fucking huge place and solidly built – I know because I helped replace a section of the roof last year. The place is massive and this man, crazy rich, and his trophy wife and two brats, live there. Just four of them, and a load of *help*," Ben made quotations in the air, "that are around all the time.

"When we did the roof job I met the guy who owned it. He deigned to come and have a sandwich with us guys who were working on the place. He stayed and chatted, but I just knew he thought he was better than us.

"Anyway, he's dead now and I live in his house. Who'd have guessed that was going to happen. The place was stocked with food and stuff and I moved into one of the spare bedrooms.

"I hung out there for a couple of days, not really knowing what to do and then I met these guys," Ben waved at Tim and Melissa. "They've joined me so there's three of us. Well, five now. Five survivors. Maybe the last five in the whole of Australia, who knows."

"How did you guys all meet each other?" Jack asked. "Just coincidence like me and Xanthe?"

"Well, kind of. It's a funny story, actually," Ben answered the question. "I was messing around in the car, the Ferrari Italia and having some fun. I always wanted to be a racing driver but you need mega cash to do it. So I worked out a circuit on the streets, you know, like a racing track, and I was racing around it in the Italia. Doing lap after lap and getting faster and faster. Felt like Mark Webber, as I was screeching around." The enthusiasm shone out of Ben's face as he spoke and mimed himself wrestling the steering wheel. Xanthe found herself smiling in response to his boyish grin but could see that Jack wasn't finding it so entertaining. Neither were Tim and Melissa for that matter. Presumably they knew the story already.

"And here I was coming round a corner, big power slide like the Stig," Ben's shoulders flexed as he counter-steered the car of his memory. "Only I've not had quite as much practice as the Stig and there was something to hit. I lost the back end and smashed into a parked car. Hurt like fuck, I can tell you. Completely totalled the Italia. Airbags went off and everything. One minute later I'm sitting in the car working out what happened, I'm OK but pretty shaken up, when Tim and Melissa here just arrive in an SUV. They helped me out of the car and took me back to my pad. They live there as well now. Don't you Timmy boy?" Tim nodded but didn't reply.

"But how did you find him? Just luck?" Jack asked Tim.

"Not really," Tim answered. "You could hear the engine noise for quite a way. We heard it and drove towards the sound and just happened to find him straight after he'd crashed. It was a mess. He was lucky to walk away from it."

"I was, that's true," Ben resumed. "That's pretty well the story up until now. We've hung out at the big house. Like you we've taken some stuff that we needed. And some things we didn't need," at this Ben nodded to the Ducati. "Yeah, we just hung out until we saw your fireworks a couple of hours ago. Then came and found you guys." He directed a smile at the two of them, although mostly at Xanthe and she, almost against her better judgement, found herself returning it.

After another round of lighting fireworks, adding logs to the fire and bringing food and drink from the Mitsubishi (Jack and Xanthe had gathered a good stock on their way, hoping for a crowd that had not yet materialised) they settled back down to hear Tim and Melissa's story.

Tim started and gave a bare-bones description of what had happened to him. He was clearly shy but managed a coherent and accurate account of events. He's much more like Jack than Ben, she thought to herself. Tim's statement was also fairly stripped of emotion. A thinker rather than a feeler or a doer. This thought was backed up by Tim's statement that he was reading physics at the University of Queensland. Jack was also a technical person, Xanthe knew, and so would presumably feel a certain kinship with Tim. Fellow geeks who contrasted sharply with Ben's extrovert existence.

Tim described his symptoms and they sounded pretty much the same as Xanthe's own illness. Tim had then run into Melissa within hours of recovering. By extraordinary coincidence the two had known each other before the epidemic had struck. They had been to the same school, although Melissa was a year or two older than Tim. They hadn't been friends but had at least known of each other's existence. Xanthe wished that she had met someone she had known before. Not instead of Jack, but as well as. It would be nice to have some kind of link back to normal life.

During the outbreak of illness Tim and Melissa ran into each other at the hospital in Brisbane since they both had taken their dying family members. Their hours in the hospital sounded similar to Xanthe's horrific experience, although they had had even less idea how to help. They had both watched their parents and Melissa's sister die and, as Tim gave this account, Melissa was wiping tears from her face, although she didn't interrupt or offer any embellishments on Tim's mechanical recount of events. After everyone was dead at the hospital they had waited one more night and then had driven to Sydney, expecting to come upon roadblocks and a quarantine border but, like Jack and Xanthe, had found only deserted roads. They had spent one night in Sydney, in a furniture shop, which Xanthe thought showed ingenuity, before hearing Ben's one-man race and finding him in the crashed Ferrari. Tim finished by giving a brief description of the house they were staying in with Ben.

"It's big. Bigger than we need really. I had to drag the family, their bodies, out of the house and into the wood at the bottom of the garden. That's why we stayed in that bed shop, so we wouldn't have to deal with corpses. But once they were gone it's a good place. It's down there," he gestured to the south, "about..."

"We'll take them and show them," Ben interrupted. "In the morning, I reckon. What do you guys think? Should we just spend the night here? Camp out under the stars?"

"May as well," Xanthe answered him. "Jack and I were thinking that too, and we brought blankets and a couple of sleeping bags, although it's a warm night. We've still got a few hours of fireworks. Is it time for another?" She raised an eyebrow in Jack's direction.

"Five more minutes," he replied, looking at his watch. Tim's whole account had taken less than ten minutes but he'd clearly finished since he was looking expectantly at Melissa.

"Well, I don't have much to add, " Melissa eventually said, her soft voice hardly audible over the gentle crack of the fire. "I work as a receptionist at a printing company in Brisbane. Well, I used to, I suppose. I'm just normal, really. Nothing special. I don't know why I survived and everybody else didn't. There's so few of us – it's really scary. But I'm glad we've met you guys." This was directed at Jack and Xanthe, who both smiled encouragement back, but that was all Melissa was prepared to volunteer.

They spent the next few hours sitting and talking about their lives before, and what they should do now. The bulk of the talk was from Xanthe and Ben, with Jack and Tim contributing rather less and Melissa almost nothing. Jack kept sending rockets into the sky every fifteen minutes, but with no results, since when the rockets ran out, shortly after midnight, there were still just the five of them sitting round the fire in the Australian night.

After the last rocket had exploded above them, they piled the last logs on to the fire and retrieved bedding from the back of the pick-up and each of them wrapped themselves up and settled down in their chosen spot around the fire. Both dogs came over and lay down near Xanthe and she felt comforted by their presence as she wormed into her sleeping bag and settled her head on the rolled up fleece she had brought. Her last thought was that it was probably going to take her a while to get to sleep, but in fact it was only a minute or two later that sleep claimed her.

Fourteen

The following day found Jack crouching behind flowery curtains in the house opposite Xanthe's parents' bungalow. A car was approaching down the street and Jack hunched lower as best he could, pressing his hand to his side as pain stabbed through him. Blood was starting to soak through his shirt, but he ignored it and he peered cautiously out of the window.

His view of the street was partially screened by bushes but Jack could see enough to watch a silver Porsche pull smoothly up beside Xanthe's parents' house, parking just behind the trailer bearing the motorbikes. A brawny man wearing a singlet, Ben, and Xanthe climbed out and looked around.

Both of them stood for few moments on either side of the car looking up and down the street. Xanthe's movements looking anxious, but Ben's demeanour could more be described as wary. Jack was struck again, as he had been the previous evening, by the similarity between the two blond Australians in their shorts and singlets. He kept his body hidden behind the curtains as he peeped out cautiously. He wasn't sure if the tension he felt was from seeing Xanthe looking so anxious and clearly looking around for Jack, or from seeing that man again.

After a few moments of looking around, they exchanged a few words over the top of the low-slung sports car that Jack couldn't hear and both made their way towards the front door of the house. The dogs, Rufus and Alf, accompanied them although it must have been a tight squeeze in the Porsche. Xanthe moved decisively, clearly keen to get inside, but her companion moved more slowly, still looking around him carefully.

Jack didn't think they could have seen the big red Mitsubishi, which was pretty well hidden from where they were, but the suntanned man was clearly looking for signs of Jack's presence. Xanthe disappeared through the door, leaving it standing open and, after a last look up and down the street, her companion followed her inside.

Jack stayed where he was, seething with indecision. What should he do? Go over and face the two of them and hope that he could avoid being killed? Jack had seen no weapons, but that didn't mean there were none. He could tell Xanthe what had happened and then maybe she would help him. Between the two of them perhaps they could overcome the powerful Ben. But then again perhaps not, and by forcing a confrontation Jack could actually be putting Xanthe in danger. At least if he stayed where he was she was safe.

These thoughts were one aspect of what went through his mind, the other being the waves of pain he had set off by moving too quickly and how painful any kind of violence would be right now. The thought of trying to defend himself at that moment was probably what kept him standing where he was.

It was only a matter of a minute or two before Ben re-emerged and came and sat on the bonnet of the Porsche. He'd obviously satisfied himself that there was nobody inside and now he was the image of a man on guard. He should have thought of this, Jack berated himself. He could have found a really good hiding place in the house and waited until Xanthe was alone before telling her what was going on. But it was too late now. Ben sat calmly on the bonnet, muscles flexed in the morning sunshine and posture relaxed, self-assured. Meanwhile Jack could see no other choice than cowering behind the curtains and watching.

Which he did for what seemed like a long time. It seemed like an hour but was probably only about fifteen minutes before Xanthe emerged back out of the house. In the meantime the man inspected the dirt bikes on the trailer, climbing up and sitting astride one of them for a few moments, before climbing back down and resuming his position on the bonnet of the Porsche. While Jack waited he looked down with some dismay at his shirt. It was soaked in blood once again and the hand he'd been holding pressed to his side was also slick with gore.

When Xanthe came back out into the sunshine she was carrying the grip she had used when they had been looting and also a suitcase, which looked heavy. Ben got up and looked at the suitcases and then at the Porsche, his thought processes clear. They exchanged a few words and then Xanthe went back into the house, leaving the suitcases in the driveway. She was another few minutes and this time paused at the doorway on the way out, calling back through the open door. Jack could just hear her voice, although not the words, but the tone told him she was calling the dogs even before they came out on to the lawn and she shut the door after them. She picked up the cases and loaded them into her parents' Toyota. Ben wandered over towards the car but didn't look like he wanted to leave just yet. The two of them had a bit of a conversation, none of which Jack could hear. It went on a minute or two and eventually Xanthe nodded and gestured towards the back of the house and the garden. Ben looked around again, and Xanthe watched him as he scanned the street. He then turned and took the path that went round the garage and was soon out of sight.

Xanthe herself walked to the pavement and stood by the Porsche a moment looking left and right and even before she put her cupped hands up to her mouth Jack had already started to realise that this might be his chance.

"Jack," Xanthe called, the sound clearly coming through the window. "Jack. Jack." He was moving as fast as he could towards the front door of the house as she called his name, the pain jabbing him viciously and making him pant, but not slowing him down.

As he came to the door he looked through the pane of glass set to one side of it and stopped, bloody hand on the door handle as he watched. Ben was walking, half running really, from round the garage towards Xanthe. He held the Honda generator in one large hand, the other was in the pocket of his shorts. Jack froze and watched as he reach Xanthe and put the generator down. Ben's right hand stayed in his pocket as he scanned the street. Xanthe too was looking around. The two of them exchanged a few inaudible words. Jack's hand was still on the door, but he couldn't deny that he was frightened and kept his body out of view. He was in an agony of indecision, but to his great, great shame, the fear won out. He was afraid, and it kept him from opening the door and showing himself.

The two stood on the pavement opposite for another minute. Xanthe didn't call out again and they didn't speak to each other, just looked left and right. But after that minute they exchanged a few words, loaded the generator into the car and climbed into the Toyota.

Last chance, Jack said to himself. But he did nothing as they started the car up and drove swiftly out of sight, leaving silence in its wake. Jack stood immobile, disbelief still strong as he thought back over how he had ended up where he was.

Jack had been woken that morning with a hand shaking him gently. It was no-longer full dark, although the sun was not nearly up yet, but the lightening sky provided just enough light to see Ben's face above him, as he stooped and shook Jack, his finger held to his lips for quiet. When Ben saw that Jack was stirring and squinting up at him, he stood up and gestured for Jack to come with him, all the while keeping a finger to his lips. Jack looked around. He could make out the bundle that was Xanthe a few yards away with the two dogs sleeping curled close by, the pre-dawn light just strong enough to show a tousled head sticking out of the end of the blanket. Further away were the formless mounds of blankets that contained Tim and Melissa. Nobody was stirring apart from Ben, who was still gesturing for Jack to join him.

Jack rolled out of his blankets, being as quiet a possible and got to his feet. He was still fully dressed, shoes and all, and so padded after Ben, leaving the blanket on the ground, curious to see what the stocky man wanted so early in the morning. One of the dogs, Jack thought it was Rufus, raised his head briefly and looked at the two men, before settling back down to sleep.

The first thing Jack noticed was that the Mitsubishi pick-up was not where it had been parked the night before, which was odd. There was enough light to see that wheel tracks in the grass ran from where it had been parked down the hill. The slope here was gentle and Jack doubted that the truck would have rolled on it's own, even with the brake off, which presumably meant that Ben had moved it.

This was sufficiently odd as to bring Jack fully awake. Why had he moved it and how? Starting the thing up would have surely woken everybody, so did that mean that Ben had physically pushed it to get it rolling down the hill? That could have been hard work, but Ben did look equal to the task, if that was what he wanted to do. Jack looked down the hill but couldn't see the vehicle anywhere.

He followed Ben with a sense of genuine curiosity, heading in the opposite direction, up the hill towards the gate. Ben was dressed in only the singlet and shorts he had arrived in, but didn't seem to be cold and Jack caught the flash of teeth in Ben's tanned face as he smiled back at him. As Jack caught up, Ben pointed at the gate to indicate that that was where they were going but didn't speak, and so the two walked in silence side by side across the dewy grass as the sky lightened behind them.

When they reached the gate Jack judged they were far enough away from the others that they could talk without being heard.

"What's up Ben? Where are we off to?" He kept his voice low, Ben's conspiratorial manner almost compelling him to a full whisper.

"I've got something I want to show you, mate. It's this way." They went through the gate, turned right and Jack kept with him.

"Where's the pick-up? The ute. Did you move it?"

"Hold on a little while, my friend and you'll see." Ben's voice was also quiet and his tone light.

They walked like that for a few of minutes, travelling up a slip road on to a broad and empty dual carriageway that curved round towards the city. The sky was lightening all the time and by the time they got half way around the curve Jack could see a vehicle ahead and make out that it was the Mitsubishi. Ben could only have got it there by driving it, so he must have pushed it down the hill to get it clear of the group and then started it up and, avoiding going near the sleepers, driven it quietly out of the gate. Why he would do this Jack couldn't guess, which was starting to make him feel uneasy, but when he looked across at Ben he got a reassuring smile back and they kept walking.

They were just passing a lamppost and were a couple of hundred yards away from the pick-up when Ben held up his hand for them to stop. The dual carriageway had a pavement for pedestrians, although Jack and Ben stood on the road, and Ben vaulted lightly over the concrete barrier, which was topped with a railing, that separated the pavement from the road. Several tall buildings seemed to loom over them in the gathering dawn, as Jack climbed across the barrier to join Ben.

As he did so Ben bent down to where the concrete barrier met the tarmac and stood up, holding something in his hand. It took Jack a few seconds to identify the object. It was a gun. A double barrelled shotgun. Ben was holding it casually, letting it dangle towards the road. He stood and returned Jack's stare.

"What's going on?" Jack tried to keep his voice casual. Seeing the gun had given him a jolt. It looked a lot like the one that Xanthe had waved at him a few days before. What the hell did Ben want to shoot at this time in the morning. Was there some Australian wildlife that should be hunted at dawn and would provide them with fresh meat?

After a few seconds, Ben spoke quietly. "You're leaving, matey."

"What? What do you mean?"

"You are going to get in that car and drive away. Now. And you're not going to trouble yourself to come back."

"What are you talking about. Why would I do that?" Jack asked this question with a horrible feeling that he already knew the answer, but was unable to help himself from asking.

"Because if you don't, I'm going to kill you. Right here. Right now. With this." Ben's voice was still quiet and conversational, but he took a step back and brought the shotgun up so he was holding it in two hands.

"But..." Jack was struggling with the whole concept. This had to be some kind of mistake. It was just too surreal.

"You're wondering why, aren't you matey boy. Well it's funny isn't it, how you with your high-power job are so slow to understand what's going on. You're thinking that it's just not cricket, aren't you pommie. Well I can tell you that this is how cricket is played now. Nobody's coming to rescue us, so we're not just some guys now.

We're a tribe. And someone has to lead the tribe, and that someone is going to be me."

Jack was totally speechless, he just gaped at Ben, who continued, his voice rising from the calm tone from which he had started.

"It's like one of those nature programmes. One of us has to be the alpha male, 'cos after all, it's hardly going to be Tim now is it. He's not really alpha male material. But you could be, so I'm going to do what the strongest lion does. I'm going to exile you from the pride. I'm telling you now that if I ever see you again, I'll kill you on sight. If I even so much as glimpse you I'll chase you down and kill you."

As he had spoken the shotgun and risen slowly to his shoulder and was now aimed directly at Jack's head.

"But. There's no need…" Jack trailed off, struggling for the right words.

"Oh, but there is need," Ben continued calmly. "The same need that the lions have. The females, mate. The sheilas. Christ I was starting to wonder how long it would be until Melissa looked good to me, and there's a scary thought. But I stopped thinking it the moment I set eyes on your pretty little nurse."

"She's not mine. I'm married," Jack eventually managed to voice an objection. Ben gave a mirthless laugh in answer.

"You're really not getting it, are you? You're not married. Your wife is dead, mate. Gone. Kaput. You may not have recognised that yet, but you will in time. And at that point I can tell you that Xanthe is going to look pretty damn good to you. I don't want you hanging around until that moment."

"But what are you going to tell them?"

"Well. I'll either tell them that you buggered off in the night without a word, or I'll tell them that I killed you. Depends on whether I wake them up now. With this," he nodded down at the shotgun.

"But she'll know what you did," Jack's voice sounded weak and baffled, even to him.

"Who gives a fuck what she knows? She's a possession now, she just doesn't know it yet. She'll end up with whichever of us is left standing and I'm telling you right now that it's me. Unlucky." As he spoke Ben had transferred the shotgun to his left hand, keeping it pointing at Jack, and put his right into the pocket of his shorts. As he said the last word he lunged forward without any kind of warning.

Jack jumped back, taken totally by surprise and just caught a flash of silver as Ben's hand, aimed for the middle of his belly, hit him in the side as Jack twisted away. Ben jumped back again and Jack clearly saw the knife in the man's hand. It was some kind of flick knife and was now red at least four or five inches down the blade.

Jack had time to see all of that and realise that he'd been stabbed before the pain started, although once it did start, it did so in earnest. He clamped a hand on the spot.

"You're fucking insane," he gasped.

"Whatever, mate. I'm bored of this conversation so you either go and get in that car and drive off right now or I am going to kill you. I could do it with the knife easily enough, or maybe I'll just shoot you. Maybe it's a good thing that nursey knows what's going on. She's going to find out sooner or later. Make your choice."

There was a long pause while they faced each other. Ben moved to the side so that Jack's path down the pavement towards the pick-up was clear. The pain was severe, but Jack tried to assess the options. He could try and jump Ben, but with the shotgun ready and pointing his way that seemed like suicide. Ben looked comfortable with the weapon and Jack wasn't prepared to bet that he had left the safety catch on. He could simply refuse to do as Ben asked and see if Ben had the balls to shoot him, but given that he had just been stabbed by the man, a bet on Ben's compassion didn't feel like a winner either. That left him only one option. Comply with what Ben was asking.

"Three," Ben said flatly. They stared at each other for a few seconds. "Two."

And Jack made his choice. He started to walk past Ben towards the car, one hand clamped over the wound, which was already soaking his shirt with blood.

"And remember, pommie," Ben shouted after him. "If I ever see you, hear you or smell you again, I will kill you. No warnings and no mercy, and I don't care who sees it. Your best bet is to head somewhere else and try and find some other people. You should be fine now that you know the rules."

Jack looked over his shoulder and saw Ben climbing back over the barrier. Jack considered getting into the car and simply running Ben down, but he had the shotgun and it seemed likely that they might both die. Equally Ben could just hop over the barrier where the Mitsubishi couldn't get him and shoot Jack in the head as he drove past. He appeared to have no option but to do as Ben was demanding.

"Shit," he muttered to himself as he approached the car, although whether this was at the situation or the pain even he didn't know, and this swear word seemed wholly inadequate to the situation.

He reached the pick-up and climbed into the driver's seat. The pain was making it hard to think. He could see Ben in the rear view mirror walking backwards up the road, his eyes on Jack, as he gestured. The message was clear. *Push off.*

Well, Ben couldn't shoot him from that range, so Jack took the time to inspect his wound. The hole was in his right hand side and about level with his belly button. It was not that large since the blade had been narrow, but it was certainly bleeding. Not squirting out, but it still seemed like a lot of blood, despite the pressure he had been applying, his T-shirt was soaked on the right hand side and his hands were slippery with the stuff.

Glancing in the rear view mirror he saw that Ben had gone out of sight, presumably to re-join the others.

What Jack really needed was Xanthe's help. She would know how to cope with a stab wound, because Jack certainly had no idea. Aside from a vague memory that you should apply pressure to bad cuts he didn't have a clue. But ironically Xanthe was the one resource that was disallowed him now. He considered simply driving the big red pick-up back into that park and calling Ben's bluff. Would he really murder Jack in front of the others – including Xanthe who was Ben's objective in this whole thing.

A week before the behaviour Ben had displayed would have been psychopathic, but it was hard now to deny his logic. Jack was not totally convinced that Ben's deduction that there was no help coming was solid, but that wasn't important. He did believe that Ben was totally convinced by his own conclusions and that meant that Ben would probably kill him as he had promised.

"Jesus," was squeezed out of him through gritted teeth, as a fresh wave of pain set in. He had to do something about this wound.

He started up the pick-up, but still sat still wondering where to go. Getting to a hospital was just too complicated. There would bandages at the house, in fact he thought Xanthe might have acquired medical supplies in their looting spree, so he got the Mitsubishi rolling, heading to what he now thought of as home.

Half an hour later he was sitting in the bathroom doing his best to bandage himself up. The wound was still bleeding and his shirt and trousers were soaked in blood. The pain hadn't lessened and Jack was finding it hard to think and function. All he wanted to do was lie down and have someone minister to his injury, but that luxury wasn't on offer. He had to keep functioning.

He'd raided the bathroom and found a fairly extensive set of dressings and bandages that Xanthe had stored. He taped the largest dressing he could find over the still bleeding stab wound and then wound the bandages round himself as tightly as he could, making it hard to breath, but he had to stop the blood from flowing. He was feeling shaky and cold, presumably shock was setting in, and was panicking that he was losing too much blood. He struggled out of the rest of his clothes and dumped them in the bath, where they joined his ruined T-shirt. He then stood in the bath himself and, using the shower head, rinsed off his legs as best he could. He used a white flannel to wipe down his arms and torso while keeping the bandages dry. The water was red as it ran down the drain, the blood from his clothes bleeding into the cold stream from the shower.

Naked and shivering he made his way slowly to the room he'd been sleeping in, crawled under the covers and lay, panting and shivering.

After a while, Jack didn't know how long, the shivering subsided and he stopped feeling so cold, although feeling properly warm was still a way away. The pain was still there, but not quite so sharp if he lay still. When he moved it felt like he was being stabbed again, but there was nothing for it but to get moving.

It had occurred to him, as he lay there, that Xanthe would be coming back here and almost certainly Ben would be with her. That meant he had to get out of the house, or at very least get ready to defend himself. Being honest with himself, he was frightened of Ben, and did not want to face the man. Ben was clearly more comfortable with violence than Jack was and Jack truly believed that, if Ben came to the house, the Australian would kill him if he found Jack there.

Moving gingerly he climbed out of bed and inspected the dressing on his side. Red was already visibly staining the bandage, but it wasn't totally soaked in blood. He hoped that that meant the bleeding was slowing. He'd also replayed the whole incident with Ben on the road through in his mind. He was fairly sure that Ben had been aiming to give him a fatal wound. The powerful Australian had lunged for

Jack's belly and only Jack's quick reaction had stopped the knife going to the hilt in his guts. He wouldn't have died on the spot from such an injury, but his chances of living long term would probably be limited. Ben had, in Jack's opinion, planned the whole incident, and part of that plan had been Jack exiting the scene with a stab wound that he would not survive.

Was this wound survivable? Jack was fairly sure that with access to proper medical care that he wouldn't die from what Ben had done to him. But with only self-help doctoring available would he recover? It didn't seem to him that the knife had hit anything vital, but in the longer term would blood loss and infection be a problem that he couldn't fix? Quite possibly.

One thing that Jack was totally clear on in his mind, despite the pain, was the fact that he did not intend to let Ben get away with this. Jack would do everything in his power to make sure that Xanthe, and Tim and Melissa for that matter, knew what had happened. His plans were still a little fuzzy on how this was going to happen, but the determination was fully formed. If he was to confront Ben there were really only two options and he didn't much like either, but already the realisation that he would have to choose was there. Trying to exile Ben, as he had done to Jack, had exactly the same drawback that Jack was hoping Ben's scheme would suffer. What goes away might come back. But Jack wasn't sure that he was yet comfortable with option two, namely killing Ben outright.

But if either of these things were to happen it was important that Ben didn't find Jack naked and unprepared in this house right now. He dressed carefully, trying to move his torso as little as possible but still wincing as the throbbing intensified to a sharp pain with any flex or twist. By the time he was dressed a vague plan had formed in his head. His plan, such as it was, was firstly to find a gun and then come and lie in wait for Ben in the house. But where to get a gun? He was in no condition to face Ben without one, in fact probably was no match for Ben even without an injury. Jack was stronger than most men, but Ben looked to be in whole different league and was likely to be armed anyway, so Jack needed a weapon.

Given that Ben and Xanthe might head here straight from the Botanics, he might not have much time. So the only plan he could come up with was to search nearby houses and see if he could find a gun. He had no idea how many Australians felt the need to own firearms. Was it like the UK where only farmers and the occasional enthusiast had any kind of weapon, or was it like the US where many people believed it was unpatriotic not be armed to the teeth? Jack didn't know, but he did know that at least some Australians owned guns since Xanthe's neighbour had had a shotgun, which had been used to threaten him twice. *So far*, he reminded himself.

He shuffled out of house slowly. If he walked faster than a man in the grip of severe arthritis then his side sent him unambiguous signals to stop, so shuffling was his current top speed.

As soon as he stood on the threshold of the front door, something else occurred to him, causing him to turn around and head for the bathroom. He needed the keys to the pick-up. If he left it outside in plain view then Ben would know for certain that Jack was inside, so he needed to move the thing.

But going into the bathroom made him realise something else. The bathroom looked like a grisly murder had happened in there, rather than the aftermath of a mere attempted murder. The floor was covered in smears and spatters of blood and the bath was full of bloody clothing. It was a sign as clear as the big red Mitsubishi outside of Jack's presence, and so he spent twenty painful minutes clearing it all up. The clothes went into a bin bag and into the bin (after he'd retrieved the car keys), and he mopped the floor and even washed the bath until the room was in its original state. He swore steadily under his breath while he worked as the stab wound spiked him again and again, but he stuck with it until he was satisfied.

He then moved the pick-up round the corner and into the drive of a house three or four along from Xanthe's parents' house. It was, if not hidden, then reasonably unobtrusive. *Now to find a weapon,* he told himself.

He started with the house where he parked the truck. It was not locked and within a second he knew there were corpses inside. With a week in the Australian warmth the smell was disgusting, coating his nose and throat and making Jack struggle not to gag. He hadn't been feeling too good before he opened the door and the presence of rotting neighbour was not in the credit column. Still, he needed to find a gun and soon. He hadn't got a very clear idea of what he was going to do once a weapon was in his hands, but he would think about that when he had one. One channel of thought was as much as his pain infused mind could cope with at the moment.

He shuffled from room to room, looking for anything that might be a gun safe. He looked in cupboards, even under a bed (although getting down on the ground was so agonising that he didn't do it again). Eventually he was forced to go in the room he had been avoiding. The bedroom. There were two corpses, both blackening and crawling with flies. The lips were starting to pull back, giving them both horrible grimaces. Jack tried not to look again after his initial scan of the room, but found it hard to resist the odd furtive, morbid glance. There didn't appear to be a gun safe, so Jack ransacked the both cupboards and all the drawers in the room looking for a handgun. He opened any boxes that looked big enough, but found only normal household items, shoes, hats, hair straighteners and other harmless items. Giving up he left the bedroom and went to find the key to the garage, which also proved fruitless, in terms of weapons.

Jack moved on to the next house, working back towards home and moving at a slow limp as he favoured his throbbing side. It contained a family of four. No need to search the children's bedrooms, no parent keeps a gun in the same room as a child. But once again he had no luck. Nothing that looked like a gun safe and no handgun in a shoe box in the parents' bedroom. Jack shuffled round to the next house.

Just an elderly couple in this one, but no gun. Jack was starting to panic a bit now. He knew that Xanthe would want to come back to the house, even if just to pick up some clothes, and thought it likely that Ben would be with her. He couldn't imagine what Xanthe was thinking about him. Presumably Ben had told her that Jack had just headed off on his own. Or maybe he had given a more elaborate explanation. Either way, unless Ben had told her that he had driven Jack away at gunpoint he couldn't imagine he was in Xanthe's good books. She would throw her lot in with Ben, Tim and Melissa for sure, but would want to come and pick up her things, and if Jack was unarmed then he couldn't see how he could face Ben.

Maybe he should have used some ingenuity, he thought, as he limped across to the house opposite; rigged some kind of trap for Ben and then triggered it at the optimum moment. *Who am I kidding*, he quickly snuffed out that line of thought. He could barely walk or dress himself, let alone produce a mantrap that would fool a man like Ben.

The house opposite was the one Jack had previously raided for car keys when he was stealing fuel, so the door was already open. He started by looking for a gun safe, but when that came up blank he was forced to go and witness the sight he had avoided when he'd been in this house before. It turned out to be a young couple, one on the bed and one on the floor. He was just starting to throw things out of their cupboard when he heard the engine.

It could only be Xanthe. Maybe she would be on her own. Yeah, right. He swept the contents off the shelf at the top of the cupboard, ripping open several boxes that spilled on the floor. Nothing. He shuffled through to the sitting room at the front of the house and crouched behind the curtains, watching Ben and Xanthe arrive.

Fifteen

After the Toyota containing Ben and Xanthe had disappeared and the silence had re-asserted itself, Jack stood for several minutes, watching through the window next to the front door of the strange house. He couldn't even have said why he was waiting. Although they might be back later for the Porsche, which still squatted, gleaming, next to the house, they weren't going to be back any time soon.

Eventually he started to move. He shuffled across the street, moving like an old man as the wound jabbed at him with each step. He needed to do something about the bleeding.

The first thing he checked was to see if Xanthe had taken the Iridium satellite phone. With massive relief he saw that she had taken the one that was still packed in its bag, but had left the one that was sitting on the kitchen table.

He was feeling cold again, which he knew was not a good sign. And so he once again found himself in the bathroom, painfully removing his bloody clothes and inspecting the wound. He really didn't know what was best, but he felt he had to do more than just bandage it up again. The only two approaches seemed to be stitches, although this thought filled him with horror, or he had a vague idea that you could glue cuts using super-glue. He'd had a couple stitches before on a stud cut in his thigh as a teenaged rugby player and one of the girls, Rose, had had a bad cut on her head which had been glued together. She'd got it, like so many other injuries, at gymnastics, although bruises and sprains were more normal than actual cuts. She'd fallen and managed to bang her head on the edge of a piece of gymnastics equipment (Jack found it hard not think of this paraphernalia as vaguely related to medieval torture) that shouldn't have been where it was. The coach, a ridiculous stereotype, being a stern East German, had phoned and summoned Jack and Jane to the hospital where they met Rose looking pale and bloodied.

The doctor had been gentle (and rather attractive, Jack remembered) and had glued the wound shut, but had definitely said something about some wounds being suitable for gluing but some needing stitches. Jack could remember the curve of her carefully plucked eyebrows, but couldn't remember if she had said what factors determined which treatment could be used.

"Oh, bollocks," he muttered as he wiped down the wound and inspected it. It was still bleeding, as well as hurting. The bandages he had removed were sodden with blood and he knew what he had to do. He had known since the blood started soaking through the bandages, he had just spent some time in denial. Stitches administered by a doctor under general anaesthetic were one thing, but doing it yourself, Rambo style, was a whole different kettle of fish. And what about blood vessels and things inside? Jack had no idea what he could do about that, and so determined that sewing the external wound shut was his only option.

It took him five minutes of shuffling around holding a reddening flannel to his side to locate a sewing box. Presumably it had belonged to Xanthe's mother. He took it back into the bathroom so he could bleed on the floor without the irrational guilt of ruining a dead couple's carpet. Inside he found a variety of threads and needles and chose the strongest looking thread he could find and the smallest needle into which the thread would fit. The needle still looked pretty substantial.

He gave a wordless shout as he first stabbed the edge of the wound. It *really* hurt and who would have guessed that skin was so tough? After working the needle through the flap of skin he realised he was going to need tools and had to go out to the garage for a set of pliers, the needle and thread hanging loose as he moved.

It took him what seemed like an age to get four sutures in, tied off and snipped. There was a significant amount of bleeding and also a fair amount of swearing. He felt light headed during the first two, but that passed and by the end he just felt cold and shaky. It was the hardest thing he had ever done, but he knew his life was on the line and there was no help coming, and so despite the pain of it, he gritted his teeth and finished the job.

When he was finished he re-dressed the wound, which was still leaking blood, despite the stitches and, as he had before, he crawled shivering and naked into bed.

He drifted in and out of sleep and by the time he felt ready to tackle getting up, all he managed was to shuffle into the kitchen. He forced himself to eat a can of cold stew before gratefully climbing back into bed.

Jack spent most of the next two days in bed. He'd made the decision after stitching himself up, that a doctor would tell him to stay in bed and so it seemed like the best plan to do just that. He did consider decamping to another house in case Ben should return, but in the end he decided to take his chances. If he was ever going to deal with the man he would firstly have to make sure that Ben's plan for him, i.e. death from a knife in the belly, did not come true.

In that two days he did little except sleep and brood. He brought a few tins of food from the kitchen, so he could eat in bed and the only sorties he made were to the toilet or to re-dress his wound. He went out into the garden and tried the Iridium phone each morning with expectations of failure, which were met. He felt like he didn't sleep well, especially during the long hours of the night, when he had to force himself to lie still, but the time passed and after two days he decided that his enforced bed rest was at an end.

The stitches appeared to be doing the job, since the wound wasn't bleeding much anymore, but it did continue to weep fluid into the bandages. Movement wasn't quite the agony it had been, although sharp stabs of pain still accompanied anything except the gentlest of bend or twist to his torso. It took him a long time to re-dress the wound (luckily Xanthe had left quite a stock of bandages) and then slowly dress himself. He didn't feel hungry, but he forced himself to eat some cereal with UHT milk.

When he stepped out of the house he stood on the step and surveyed the start of another beautiful day in the deserted city. The air was crisp, although with promise of heat to come later in the day, and just breathing it improved Jack's outlook on life. The plan he had made, which had seemed next to impossible while he was struggling to put his T-shirt on, seemed more feasible now he was outside.

He retrieved a couple of bottles of water from the kitchen and then went in search of the first item he needed. A car that was a bit less distinctive than the Red Mitsubishi ute.

It wasn't that long before Jack was pulling up in front of the enormous chicken barn in a dark grey Holden that he had taken from one of the houses he had ransacked in search of a gun. His objective here was not, however, related to chickens. He was still looking for weaponry and the best plan he could come up with was the idea that farmers generally owned guns. He had found a gunsmith in the yellow pages but his worry about that was the time and effort it would take to break into such a place. Whereas a farmhouse would have only normal house security, leaving just the gun safe to deal with. Hopefully.

The house itself was, like so many dwellings in Australia, a predominantly wooden bungalow, and was set a reasonable distance from the actual poultry sheds themselves, behind a stand of trees.

Jack moved gingerly around the building looking for an easy way in. He didn't feel up to kicking in any doors and was disappointed that the front door was locked. However he had more luck around at the back, where a neat little garden, entered by a gate at the side, gave him access to the back door, which was not locked.

Inside the house the now familiar smell was present and intense, but Jack delayed finding out who the dead occupants were by looking for a gun safe. This didn't take him long at all since it stood in clear view in the utility room, alongside the washing machine and freezer. Locked, unsurprisingly.

He could go and retrieve the break-in kit that he had brought in the Holden, or he could go and rummage around amongst the dead people's things to try and find the keys. Given how hard movement was and how many corpses Jack had seen recently, the key search seemed like the easiest option. He quickly located the master bedroom which contained a surprisingly young couple (Jack had an image of a large, middle-aged farmer but the reality was a muscular young man and his slender wife rotting in the bedroom), although it was getting harder to tell every day that passed as the corpses blackened and started to bloat.

The key search, it turned out, was not so easy but Jack eventually found a large key ring in the pocket of a brown work jacket that was on a chair in the kitchen. The key to the safe was on the ring and so Jack opened the safe. He had his weapons.

There were two guns in the safe and both exceeded Jack's

expectations of what he was looking for.

He had expected a twin barrelled shotgun or maybe some kind of small calibre hunting rifle but the two guns he was presented with didn't really fit these descriptions. There was a shotgun, but it was a pump action weapon. In Jack's opinion it looked more suitable for robbing a bank than controlling vermin on the farm, although he would have been the first to admit his ignorance of the whole subject. Jack hefted the lethal object. He'd never handled such a gun before but he'd seen enough TV to make him think he knew roughly how it worked.

Leaning the shotgun back in the safe he took out the other gun and examined it with some trepidation.

It was, presumably, a hunting weapon, but to Jack's inexpert eye it seemed more military than anything else. It had the expected large telescopic sight, but instead of a single shot bolt-action mechanism, he could see this was a more serious piece of equipment.

It had a green sling for carrying and a largish magazine stuck out of the underside and the gun was clearly self-loading, since there was no bolt, only a cocking lever. Instead of the expected wooden parts, there was camouflage pattern plastic, which had a grippy, rubbery feel to it, and the whole heft of the gun in his hands was both intimidating and exhilarating. He realised that if he was going to use either of these guns as a weapon, then a bit of practice was in order and so he first sat on a chair and learned how to load and unload each one. This was actually rather trickier than he expected on both guns but eventually he had loaded, unloaded and reloaded both of them. There were three or four boxes of ammunition for the rifle and even more for the shotgun. Far more than he needed, but he would take it all anyway.

Leaving the rifle propped in the safe he first took the shotgun outside to try it out. Jack had only ever fired a firearm once before in his life, which had been a .22 rifle as a school cadet. He hadn't deliberately avoided doing so, but the opportunity had just never come up and Jack had had no interest in seeking it out. So it would be fair to say he got the fright of his life when he finally managed to get the gun to go off.

His initial attempt was unsuccessful since he forgot that guns had safety catches, his nervousness having driven even this knowledge from his head. So the first try resulted in him pulling the trigger harder and harder but with no effect. Once he had realised his mistake and identified the safety, he put the gun to his shoulder and before he was really even ready, it seemed, it gave him an enormous thump in the shoulder and left his head ringing from the noise. It took him several minutes to pluck up the courage to try again. For want of something better to shoot at, he shot out the windows of the farmhouse that the young farmer couple owned. They wouldn't mind.

This was, he had to admit, enormously satisfying, as each thunderous bang was accompanied by the crash and tinkle of broken glass. By the time he'd emptied the gun he was starting to get slightly less afraid of the recoil and noise. He couldn't deny that this was more exciting than he expected, but after he had pulled the trigger and got nothing but a click from the empty shotgun, he started to become aware of the ringing in his ears and the pain in his side, presumably from just clenching his muscles against the recoil.

He painfully made his way back inside and swapped the shotgun for the even more scary hunting rifle and then surveyed the garden for targets. Stepping through the gate and out of the garden, he slowly, and rather painfully got himself down on the ground. There was a house about a hundred and fifty yards away and he reckoned that blowing the windows out of that building would make suitable target practice. The first trigger pull produced the same result as the shotgun. Nothing.

"Bollocks," he muttered to himself, as he located and released the safety catch. However the second trigger pull produced the same result. Was it broken? No, he'd just forgotten to cock it. He pulled the cocking lever back and tried again but with the same result. With a frustrated groan he examined the weapon again. The safety catch had re-applied itself. Well that made sense, Jack reasoned out, that the gun would make itself safe when it was cocked.

"OK," he said out loud. "Remember, Jack Stevens. Cock it, then safety catch, then fire."

He lined it up on a window of the distant house and pulled the trigger. The gun worked this time, with the spent cartridge ejecting out of the side. He squinted through the scope again and looked at the window he had aimed for. It appeared undamaged. A second shot also produced no visible damage, as did the third. He could see the windows clearly through the sight, but the gun was wobbling just too much. He tried to calm his breathing.

"Take your time," he told himself. The fourth shot did, to his enormous satisfaction, shatter the chosen windowpane. He emptied the entire clip at the various visible windows and only missed with one more shot. A window was a bit bigger than Ben, but Jack reckoned he would have a fair chance of hitting a man, a particular man, at that range.

He struggled painfully to his feet, moving even more gingerly than he had before playing with the guns. He had what he needed.

Jack wanted to get on with the next part of his plan, but before leaving the farm he felt he should check in on the chickens.

There were still plenty of cats hanging around and Jack fought off the urge to start shooting them with the shotgun. He'd never been a big fan of cats, their supercilious nature had always somehow rubbed him up the wrong way. Did they know who was in charge? And for that matter, who was in charge? As the saying went, dogs have masters but cats have staff.

However he didn't blow away any of the felines prowling the chicken sheds who were clearly missing their former servants. Instead he ducked quickly through the door to see if the chickens still had food.

The answer turned out to be a no. The shed was still noisy with the clucking and squawking of the thousands of birds. In fact the din rose considerably as he closed the door behind him as the hens reacted, in Pavlovian fashion, to the noise of the door. A quick inspection showed him that nearly all the pens had run out of food and that there were, in fact quite a few dead chickens in most of the pens. There was still water in the long troughs, although it looked like the water was no longer flowing in, but enough remained.

The problem was one of plain numbers. There were just too many chickens, and so if he was to avoid coming back here to refill the food hoppers every couple of days, he had to reduce that number. He went down the row opening the pens so the chickens could get out into the barn proper, and then back down the other side, until all the pens were open and the chickens were starting to emerge to mill about the concrete aisle-way that ran down the centre of the cavernous shed. He then slipped back outside, taking care to make sure no cats got in, to retrieve the shotgun from the car.

Back in the shed he went to the big doors at the end that he and Xanthe had used to bring the forklift into the barn last time and, with chickens milling around his feet, he rolled the door right back. Several cats were close by, but Jack fired the shotgun into the air and they shrank back. This gave him enough time to drive the first batch of hens out of the door and into the daylight. Once this process was started, Jack reasoned, the cats would not come into the barn as they would be busy chasing the chickens that were outside, and so it proved.

He spent the best part of twenty minutes trying to drive as many birds as possible out of the door. He shouted and even fired the shotgun into the roof a couple of times.

"Get out. Get out. It's quite safe. You'll like it, I promise. Get out. Out. Out." he bellowed at them, despite the patent lie that this was. He knew many would die. Some immediately at the claws of the gathered predators and many more over time, but it was better than leaving them to die of starvation. Once he was satisfied he had thinned the numbers enough, or being honest with himself, he had had enough and wanted to sit down so his side would stop throbbing, he brought the loader in the shed. He crushed several hapless hens in the process but he was getting past caring. Retrieving a knife from his break-in kit he simply slit the enormous bag of feed open and let it all run on to the floor to form a huge mound of chicken pellets.

The chickens still in the shed immediately went berserk, attacking the pellets as if they wanted to kill the mound of food and not just eat it. Jack did a final inspection to make sure no cats were inside (he was ready to use the shotgun) but found none and so left the depleted chicken numbers shut up in the shed, gorging themselves.

Outside the clouds were piling up and the air had that under-water quality that, certainly in England, meant it was going to rain. There was also a breeze starting to rise. The farmyard held surprisingly few of the evicted chickens, given the hundreds, maybe thousands – Jack hadn't been counting – that he had driven out. That was undoubtedly as a result of the cats' handiwork. Interestingly a few cats had managed to kill a chicken, but a surprising number seemed to have failed to do so. Maybe the chickens had turned out to be not such easy prey as the cats had hoped. Fights were starting to break out over the carcasses of the victims.

"Is that better, you guys," he asked them out loud, causing one or two to turn their heads to give him that cool look that he so disliked. Jack's side was really throbbing now and he was sweating hard. He climbed into the car, stowed the shotgun on the back seat alongside the hunting rifle and, after a minute to recover, embarked on the next part of his rather sketchy plan. Now he needed to find where Ben, Xanthe, Tim and Melissa were living.

Sixteen

Although Jack didn't know where the others were, he did have a rough idea of the section of Sydney he was going to search. Thinking back over the evening conversation when the five of them had been together Jack realised that not only had they not said exactly where they were living, but Ben had been deliberately evasive. This implied that he had made his plans within hours or even minutes of meeting Jack and Xanthe. While they had all been talking about how they came to be sitting in the Botanical Gardens shooting fireworks into the Sydney night sky, Ben had clearly been thinking through how he was going to deal with his rival for the alpha-male position. The ironic thing was that Jack had not seen it that way before Ben's plans came to pass, but he certainly did now. There was no way the two of them were going to rub along together after this, as the blood, still soaking slowly through the dressing on Jack's hand-stitched wound, attested. He did not have those guns on the back seat in order to establish a friendship with Ben.

No. Ben was going to leave town or die. Jack's mind gnawed on that decision but he was still struggling with both options. Although he didn't like either choice, he was determined that Ben would not get away with what he had done, and so one of those two things was going to have to happen.

However, first he had to find them and Jack wasn't fooling himself that this would be a quick task. All he knew was that they were in a large and expensive house somewhere south of the botanic gardens. He also knew that it had been a little over half an hour from when they first starting lighting fireworks until they had heard the engine of Ben's Ducati. That and the fact that Ben, Tim and Mellissa had seen the rockets at all limited both the range and aspect of where they were staying. Jack had no way of knowing which rockets they had seen, but it must have taken them some time to see the fireworks and get themselves moving. The house also had to be somewhere that had a view of the sky above the Gardens. This still left an enormous area but Jack was hopeful that Ben's car fixation would allow Jack to home in on the group.

The chicken farm was on the north side of the city and so it took him a while to drive to the address he had set the Garmin to locating. He was finding that the combination of the Yellow Pages and the Garmin was an extremely effective tool kit for navigating this strange city. It was how he and Xanthe had gone about their looting spree and also how they'd stocked up on fireworks for Jack's ill-fated plan. It didn't take long for him to locate a likely candidate for the car dealership that Ben had taken the super-cars from.

He set off with pain still throbbing through his side and spots of red blood marking his white T-shirt over the dressing. The pain seemed less intense, less focused, but was now coming from the whole side of his torso. He tried to ignore it as he drove the Holden, following the Garmin lady's instructions. The car owner had a selection of CDs, but they all seemed to be country music, which was not Jack's taste, and so he turned the stereo off and wound down the window. Although he knew it was unlikely, he wanted to maximise his chances of hearing another vehicle.

As he drove it started to rain, big drops splattering on the windscreen from the heavy sky. Jack drove slowly but saw and heard nothing. When the Garmin told him he was less than a mile from the Ferrari dealership, he pulled over and parked the Holden. It was, deliberately, an inconspicuous car and he parked it between two other cars to minimise the chances of Ben noticing a new car on the road. He knew he was being paranoid. Ben had probably never driven up this road and certainly not noticed exactly what cars were there, but Jack didn't want to make a stupid mistake and alert the man.

He got out and stood in the rain for a minute, hunting rifle over his shoulder. The big tropical drops soaked him to the skin very quickly, but it was not cold. He set off with his T-shirt stuck to his skin and decorated by a large pink stain on his right side. Walking slowly, soaked and wounded, the loaded rifle slung over his shoulder and murder on his mind, he for a moment thought back to before the epidemic. Less than two weeks ago he was sitting in an office programming door security. The contrast between that Jack and this one was so stark that he found himself smiling a grim smile as he trudged along, listening and alert.

It was less than two weeks since he had spoken to Jane, exchanging the usual trivia of life. Less than a fortnight since she had chattered on about Rose's gymnastics and the fallout the twins had had with their best friend at school. In fact it was only two weeks since he had arrived down under, by Jack's calculations, so just over a fortnight since he had sat and shared a last meal with Jane and the girls, and then kissed them all goodbye before climbing in to a taxi for Heathrow. It seemed like a lifetime.

Would she even recognise the man who was hunting his enemy through the warm tropical rain, seeking revenge? It was hard to believe it was such a short time, and that so few days could change him so much. Or maybe he wasn't changed, he mused. Maybe this Jack had always been inside him and only now was seeing the light of day. And perhaps the same was true for Ben.

As he walked he stayed close to the parked cars and the side of the street. He was aware all the time of the nearest cover, should a car suddenly appear on the street. But no car did appear and the streets were as silent as ever, with just the patter of the rain. Even the usual occasional cat was absent as they no doubt sheltered where they could.

He hadn't brought the Garmin, since it was too valuable to him to allow it to get wet, but he had memorised the simple route to the dealership, and it was not long, even at his slow pace before he saw it a few hundred yards ahead. It was a large glass fronted building set on the corner of two streets. The glass was dark and reflected the street scene rather than revealing any of the interior, but the words "Ferrari Maserati Sydney" were clear.

He unslung the rifle and cocked it. He cradled it as he had seen soldiers do on countless films.

"Remember the safety. Remember the safety," he muttered to himself as his thumb found the catch, although he left it engaged. He knew it was unlikely that Ben was in the building, but it was as well to be prepared.

The front door in the rounded glass wall that fronted the building was, as Ben had said, unlocked, and so Jack crept inside, nerves jangling despite telling himself that nobody was there. It felt like he was entering enemy territory, but without an intercom that he could use to say "Entering the building now. What are your orders, Control?"

It was surprisingly dark inside, despite the large glass walls. Rain was running down the glass and the gloom outside was magnified in the showroom, but it was utterly silent, with just the noise of the rain outside and of water hitting the floor where Jack stood, as he involuntarily marked his trail with drips. Several cars stood around the room, looking predatory in the bad light, their sleek lines ready to pounce on the unwary. He crept past the vehicles barely giving them a glance, rifle still at the ready, towards the back of the showroom where there were several counters and doors, which presumably led to offices.

It took Jack about ten minutes to search the building thoroughly and establish that he was alone. By the time he had finished he was really not feeling well. His wet clothes had chilled him and he was shivering and also dealing with a thumping headache. Blood continued to ooze through the soaked dressing and he was becoming aware that he would have to change it soon. But first he needed to recover, so folded himself into luxurious passenger seat of a Maserati to have a quick rest.

When he woke it was to absolute blackness, disorientation and a headache. It took him a few moments to even remember where he was, although before he started fumbling around in the dark he took the time to think about that particular issue. It was the solid mass of the rifle resting across his thighs that reminded him that he was sitting in a Maserati on a stake out. He fumbled for the door catch with fingers that were numb from being wrapped around the rifle.

The door catch was difficult to locate, but when he eventually did find it the interior of the sports car was flooded with light, making him squint in the brightness. A quick check on his watch showed him it was only 8 o'clock, although it felt like three in the morning. He struggled from the car.

"Oh God," he groaned as the movement from the lowdown seat jabbed his side. Peering back into the interior he saw that he had left a smear of blood on the dark leather next to the passenger seat, and so he stripped off his T-shirt and spent a minute using a clean patch to wipe away traces of his presence.

It seemed too painful to put the shirt back on and so Jack walked back to the Holden still freezing cold, clutching the rifle. The rain had stopped, but the night was black and windy with solid cloud cover ensuring there was no moon or stars. It took him the whole drive home to stop shivering and, on arrival, he changed his blood soaked dressing as quickly as he could before falling into bed and sleeping.

The following day was one of the worst of Jack's life. *So far,* he reminded himself, as he drove back home, exhausted and in pain.

He had spent the day on the south side of Sydney hoping to catch a glimpse, or even a distant engine note, of the survivors, but he had seen and heard nothing. He'd parked opposite the luxury car showroom and spent an hour or two just sitting in the Holden looking through the rain, which continued to fall, at the deserted street.

He then got out and walked south for a while, but all he achieved was soaked clothes, a pain in his side and more blood stains. He'd walked for longer than he intended and by the time he got back to the car he wasn't feeling too great. His head was starting to pound again and he was getting cold. He wasn't sure if his shivering was because it genuinely was cold and he was in soaking wet clothes or for more worrying reasons. He'd heard somewhere in a film he had watched that blood loss makes you cold, but had he lost enough? He had no idea, although he did seem to be continuously dealing with the oozings from his roughly stitched stab wound. If he was losing too much blood then what could he do about it? He didn't even know his own blood type and so didn't rate his chances of finding blood in a hospital that would do him any good. And anyway, didn't it need to be refrigerated? What was the shelf life of blood? Jack had no idea. This had got him thinking about the whole subject of expertise.

Removal of most of the population had brutally shown him how little he knew.

This was not comfortable for him since Jack had always thought of himself as a man who knew things. A practical man. But he now realised how much he didn't know, not just about medical matters, but on so many useful and practical subjects. And Google, both verb and noun, was gone, from Australia at least. Things had reverted to the time when WWW might be an acronym for something to do with wrestling, and when questions came up you had to just accept that the knowledge was not available.

Xanthe, of course, would know more about dealing with his injury, and as the blood continued to flow and he felt worse and worse, he was starting to realise that finding her was rising in importance. On inspecting his wound the previous night he'd noticed that it was starting to ooze other fluids as well as blood. Was that normal? It was hard to imagine that it was a good sign.

After he arrived back at the Holden he went in search of some food. He didn't really feel hungry, but he knew he had to keep eating. There was nobody to look after him and so he would have to look after himself, if only for Jane and the girls, all those miles under his feet. He couldn't raise the will to go and find (and break in to) a suitable shop, so he brought his break-in tool kit to bear on one of the small houses opposite the car showroom. It wasn't hard to get the door open, although even that work with the crowbar made his head pound harder.

There wasn't a great deal inside, apart from the ever-present smell of the dead, but he did find a couple of cans of soup, which were exactly what he needed. The gas even worked on the hob, although he had to spend five minutes searching for matches, which he luckily located without having to go upstairs to the source of the smell. The hot soup was good and he sat with his wet shirt draped over a chair in the small front room, looking out at the glass fronted car dealership. After he'd finished the soup he picked up the rifle and squinted through the telescopic sight at the scene across the street. Could he hit a man at this range? He thought he could. He opened the sash window, moved the sofa so that it was made a convenient rest, and then knelt behind it and sighted again. Although the window was open he thought that he would hardly be visible in the dark room to anybody looking from the street. The rifle was steady on its rest and, despite having a limited field of view, he was reasonably confident he could hit what he could see. He resisted the urge to take a test shot, but couldn't help but smile as he stood back up. Programmer turned sniper in two weeks.

For the afternoon Jack drove cautiously around the suburbs of Sydney. When he found an area that seemed affluent he got out and walked the streets for a while in the hope of seeing some sign of habitation. The rain continued and the wind was now picking up as well, driving water into his eyes and chilling his wet clothes. He saw some expensive looking houses but nothing that showed any sign of current habitation. He kept his eyes open for Xanthe's parents' grey Toyota, but didn't see it parked in the driveway of any of the large houses he passed.

By five o'clock he was shattered and feeling terrible, and so headed home. However, during the drive and his evening routine of a wound-dressing change, some tinned food and sleep, his mind was working at the problem that lay before him. Sydney was a big city and random searching might take him weeks. Time that he was no longer sure he had, given his health. He had to be more inventive and think of how to locate the survivors. Despite his weariness, his mind raced, keeping him awake as he lay in bed and it was a number of hours before he drifted off, a new plan now formed.

It was hard to get out of bed the next day, but Jack forced himself.

The headache was still severe and he was feeling cold all the time. He knew that that meant he had a temperature but there didn't seem to be much he could do other than take some painkillers, which he did. Xanthe had laid in quite a stock of drugs, as well as other medical gear, but most simply had the names on the packets and so Jack had little clue what they did. He ended up taking both paracetamol and ibruprofen in the hope that they would help with the pain, which was constant, as well as the fever. His bones ached as he slowly got himself dressed and forced down some unappetising breakfast. He then set off to put his plan into motion.

The weather was better today, although still quite overcast, as he crossed the Harbour Bridge and looked down at the famous Opera House. He'd set his destination and wasted no time getting there and breaking in to his target, which was entitled Bob Jane T-Marts and was in Bondi Junction. This wasn't the easiest piece of breaking and entering he had done, and he was starting to consider himself an expert, but eventually he was backing the Holden into the large dark interior of the auto shop. Although the establishment claimed to be a specialist in wheels and tyres, Jack was interested in neither of those items, but it did not take him long to find what he was looking for, which was car batteries. He loaded fifteen into the back of the Holden, a process which made his head spin and created a few waves of nausea, but he pressed on. He also found several packets of assorted jubilee clips and some bright red cable ties, which he loaded up, along with some extra tools that he thought he might need.

Next he re-programmed the Garmin and found his way to a large electronics shop, called Dick Smiths, into which he broke with some ease. It took him slightly longer to find what he was looking for and he needed to take a variety of products out into the street so he could easily read the details. Eventually he found what he wanted and loaded ten webcams into the car. A few more trips and he had ten small laptops (he stripped them out of the packaging and threw them and their chargers on to the rear seat, and finally a whole load of car adapters which claimed to be compatible with the Acers. He ripped one out of it's packaging and confirmed the fit before slamming the door closed and climbing gratefully back into the driver's seat. He dry-swallowed some more pills and let the shivers subside. As he sat there one more idea popped into his mind and so he headed back into the shop for one more item.

Jack headed straight to the car dealership and back into the stake-out house into which he had broken the day before. He parked as close as he dared and then carried a single car battery, laptop and accessories into the house in two journeys, with the hunting rifle slung over his shoulder the whole time. Once settled on the sofa with the window open so he could hear anything that happened outside, he got to work.

His plan was reasonably straightforward. Instead of relying solely on his own eyes and ears, he would widen his net by including some additional cameras to create a surveillance network. Although this would take some time and effort, it was not wasted since he would be doing it in areas he wanted to monitor anyway, just as he was at the moment, and in going back to check the cameras he would be visiting his best guess places. So nothing lost and everything to be potentially gained.

The first task was to power the laptop up and so he took the car charger he had looted, that was compatible with the laptop, and snipped off the cigarette-lighter plug. Five minutes work with a pair of pliers and a screwdriver and he had the stripped wires clamped to the terminals of the car battery using two jubilee clips. The light on the little transformer was on – a good sign.

He plugged the cable into the laptop and pressed the power button. The machine went through its boot-up process and Jack found himself whisked back to a world where this was what he did. It was obviously crazy to get emotional over the noise Windows makes when it starts, but it brought a lump to his throat to hear it and see the chirpy welcome message.

"Get a grip, Stevens," he growled to himself.

He ripped open the box to the webcam he had brought in and inserted the CD in to the laptop. Installing the software took five minutes, during which he read the instructions that came with the camera. Once the camera software was installed and the USB device was plugged in and clipped to the top of the laptop screen, Jack found himself looking at his own image on the small laptop screen.

"Jesus! You look rough," he commented, and there was no doubt that that was true. His face was pasty grey and sweaty, with a hollow cheeked look he hadn't had two weeks ago. There were dark circles under both eyes, and he could see his concern reflected in the image's face. After a few more moments of looking at himself mournfully, he shut the window down and tried to concentrate on what he needed to do.

The software was not complex and he quickly found the features for which he had selected that particular camera. It said on the back of the box that it did motion-activated recording and sure enough he found the feature in the software's menus and activated it. Since Jack came from a technical background he was a firm believer in the old adage, 'If it's not tested it doesn't work', and so he clipped the camera to the window frame, looking out into the street and peered at the screen. It didn't appear to be recording. He slung the rifle over his shoulder and went outside to test. He wandered around in it's field of view, walking across the camera's line of vision at various ranges, right up to the showroom across the street and came back inside to see the results.

What he found was that past a range of about twenty-five yards the camera switched off, since it obviously judged that to be insufficient motion.

"Good to know," Jack commented. Although he was still feeling rough, it was good to get his teeth into a technical issue he could solve. His situation had been steadily spiralling out of control and technical challenges were a way to get at least the feel of some power back. Whether this idea could work, or even made any sense, was impossible for him to judge, but he had thought up this plan lying in bed the night before and now he was going to execute it.

Twenty-five yards was too far away from the window since, if Ben entered the showroom from the front door, it wouldn't trigger. The objective of this was to see which way he went afterwards, so Jack needed to find a better place to put the camera. The ideal would be close to the exit ramp so that as Ben took a car, which was the only reason he would come here, Jack could see which way he drove.

A few minutes of reconnaissance and he settled on an unremarkable parked car near the bay doors of the car dealer. These doors were the only way a car could leave the building without smashing through one of the full length windows. The car was locked but this was the work of a few seconds in which Jack just staved in the passenger side window with his trusty crowbar. Shockingly, although why Jack was shocked he couldn't have said afterwards, the car burst into alarmed life and it was another two minutes of fumbling under the bonnet to get the battery disconnected before the street was plunged back into silence. The echoes of the alarm still seemed to ring in Jack's ears long after the physical noise had ceased.

Jack swiftly picked the rifle up from where he had left it and stood nervously for a minute. How far would sound like that travel? A mile? More? The streets were quiet, but there was still a breeze, the aftermath of the weather front that had passed through the day before. It might have muted the sound a little with the white-noise from moving leaves.

When nothing happened Jack went back to his task. He fetched a fresh battery, connected it up to the laptop and got it booted up and working. He clipped the camera to the top of the steering wheel and checked the field of view on screen. A couple of small adjustments and he had a good view of the bay doors as well as the junction in front of the showroom. Hopefully if Ben decided he needed another sporty car then Jack would see which way he went. He got out and checked the hidden camera from the street. You would have to look very closely from the street side to see either the camera or the staved in window and the battery and laptop were totally hidden in the foot-well.

"OK. That's number one," he announced to the world as he headed back to the stakeout house.

He did the software install on the remaining laptops in the stake-out house, after a lunch of tinned fruit. By mid-afternoon he had all of them installed and ready to go. He had worked with the window open, hoping to hear a distant engine, or perhaps a not so distant one, but by the time he was ready to move the only thing he had heard was a distant dog barking.

He was sweating heavily and not just from the heat. His headache remained in force and now the occasional bout of dizziness swept over him as he worked. After each laptop he took five minutes to just sit and stare out of the window, but all that did was make him think about how bad he was feeling. He had to keep moving. The wound was still seeping pinkish fluid into the dressing and pain was always there. This evening he would take his best guess on which pills to take to fight the infection that was definitely setting in.

Jack was starting to care less and less about bumping into Ben, so he brought the Holden down to the house so he could load the laptops back up easily, and then set off to find good spots to put the cameras.

When he envisaged the plan he had imagined finding high buildings in to which he would position the cameras to spy on the main roads in the south of Sydney, but the reality was that this seemed like too much effort. Instead he went mostly with repeats of his first option, using parked or even crashed cars as hosts for his spyware. He used the GPS to target major roads in and out of the city, positioning each one so that it got a view down the road in order to maximise the footage he would get of any vehicle travelling that way. Each laptop got a camera and a car battery and he carefully turned the screen backlight off on each laptop once it was running. This was partly so that no screen glow would alert Ben if he passed at night, and partly to maximise the battery life. Jack had no idea how long a car battery could power a small laptop, but he hoped it would at least be a day. He could change the batteries every day as he checked for motion-activated video.

Only one camera went into a building. He found an apartment block above a large intersection, near the hospital, which was perfectly positioned and so he expended the effort to break in. This would not normally have been an onerous task but he was getting tired now and both his strength and the will to exert it were starting to ebb. However, eventually he got all the cameras positioned and was ready to head home, having marked the location of each as a "Point of Interest" to Miss Garmin. He drove back north with a glorious sunset on his left, but he was finding it hard to see the appeal in anything at the moment. Despite having brought his plan to life Jack was not feeling good about life. He felt tired and sore, as well as alternately hot and cold, and the gnawing worry that he was ill equipped to deal with his current troubles was starting prey on his mind.

He was totally alone and felt it. The loneliness was starting to take its toll and he was finding coping more and more draining. But this was not a voluntary isolation and so he had no choice but to endure.

Changing the dressing he was now starting to become aware of the smell. Not just of his unwashed body (and God knows, he thought, that's bad enough) but a sickly smell coming from the old dressing. He examined the contents of the medicine cabinet that Xanthe had stocked and found few clues, but eventually found a packet that said Amoxicillin on it. It seemed likely that this was related to Penicillin and so Jack took two. There were no instructions with it so Jack arbitrarily decided to take two each morning and each evening and see how it affected him. After a supper of cold tinned stew he fell into bed and was asleep in seconds.

The next morning marked two weeks since the Last Day of Civilisation. It was, by Jack's calculations, Wednesday 24th of November and Wednesday 10th had been the last day that Jack, or anybody else in Australia, had gone to work as usual. His mood had not improved over night and neither had his health and he found himself fighting a wave of homesickness, as well as more physical symptoms, as he forced some breakfast down. He was homesick for home itself, of course, for Jane's arms around him and goodnight kisses from his girls, but he was also homesick for other aspects of his normal life. Friends, travel, work; the full package.

He remembered so vividly that final day in the office with Rick and Cynthia. Eating a sandwich at his desk, white-boarding the plans for the project with the client managers (who were both drooling over Cynthia in an almost laughable way). The whole day had just been so, well, *normal* was the word for it, and Jack found himself wiping away tears as he thought about it.

"What the hell's wrong with you, Stevens," he chastised himself. He hadn't even really liked his job and so why the hell he was getting emotional about it he didn't know. Maybe he was sicker than he thought and so couldn't control his own self-pity, or maybe, just maybe, it was for Rick, Cynthia and the others that he was crying. He couldn't think of his two colleagues now without the images of their corpses that had so shocked him in those first few hours.

His head was still pounding and the deep bone-ache that was starting to govern his days had not receded. He dry swallowed two more Amoxillin and some Ibruprofen before loading some snack food into the Holden's passenger seat, which was already awash with discarded packaging, and setting off once again.

Having worked quite hard the previous day, his plan for this one was to take it a bit easier. He would check the cameras and simply keep his ears and eyes open and hope that some clue came his way. But first he had to re-fuel the Holden, which he did about half a mile from home, using a smart black and shiny Mercedes four wheel drive as the donor vehicle.

The smell of the fuel seemed even stronger than usual and he had to let some just spill on the ground as the the nausea overcame him and he vomited in the flowerbed next to the vehicle.

"Jesus," he commented, as he wiped his mouth and tried to get back on task.

The Mercedes had a big tank and completely filled the Holden, which was good, and then Jack was off on his way again. *Feeling grim but still functioning*, he thought to himself.

His first stop was the Bob Jane garage, where he loaded more brand new batteries into the Holden. He planned to replace the batteries each day so that power outages wouldn't cause holes in his spy network. He didn't know how long one battery would last, but since there was, in effect, an unlimited supply of new ones and they were free, apart from the effort of moving them, he may as well play it safe. Once they were loaded into the boot he set off to begin the check of the cameras, one by one.

He started at the Ferrari dealer, the first camera he had set up. Jack settled into the passenger seat of the parked car he had used, pulled the little black laptop on to his lap, rifle propped on the driver's seat, and turned on the screen, wondering what he would find.

"Well, we've got something," he commented to the world as he found there was about fifteen minutes of video that the machine had captured. It was getting hot in the car and he was sweating heavily, but despite that, the headache, the pain in his side and the ever-increasing nausea and dizziness that was starting to affect him, he still felt a quickening of excitement.

However, it was misplaced. The video held no images of Ben, Xanthe, or any other people. Most of it was just a plain view of the street, with no clues as to why the motion sensor had been triggered. There were two short clips of different cats, one white and one tabby, sauntering across the street, and one even shorter clip of a large bird, species unknown to Jack, swooping low over the camera.

"Bollocks." There is nothing worse than having your hopes raised and then brutally dashed. Jack hadn't realised the extent of his loneliness, and the intensity of hope the video produced, until he found the tears coursing down his face as his isolation came crashing back. He had been trying to hold it together, do the sensible thing, but it was getting harder and harder to motivate himself.

"Oh, Jesus. Pull yourself together, Jack," but even this came out with a sob in his voice. He was starting to lose it, no question.

He also knew he was talking to himself more than he ever had before, but since there was nobody else to talk to, it wasn't worrying him overly. The myth about it being the first sign of madness was the least of his troubles.

He deleted the video and changed over the battery to the new one, and then just sat for a few minutes, contemplating the street and gathering his strength for the next leg.

The second camera was also in a parked car, looking at a junction on a main road. It was mid-morning now and the sun was starting to really heat up in earnest. The inside of the car was really uncomfortable despite the window Jack had smashed to get into the car. Since the car had been parked there were no keys in it, so he couldn't even start it to get some air-conditioning running. He left the passenger door open while he manoeuvred the heavy battery into the driver's foot-well, next to the one he put in yesterday. The pain in his side stabbed him fiercely but he was getting more used to it and so just gritted his teeth and carried on. Once the battery was in place he retrieved the shotgun, which he was finding a serious encumbrance, from where he had propped it on the wing of the red Honda he was using. The metal of the car was now hot to touch as he picked up the gleaming weapon and climbed back into the passenger seat and stowed it on the back seat.

Although he was finding the gun a pain while he fetched and carried equipment, to go with all his other pains, he had made a decision that he would keep one of the guns with him at all times. The shotgun was marginally lighter and easier to carry about and so this was the one he was slinging over his shoulder to make sure he would not be caught out again.

He settled into the passenger seat and fired up the laptop to see what it had captured. This one had even more video than the first, with over twenty minutes of motion-activated film.

"Come on. Come on," he found himself muttering as he started the first clip running. But he was disappointed once again. The tally on this camera was one cat, one large dog, two birds and a small kangaroo or maybe it was a wallaby (Jack was no expert on marsupials).

With the disappointment came a physical wave of tiredness that Jack found it impossible to fight. The car was boiling hot, although shivers still periodically came and went, and the throbbing in his side seemed to intensify. He put his head back and gave himself up to the urge to just sit, eyes closed, and let the dizziness, reminiscent of bed-spins from too much alcohol, take him.

When Jack came properly awake he wasn't sure if he had been sleeping or just in a stupor, but the sweat was rolling off him and his mouth was bone dry. He didn't think it had been too long, but he didn't bother checking his watch and doing the calculations. The pounding in his head and throbbing in his side made any non-vital movement seem not worth the effort.

Moving slowly he changed the laptop over to run on the new battery and deleted the pointless video files. He then painfully retrieved the shotgun and hobbled back to the Holden. He had to stand next to the camera car and let the world stop spinning when he first stood up, but after a few seconds his equilibrium returned and he was able to move slowly and painfully across the street.

"Thank God," he croaked as he saw that there were two large bottles of water on the passenger seat, since he couldn't remember if he had actually put them in this morning or just thought about doing so. He greedily drank half of one straightaway, spilling some of the lukewarm water down his red T-shirt but not caring in the slightest. It was already stained a deeper red at his side as his wound continued to ooze bodily fluids in a seemingly never-ending leak. He wiped his hands on his shorts and then fished out the blister pack of Ibruprofen he had put in his pocket that morning. He washed down three with some more water before selecting his next point of interest, the next camera, on his one true friend, the Garmin.

The third camera Jack had set up was in a crashed car, a white Jeep 4x4, that was slewed across the main highway that ran south and then west out of the city. The Jeep was nose into the central barrier, both nose and barrier rather crumpled, and luckily the occupants were nowhere to be seen. He wasn't sure if he could have made himself set up a camera in a car with corpses rotting in the heat, despite the good cover it made for his covert addition to the vehicle.

He parked right next to it and, shotgun slung over shoulder, did the now-routine battery transfer from the boot of the Holden. He retrieved a bottle of water and, getting wearily into the passenger seat, set about reviewing what there was. The first clip was a kangaroo and the second was one of those mysterious scenes where nothing seemed to be in motion, although the laptop obviously thought that something was. The third was another kangaroo (or maybe the same one) and the fourth was a bright red BMW barreling down the highway right past the camera.

Seventeen

Jack had to watch the video clip three times before he truly believed what he had seen, his hands trembling. The car didn't appear to be in a tearing hurry, although it wasn't dawdling either and, according to the timestamp on the file, it had passed by two and half hours before. Adrenaline coursing through his body he reviewed the rest of the clips, but there was nothing except animals and phantom activity. He went back to the BMW.

He couldn't see properly through the windscreen due to the reflection of the bright sky, although examining the clip frame by frame, he thought that there might be a hint of a face on the passenger side. At least two people then. He sat for a moment wondering what he should do with this information.

He didn't know who it was. It was possible it was someone Jack had never seen before, but the endless silence of the city made him think otherwise. It was surely two or more from the Ben/Xanthe/Tim/Melissa group. And did it matter? He'd been on his own for days, it felt like weeks and was desperate for human contact. In fact if it wasn't them so much the better since another group might not contain someone who wanted to kill him.

If this car had travelled up this highway this morning then there seemed a fair chance that it might also come back this way.

That meant he had a choice, he could either stay where he was and hope that either the car didn't contain Ben or, if it did, that he was more heavily armed and prepared than the Australian. He held out his hand in front of him, which trembled to the point where you could call it a shake. Did he want to risk a confrontation like that? Perhaps get into a gunfight here on the highway? He would be outnumbered and if he laid an ambush and started shooting then whoever was in the car would want to try and defend themselves. And if they were unarmed would he just kill Ben in cold blood? Jack still didn't know the answer to that question, although he also didn't really see a viable alternative.

No, an ambush here on the highway was not a good plan. He couldn't shoot at a car that contained other people and if he allowed time for people to get clear then he might find himself in a gun fight he was not in good shape to win.

"I've got to get off this road," he concluded, looking through the windscreen and then twisting the rear-view mirror to show the empty highway, heat shimmering off the grey surface, which stretched away in both directions. To his left was a wooded bank and he eyed it up as a potential hiding place. Could he get the Holden up into the undergrowth sufficiently to hide it? Maybe, maybe not.

Up ahead was a bridge and beyond that a junction. He ran the video clip a couple more times but unfortunately the camera activation hadn't happened until the car was well past the junction. This meant he couldn't be sure it didn't join the highway there, but the angle and steady speed seemed to imply to Jack that it hadn't come down the slip road but had already been on the highway.

"Yup, that's it," he told the laptop. Suddenly worrying that the car would come back any minute he hurriedly shut the laptop screen down, decided he wouldn't bother connecting the new battery, and hurriedly returned to the Holden. He threw the shotgun onto the passenger seat, started up the car, slammed it into gear and headed at full speed down to the junction where he swept up the slip road, braking sharply at the junction at the top.

The junction was a large road that simply crossed the main highway, on a wide bridge that was bathed in the bright afternoon sun but totally deserted. Not even a parked car. But the bridge did have a low concrete parapet topped off with a high wire fence and this, Jack reasoned, should mostly hide the Holden from anyone down on the carriageway, especially if he didn't park right next to the parapet. He came to a halt about ten feet from the concrete wall on the far side, killed the engine, and climbed out of the car as quickly as his wounds and dizziness would allow, shotgun in hand.

He crossed to the wall, which was about three feet high, and looked down on the deserted road. Well, not quite fully deserted. Another kangaroo was visible a couple of hundred yards down the highway on the verge. It was looking alertly in his direction although whether it could see him as he squatted behind the concrete boundary, or had just heard the car he couldn't tell.

The silence was oppressive and seemed even deeper after the noise he had made getting to his vantage point, the only sound now was the ticking of the cooling car engine. The sweat trickled between his shoulder blades and his head started pounding more vigorously as the adrenaline in his blood ebbed away. After a couple of minutes of contemplating the empty road he went back and sat in the driver's seat of the Holden, leaving the door wide open for air. He swapped the shotgun for the hunting rifle, putting it across his knees and swigged some tepid water from his remaining bottle.

Time passed slowly in the heat of the afternoon and nothing happened. No car swished by underneath the bridge as Jack fought to stay awake. He periodically walked around the junction, but it was hot and his head hurt. He finished the water and the snacks he'd brought with him. There were some houses a few hundred yards away, but he didn't dare risk missing the car returning and so he waited.

He waited all afternoon and then watched the sun set. It was a spectacular display, fantastic pinks reflected off the light streaks of cloud in the west. He told himself that when it was fully dark he would head for home, by the back roads rather than up the highway, and then he could come back and concentrate his cameras in this area tomorrow.

The sky was still light, although he had seen the last direct rays of the sun a good ten minutes previously when he heard the sound. There was no mistaking it. A car was coming and as he watched he could see headlights sweeping towards him along the highway. Jack crouched down, worried that he might be silhouetted against the sky.

The car passed under the bridge without any change in the engine note, as it tooled down the right-hand carriageway. Jack climbed into the driver's seat of the Holden and set off in pursuit.

The whole reason for waiting had been to follow the car as far as he could when it returned and he now realised that the fact that it was dusk was hugely to his advantage. This piece of luck meant that it was bright enough to follow with his lights off, but also dark enough that he could clearly see the lights of the car he was following. For the moment, at any rate. He knew that he had to stay well back and it was better to risk losing the car then being seen. If it was Ben driving it and he spotted Jack in his rear-view mirror then the ambush would be reversed and Jack didn't rate his chances in anything like a fair fight, guns or no guns. It seemed very likely that Ben would be armed, at the very least with Xanthe's shotgun.

Jack swung the Holden down on to the left-hand carriageway,

reasoning that being on the other side might make him harder to spot.

"Thank God it's not a Volvo," he said to himself, thankful the Holden was a car where you could drive with no lights.

He had to get up quite a speed to keep the rear lights of the BMW in view, but he managed. As he drove he got the Garmin up and running. When he did lose his target he would need to mark the last place he had seen it, so he could come back and find it tomorrow. If he could just keep it in sight until it left the highway then surely he would have a much narrower area in which to hunt down the little group of survivors.

Jack barrelled through one junction but a minute or two afterwards he clearly saw brake lights on the car ahead light up. Jack slowed, squinting forward, trying make out what was going on. It was hard to tell in the gathering gloom, but he thought the car had taken the ramp beside the highway. He slowed further, letting the Holden coast, and his theory was confirmed. He clearly saw the lights cross a bridge above the highway, having turned left, and pass out of sight as the car drove south on the road above. Jack speeded up again and went up the slip road on his side faster than was comfortable in the poor light, but he was desperate to get on to the same road as the BMW so he could see where it turned off.

The junction at the top had a central island, which Jack saw too late and couldn't avoid slamming the two driver's side wheels on to the low curb. There was a bollard and a lamppost, which he did just manage not to hit, before shooting out on to the road at the top of the ramp, just managing to miss the central reservation which was only visible as a darker strip down the middle of the road.

"Shit," he swore to himself. Hitting the curb had made the most god-awful noise inside the Holden and must have made quite a thump outside. Would it have been heard?

The taillights were still visible ahead and there were no brake lights, so that was a good sign. Jack eased off the throttle. It was almost completely dark now, although there was a bit of a moon, and Jack felt insanely reckless, careering down the road with the lights off. But he was past caring. He knew his health was deteriorating and that without help he might not recover. Maybe he was already past the point of no return. The wound was clearly starting to become infected (the smell as he changed his dressing last night told him that) and so while he'd waited on the bridge he had acknowledged to himself a fact he had been carefully denying for at least a day, maybe more. Finding Xanthe was more important than getting revenge on Ben, or even than countering the loneliness that was becoming an almost physical presence as he moved from one solitary activity to another. Xanthe had medical training and he needed medical help urgently to avoid becoming a secondary victim of the plague.

The road they were now on was wide, with dark buildings on either side which looked like they might be large retail outlets, but it was hard to tell in the gloom. The taillights ahead disappeared round a curve to the left and Jack couldn't help speeding up in agitation, only to ease back down again as he rounded the gentle curve himself and saw the lights ahead closer than he wanted. No brake lights appeared and the BMW held a steady speed.

Jack judged that they had travelled perhaps a couple of miles when the buildings gave way to trees and then the surrounding view suddenly opened out as they crossed a bridge spanning some kind of river or sea inlet. Jack could clearly see the moonlight, which was strengthening even as the sky darkened, shimmering off the water.

Into the trees on the other side and it was less than another mile before the lights dipped down out of sight. As Jack approached the place where he judged he'd last seen the car lights he was faced with a choice and hadn't a clue which way to go. A slip road ran straight on, sloping downward, while the main road, a single carriageway now curved down and round to the right.

"Well, made a lot of progress, anyway. Don't want to go too far," he muttered as he took the slip-road. It was better to stop short than over-run, and so he eased off the throttle and coasted down the slip-road, which was narrow and dark, over-hung with trees that were blocking out the moon. At the bottom was a roundabout, barely visible and Jack, accepting that he'd lost the BMW, slowly circled it. But as he did so he caught a glimpse of lights on the road to the left.

He quickly accelerated on to that road, which was just a lighter grey strip between darker grass verges and trees, with some low buildings, probably private houses set further back. He hugged the left hand edge to give himself some reference, which paid dividends when he narrowly missed an island with bollards in the centre of the road, which he didn't see until he was practically alongside. The lights were still visible ahead down the straight road and Jack glanced continuously between the distant red pinpricks and the grey shapes rolling past his open window.

The lights were out-distancing him but at that point he had a stroke of luck. The driver of the car, obviously not paying very close attention and running, to some degree, on autopilot, switched on his left indicator. It flashed three times clearly before the brake-lights shone out and the car vanished from Jack's view.

Jack cruised down the road gently, trying to gauge the exact point where the lights had disappeared. He was aware that as soon as the BMW arrived at its destination and the driver killed the engine then his own car would be the loudest thing around and so he couldn't go charging forward, engine revving. He arrived at a turning on the left that could well have been the one the BMW took. There was nothing to be seen and so Jack shut the Holden down and let it coast to the side of the road.

He sat in the silence for a minute just listening. He could hear nothing other than the occasional creature in the night. There was no wind and so even the trees were silent. Sweat was dripping off him, despite the open window and he was finding it hard to control the shivers that were coming more and more frequently. A leaden tiredness filled Jack and he had to fight against it to make himself retrieve the hunting rifle from back seat and climb out of the car. He pressed the door closed as quietly as he could.

Slinging the rifle over his shoulder, he leaned against the Holden to let the dizziness pass. Maybe he should just mark this spot and come back tomorrow. Was he up to sneaking around at night? But then again, would he feel any better tomorrow? Logic told him that he was likely to be worse, not better, and so he had to make himself act now. He had just made this decision and started to move quietly along the grass verge when he heard clearly, although the noise was distant, a car door slam. The noise came from somewhere along the road he was looking down, confirming his estimation of the turning.

"Oh, thank God," he whispered to himself. He had found them, or at least found *somebody*. The slamming door couldn't be more than 500 yards from where he stood, and there were only so many places there could be in that area. Relief was flooding through him, as well as a healthy dose of adrenaline, which certainly helped a little with the tiredness and aches that filled him.

He trudged down the road studying each house as he passed in the moonlight to see if it was large and grand enough to meet Ben's description of the house they had taken over. The houses looked large and solid, two stories for the most part, but not really in the league that Ben had described. However after a couple of hundred yards he came across a set of wrought iron gates, behind which he could just make out a pale drive-way retreating between the trees.

Jack pushed the rifle through the bars at the bottom and laid it gently on the ground, before slowly and as quietly as possible, climbing the gates. They were solidly made and there was no noise, aside from his muted grunts of effort and pain, as he crossed them. Dizziness forced him to pause on the top, lying along the iron with a leg on either side, before he recovered enough to lower himself down inside and retrieved the rifle. He hefted the rifle for a moment before cocking it as quietly as he could, although it still made an audible clicking, and then shouldering it into a semi-firing position, thumb on the safety catch. Hugging the trees and walking on the grass he made his way up the drive, round the bend until he had a view of the main house.

This was more what Ben had described, a hulking shadow that blocked out a good portion of sky, starlight reflected from the many windows looking darkly out on to the paved parking area in front. Three cars were parked there, although whether any were the red BMW Jack couldn't tell in the darkness. There was no hint of any light or life from the silent building.

It took Jack about ten minutes to establish that this was not the right house. He circled round to the back and found the back door unlocked, but moving around in the utterly silent and almost totally black interior told him that the house was deserted. That and the smell, which emanated down the stairs from where the owners no doubt rested in their beds. The only thing of value he found was a torch on the windowsill next to back door as he was leaving. He was deliberately looking for just that, knowing that next to the back door was the kind of place people might leave a torch, and so was pleased with himself when his hand closed on the cold metal and the beam stabbed out dazzlingly bright after the darkness. He quickly turned it off and debated doing a more thorough search using its light, but he was sure this house was empty and he just couldn't be bothered, so he pocketed the torch and moved on.

The next house was almost the same story. A set of wooden gates were more difficult to climb and he had to grit his teeth to avoid crying out when the pain in his side stabbed viciously at him, as he pulled himself over. There were four cars here on a tarmac driveway and Jack crossed to them to check something. It was the work of moments to establish that all were stone cold, with no hint of engine heat coming through the bonnet or dissipating hysteresis in the tyres.

"Not this one either," he muttered, slinging the rifle over his shoulder. He still went to try the front door, which was not locked, but once again the smell and the silence told a story which meant he didn't need to look for long.

Back on the street it was only a few hundred yards until he reached another set of gates.

"How many of these are there?" he spoke aloud, but his voice was a barely audible whisper. This was obviously a place millionaires in Sydney came to live. The gates stood open, which was welcome, as climbing the last wooden set had been painful on both entry and exit, but here he was able to walk straight up towards the house, keeping to the grass verge, rifle held at the ready.

As soon as he rounded the last of the bushes screening the house he knew he had found it. The house was at least as large as the previous two, maybe even bigger, but the difference was that one of the lower windows held a glimmer of light. It wasn't bright and it was only one window on the ground floor, but it was enough. Once again Jack felt a combination of fear and excitement clutch his insides. The light looked liked it might be candlelight, as it flickered uncertainly, and it clearly came from deeper in the house, rather than the room with the window.

He stole across to the group of five or six cars that were parked on the huge asphalt area in front of the house, and the first one he came to was the BMW that he had followed. He crouched beside it, although logic told him that anybody looking out of a window would be able to see virtually nothing in the night. He couldn't see the colour or make in the moonlight, but the bonnet heat touched the skin of his hand even before he laid it against the warm metal.

There was an open space, a lawn, he supposed, to one side of the house and Jack headed out on to that, heading for the gloom under the trees and intending to circle round the house and get a look in through the windows. He was about halfway across the lawn when there was the distinctive sound of a door opening behind him. Obeying some instinct he hadn't known he had, Jack dropped to the ground where he stood, sending pain exploding through his body, but managing to keep silent and also turning his head as he fell so he could lie still but still see back towards the driveway.

Standing in the doorway was a man holding a battery-powered lantern. It was Ben. He was dressed the same as the last time Jack had seen him, when Jack had cowered in the house across the road, pinned down by fear, covertly watching Ben and Xanthe.

And the fear was there now. Ben was only about thirty yards away and Jack felt it slide a cold hand up his spine as he watched Ben hold up the lantern and look around. Had the man heard or seen something? There was something lazy about his movements that made Jack think that he had not. His powerfully muscled shoulders looked relaxed and Jack could clearly see his face, which seemed to hold a small smile. Ben looked left and right one more time and yawned, before stepping forward off the step, flip-flops slapping, and he walked past the cars towards the trees, lantern held at half-mast.

Ignoring the pain thumping through his head and torso, Jack rolled over, not so fast as to make a lot of noise, but not too slowly either and got himself into a firing position. He didn't know if Ben could see him lying here on the dark lawn, but he needed to be ready in case he did. Jack brought the rifle up and looked through the scope, getting a shockingly clear view as Ben put the lamp down, took another two steps forward and started to urinate, his back half to Jack.

Jack's thumb found the safety catch, which made a tiny click as he disengaged it, but Ben's urine stream remained uninterrupted as he emptied his bladder in blissful ignorance of the danger lying on the lawn behind him.

This was an easy shot, even for Jack. He was confident he could hit Ben in the head from here, but he sighted on the centre of his body. There was no point in taking an unnecessary risk. And so it came to decision time. He could kill Ben now with no risk to himself and make this whole problem go away. He could then walk in the house and tell the other three what had happened. The evidence was festering under the bandages under his shirt. Jack put his finger on the trigger as Ben finished his business. Now was the time, but still Jack hesitated. He'd heard people in films say that it was hard to kill a man, but he had always imagined that to be movie-speak. Surely in a life or death situation it would not be an issue. And yet here he was watching the man who, without provocation, had tried to kill him, who had sworn to kill him if he ever saw him again, and Jack was hesitating, finger on trigger. The gun followed Ben, keeping the cross-hairs steady on his body as the Australian retrieved the lantern and sauntered back towards the house. He stopped, put down the lantern again and opened the door to one of the cars. The light came on inside the car, giving Jack a crystal clear view as Ben reached inside and retrieved what looked like a packet of sweets from the car. He closed the door again and picked up the lantern.

Jack was still undecided. He hadn't decided not to kill Ben, but he also hadn't quite decided to kill him, and that was how it remained. By the time Ben went back through the door and shut it behind him, leaving darkness outside, Jack had still not quite decided to kill Ben, and so the big man was still alive. Jack re-engaged the safety on the rifle, unsure whether he had just been weak or strong. Had he failed to assert himself as a man or had he just done the right thing? What did it matter? By not choosing he had made a choice, at least for the moment.

Jack lay there for a few moments before levering himself painfully to his feet.

Following his original plan he circled the large house, keeping well back from the windows until he had a clear view of the back, where a single lighted window shone out of the darkness. From the edge of the trees on the other side of the lawn Jack lifted the rifle and used the scope to look through the window. What he saw almost brought tears to his eyes again.

He had a clear view of Xanthe's head and shoulders as she sat, presumably at a kitchen table, although Jack couldn't see the table. Beyond her sat Tim and they were both sitting, clearly listening to someone else speak. The candlelight that lit the room was warm and inviting. Xanthe looked so lovely Jack could hardly believe it was the same girl. *Maybe that was just a function of being on your own too long,* Jack at least had the presence of mind to think.

The warm candlelight drew him closer like a magnet, and soon he found himself crouching beside the wall peeping through the window. The room was indeed a kitchen, large and tasteful with many candles burning, and the four survivors were sitting at one end of a scrubbed wooden table. Xanthe and Tim were on one side and Melissa and Ben the other. As with the night in the Botanical gardens, Ben was doing most of the talking but occasionally one of the others, most often Xanthe, would interject a comment. Jack found himself just watching and drinking in the scene. None of them glanced his way and he almost forgot that he could be seen.

Eventually, however he started to think about how he was going to play this. The door to the kitchen was ajar, presumably leading out into a hallway, but Jack could only see darkness beyond the door. He watched for another couple of minutes, weighing up his options and finally managed to make a decision on what he was going to do.

Jack padded back round on the lawn. At one point he stumbled, although whether it was due to an uneven patch of grass or the dizziness, which was almost continuous now, he didn't know. He managed to avoid jabbing the barrel of the gun into the ground, which he had a feeling was not what guns liked, but the pain was excruciating. He lay on the cool grass for a minute before summoning the strength to rise and move on. He arrived at the front door and slowly and carefully tried the large doorknob. It turned and the door swung silently inward, revealing nothing but blackness. Jack slipped through the gap and closed the door carefully behind him, using the handle to avoid any noise from the latch. He stood in the darkness, clutching the rifle and trying to breathe as quietly as possible.

The hallway actually wasn't totally dark, now that Jack got a chance to adjust. It was a huge space, with a dark floor and walls, and candlelight was leaking in at the far end. Presumably that door was to the cosy kitchen scene he had just illicitly watched. Jack could hear voices emanating from that direction, although he couldn't make out what they were saying. A large staircase lead from Jack's left in a curve around the hall, disappearing in the gloom, and that was exactly what he hoped he'd find. Without wasting any more time, since time might be an issue here, Jack headed up the stairs. He moved slowly, partly because he wanted to be silent, and partly because he really wasn't feeling too steady on his feet. A stumble could be a disaster, as he certainly didn't want to get into a gunfight here in the hall, luckily the stairs were thickly carpeted and solidly made, with no creaks or groans as he ascended.

He made it to the top of the wide staircase, one hand holding the rifle and the other clutching the smooth and solid wooden banister. There was very little light here and so there was nothing for it but to use the torch. He slung the rifle, which was getting heavy anyway, over his shoulder and retrieved the torch from the pocket of his shorts. His hands were slippery with sweat, as he covered the lens and switched it on, deliberately looking away so that he minimised the damage to his night vision. The blood-red wasn't really enough to let him see anything, but letting a small amount of light leak out showed him what he needed.

The top landing he was standing on had a number of doors off one side and a continuation of the solid wooded balustrade on the other, forming a kind of mezzanine level that looked out over the cavernous hallway. Leaving the torch on but covered and letting out only the occasional beam of light, Jack found the first door and entered the room. He turned off the torch and closed the door behind him (although he didn't click it shut) and switched on the torch properly. He was in a large and well-appointed bathroom, which was not what he was looking for.

Back into the hall with a smothered torch. The next room was a bedroom, quite large but clearly nobody was staying there. Jack's torch beam revealed a made bed and pristine floor and surfaces. He carefully opened a drawer to see only paper lining the bottom. The next was another bedroom, much smaller than the first but someone was staying here. There was a pair of jeans on the floor and the bed was not made. Jack inspected the jeans. They looked new, no surprise there since they would be newly looted, but they were for someone far taller than Xanthe, taller than Jack even. They must be Tim's. Jack moved on.

The next door was to an airing cupboard, although cupboard might be too small a term for the spacious shelved interior that Jack lit with his torch. That took him round the corner and into a corridor which Jack's muted torch beam showed had rooms on either side. The first on the left was another bedroom with an en suite bathroom. This was also inhabited but tidier than Tim's room and so Jack knew he had, perhaps, found what he was looking for. He carefully, and as quietly as possible, opened drawers until he found a pair of trousers and held them up for inspection. This was Melissa's room. Jack and a friend could have fitted in those slacks.

He went for the room opposite and immediately identified his objective. The room was large and tidy, also with a door that looked like it lead to an en-suite bathroom, and had a large double bed against the far wall. The bed was made and there were no clothes lying around but next to the chest of drawers was a suitcase, which was a distinctive red and blue. The very same one that Jack had watched Xanthe carry out of her parents' house, the best part of a week before. This was definitely the room Xanthe was staying in, unless she had already moved in with Ben and was simply storing her clothing here.

Without disturbing anything else Jack padded over to the double sliding doors, which hid the built in wardrobe, and slid the doors aside. One end of the cupboard held a selection of clothing, probably Xanthe's, but the other end was empty, with just a couple of vacant wire hangers hanging on the metal rail. Jack got himself into the cupboard, shut the cupboard door, which was louvered wooden panels, although didn't allow any view through, and lowered himself so that he was sitting leaning against the end wall. It was good to sit down after his efforts, and so Jack adjusted the gun to lean against the wall beside him and settled down to wait.

Eighteen

The next thing Jack was conscious of was someone shaking his shoulder.

"Jack, what the hell are you doing here? Wake up." He recognised that voice, but didn't want to do what it was asking. He squinted into the light, but couldn't work out what he was seeing. His head was pounding ferociously.

"God, Jack you look terrible. What's happened? Why are you in the cupboard? Jesus, Jack, why do you have a gun?" It was Xanthe, of course, speaking in a low but urgent voice. He remembered now why he was in her cupboard. His mouth was dry and no words came out as he looked up at Xanthe squatting in front of him holding a lamp with one hand and his shoulder with the other.

"Hold on, I'll get out. Keep quiet," he meant to whisper, but it came out as a barely intelligible croak and he didn't even know if she had understood. Maybe she had, since she straightened up and gave him space as he levered himself painfully out of his hiding place. Rufus was also in the room and the small dog growled at Jack but thankfully didn't bark. Xanthe stroked him and murmured something Jack didn't catch, calming the little animal. There was concern on her face as she watched him, but also suspicion and confusion. He left the rifle propped in the cupboard, as he didn't want to alarm Xanthe any further than he already had.

He had to steady himself against the wall to keep from falling. His knees felt inexplicably weak and the room was spinning around him, so he just leant against the wall and tried to recover himself. Xanthe could obviously see that he was in difficulty as she started forward and grabbed his arm and helped steady him as he swayed.

"Come and sit down," she helped him towards the neatly made bed. "And then you can tell me what the hell is going on." She kept her voice low, but Jack was still nervous about being overheard, so he put his finger to his lips as he sat down and tried to gather his thoughts. Strangely he had not rehearsed this part in his mind and so was not really sure where to start. Xanthe set the lamp on bedside table and stood back, arms folded and one eyebrow raised.

"I..." his voice came out cracked and scratchy from his dry mouth. Xanthe handed him a glass of water that had been sitting on the bedside table. He took a grateful sip, using the time to try and martial his thoughts around the headache and dizziness.

"I didn't want to leave," he eventually managed. "I had no choice."

"So why did you leave then?" Xanthe asked, but before Jack could answer, another voice cut in.

"Yes, Jack. Why don't you tell me and Xanthe why you had to leave us?" Ben stood by the doorway wearing only a pair of shorts. His heavily muscled arms were folded, but he looked tense, ready. There was a long pause while they all looked at each other, faces eerily lit by the camping lamp.

"I'll tell you why Jack had to leave," Ben continued, his voice loud and hostile. "He woke me up the morning after we met and told me he had something to show me. He took me off to where he'd parked that big truck he was driving. He then explained to me very carefully, didn't you Jack, that there wasn't room for the both of us in the group and told me that I had to make myself permanently scarce. To cut a long story short, I said 'No way mate', he threatened me with a shotgun he had in the truck and we had a fight which, if I say so myself, I won, didn't I Jack? It was obvious that the two of us were never going to be mates, so I gave him his marching orders and, like the coward he is, he left with his tail between his legs."

"Jesus, Jack. Is that what happened?"

"No. Well partly," Jack croaked. His mind was on the rifle propped in the cupboard and he realised that that had not come out well. He tried again.

"No. It was him who did the threatening. He woke me up and threatened me with the shotgun. He also stabbed me," Jack indicated his side.

"Oh, that is such bullshit, Jack and you know it. Stabbed you? Christ, I don't know what you've done to yourself but it's got nothing to do with me. I did threaten you, it's true, but only after I'd managed to get the shotgun off you. After I'd got tired of you showing me the business end of it. Jesus, I can't believe you would lie, like that."

Ben took a step forward, looking threatening. Xanthe looked from one to the other, confusion on her face. Jack looked at Ben and then Xanthe and tried to avoid looking at the rifle in the cupboard, which Ben couldn't see from where he was standing and Xanthe appeared to have forgotten about.

"Xanthe, it's Ben that's lying," Jack tried to keep his voice calm and reasonable, but without much success, as he heaved himself off the bed and stood swaying. Ben's eyes narrowed and he took another step forward. "He wanted to get rid of me because he wanted you to himself, he said." Jack took a step sideways towards the cupboard, keeping his eyes on Ben and trying to make it look like he was just giving himself some room. He didn't want to alert Ben to the weapon's presence, so he continued to talk.

"I was keen to increase the size of the group. You remember that the fireworks were my idea." He looked into Xanthe's eyes as he made this last point and saw that it connected somewhere behind them.

"Lying pom," Ben snarled and took another step forward. Jack judged it was now or never and lunged for the cupboard, ignoring the pain in his body. He got his hands on the rifle barrel but before he could get anything close to pointing the rifle anywhere, Ben's shoulder hit him, slamming him against the wall, and making the world fade in the white glare of agony from his knife wound. He felt the gun ripped from his grasp and then a savage blow to the side of his head smashed him to the floor.

He wasn't sure if he had lost consciousness, but if he had it can only have been for a few seconds, because when he opened his eyes, Ben was standing over him, holding the gun loosely in one hand and looking down at Jack, a sneer on his face. Rufus was barking, although the ringing in Jack's ears nearly drowned out the little dog.

"Wake up, my friend. You need to pay attention now, because soon you won't be able to." Jack could hear that OK.

"Ben, you can't kill him," Xanthe's voice sounded frightened, a noticeable quaver in it. "Look at him, he's no threat to anybody."

"He's not now, love," Ben answered, his voice now matter of fact. "But he will be. What's the alternative? You nurse him back to health and the crazy bastard's going to have another go at me. There's no cops now to lock him up, it's the law of the jungle. Him or me. I don't want to but I've got no choice. You can leave if you don't want to watch." Jack squinted upward from the floor, fighting off the waves of blackness that threatened to engulf him. He could no sooner rise from where he lay than he could teleport himself back to England.

"But you can't. I won't let you," and Xanthe made to get between

Ben and Jack, but Ben shoved her easily out of the way with his free hand.

"Don't be stupid, love. This is between me and him. He came tooled up to kill me and so I have to kill him." Ben cocked the weapon and Jack saw the unspent cartridge that had been in the chamber fly, glinting, out of the lamplight.

"No," Xanthe shouted and lunged for Ben again, but this time he saw her coming and hit her a stinging blow across her face with the back of his hand. She was knocked on to the bed with a wordless cry and Ben raised the rifle to his shoulder. Jack looked helplessly up at the muzzle of the gun, just a few feet from his face. He closed his eyes, tried to fix a picture of Jane in his mind and let the darkness take him as he felt, more than heard, the concussion of the gun going off.

The first thing Jack became aware of was light coming though his eyelids. It was bright and insistent and he fought it as long as he could but eventually recognised that he was awake and so he opened his eyes. They didn't open easily but were gummed together and the light was very bright and so it took him a few seconds of blinking before he got to actually see anything.

He was looking at a white ceiling with a rather ornate moulding running around its edge and lit by sunshine that was streaming in through a window on his left. He couldn't see much else without turning his head and, for some reason, this seemed like a barrier to finding out more about where he was, and so he just lay for a minute or two looking at the ceiling and trying to piece together where he was.

The last scene he remembered was the confrontation with Ben and the very last event was Ben shooting him in the head at point blank range with a high-velocity hunting rifle.

Jack didn't believe in an afterlife, it had always seemed just a bit too much like wishful thinking, and, of course, the whole Heaven and Hell thing was just an obvious mechanism for getting the medieval masses to toe the line. However, despite this disbelief, he was now lying in a sunny room and so it was either the afterlife or he had somehow survived a seemingly fatal bullet in the head. This line of thought was sufficiently interesting to him to attempt to move his head and so he turned it towards the window to see what else he could see.

The room he was in was large and tidy, with a thick dark-blue carpet and magnolia coloured walls. He could see an expensive looking desk, which had a row of paperback books and a vase with some flowers on it, standing in front of a carved wooden chair. There was also a large solidly built wooden wardrobe that looked like it might lead to another land if you crawled through it. The large window was partly open and he could see trees that were moving gently in the sunshine framing, rather than blocking, the blue sky that held one perfect white cloud. This cloud was shaped, to Jack's mind, rather like a piggy bank.

He contemplated this view for a minute. It seemed very earthly but the improbability of him remaining alive was undeniable and so Jack reserved judgement on the whole afterlife question until more evidence was available. The freshly cut flowers seemed particularly unlikely in any kind of reality consistent with his memory, but there was no denying the appeal of the view. The cloud was gradually morphing so that it looked less like a pig and more like a fish.

After a minute of contemplating this view he mustered the will to look the other way. Once again head movement seemed like a challenge but he managed it and this answered the question about whether he had died or not. Tim was slumped in an armchair reading a book, his scrawny body totally relaxed in the way someone can only be if they are truly bored. Tim obviously caught movement out of the corner of his eye because he looked up sharply. The two of them studied each other for a moment and then Tim's face split into a wide grin. Jack didn't think he'd seen Tim smile in their brief previous meeting and it was interesting how much better his pockmarked face looked when it was lit by a friendly expression.

"Morning, mate," he said in a quiet, conversational tone. " How're you feeling?" Jack tried to reply but his mouth seemed glued together and the noises he made weren't words that Tim could possibly decipher. A look of concern flitted across Tim's face.

"Hold on," he said, getting up from the chair. "I'll get Xanthe," and he headed out of the room, his long limbs carrying him at some speed. Jack contemplated what else he could see. The first thing that caught his attention was the IV drip that was hanging next to the bed. The bag was full of a clear liquid and a transparent tube snaked down towards him. Jack looked down and saw that it was neatly taped on to the back of his right hand, which was sticking out of the sleeve of a red stripy pyjama top and lying on the patchwork bed cover.

So, not dead then. Neither Tim nor this piece of medical paraphernalia had any place in an afterlife, not to mention the stripy pyjamas, Jack judged. But what were his injuries? You don't get shot in the head and come away like nothing has happened. How much of his head and face remained? He felt like he was thinking in a reasonably normal way, although if he wasn't would he be able to tell? There certainly was a strong sense of disconnection from his body and the rest of reality. His head had moved when he commanded and, despite feeling like he was on some high-gravity planet that was pinning him to the bed far more firmly than would happen on earth, he felt no pain. He looked at his fingers and was pleased to see them lift up when he commanded them. He wasn't totally paralysed it seemed. So the next question was how much of his head was left. He had a mild headache but nothing alarming. He could feel the back of his head where it rested on the pillow and his mouth felt reasonably normal as he explored the inside with his tongue and pursed his lips. He could see out of both eyes and close them both as well, which seemed like a good sign.

"So, Tim tells me you're awake," Xanthe announced briskly as she came bustling into the room, Tim trailing in her wake. She stopped by the bed and looked down at him.

"How are you feeling," she asked, her voice softening.

"Weird. Hard to move," he managed. It came out rather slurred but intelligible.

"Mmmm, that'll be the Bromazepam. It'll wear off slowly. D'you think you can manage a drink of water?"

"Yes."

"OK. Tim, can you get Jack a glass of water?" Tim left the room and there was a silence. Xanthe just looked down at him, her face unreadable. A minute later Tim returned with a glass and Xanthe expertly slipped her hand behind his head and helped Jack to drink. Some got spilt but the lukewarm water that he managed to get into his mouth tasted great. Xanthe laid his head back on the pillow and handed the glass back to Tim. She looked tired, Jack thought, as she stood for a moment again.

"Tim, can you go and get Melissa? I think she should be here while we have this conversation." It was interesting the authority that Xanthe's voice held as she issued these instructions, and Tim immediately jumped to it, hurrying off again. Once again Xanthe was silent in his absence and her face held carefully impassive, but the sunshine coming through the window showed how pale she was and the dark circles under her eyes showed that she had not had much sleep recently.

Several minutes passed before Tim led Melissa back into the room. The three of them stood and looked down at Jack, who felt self-conscious under their combined gaze, although Melissa did offer him a small smile. After a pause, Xanthe started to speak.

"I don't know how much you remember about what went on, so I'm going to run through what happened here and then, hopefully, we'll all be clear. I'm not going to get you to try and explain anything because you've been sedated and it's still wearing off. By this afternoon you should be fine and then I will be asking you questions.

"Anyway. First thing is you've been unconscious for two nights and a day. Your wound was badly infected and I think you might have had some concussion. But you seem to be responding well to the antibiotics," Xanthe gestured at the IV, "so I don't see why you shouldn't recover fully. I think you've been lucky. Another day and I think the infection would have been past treating."

Xanthe paused and glanced at the other two standing beside her. She really did look tired. In fact positively haggard, Jack thought.

"I suppose the key piece of information here is," Xanthe paused again and took a breath before continuing, "Ben is dead. Do you remember that happening?"

"No," croaked in reply. "No, I don't."

"Do you remember hiding in my cupboard?" Xanthe asked him.

"Yes," Jack replied. "I remember that."

"Well, after I found you in the cupboard Ben came in and the two of you argued over why you had disappeared last week. You went for that gun that you'd brought with you, but Ben took it off you. He hit you and was going to kill you, to shoot you in the head. But he never did because..." she paused again and glanced at Tim and Melissa who had both been totally silent since they entered the room.

"...because, well because..."

"I killed him," Melissa interrupted in her little girl's voice. "Tim and I had been into town that day and we had been to a gun shop. We both got ourselves guns. Hand-guns, that is. We heard the shouting that night and both of us came out into the hall. I brought my gun because, well, because I was scared.

"We heard what you and Ben said, but I didn't believe him. I believed you. He was a liar. We heard him tells lots of lies, so when I heard that he was going to kill you I went into the room and shot him. In the head." She paused for a few seconds. "It was messy," she finished in a small voice.

At this last Xanthe managed a wan smile.

"That's true, it *was* messy," Xanthe took over the narrative again. "Anyway, I took a look at you, worked out what was needed and went and got the necessary stuff from the hospital. I've re-stitched your wound, by the way, although I have to say that that wasn't a bad effort for a first timer. It can't have been much fun to do that to yourself."

"I think we should leave you for a few hours to let the last of the Bromazepam work its way out of your system, and then you can tell us what really happened. Tim, will you stay with Jack? I could really do with some sleep."

"No problem, I'll stay with him," Tim answered, the first words he'd uttered during the whole exchange.

"Is there anything you need?" Xanthe turned back to Jack.

"No. I think I'm fine," croaked Jack, his mind still reeling from what he had just heard.

"OK, I'll see you later."

Nineteen

When Jack awoke again he felt much more alert. The disconnection with reality had gone and he felt rested and better than he had for some time. The pain in his side had returned to some degree, but it was definitely reduced from when he'd arrived at the house, and the pounding headache had also receded, although not totally disappeared.

Tim was asleep in the chair and Jack just lay for a few minutes thinking about what he had heard that morning. The irony of the fact that all of his plans had been a waste of time was not lost on him. He had found and practiced with the guns and as a result had come within a hairsbreadth of being killed with one of them. And then had been saved by the most unlikely of sources. He had to admit to himself that he had not paid Melissa, or Tim for that matter, much attention. She was an overweight girl, short of confidence and seemingly with little to say for herself who had been wholly eclipsed by the force of Ben's personality at their first meeting. But there was obviously more to these two than met the eye. Tooling up with a pistol and then shooting an armed man in the head at point-blank range was the very definition of a decisive act and revealed an inner steel in Melissa that he would not forget was there.

And why had she done it? She hardly knew Jack whereas she must have known Ben pretty well by now. An inescapable conclusion from this was that her action was less about saving Jack and more about killing Ben. She had said that the pair had armed themselves that afternoon, which was before Jack had turned up, and so there were obviously already things going on in their minds. A hand-gun is not for hunting, it is for self defence or short-range killing. Jack knew for sure that Ben was a nasty piece of work and obviously Melissa and Tim had come to the same conclusion. In fact they had concluded that not only was he a nasty piece of work but also a direct threat. But what had Xanthe concluded? Jack would find out soon enough.

Tim slept for quite a while longer (Jack had no way to gauge time) but after a long period of time in which Jack rehearsed what he was going to say to the group, he rolled over and got himself a sip of water. This woke up Tim who, blearily rubbing his eyes, got to his feet.

"I'll go and see what the others are doing," he told Jack. "Xanthe was in here all night with you and so I think she might still be sleeping."

Tim disappeared and left Jack to consider that last statement and what he was going to say when the group were assembled.

This happened soon enough, with the three filing in together a few minutes later, accompanied by Alf but not Rufus.

"Feeling better?" Xanthe was all business.

"Yes, much. Thank you." Jack was aware he sounded very formal but didn't really know how to get past that.

"I'm sorry, Jack," Xanthe continued. "I could do the whole nurse thing, and check you over and get you what you need, but I just have to know what's happened to you over the last week. Can you tell us first and then we'll do the medical bit. Is that OK?"

"Yes. That's fine," he matched her matter-of-fact tone. "I want to tell you. Do you want to sit down?" His voice sounded much more like his own, although he managed another sip of water while they sat, Melissa in the armchair, Tim on the desk chair on the other side and Xanthe on the bed, way down at the foot, as far from Jack as she could get.

"So first, I want to tell you that what I'm about to say is the unvarnished truth. I can't prove all of it but, although I have many faults, I am not a liar. I know that even saying that casts doubt on what I'm going to say, but I suppose it's still better to state it." He took a deep breath and began.

"I'll start with when Ben woke me up quietly that morning and told me he had something to show me. It was really early and you three were still sleeping. The first thing I noticed was that the red ute we were driving, which I've still got, by the way, was not where we had left it. Ben must have moved it in the night and he must have pushed it for the first part since the engine would have woken us up."

Jack went on to tell them about the confrontation he and Ben had had on the road. He tried not to put spin on the story but just gave them the facts; the speech Ben had given about alpha male status, the shotgun, the stabbing and Jack's eventual compliance with Ben's instructions.

"I've gone over it in my mind, but I don't know what I should have done differently. I believed at the time, and I think I still believe, that he would have killed me if I had refused or fought. I don't know if that makes me a coward. I think it probably does but that's just what it is. Later on I watched you, Xanthe, and him arrive in the Porsche and collect your stuff. I was in the house opposite looking for a weapon, a gun. But I didn't find one and I was too frightened to come out because I thought Ben would kill me. I suppose I'm embarrassed now that I was such a coward and I'm sorry that I didn't do more."

There was a long pause after this while they sat in silence. Eventually Tim stirred and, reaching into his pocket, he pulled out something.

"This is the knife," he said simply holding it up. He pressed the stud and the blade flicked out. "It was in Ben's pocket when I... When I buried him." Tim held it up for a few seconds longer before folding the blade away and putting it on the desk beside him, the light tap of it hitting the wood sounded loud in the silent room.

"I saw him that night," Xanthe eventually commented in a slightly hollow voice. "I woke up in the night and saw Ben moving around. I assumed he was going for a pee and didn't think much about it. I just turned over and went back to sleep. I haven't even really remembered that until now. I didn't connect it with you disappearing. I also saw blood at Mum and Dad's house. There were droplets on the floor of the kitchen.

"I wondered if it could be you, but there were no other signs that I could see, so I thought perhaps it was one of the dogs the day before."

"Well, anyway," Jack continued, "after you'd gone I stitched myself up and spent the next couple of days in bed. Then I went back to the chicken farm that we went to and the farmer had two guns, which I took. Then I looked for you in earnest and eventually, a few days later, I found you."

"How?" asked Melissa. "How did you find Saltview? It can't have been easy."

"Saltview? Is that the name of this house?" Melissa nodded in answer to Jack's question.

"Well I knew you were somewhere in the south of Sydney, so I concentrated in that area." Jack explained his scheme with the cameras and laptops and how he'd eventually captured the BMW on camera.

"That was us. Me and Tim," Melissa exclaimed.

"And that was pretty clever. What you did with the cameras," Tim commented. "I don't think I'd have thought of that. Didn't they just run out of battery?"

"I got car adaptors from the shop and wired the laptops to car batteries. Seemed to work."

"Well, yes. I can see that it would. In fact it definitely did, since you're here." There was something like respect in Tim's voice.

"And that's pretty well it. The rest you know," Jack finished. "What's your story? What have you guys been doing since, well, since that morning."

Between them the three of them recounted their tale, although in truth they had done little since waking up and finding Jack missing on the morning after meeting in the Botanical Gardens. Ben had driven Xanthe to her parents' house to get her clothes, and then they had spent most of the time back at Saltview where the little group of survivors had made a home.

"Ben said that we should just hang-out and see what happened," Xanthe told Jack. "He said that either there were people coming or there weren't. And either way there was no rush and I think we all just naturally accepted his leadership. He was very, well, forceful and pretty convincing."

"He was different when you weren't around," Tim sounded almost apologetic. "You didn't see it, Xanthe, because he cared what you thought, but when it was just Melissa and me he dropped the act and was different."

"That's right, " Melissa jumped in. "Before we met you guys he was difficult. Pushy and aggressive. But once you were here he changed. When you were in the room he was all smiles and charm, but as soon as you left it was like Tim and me weren't even there. He just ignored us like we didn't exist. It was weird and quite frankly, pretty scary. I didn't feel safe around him at all because he clearly thought we were so unimportant. It's why we went and got those guns." Xanthe took a few seconds to absorb this.

"I don't really know what to say," she said slowly. "I knew Ben was making an effort, but I didn't really realise… " she petered out and so Jack spoke up.

"I've got two things I want to say on this subject. The first is to say thank you, Melissa, for saving my life. It can't have been an easy thing to do but you did it, so thank you. I'm afraid I don't think there's anything I can do in return, but if ever there is then just ask and I will do it."

"You don't have to say that," Melissa replied, her face serious. "It was the right thing to do and I don't regret it."

"*You* may not think that I have to say it, but I think I do. So thank you." Jack gave Melissa a smile, which she returned, blushing a little. "The second thing I want to say is this. Let's put the whole thing behind us. It's over and done with now so there's point in raking over it. I move that we don't talk about it any more. We're still survivors of the plague and have enough to worry about. What do you think?"

"I agree," Xanthe looked grateful and was busy re-knitting a business-like face.

"Me too," Tim came in straight away.

"And me," Melissa agreed.

"OK, then. That's agreed," Xanthe had her nurse persona back on securely. "We've got to leave this guy to recover, so you two out. Jack do you need anything?"

"Um, no. I think I'm fine.

"Then I'll leave you alone to rest and come and check on you later."

Jack spent the next four days in bed under nurse's orders. After the stress of the previous week it was an unspeakable physical luxury to lie and not have to force himself into action. The others all visited him, even occasionally the two dogs and he enjoyed their visits, but he also enjoyed reading a book (he went through two novels) and just losing himself in the plot and trying to forget about the current reality.

However behind this appearance of recovery and recuperation Jack could feel something darker moving, like a dark shape under water slowly becoming clearer. Whenever he thought about what was going to happen when he got out of bed the shape was there and each time a little bit more threatening. And so it would be fair to say that Jack spent a good deal of the week in denial, trying to distract himself from an emotional pressure which increased day by day, as his physical strength returned.

Although the worst of the wound and infection was behind him, Jack did still feel a deep tiredness, which seemed like a weight on his body. Far from feeling impatient to be up and about, he was more than happy to just lie still and he spent plenty of time in the day sleeping, although that did lead to a couple of long stints in the night, desperately trying not to think about the subject that he knew he had to think about.

And so Jack's efforts to treat his recovery time spent in his sunny bedroom as a holiday could have been said to be partially successful. There was little he could do and no immediate threat to any of them and so he tried, as much as was possible, to put planning and worrying on hold and just live in the moment, as he had done pretty well since the plague. But re-capturing that feeling was getting harder. Xanthe was business like. They didn't discuss anything other than his recovery and even that in fairly brief terms.

"You're responding very well to the antibiotics," she told him. "Another couple of days and I'll remove the IV, but I think we should leave it in for the moment. The infection really was quite severe and I want to make sure it has completely cleared up. You need to stay in bed as well and try and move around as little as possible. Let's give the wound a chance to heal up." Jack was entirely passive and just accepted the care gratefully without broaching any uncomfortable subjects.

The person he did have some lengthy conversations with that week was Tim. The young man wanted to get busy with the practical side of life on their own, and was keen to hear Jack's advice on what could be done to make their lives as comfortable as possible. And Jack, for his part, was enormously grateful for the distraction that Tim's practical problems represented. The first major topic he wanted to tackle was the water issue.

"There's been no water in the tank for well over a week now," he told Jack in his earnest and slightly pedantic voice. "We've got jerry cans that we've been filling but it's a bit of a pain to refill them. Taps work in some houses, the ones that have tanks in the roof, but no mains taps work anymore. The girls have both commented on how they'd like a bath or a shower, but there's no way we can spare the water at the moment. We've all been for a swim in the river, but it's salt and so not the best."

"Mmm. I take it you've checked the area for some kind of fresh water. A stream or something," Jack asked.

"Yes, but there's not really anything. There is a stream in the hills over that way but it's a couple of miles away and I don't see that I can easily lay a pipe that far."

"Well, let's think about that. How would you go about it," Jack mused. "The easiest would be garden hose, I suppose. I wonder how long a garden hose is. Let's say a nice long one is fifty meters. Sound reasonable?"

"I suppose so, yes."

"Well if the stream is two miles away, let's say three kilometres, you'd need, um, sixty of them to stretch that distance. That's quite a few and so you'd probably have to raid quite a few garden centres to get enough. And you'd need connectors as well, of course. I wonder where you could find a more substantial roll of pipe. Maybe some kind of council depot, if you have such things in Australia."

"Of course we do. That's true, a place like that might have big rolls of pipe and we could just roll them down the road to lay the pipe. Not sure how we'd find a place like that though." Tim's sudden burst of enthusiasm was damped.

"Me neither. And I think you might find that laying the pipe and joining it all up, even on the ground, might be trickier than you think. I wonder if there is a different method."

"Like what? I thought that perhaps we should just move to a house that's nearer a stream. I mean we don't need to stay here at Saltview, do we. It's just where, well, it's where Ben chose. But I suppose we need to stay here until Xanthe says you can get out of bed."

"That's true, we can't defy Nurse McDonald."

"Is that her name? Xanthe McDonald?" Tim sounded surprised.

"It is. No prizes for guessing where her ancestors came from."

"No. It's weird but I didn't know. My surname is Carrick. Tim Carrick. What's yours?"

"Stevens. Nice to meet you Tim Carrick." Jack held out his hand and Tim shook it self-consciously.

"So on this water thing," Jack continued, "I actually agree with you that finding a house that has access to fresh water is a good idea, but in the short term I wonder if there's a way we can easily just fill the tank. Without laying miles of pipe, I mean.

"How about," Jack said slowly, thinking and talking at the same time, "we get our hands on one of those tanker trucks. One that's used for fresh water. They have to exist, don't you think?"

"Definitely," Tim sounded excited by this idea. "And one of those things could hold loads. Probably fill the tank up in the roof ten times from one load."

"Yes, I would think so," Jack was slightly less enthusiastic. You've still got the problem of finding one and then if you can find one you've got to somehow fill it and then pump the water up into the tank."

"Well, do you think the truck itself would have a pump as part of it?"

"It might do." Jack was still thoughtful "It might well do, if you could find a suitable tanker."

"I bet they've got serious pumps on them. They'd have to be able to empty and fill themselves." Tim was still all enthusiasm.

"Do you know what, Tim? You've given me an idea. I know what it is we need. It'll have the carrying capacity and the pumps to fill itself, and then pump the water up to the tank in the roof. And it's not a water tanker."

"Really? What is it then?"

"A fire engine."

"A fire engine," Tim sounded nonplussed. "Are you serious?"

"Absolutely. It should be a lot easier to find a fire engine than to find a water tanker, and you know for certain that it'll be able to suck up water from just about any source and then pump it out wherever you want."

"And will it hold enough?"

"Well, I obviously have no idea what the carrying capacity of your average fire engine is," Jack admitted. "But the whole point is to squirt a large quantity of water at a fire, so I'm guessing they can hold quite a bit. And another bonus is that they probably keep them topped up so they're ready to go. I doubt you'd even need to fill it the first time."

"That's true. You know I think that might be a really good idea. I'll get Melissa and see if she wants to help me find one."

That conversation happened in the morning and it was only mid-afternoon on the same day that Jack heard, through the open window, the grunting and roaring of a heavy diesel engine as a vehicle manoeuvred outside.

After a reasonably lengthy period of the engine revving as, presumably, Tim got the thing parked, there was then a long period where the engine note was steady as it idled. It then stopped a couple of times but was re-started and finally revved loudly and kept roaring. Jack could just hear shouts above the noise, but he fought the urge to get out of bed and see what was going on. After a few minutes of that the engine was shut down, leaving a thick silence in its wake. Jack lay back and waited for them to come and tell him what was happening.

He didn't have to wait long before Xanthe came into the room on bare feet. She was wrapped in a towel and her hair was wet.

"Tim and Melissa found a fire engine. We've just been squirting each other," Xanthe beamed at him. It was the first smile he'd seen on her face since the two of them were in the Botanical gardens. "I haven't done that since I was a little girl. It was fantastic! So good"

"You played with fire engines when you were a little girl?"

"Well, no. Garden hoses. You know what I mean."

"I do. I'm glad you enjoyed yourself."

"It was great," he got another smile. "Tim says it was your idea, so I just came up to say thanks. Not only fun, but Tim is taking the hose up to the tank at the moment and once it's full we'll have running water again. Luxury."

"We aim to please, Madam."

"You certainly know how to spoil a girl," and Xanthe gave his shoulder a squeeze with a damp hand before disappearing and leaving him on his own again.

The next morning Tim was back with more plans.

"The fire engine is great!" he enthused. "It wasn't that difficult to drive, although getting it into the driveway here was a bit tricky, and getting out again was even more difficult. Melissa had to guide me out." Jack had heard Tim backing and filling last night as he moved the big vehicle out on to the street. "But it has a huge capacity. We spent some time learning how the pumps work and, well, playing with them. But even after that and filling the tank it's still well over half full. I reckon we can fill the tank twice more before needing to find some more water."

"That's good," Jack couldn't help smiling at Tim's infectious enthusiasm.

"Yeah, it's great. It means we can use the toilets again, which is a big bonus. It was a really good idea."

"Well, I'm happy to help. I can't do much else so thoughts are about all I can contribute at the moment."

"Well, on that note, Xanthe said you rigged the generator up so you could get hot water at her parents' house. How did you do that? The girls would love hot water and I have to say that I wouldn't mind either."

"It actually wasn't that tricky. First you have to find the hot water tank and establish if it has an electric immersion element. That's basically the same thing that you have in the bottom of an electric kettle. If it does then wiring up the generator is really not that tricky."

"And what will the immersion unit look like? I can't look inside the tank can I?"

"No, you can't," Jack was trying hard not to patronise Tim, who was obviously not a handy man. "It will be mounted on the side of the tank, probably near the bottom. It's a device that sticks out of the side of the tank and has a cable going to it."

"OK. I'm not sure where the hot water tank is, but I'll see if I can find it."

Ten minutes later Tim was back. "I've found it, I think. And I think it has an immersion unit. Certainly it has something mounted in the side which has a cable going to it."

"OK, good. I have to say, Tim, that the little generator Xanthe and I were using is probably not powerful enough. This house will have a big tank and it will take a long time to heat it up. I suggest you try and find a bigger one."

"A bigger generator. OK I can do that. I'll see if Melissa wants to come."

"I have a suggestion, Tim, if you don't mind me making one."

"Of course not. What is it? Do you have an idea on where to find a generator?"

"No, I'm afraid not. My suggestion is that we make it policy not to go off too far on your own. We have no way of contacting each other and so if something happened it could be awkward."

"Yeah. That seems sensible. We've sort of been doing that, although we haven't made it a rule."

"I can't make it a rule. It's not my place to do that. But it is a suggestion."

"I agree. I'll go and find Melissa and see if she wants to join me looking for a generator. How big do we need?"

"I'm afraid I have no idea. Have a look at the one that Xanthe and I were using and go for one that is physically bigger than that. Maybe twice as big. There has to be a correlation between size and power output."

"Makes sense. OK. I'll see you later."

"And I'd suggest you try and get your hands on a good long extension lead. Or even better a roll of cable if you can find it. There may be an extension lead here but it's unlikely to be long enough. We want the generator as far from the house as possible."

"Roll of cable. Good thinking. That should be easy." Tim was half way out of the door, keen to be on his way.

"And are there tools here? You know, screwdrivers, pliers, those things?"

Tim paused in the doorway. "Yes, there's a whole work room full of stuff like that. The people who lived here had everything."

"One last thing, Tim."

"Yes?"

"Do you have a phone with a camera?"

"Of course. But it's not charged."

"Do you have a car charger for it?"

"Sure. But what for?"

"Well if you charge it up on your way to find the generator then when you're doing the job you can show me pictures of what you're up to and I could help. If you need it, that is."

"Okey dokey. I'll charge it as we go."

Later that afternoon Tim and Melissa were back, having successfully looted a generator and a huge roll of electrical cable.

"So explain what I'm looking for in the immersion heater and I'll get to work," Tim was eager. Melissa stood in the background, smiling encouragingly at Tim, but not looking like she actually wanted to participate.

"Well, I've been doing a little thinking and I have a different idea."

"Oh, what's that? Hot water would really go down well, I think," Tim observed, and exchanged smiles with Melissa.

"I'm sure that's true. What size of generator have you got?"

"You mean it's physical size?"

"No. I mean how powerful is it?"

"Well, it was the biggest one there. It's really heavy and was difficult to get up on the truck, although we managed eventually. It says that it is seven Kilovolt Amps."

"OK," Jack wasn't sure exactly how much was enough, but that seemed like quite a lot. The only reference he had was that a kettle used three kilowatts. He thought that a kilovolt Amp was the same as a kilowatt. "So why don't we try and wire up the whole house rather than just the immersion heater? Then we'd have power for other things like lights and washing machines when the generator was running, as well as the hot water."

"Oh, that would be fantastic if we can do it," Melissa commented.

"Well, it's probably easier than wiring the immersion heater to be honest."

"So presumably we need to find the meter and wire it up there?" Tim sounded a little unsure of this idea.

"Yes, indeedy. You'd want to cut the wires on the house side so that we are not trying to power up the whole city and then connect the stripped wires from the end of the long cable to the live and neutral cables running into the house. I'm assuming that this house is single phase."

"OK. And how would I know which ones are the neutral and live?"

"Well. Why don't you find the meter and take some pictures and then we can see if we can identify which ones are which?"

So the next couple of hours for Jack was spent alternately reading his book in the slowly fading sunshine and remotely advising Tim on how to wire up the house mains circuit to the generator. After many examined photos, lengthy discussions on alternative connection techniques and a full sweep of the house by all three of the able-bodied house-mates (to turn off everything they could find) the lights at Saltview were finally on.

The generator was gently chugging in the garden and power was restored, at least for as long as the generator was running. The electric lights seemed fiercely bright after so long with just lamps, torches and candles after dark. Everyone was smiling and even more so when Tim reported that with power available the gas-fired hot water boiler was working, giving them all the chance to bathe or shower in steaming fire-engine water.

"I think you only need one more day in bed," Xanthe pronounced as she performed her daily inspection of Jack's healing wound and changed the dressing. She had efficiently removed his IV that morning, leaving a small plaster on the back of his hand and making him feel that things were looking up. The morning sun was beaming through the open window as the Australian summer day heated up outside. "That's healing up nicely and so long as you don't overdo it you should be fine to be up and about. Probably in three or four days I'll be able to take the stitches out and pronounce you as good as mended. You'll have a smallish scar, but no other lasting damage."

"Thanks, Nurse. You've been great."

"Yes, well. It's good to keep busy I suppose," she looked a bit pre-occupied Jack thought, but then she suddenly looked him in the eye. "I think it's time for us to have a meeting. We said, me, Melissa and Tim, that is, that we wouldn't decide anything until you were recovered and I think that you've recovered enough to talk about what we're doing next. We can't pretend that nothing is wrong."

"OK," Jack matched her serious tone. "I agree. Let's talk about it."

Twenty

Two minutes later the four of them were assembled, with even the two dogs padding in to curl up at Xanthe's feet and join the gathering.

There was a pause while they looked at each other wondering who was going to start. Jack didn't want to be the one to speak first and eventually it was Melissa who broke the silence.

"OK. I'll ask the question we're all thinking. Do we think we will be rescued? Is there anybody out there, in other countries, or is the whole world like this?" She gestured with her hand although Jack didn't know if the gesture meant the whole of Sydney or even all of Australia. Not that it mattered. They all knew what she meant.

"It's been two and half weeks now," Xanthe stated. "In that time we've seen nothing at all. That's certainly not good news, is it?" Another silence greeted this sombre statement.

"It's not," Jack agreed. "But it doesn't mean we can assume that what has happened here has happened everywhere. Can we? I think we can certainly say that it's not just limited to Australia, but we don't really know more than that. Things could be very different on the other side of the planet." Even Jack could tell that this last sentence was delivered in a slightly desperate voice. He could tell by their faces that they were acutely aware that he had a family on the other side of the world and so the debate about northern hemisphere survival was uncomfortable territory.

And, as he looked at their sympathetic expressions, in only a matter of moments that particular door in his mind finally opened fully. As he sat in the bed he could see the faces of Jane and the three girls in his mind's eye as clearly as he could see the real faces of the survivors in front of him. "There's no real point in speculating about what's going on elsewhere," he managed to get out, but his voice was hopelessly broken. Whether it was an in-built survival mechanism that was released now that he was safe, or some other subconscious tactic that his mind had employed Jack couldn't say, but suddenly he was missing his family so acutely it was practically physical. "Let's..." he managed, but now tears were streaming down his face and he couldn't finish the sentence. There was a pause as the others looked on with a mixture of concern and worry. Only Xanthe's face showed any understanding. Jack sniffed and wiped his face on the sleeve of his pyjamas.

"I agree," Xanthe said gently. "I think we have to go back to the idea that you had before... when we first met. Decide what our planning horizon is and make a plan for it. It's really all we can do." Jack nodded, grateful to talk about practical things. There was another pause while the three allowed him to get a hold of his emotions.

"Well, if we're doing that," Tim eventually broke the awkward silence, speaking for the first time in the meeting, "and I agree with the planning horizon idea by the way, if we're setting ourselves a task, I think we should do an organised survivors sweep. You know, go out and search for survivors in as many places as we can. We surely can't be the only ones, but imagine what it would be like if you were on your own."

"I agree with Tim," said Melissa in her soft little voice. "We've been talking about it, me and Tim, and we think we should spend some time driving around looking for survivors. If we don't find any then nothing lost, but if we do..." she trailed off.

"We thought the fireworks you guys used were a really good idea," Tim took up the thread. "We could take big utes and load them up with fireworks. Fire off a few in each town. Make sure nobody is stuck on their own. That would be just awful."

"That is the right thing to do," Jack spoke slowly, trying hard to re-close the door behind which the emotional overload had been lurking, and focus on practical things, "but I'm afraid I'm not going to join you. It's been two weeks now and I just can't stay here. In Australia, I mean. I've got to start planning how to get home." And strangely just saying it eased the pressure that had overwhelmed him. Whether it was the thought that he could take some action, or the thought that he could take refuge in the mighty practical problem he was facing, did not matter to Jack. Just articulating the intention to set off for home re-checked the 'manageable' box on his homesickness, which had been, for a few minutes, quite decidedly and rather embarrassingly, unchecked.

"OK. We understand that you have to do that," Xanthe spoke slowly, clearly thinking, as the other two nodded their understanding of his decision. "But maybe I've got a different suggestion." She paused and licked her lips. "How about you wait one more week, Jack. It's been less than three weeks and rescue could still be on the way. We could really do with your help to, to look for survivors, I mean, so why don't you stay with us one more week, help us search, and then if rescue hasn't arrived you can set off home?"

This last was said with little inflexion, Xanthe's voice strangely business like, considering the subject being discussed.

However the suggestion was greeted by silence, as both Melissa and

Tim waited for Jack to think about what Xanthe had said. Jack himself considered what it meant and also wondered how much of this they had already discussed. His brain was starting to function now that it had a plan to work on and the first thing that occurred to him was that leaving Australia was a non-trivial challenge. Looking for survivors was certainly a worthy activity and the time would allow him both to recover physically and also think through what he was going to do.

"One week, is what you're suggesting?" The moment the question was out of his mouth he saw the tension around Xanthe's eyes ease. Asking it revealed his decision to himself as well as to the other three.

"Absolutely," Tim answered. "Well, maybe a couple of days to get ready and then a week to search. Then we'll meet back here."

"OK," he took a deep breath. "I'm in. I agree that we should try and find people. Do a survivor sweep, as you say. But we have to keep to the time limit. We can't search the whole country."

"Agreed. One week it is." Xanthe asked, looking at Tim and Melissa, who had clearly been planning this together, although Xanthe's level of involvement wasn't so obvious.

"Yup. One week," Tim agreed, although a bit hesitant. "Like Jack says, we can't do everywhere, but we could go to quite a few places in a week on the road."

"It's a plan then," Xanthe thought for a few seconds and then continued. "But we would cover more ground if we split up. Was that what you two thought?"

"Yes," Tim sounded distinctly pleased that Xanthe had asked that question. "We thought we'd be best dividing into two couples, I mean," colour flowed into Tim's face, "I mean two pairs. That way we could, um, maximise the area we can cover."

"I agree," Xanthe ignored Tim's embarrassment and re-assumed the role of leader that she had held at the start of the meeting. "I suggest that the two of you go together and Jack and I will do the same. We need to think a bit about the practicalities. Get good vehicles and stock them with what we need. We can do that today and tomorrow and then leave the day after that. You agree Jack?"

"Yes, sounds OK. Will we camp? You know, take tents with us? Or just camp in whatever house we can find?"

"Well, we were just thinking we would use whatever houses are there," this from Melissa. "But I suppose you could camp if you wanted."

"Actually, now that I think about it, I've got a better idea. How about camper vans?" Jack was suddenly enthused as the idea occurred to him. "Some of those things have everything, they're like mobile houses with all the mod-cons. That would be travelling in style. What do you think?"

"You mean a motorhome, don't you? A camper van in Australia is a small thing for backpackers. But that's a fantastic idea, Jack," Xanthe eyes told him that either she was pleased that he was engaging in the conversation or perhaps it was just that a bit of comfort wouldn't go amiss for her. "Tim, Melissa, do you think you two could rustle up a pair of great big luxurious motorhomes?"

Tim grinned. "I reckon we could."

Tim was as good as his word, and later that afternoon he and Melissa arrived back at the house, each sitting at the wheel of a large six-berth motorhome that they had acquired from a rental agency out of the yellow pages. They certainly were large and there needed to be a fair bit of car shuffling to get them in. When all was finished the two were parked side by side on the tarmac outside the front door, while all the various cars were out on the road next to Tim's fire engine.

Xanthe allowed Jack, for the first time, to do more than just shuffle to the toilet, and in fact suggested that he have a shower and then go and inspect the new vehicles. She fired up the generator so there would be hot water for him and Jack enjoyed the luxury before shuffling back into the bedroom, wrapped in a towel, to get dressed.

There were no clothes in evidence but when he opened the wardrobe to see if there was anything he could wear he was mildly astonished to find that it was full of clothes. His clothes. He recognised the loot that he and Xanthe had acquired together and concluded that without telling him she had driven back to her parents' house and collected all this stuff. He thought back to the shocking state it had been in when he last saw it, and felt a twinge of embarrassment. He'd lived like a slob, even the bloody clothes and dressings from his wound just strewn around the house. But here were his clothes, even the ones that had been dirty, washed, although she must have thrown away some of the ruined shirts.

Jack dressed and shuffled down the stairs to look at the motorhomes. He could definitely still feel the wound as he walked, but the stabbing pains he had been suffering had receded to a dull ache, which was quite manageable. Under Xanthe's directions he was taking antibiotic tablets, but painkillers were not necessary any more. His legs felt a little weak but maybe that was just from lying in bed for the last few days.

The motorhomes were even better than Jack had envisaged. Each had a shower, a toilet a fridge and many other creature comforts besides. They were empty of supplies except for several gas bottles that Tim and Melissa had liberated and some bedding, which they thought they would need.

"These'll be great," Tim still had a smile on his face. It means we can sleep in the same bed every night but still cover good mileage. They're pretty easy to drive. Especially since there's no traffic."

"They're diesel, right?" Jack asked.

"Yeah, but that should be OK shouldn't it," Tim didn't want to find any flaw in his new toys.

"Diesel is fine. We should sit down tonight and go through a list of what we need."

"Great. Then me and Melissa can collect the stuff tomorrow. We're getting pretty good and finding what we need. Even without Google maps."

"I can see that," Jack smiled, patting the side of the nearest van.

That evening Jack joined the other three for a meal downstairs. They left the generator turned off and had a candlelit dinner in the large and beautiful kitchen. Jack couldn't help thinking about how a week earlier he had peered through the window and ached to be included in the scene. And now he was in the house and Ben was in the ground. He said nothing of his peeping Tom efforts but couldn't help but take the odd irrational glance out of the dark window, just to be certain that no face was looking hungrily in on the domestic scene. The food was tinned, as almost all their food was now, heated up on the large gas range that continued to work from mains' gas. Although mains' water was now a thing of the past, mains' gas seemed to be working well, with no discernable loss of pressure. Tim commented on it and wondered aloud how long that would last. Jack knew nothing about how gas pressure was maintained and so didn't comment. On the face of it a single house with four people would take hundreds of years, maybe thousands, to use an appreciable amount of the gas that a large city like Sydney had in the mains at any given time. But Jack suspected that leakage, and maybe other factors, would end that luxury in much shorter timescales than that.

There was fresh bread, which Xanthe had baked that afternoon, to go with the canned stew. Irritatingly the ovens were electric and so she had had to run the generator to bake it, but it was certainly welcome, albeit a bit on the dense side.

"So," Xanthe launched in as the meal came to a close. "We're obviously going to need food and water for a week in the vans, to save us having to find it as we go. We're also going to need fireworks, and lots of them. I can tell you where Jack and I found the last lot, which had stacks of them. More than enough for us. What else?"

"We'll need tools," Tim contributed. "You know a break-in kit in each van so we can get into buildings when we need things."

"Agreed. What else?" Xanthe was assuming chair of the meeting, which was fine by Jack.

"Pumps," Jack said just the single word.

"Pumps? What kind?"

"We'll need two pumps each. One for diesel and one for fresh water. They need to be twelve volt ones so we can run them from the van's power and fill the water and fuel tanks. It's a real pain to do it by hand and a pump would make both jobs a lot quicker."

"Makes sense. Let's make a list," Xanthe rose and rummaged around in kitchen drawers until she had found a piece of paper and a pen. They listed out a few more items, binoculars, sunblock, a satnav, and even agreed that each van would carry a gun.

"Anybody been tempted to try and find some fresh meat?" Jack asked.

"Mmm, we did talk about it," Xanthe answered. "None of us have ever butchered anything before. Have you?" Jack shook his head.

"Well, I'm prepared to give it a go," Xanthe said in a matter-of-fact voice. "I'm not squeamish, so if you can shoot something I'll try and cut it up and we can cook it.

"OK. Me hunt game," replied Jack in his best Neanderthal impression. "Better add matches and firelighters to the list. Right. Do we have a map we can look at to decide where we're going?"

Towards the end of the meal the conversation turned more philosophical, passing through a debate on the likelihood of finding more people and then on to the topic of the source of the plague.

"The more I think about it the more I start to wonder if this isn't something of our making," Tim declared. "I mean think about it. We've been on this planet for millions of years with relatively minor health issues and then suddenly wham, within a hundred years of discovering proper medicine the whole population is wiped out."

"Minor health issues?" Xanthe was performing her trademark eyebrow raise.

"Well, you know what I mean," Tim continued. "I'm sure the Black Death was unpleasant for the people involved, but it was nothing like this, in terms of speed and mortality rate. The point I'm trying to make is the coincidence in the timing. The species exists for three million years and then within fifty years of us starting to muck around with biology we all get wiped out. It just seems like too much of a coincidence. I'm not saying it's a military thing, although it could be, I just think it's likely that it's something we have done somehow."

There was a pause, which Jack finally broke.

"Maybe you're right, Tim, although maybe we were just too successful."

"What do you mean?" the young man asked.

"Well, obsolescence is a common theme in nature. So for example humans are designed to die to clear the way for the next generation, and maybe it's the same in species. Maybe all species have an in-built 'emergency eject', if you like, and if they get too successful and start hindering the development of the whole ecosystem it gets triggered."

"Are you suggesting that the human race has been wiped out by Gaia because we were getting in the way of progress?" Xanthe frowned. "Doesn't that rather go against the 'selfish gene' idea?"

"Maybe. I'm not really suggesting anything. I'm just wondering if Darwin got the full story. We know that we share a massive amount of genetic material with everything that lives, and we don't really understand what it all does. And we still don't really know what killed the dinosaurs."

"You think that we are dying to make room for other species to evolve? But why would evolution want to kill off the most successful species?" this from Melissa.

"We think of ourselves as the pinnacle of evolution, but another way to look at this might be that we're the best that has come up so far. But we would never have evolved if raptors and tyrannosaurs had hunted stone-age man. They were the pinnacle back then, but they needed to make way for us. It's probably just idle chit-chat, but clearing us away would certainly make room for whatever might come next."

"You're kind of implying that we have been designed with an evolutionary fail-safe. But I don't believe we have been designed at all," Tim stated.

"No, neither do I," Jack hurriedly set the record straight on that one. "But a lot traits that we have developed appear at first glance to have a design behind them. That's why there are so many creationists."

"But for us to have evolved the fail-safe you're talking about, it would have to have happened before. Several times. I'm not sure it makes sense." Tim was sceptical.

"You're quite right," Jack agreed. "It would have to have happened before. Many times. But if it had would we know? Maybe lots of very successful species, from microbes in the primordial soup through insects and on to dinosaurs, have been wiped out already by evolution's fail-safe. Would we know?"

"No. I suppose not," Tim conceded.

"So how many of us would have to survive in order for humans to come back and dominate again?" Xanthe asked. "And how long do you think it would take to get back to, you know, where we were?"

"Well, on the first question, I don't reckon too many," it was Tim who answered. There were hardly any people in medieval times, and so a single tribe could, over time, re-populate the planet. The second one is a bit tougher. I suppose it depends upon how many are left."

"I agree," Jack's voice was thoughtful. "The fewer people who survived the further back we would go. So half the population might take us back to, say, the second world war. Three quarters might take us back to the nineteenth century. And so on. The trick for the survivors would be to judge what level of information to try and retain. There's no point in trying to retain information about cars if the survivors aren't going to be able to mine and refine metal ore."

"Not 'would be'. Is." Xanthe had a frown on her face as she spoke. "You said that 'the trick for the survivors would be', but this isn't just an academic discussion. It's not a problem they would have. It's a problem *we do* have. So what level of technology would last if the survival rate globally was what it is here?"

There was a long pause before Jack answered. "I think if it's like this everywhere then our descendants are going back to the stone-age. That is if we could survive it at all. Let's hope there are more."

Two days later just after dawn they were packed and ready to go. They had all taken part in the looting spree needed to equip themselves, and even Jack had been allowed to get involved, although Xanthe was explicit that he still had to take it easy so as to avoid re-opening the wound. The bulk of the collection had been done by Tim and Melissa, with Xanthe and Jack having relatively little to achieve. They had picked up the items on their list quite quickly and that had given them enough time to collect fifteen chickens from the farm that was becoming familiar territory for Jack now.

The barn still had lots of living birds in it and so Jack had watched Xanthe run around and catch chickens and pack them into crates they had found in the equipment shed. These were now locked in the spacious garage back at Saltview with a large supply of food and water. They had left the huge shed open so that the remainder of the birds were free to make their way in the world, which probably meant ending life as predator fodder, but what else could they do.

Once they had pretty well everything on their list the four had spent the previous evening route planning. They had a detailed map each with their own planned route and that of the other pair marked out.

"So we're agreed," Xanthe said as they stood together next to the motorhomes with the early morning sun hitting the house. "Whatever happens we'll come back here. Meet here in exactly one week. Everyone OK with that?"

They all agreed that they were. There were general goodbyes, Jack getting an awkward handshake from Tim and even more awkward kiss on the cheek from Melissa.

"Take care guys," Jack told the other two. "Drive carefully and stick together all the time. Don't go off on your own too far." They assured him that they would be careful and Melissa even wiped a tear away after exchanging a heartfelt farewell hug with Xanthe. And then they were on their way, Xanthe driving the big van, Jack sitting beside her and the two dogs lounging on the bunk in the back as they trundled north towards Brisbane.

Jack found his spirits rising as they drove north on the Pacific Highway, through the heavily forested suburbs of Sydney. The activity of preparation had taken his mind off his homesickness and now he found he was able to effectively leave it behind. He'd committed to a week on the road and so he could almost feel the live-for-the-minute attitude that he had achieved in week one (as he now thought of it) settling back on to him. It didn't mean he wasn't thinking about how to get home, but there was nothing to be done now.

Xanthe too looked like she felt the load easing as she drove and they chatted easily, carefully avoiding any topics that would remind them of their status as lonely survivors. They talked about all kinds of other subjects though; sport, music, even politics and there was more smiling and laughing than either had enjoyed for what seemed like a long time.

They'd agreed that they couldn't stop everywhere and so they drove for a couple of hours before their first stop, which was planned as Newcastle. Even the occasional crashed car, sometimes with a grisly load, was now a familiar sight to both.

"It's amazing what you get used to," Jack commented as they past one such vehicle with the remains of the occupants still visible inside. He regretted it instantly, as he saw Xanthe's face fall.

"Yeah, but we're doing the right thing," she replied. "Let's hope we find lots of people." There was a brief silence, but Xanthe was determined to remain positive and soon weighed in with a question about what CDs Jack would loot when they next passed a suitable shop, since music was one thing they had not remembered to pack.

As they approached Newcastle, which seemed very different from its Northern Hemisphere namesake, what with the virtually tropical forests and leafy suburbs bathed in southern sun, Jack spent a bit of time fiddling with his friend the Garmin trying to identify a suitable firework spot. They needed somewhere that was easily visible from the town and, ideally, not so far away that the bangs would be inaudible.

In the end they spent an hour launching some of their huge stock of rockets from the middle of Broadmeadow Racecourse, but nobody came to investigate the bangs or the small puffs of rather dirty cloud that they generated. The two dogs had a nice time exploring this new landscape but didn't stray too far from the van and their beloved Xanthe. They stuck to their one-hour time limit before mounting up and heading north once again.

Their route out of town took them through a shopping area and while the two maintained some banter about the need for a music shop Jack was watching carefully, and assumed Xanthe was too, for signs of looting. But there were no obvious smashed windows or any other signs that survivors might have made, and so they pressed on north.

The following week blurred together into a routine of driving, stopping, driving and stopping. Jack was mildly amazed at how quickly he could feel the strength and stamina returning to his body. So much so that after only a couple of days on the road he found it hard to believe that he had been at death's door such a short time before.

The weather stayed hot and sunny with large cumulus clouds building up each afternoon but never quite managing to rain. At each stop in the major towns they launched some rockets, waited an hour and then hit the road again. Jack regularly filled the van with fuel and they were always on the lookout for diesel vehicles, HGVs or large vans that would be donors. When they saw one they would top up their tanks and also their five jerry cans, if any were empty.

Each evening they would stop in a town, launch their rockets and then build a fire and sit and watch the bright southern stars wheel overhead. Once supper was over and it was evident that nobody was coming to answer their call they would turn in.

Xanthe commandeered the large bunk over the cab of the vehicle as her private domain, leaving Jack in the rear bunk. The interior, though large, was cluttered, since their supply of fireworks took up a good portion of it. After they had said goodnight each evening Xanthe would draw the curtain and not emerge until dawn broke and then she would appear, dressed in her running gear.

On the first evening she had declared her intention to go for a run each morning, since it was 'time to start exercising again'. There was no arguing with that and so Jack suggested that he would accompany her, if he could keep up.

"I don't think so," Xanthe answered, after thinking about it for a few seconds. Give it another couple of days."

Once she was back at the motorhome, they had breakfast as she cooled off. Each morning they also performed Jack's ritual test of satellite communications with an identical result to that first day at the Flying Doctor centre, and then they set off, Xanthe showering while Jack drove.

Since any laws about remaining strapped up were entirely obsolete, whichever of them was not driving would keep the other supplied with snacks and cups of tea, while the driver selected the music from their looted collection.

On the second day Xanthe broached a subject that she had obviously been thinking about carefully. Her tone was cautious as she broke a lengthy silence in which Jack was driving and Xanthe humming vaguely to herself in the passenger seat.

"Jack, I know you said you didn't want to talk about it, but there's something I have to say." Jack looked over at her but didn't speak. She looked back earnestly and so he waited to see what was going to follow.

"I want to say that I'm sorry," she continued, "about what happened with Ben. And I don't mean sorry in an abstract way. I mean I want to apologise for my part in what you went through. I feel really bad about it."

"You don't have to say that. None of it was your fault."

"Well, I see it slightly differently, so hear me out. What Ben did that morning in the park wasn't my fault, but the next day I saw drops of blood on the floor at Mum and Dad's house and I wondered, I even shouted your name out to see if you were nearby, but I did nothing else. And then I let Ben hurry me away.

"I had a vague plan to come back and check later, and that's what I really want to apologise for. I really did want to come back, but instead of doing it I let Ben railroad me into not going. He was

249

forceful and confident and I didn't really push it. Each time I said I wanted to visit Mum and Dad's to see if you were there he had a reason why I shouldn't. Twice he said he was heading that way anyway and he would visit. I'm guessing he never did?"

Jack looked over at her serious face and then back at the road without speaking. After a moment Xanthe carried on. "I even wrote a note with a map of exactly where we were and he said he pinned it to the door, which he obviously never did, but at the time I believed him. So I want to say sorry for buying Ben's shit. I kind of knew something was not right, but I was angry that you had vanished and I suppose a bit apathetic as well. I wish now that I'd got off my arse and just driven up to the house to check for myself."

"You don't have to…" Jack started, but Xanthe cut him off.

"Don't tell me that it wasn't my fault. Just accept my apology, if you can, and then we won't need to talk about it again."

Jack thought about what she'd said for a few moments, looking alternately at the road and her slight, anxious, face, before he answered.

"Thank you for your apology. I accept." Some of the anxiety definitely left her face with his answer, and she gave a small nod. They said no more about it.

By the evening of the second day they were in Brisbane and so had, once again, to find a good spot to launch from.

"Let's go up a skyscraper," Xanthe suggested. "Let's climb to the roof and launch from there. Then it will be visible for miles."

"Well, yes. But it will be quite a climb."

"It'll be good for us. We've been sitting in this van for days. Come on Jack. Let's."

"The dogs can't come with us."

"That's fine, we can just leave them in the van. We'll only be gone a couple of hours."

"OK. But you do know that the lifts aren't working, don't you?"

"Of course I do," she punched his arm lightly.

"But my doctor says I have to take it easy," Jack tried one more time.

"Well she now says that a bit of exercise will probably do you some good."

So after packing what they needed for supper, breaking-and-entering gear, stuff to light a fire, two torches and, of course, the necessary pyrotechnics, into two large bags, they set off to climb the biggest skyscraper they could find in Brisbane, identified by the words Aurora Tower over the entrance.

Finding the stairwell was a challenge and they had to climb in torchlight, but by the time they emerged after thirty minutes of trudging up stairs the sun was just starting to set over the city. They were both sweaty from the climb, but Jack had to admit that it felt good and Xanthe was buzzing. After a rest they went back down one floor and broke into the penthouse that occupied the top floor of the building. It contained some ludicrously expensive looking furniture, which they duly carried up on to the roof and burned.

Having eaten supper straight out of the tins that they had heated on the fire, and launched their first batch of rockets, they sat and looked out over the dark and silent city.

"I wonder how long buildings like this will last if the whole world is like this," Xanthe eventually broke the silence.

"Who knows? Twenty years. Fifty, maybe. Until they are Ozymandias remnants, I suppose."

"Ozymandias? That rings a bell. Remind me what it means?"

"It's a poem. By Shelley."

"Oh yes. I think I remember something about that from school. But you don't strike me as a poetry kind of guy, I have to say."

"I'm not really. But it's a good one and rather appropriate when we're standing on this building."

"What's it about?"

"I was made to learn it at school, but I can't remember it all. It starts:

I met a traveller from an Antique land,
Who said: "Two vast and trunkless legs of stone,
Stand in the desert…"

"And then I can't remember the next bit, but it's about an enormous statue, with the head lying nearby and a sneer on its face. And then the really famous bit is written on the statue's pedestal. It goes:

`My name is Ozymandias, King of Kings:
Look on my works, ye mighty, and despair!'
Nothing beside remains. Round the decay
Of that colossal wreck, boundless and bare,
The lone and level sands stretch far away".

After a silence Xanthe sighed and murmured, "I do remember that now. I see why you thought of it. Appropriate."

"Only if the whole world is like this," Jack gestured at the view, and there was another long silence.

"So, do you really think the whole world is like this?" Xanthe eventually asked.

"I don't know. Maybe," Jack was calm. Now was the time to talk about it. "But also maybe not. Whether people arrive or not I have to hope that things were different elsewhere. At home I mean."

"Do you believe what Ben said, Jack? That if there were places that were untouched that they would be here by now?"

"Well, to some degree I do. If most of the world was unaffected, so it was just a local thing to Australia, or even just one side of the planet then I think people would probably be here. Probably, but not definitely. But what if the level of affect was different in different places? I mean here the fatality rate was virtually total. Survival rate of maybe one in a million. But in other places it could be much less.

"If a country like the US had a survival rate of, say, one in a hundred then there still would be three and half million people there, which is quite a few. But if that had happened then they certainly would have no interest in going out to other countries to help them out. In fact if the death rate was as high as fifty percent then that would be enough to stop them mounting expeditions, I think. They would be too concerned with what was happening at home."

"So you think that the survival rate might be higher in other places like the US or Europe?" Xanthe asked gently.

"I'm not saying it was," Jack took a deep breath. "There's just no way of knowing. Maybe it's worse in other places and absolutely nobody survived. It's all just guess work. I'm not going to make any assumptions until I know. One way or the other." There was a pause in the conversation.

"My Dad always said I was one in a million," Xanthe reflected. "It used to really annoy me when I was a teenager. 'I'm not one in a million,' I once shouted at him. 'I'm just like everybody else.' But it turns out he was right after all."

Jack gave Xanthe's shoulder a squeeze and they sat in silence for while.

Twenty One

After Brisbane they started back towards Sydney via what Jack referred to as the 'scenic route'. And very scenic it was, but utterly devoid of people. There seemed to be plenty of wildlife, and even some domesticated cattle and sheep, but none of the towns they stopped in had any sign of life. The town names were a strange mixture of English and exotic. Ipswitch, Toowoomba, Pittsworth and Goondiwindi.

Jack and Xanthe spent the night parked on Goondiwindi golf course before setting off again the next day. Jack once again suggested that he run with Xanthe and this time she agreed.

"If I can keep up," he qualified his suggestion.

It turned out that he was just about able to, arriving back at the motorhome significantly sweatier than Xanthe, but still with her. In fact he rather enjoyed the run in the cool of the early morning and he and Xanthe chatted as they ran, although in the second half it would be fair to say that Xanthe had to hold up both ends of the conversation, as Jack focused his efforts on keeping up with the Australian girl. He was pretty sure that she went easy on him, given his convalescent state.

After breakfast they were off on their way again, headed for Moree and Narrabri, but in the latter of these towns their routine was, to some degree, broken.

They parked the van next to a cricket pitch near the river that flowed through the little town. The grass was starting to look a bit shaggy, now that it was a month since anybody had cut it, but they still trundled over as near to the river as they could get. A set of neat white railings blocked them from getting any closer. Jack stretched as he swung down from the driver's seat. Once they'd done the firework thing they needed to find a diesel donor and, ideally some fresh water. Jack strolled over to the riverbank to see how the water looked, accompanied by Alf who was very interested in all he could smell, as he always seemed to be. Rather brown and murky was the answer. Not really suitable for filling the tank in the van, he concluded.

When he got back to the van Xanthe was leaning against the side, watching Rufus as the little dog busied himself defiling the cricket square. Jack crept up behind her as quietly as possible, the grass killing any sound of his footfalls. He was just about to poke her in the side when she spoke.

"Don't even think about it, Stevens," she looked round, smiling at his rather sheepish expression. "Right, mister. Time to get those stitches out, I think. Get your shirt off and let's have a look at them."

"Let's launch a couple of rockets first so we don't waste time," Jack suggested.

"OK. Good idea."

Once the rockets had been turned into small puffs of cotton wool in the sky above the cricket square, Jack took off his shirt and lay down on the grass. Xanthe knelt beside him with a small pair of scissors and some tweezers from her medical kit.

"Yes, these are definitely ready to come out," she said, laying her hand on his belly and studying the healing wound carefully. "This shouldn't hurt much."

Far from hurting Jack was rather enjoying the physical contact when, after the second stitch came out, Xanthe suddenly sat up.

"What's that noise?" And now Jack could hear it too and both dogs were on full alert. There was no denying what the noise was. It was the clip-clop of a horse's hooves hitting tarmac. They both scrambled to their feet and looked around, trying to pinpoint where it was coming from. It was getting louder and coming from the direction of the town.

"Come on," Xanthe set off at a run with Jack, shirt in one hand, hard on her heels, and the two dogs racing ahead.

When they reached the road the horse was already in sight. It was a plain brown animal and seemed on the small side to Jack's inexpert eye. It was trotting down the middle of the street towards them and on its back sat a person. A girl in fact, with dark hair tied back and a dirty white T-shirt and jeans. Her feet were bare.

She stopped the horse about thirty yards from them and slid agilely off the animal's back. She stood for a few moments holding the halter of the horse, which Jack could see had no saddle, with her head close to that of her mount. She might have been talking to it as she looked at them slightly sideways and they stared in return. Jack could see that she was small, a child in fact, but from here he couldn't see how old. Xanthe stepped forward, the dogs clustered close to her feet. Jack followed a few steps behind, not wanting to intimidate the child. She stood and waited for them, still whispering to the horse, which was eyeing the dogs but standing calmly enough.

When they were about ten yards away they stopped. Jack could see her clearly now and she looked back at them both with open curiosity. She looked to be about Rose's age which made her nine or ten, and her skinny frame was held taut as a bow string, as if she were ready to leap back on to her mount and gallop away.

"Hi. I'm Xanthe and this is Jack. What's your name?" Xanthe kept her voice calm.

"Emily," came the reply with a strong Australian twang.

"Hi Emily. Are you here on your own?"

Emily didn't reply, just stared.

"Emily, we're travelling around looking for people. Did you see our fireworks?"

"I heard them first. Then I saw the smoke."

"And who's this?" Xanthe indicated the horse, which was probably more of a pony.

"William," Emily replied. "He's mine."

"And is it just you and William here?"

This time Emily nodded. Xanthe took a couple of steps forward and the little girl didn't retreat. Jack stayed put, not wanting to frighten this poor little girl who had been on her own for over three weeks.

"Emily, we're survivors just like you. We're not part of a big rescue party, but we are travelling around looking for other survivors. In that van over there," Xanthe pointed. "Would you like to come and have some lunch with us and we'll tell you what we know, and you can tell us what you know?"

Emily nodded again, and they all turned and set off across the cricket pitch towards the motorhome.

"I always wanted a pony like William when I was a girl. You're a lucky girl."

Emily gave Xanthe a look that showed how ridiculous she thought that statement was, but her hand did stray to William's neck as she led him across the grass. The dogs kept their distance from the horse's hooves, but Emily seemed unconcerned by their proximity to her bare feet.

"Are you the only ones?" she asked in a business-like tone. "In the whole of Australia?"

"No, we're not. We have found two others who are also off looking for people. But obviously we haven't searched the whole country."

"I was starting to think I was the only one." For the first time her matter-of-fact tone was starting to slip a little. There was a trace of a wobble in her voice.

"You're not the only one. We're in this together. There's not many of us but we can look after each other."

"I've been so lonely." Her self-control was really slipping now and Xanthe took a step towards her. Emily responded by dropping the pony's lead rope and stepping into Xanthe's arms, her face crumpling as she buried in against Xanthe's singlet. Xanthe held her tight, her own eyes filling with tears as she looked at Jack over the girl's head.

Five minutes later they were sitting round the table in the motorhome with Emily drying her tears, although her breath was still shaky as she recovered. They'd left William contentedly cropping the uncut grass outside and installed themselves inside. Xanthe had put out some slices of malt loaf and Emily was already several bites into the first one, despite her tears. Jack and Xanthe sat opposite her.

"Would the best thing be for Jack and me to tell you what's happened to us and then you can tell us what happened here? Is that OK?" Emily nodded past her mouthful of malt loaf and wiped her nose on the back of her sleeve.

Xanthe started off and gave a redacted version of happenings since the plague. She told how she was a nurse in Melbourne and how she had tried to save people. She didn't give a lot of detail, but she also didn't shy away from the fact that people had died. This child clearly knew that already so there was no point in denying it. She gave a brief account of how she met Jack and then subsequently met Melissa and Tim. She also gave a short description of their plan to find other survivors and in doing so described why Tim and Melissa weren't with them.

"And our plan is to all meet back in Sydney in a few days," she finished. "We don't know if Tim and Melissa have found anybody else, but you're the first person we've met since we left Sydney. Jack, your turn."

"Well, I was working in Sydney," Jack started, the first words he had spoken since meeting Emily. "I'd been there a few…"

"Are you English? Like from England?" Emily interrupted.

"Yes, I am. I'm from England."

"Are you two married?" This caused Xanthe and Jack to look at each other for a moment before Xanthe replied.

"Jack is married. His wife lives in England. We're not married to each other. And you have daughters, don't you Jack?"

"I do. My eldest daughter, Rose is nine. How old are you, Emily?"

"I'm ten," she announced, as if this should be obvious to anybody.

"So you're a bit older than her. I also have twin daughters, Daisy and Sophie. They're seven."

"And are they all in England?"

"Yes, they are."

"So you don't know if they are alive or not, I suppose?" This was delivered as a simple statement.

"No, I don't know that."

"Well, that's better than knowing," Emily declared, a little defiance creeping into her voice.

"Maybe," was all Jack could say to that. "Anyway I was working in Sydney and staying in a hotel when it happened. I got pretty sick, more sick than Xanthe, I think, but when I recovered everybody was dead. I set out to drive to Canberra to see if I could find people alive and I met Xanthe on the road. She was a bit nervous so she pointed a gun at me, although I notice she left that part out of her story, but luckily she didn't shoot me, and here we are. Looking for people like you."

"Why did you point a gun at him?"

"Well, look at him," replied Xanthe with a twinkle. "Wouldn't you have pointed a gun at him today if you'd had one?" This did get a small smile, through the malt-loaf and snot. "Actually it was just because I was feeling nervous, just like you were when you first met us." Emily gave a single nod to this, a rather adult gesture.

Once enough malt loaf had been consumed and Xanthe had used a bottle of water and some tissues to give Emily's face a bit of a wipe, Xanthe gently prompted for the little girl's story.

"Well, it started just like you described. I went to school like normal but I wasn't feeling very well. Everybody seemed to be feeling bad. But I went home like normal – Mum picked me up. And when we got home we all started feeling worse and worse. Dad came home from work and Nathan, that's my brother, started being sick. We all felt bad and went to bed. The next day I felt really bad. I was sick but Mum and Dad were too ill to drive us to the doctor. We tried to phone but the phones weren't working. And then when I woke up again I felt better but I couldn't wake Mum up. I think Dad and Nathan were both dead because they were cold and not breathing. I tried to drag Mum to the car but she was too heavy and I couldn't do it. She died in the day. I heard her stop breathing."

This was all delivered in a voice that sounded like Emily had rehearsed the whole statement carefully in her mind, or possibly even out loud. There was no emotion in it, just a statement of bald facts. Xanthe reached over the table and squeezed her shoulder, but Emily ignored the gesture.

"I stayed in the house for three days, but no one came, so I went into town. I tried to drive Mum's car but I couldn't see very well, or reach the pedals properly, and I hit a fence. So instead I took William. Everybody was dead here in town, but me and William have been living here ever since. I've had to steal food from Cole's and also food for William from the feed store. There's no water or electricity. I've been waiting but I was starting to think that nobody would come." Emily looked them both in the face and then said simply "I'm glad you're here."

"We're glad we've found you," Xanthe smiled encouragingly across at Emily's serious little face. "This van's got a hot shower, if you want one. Jack, is there enough water? I know that's what I missed."

"I should think there is, yes. It'll be hot as well because the engine was running."

"OK," Emily didn't sound overly enthused, and Xanthe was quick to pick up on it.

"Or perhaps we should go and get your clothes first. We'd need to go back to your house. Would that be OK? Or we can get you new clothes when we get to Sydney if you'd rather do that?"

"What about William?" Emily asked.

"What do you mean?" Xanthe looked nonplussed but Jack guessed where this was going.

"What about William? How are we going to get him to Sydney?"

"I really don't think William can come with us," Xanthe's tone was gentle. "I think…"

"I'm not going without William," there was a sudden edge of panic in Emily's voice and her lip was starting to quiver again.

"We won't go without William," Jack jumped in, only to receive a bit of quizzical look from Xanthe and suspicion from Emily.

"This van has a tow-bar. We can bring him with us. Do you have a horse box we can use to put him in?"

"No, we don't have one. When we move William we borrow the Mitchell's truck."

"And is that an all-in-one truck? You can't separate the horse part from the driving part?"

"No. It's all one piece. It's really big."

"OK. We can use that if we have to," Jack was thinking aloud. "Does anybody you know have a horse-box? One that we could tow behind this van?"

"Jane Parker from school has one. I've seen her arrive at polo-cross with it." Jack had no idea what polo-cross was, but it sounded like a viable option.

"And do you know where Jane Parker lives? Could you take us there?"

"Lived. She's dead now like everyone else." That same defiant tone, but Jack didn't comment and after a moment Emily carried on more calmly, "Yeah, I know where the Parkers live."

"OK. Can we leave William here while we go and collect the horsebox?"

"I'll ride him back to the school where I've been keeping him. I've been staying in the Collier's house because they're away on holiday and live right next to the school. I mean, they were away when it happened."

"So is your house out of town?" Xanthe asked. "How far away is it?"

"About five miles that way," Emily waved. "I've been back a couple of times but it's a long way for William and so I've been staying here more and more because there's food for me and him."

"Are you hungry? Do you want more to eat?" Xanthe asked the little girl.

"No. There's plenty of food at Cole's, although I had to climb through a window to get it."

So they packed the dogs back into the van and Emily jumped up onto William's back with impressive ease and they set off. The motorhome, with Jack at the wheel, idled along behind the girl on the pony. Since the barefooted Emily was riding William without a saddle or bridle – the pony just wore a halter – Jack marvelled at the apparent ease with which the horse went where the little girl directed. In fact there was little sign of any rider input at all, the two seeming to be joined by some kind of telepathic link that they were both very comfortable with. Presumably there were signals that Emily gave William, but they weren't apparent to the untrained observer.

Very soon they arrived at the school, a two-story brick building with a white statue of a woman in flowing robes standing in front of it. The woman had her arms outstretched and looked up at the building with an arch expression on her face, as if greeting her husband after an evening where he had stayed out too long and drunk too much.

Emily, with the familiarity of a thousand passings, slid off William and led him past the statue to the low wire fence bordering the field beyond. She led him through a gate and then, after a pat on the neck and a brief whisper to him (to which William paid close attention) she left him to it, shutting the gate behind her. William ambled over to a pile of hay nearby and turned his equine attention to it.

Jack and Xanthe meanwhile had parked the motorhome and climbed down. They waited beside it while Emily padded back on her bare feet and joined them.

"Where have you been staying, Emily?" Xanthe asked.

"Just down there." Emily pointed down the road.

"Shall we go there now? Are there things you want to collect?"

"No," the girl replied, rather too quickly. "There's nothing there. I don't want to go there." Jack wondered what was there that she didn't want to see again, or perhaps didn't want them to see. Maybe just a mess, given that she was only ten and had been living alone without power or running water for three weeks.

"Right," Xanthe took this in her stride. "What do you want to do? Shall we go and get the horsebox? Would you like to get clothes from your house or shall we just go to a shop and get new clothes for you?"

"New clothes," Emily almost whispered, her gaze far away, presumably seeing the grisly scene she had left at her home.

"New clothes it is. Jump into the van and you can show us where you usually buy clothes from. Jack is very good at getting into places so you don't need to worry about that."

As it turned out a fair number of the shops in Narrabri were packed into one short street and so it didn't take long to visit them. Jack didn't even need to break into the first clothes shop, named Crazy Clarke's, and the second and third were a matter of moments. After that they visited a shoe shop and emerged with two pairs of Emily-sized cowboy boots and two pairs of running shoes.

At this point Xanthe insisted on a shower for Emily and so Jack left the girls to it and wandered the neat, but deserted, Narrabri main street. By the time he returned Emily looked rather different, her grubby T-shirt, jeans and bare feet replaced by a new white blouse, some brand new jeans and bright white trainers over pink socks. Her hair was still wet and Jack could see that hot water, soap and clean clothes had gone some way to restore Emily's spirits. Children are amazingly adaptable, he thought to himself, but also couldn't help wondering how Rose would cope in this situation, and didn't know whether to hope she was having to do so or not.

They then had an afternoon of various tasks, mostly revolving around William. They collected the horsebox, with Emily squatting between the front seats of the motorhome directing Jack. Next they loaded William himself into the trailer. Once again this operation, which would have filled Jack with dread, went very smoothly as William docilely followed Emily up the loading ramp and into the large two-horse trailer. William's saddle and bridle (or 'tack' as Emily called it) were also there in the field and so went into the empty compartment beside the pony. Finally they visited the Narrabri Farm Centre and loaded various foodstuffs that William apparently needed, including a number of bales of hay which Jack moved using a large trolley rather than risk hurting himself. Finally they were back in the van and ready to go.

"Are you sure there's nothing you want from home?" Xanthe asked Emily gently.

Emily paused for a long time, looking first at Xanthe and then Jack. Eventually she said in a small voice, "I'm never coming back here, am I?"

"I don't know, Emily, but we won't lie to you. You might not be back for a long time. Maybe never. There's nothing here for you now with all the people gone."

"Then I do want to go and get something from home." She was dry-eyed as she said this although her voice was little more than a whisper.

Jack drove steadily with Emily directing in that slightly random way that non-drivers have, although he was used to it, having had the same experience many times as Rose directed him to one gymnastics venue or another. Emily's house was out in the countryside a couple of miles north west of the little town. They were cruising along a small, but paved, road when she suddenly pointed, from her squatting position between Jack and Xanthe.

"Down there," she said, her voice flat.

Jack turned the big vehicle and its trailer slowly on to the dirt drive and through the gate that stood open. A small red hatchback had buried its nose into the fence next to the gate, doing minor damage to both car and fence, but neither Jack nor Xanthe commented on it. The drive snaked through some trees for about a hundred yards, with Jack going very slowly so as not to bump William too violently through the potholes, before they came to the house itself.

It was a large bungalow, painted a cheery yellow colour with a dirt courtyard in front between the house and some kind of outhouse which supported a car-port. A dusty white Toyota Landcruiser stood in the courtyard. Beyond Jack could see a small garden, clearly well watered, which stood out a vivid green amongst the burnt colours of the more normal Australian summer. At the end of the courtyard was a gate leading into a large paddock that was, presumably, William's normal abode. Jack pulled the van and trailer to a halt and shut down the engine, leaving a thick silence over the sun-drenched scene.

"Would you like me to go and get something," Xanthe asked Emily, looking at the little girl's face, which was set in a determined expression. "Or come in with you?" Emily shook her head but didn't speak. Jack climbed out of the driver's door and then lifted Emily down and she headed straight though the double door of the house, a screen door on the outside and wooden door on the inside. The windows showed only the reflection of the sunlit scene outside and the silence and heat were intense as Xanthe and Jack waited.

It was five minutes before Emily emerged. She had in her arms a bundle of soft toys. Jack could see several teddy bears, a camel and a monkey. Jack went round and opened the side door of the van but stayed silent while Emily climbed the steps and then emerged a moment later. Without a word she headed back inside the house. Jack and Xanthe exchanged a look, both of them clearly feeling her pain but helpless to do anything but wait.

Another ten minutes passed, leaving Jack with his shirt sticking to his back, and wondering if he should go inside and find her, before she emerged again. This time Emily was dragging a black, medium-sized roller suitcase, which seemed enormous for the little girl. Both Jack and Xanthe leapt forward to help. Jack took the case from her hand, as Xanthe enfolded Emily in her arms. Tears were streaming down her face and her body was wracked by sobs as she cried. They stayed that way for a long time and Emily was still crying when they climbed back into the van, Xanthe lifting Emily's skinny frame onto her lap as she sat in the passenger seat. Emily craned her tear-stained face to look at the house for every available second, as Jack slowly, and rather clumsily, reversed the motorhome and horsebox to get the assembly turned round. As the house passed out of sight again Emily buried her face back into Xanthe's shoulder with a fresh outburst of crying that seemed too intense for any of them to bear.

Twenty Two

The journey back to Sydney was disappointingly uneventful. They stopped in a succession of countryside towns with names like Dubbo, Peak Hill, Parkes and Forbes. In each they fired more rockets but nobody was there to see or hear. Each evening they made a fire and ate some supper, while Emily unloaded William and let him stretch his legs and crop the grass, which was becoming longer and longer in each site. After supper Xanthe put Emily to bed and then the two adults cracked a cold beer each (having a working fridge was a blessing). They chatted under the stars, the dogs curled on the ground next to them, before turning in themselves. Emily had joined Xanthe on the bunk above the cab, making it the girls' cabin and left Jack occupying the lower section of the motorhome, which was becoming more and more spacious as the firework boxes were emptied and then burned on their evening camp fire.

In the days after leaving her home Emily was subdued. She answered when spoken to, but never volunteered information. In fact the only thing she showed any interest in was William, who she cared for with real focus, often calling for a stop so she could check he was alright, and make sure he had enough to drink.

After the last night, spent in a town called Bathurst, they set off for the final day's travel into Sydney. The atmosphere in the motorhome was quiet, and after half an hour Emily went back into the main cabin and appeared to fall asleep on Jack's bunk. Xanthe set a CD playing, choosing Midnight Oil which had been one of Jack's selections, the Australian band being a bit before Xanthe's time. After the first track, which ironically seemed to be about global warming, Jack reached over and turned the music down.

"OK. I think it's time to talk about what happens next," he started.

Xanthe glanced at him and then out of the window again. "What's that then?"

"You know what. When we get back to Sydney, and assuming Tim and Melissa don't have any more insight into what is going on, I'm going to set off for home. Back to England."

"How?"

"I haven't worked out exactly how yet, although I have been thinking about it, but I have to go. I don't want to abandon you. Or Emily. Or Tim and Melissa either. But I have to go. I'm not going to hang around long. As soon as we get back I'm going to get started."

"Well, I've been thinking about it as well. And I have a different idea on what's going to happen." Xanthe turned to face him. He glanced across but her rather intense look chased his gaze back out of the windscreen.

"Yes. I'm going to suggest to Tim and Melissa that we all come with you."

"What?"

"Well what have any of us got to stay for?" she asked him, a touch defiantly. "Do you think we don't want to know what's happened in the rest of the world? It's been a month since the plague, or whatever it was. We're in this together now and I'm coming with you, mate, and unless Tim and Melissa have had a wholly different experience to us and found thousands of survivors, I am going to suggest that everybody comes with you. We can't just hang around in an empty Australia for ever, waiting."

"Well, that's…" Jack trailed off.

"That's what, Jack Stevens? What were you going to say?"

"It might be dangerous. Too dangerous."

"Why? How're you planning on getting home? Swimming?"

"I do have a couple of ideas."

"I'm sure you do, Jack. You're always full of them. But now you have to extend your plans to include us as well. Better get thinking."

"I will," he couldn't help smiling. "And I…" he trailed off once again.

"What?"

"I didn't expect it," he tried again, "but it's great. Fantastic. Thank you." Xanthe didn't reply, just laughed, got up from the passenger seat and planted a kiss on the side the side of his face. Without further comment she went back to busy herself in the main cabin of the motorhome.

Their arrival back at Saltview was something of an anti-climax, since there was nobody else there. The fire-engine and cars were still parked outside and were all in exactly the same spots they had been. The grass was one week longer, but that was the only apparent change. Jack helped Emily unload William, while Xanthe moved clothes back into their rooms in the house.

"I think there's a perimeter wall that runs all the way round the property, so if we close the gates William should be able to wander wherever he wants. Will that work?" Jack wasn't too familiar with horses' needs.

"Yes, that'll be fine. We'll need to make sure he has some shade and a water trough," Emily told him.

"There's plenty of shade. I'll try and find something we can use as a water trough."

Once that was complete and William was happily cropping the grass on the lawn, the two of them headed inside to join Xanthe.

"Jack, can you get the generator running so we can use the washing machine?" Xanthe asked.

"It shall be done, my lady."

Tim and Melissa did not arrive that day and so by evening the two adults in the house were starting to feel a bit edgy. What if they didn't come back? Should they write a note and then set out on the route they had agreed the other two would take? The younger pair's route had included Canberra, Melbourne and Adelaide, but should have been feasible in the week. It was a strange and uncomfortable feeling, just not knowing what had happened. Supper that evening was a subdued affair.

Emily had been in bed in her new bedroom for nearly two hours when they heard the sound of an engine outside. The two jumped up and hurried outside to greet the arrivals, who were negotiating the closed gates.

Once they were inside Jack re-closed the gates again to keep in the beloved William, while he could hear car doors slamming and voices. He went back to the house to find Tim, Melissa and Xanthe standing in a huddle, Xanthe holding up a camping lantern, which was illuminating the tired faces of the new arrivals. There was nobody else there.

However, after a brief handshake from Tim and a surprisingly warm hug from Melissa, Tim turned and opened the side door of their motorhome, looking up into the interior expectantly. This action was enough to tell them that Tim and Melissa hadn't entirely wasted their week.

Sitting round the kitchen table in the candlelight they got a chance to inspect the new arrival. He was about sixteen, Jack judged, and he introduced himself as Shane. He was a strong looking lad, with blond hair and a regular face that must have worked well with the girls - when there were some. The first thing to notice was that he moved on crutches, his right leg below his shorts encased in a filthy looking plaster cast. It had faded signatures on it, hardly visible below the grime.

"So, Shane, what did you do to your leg?" Jack asked him. He knew how to speak to Emily, since he had children of a similar age, but hadn't had much experience of teenagers since he'd been one himself, which was now quite some time ago.

"Football," Shane said, glancing up at Jack and then back down at the table.

"Football as in soccer?"

"Nah. Aussie rules. Got hit by two guys at once. Shattered my femur."

"Ouch," was all Jack could of think of in reply to this.

"How long does that cast need to stay on?" Xanthe asked him.

"They said at least six weeks, depending on how quickly it healed. It happened a week before…" he didn't finish his statement.

"Well, I don't think we can do an x-ray," Xanthe commented, "but I'm a nurse so we should be able to see how it's doing."

"Yeah, Melissa said," Shane grunted, not looking up from the table. Having seen everybody he knew die and then living on his own for three weeks gave Shane some latitude, Jack decided, and so didn't pass any judgement on the surly youth.

The two groups swapped stories. Jack and Xanthe first, recounting their climb of the skyscraper and the finding of Emily, and then Tim and Melissa. They had found Shane in Adelaide, which was his home. He had come screeching up in his parents' car within fifteen minutes of the first rocket going up from viewpoint overlooking the now-dark Adelaide. His answers to questions were so monosyllabic that Melissa supplied much of the detail. Interestingly Shane, like Ben, had hardly got sick at all, but had watched helplessly as his family, and the rest of the city, died around him. He had driven to Melbourne and found nobody, and then returned to Adelaide, for lack of any other ideas.

As this story was coming to a close, a movement caught Jack's eye by the door.

"And this must be Emily," Melissa announced. Emily nodded and crossed to stand close to Xanthe.

Once introductions were done for the little girl, Jack had a suggestion for the group.

"Since we're all here I think we should sit and talk about what we're going to do. Tomorrow and after that. I know it's late, but hey, none of us have got work or school tomorrow.

"Xanthe and I have been talking and I have a suggestion. My family are in England and I have no choice. I have to go back there and find out what has happened. My suggestion is really more of an invitation. I want to invite you all to come with me." There was a bit of a silence, which Xanthe eventually broke.

"I think we should all go. There's no reason to stay and we need to find out what's happened. It's been nearly a month now and nobody is coming to rescue us, so if the world is not coming to us let's go and see the world."

This was greeted by a long silence. Eventually Tim spoke up.

"Makes sense to me. How?"

It wasn't until the next morning, after Jack and Xanthe had been for their run, that they really got round to discussing details. There had been general agreement that they would go together, although conspicuously this was only from the adults present. Neither Shane nor Emily offered an opinion on whether they wanted to travel or not.

So there's three possible ways," Jack started, as Tim fried fresh eggs that their chickens, now released from their imprisonment in the garage, had produced. "We could go by land, sea or air, and I think we should think about all three and decide which one is best."

"Well, nobody here's a pilot, so air is out," Xanthe said, around a mouthful of fresh bread she had baked and was now eating and feeding to Emily.

"Well, not necessarily," Jack replied. "There are no rules now, so the question is whether we are able to do it. A licence means nothing, as Shane demonstrated when he drove to Melbourne." Shane gave Jack a blank look but said nothing. "And a lot of the complexities, air traffic control and stuff, are probably not relevant. So the question is just whether we can get in a plane, take-off from A and land at B."

"With some degree of safety. And several times over. You can't fly to London in one flight," Xanthe pointed out.

"Agreed," Jack conceded. "So there's flying, which is far and away the quickest, but maybe has some challenges. Then there's driving, which has one very obvious drawback."

"That Australia is a separate continent?" Melissa commented, drily. In the morning sunlight Jack noticed a change in Melissa. She had some colour in her skin, which had not been there when they had met. Obviously she had spent some time in the sun in the last week, but the difference was more than that. It seemed unlikely that she could have lost much weight in the two weeks since Jack first saw her in the Botanical Gardens but somehow, although she was still overweight, her movements and posture seemed more positive. She undoubtedly seemed more confident and less 'apologetic' was the word that Jack felt described her earlier persona.

"Exactly. So if we're going to drive, we're going to have to do something else as well. Either air or sea to get somewhere we can drive from. Do you think there's an atlas here somewhere?"

"Maybe." This from Tim. "There is a kind of library that has a load of books in it. I'll go and look." Breakfast continued for a few minutes before Tim came back with a big book in his hands.

"Yup. Check it out. This has got maps of everywhere." They spent a while leafing through the beautiful book looking at maps.

"So," Tim eventually summarised, "if we want to drive, we need to drive to Darwin and then either sail or fly to Singapore. From there we can drive all the way to France. Theoretically."

"And how far is it from Darwin to Singapore?" Jack asked.

"Mmmm, let's have look," Tim was measuring lengths and comparing them to the scale at the foot of the page. "At least two thousand miles, I would say. Maybe a bit more."

"So that means we have to either sail or fly anyway, so let's do some research on those two methods and see which we prefer. None of us are pilots and none are sailors, but by the time we get to Singapore…"

"Who said none of us were sailors?" Tim interrupted.

"You're a sailor?" Xanthe asked, although the answer was obvious from the question Tim had asked, as well as his rather smug expression.

"Yes. My Dad and his brother are really keen. Were really keen. I used to get dragged along all the time when I was younger. I never really got that into it, but I did quite a bit of racing and even some cruising."

"And do you think you could sail a boat two thousand miles. You know, as skipper?" Jack asked.

"Well, I've always been crew, I haven't done a great deal of navigation and stuff, although I have done some."

"Mmm, sounds like quite a step up," Jack pointed out.

"It is," Tim agreed, "but I'd feel more confident about sailing a boat to Singapore than I would flying a plane, which none of us have done."

"It's a good point, and well made," Jack smiled. "But actually I have flown a plane. I'm not a pilot but I did once have two lessons. My father-in-law, may he rest in peace, gave me two tester lessons as a present. I've also been up with a friend of mine who is a hobbyist pilot."

"He might still be alive. Your father-in-law," Melissa pointed out earnestly.

"Unlikely, unless the old codger faked his own death. I went to his funeral three years ago." Jack smiled as he delivered this to show he wasn't remotely offended.

"Well, maybe he did," Melissa smiled in return. "Let's just move on from that shall we?"

There was a bit of a pause in which Jack felt that eyes were on him. It had occurred to him that he appeared to be the oldest person on the continent, and so there was definitely some pressure for him to show a little leadership.

"I suggest we check out both alternatives," was what he finally came up with. "Although it might make sense to drive to Darwin first, I think we should make a decision here on how we are going to do it. So we should go and look at some planes and some boats and decide which method we think is best."

"And what about me?" Shane suddenly asked. The teenager had been silent up until now and this question was blurted out, leaving an uncomfortable silence in its wake.

"What do you mean, Shane?" Xanthe asked, her voice fairly neutral, if a touch guarded.

"Do I get a say in this or are you all going to just decide for me?" Shane was looking at the table as he spoke, but his tone was a mixture of aggression and worry. The others exchanged looks before

Jack spoke up.

"Shane, how old are you?" he asked.

"Fifteen."

"Well, this is probably as good a time as any to talk about how this works. All the adults in this group get an equal say in what happens, and there is no compulsion on any of us to do anything we don't want to. You, Shane, are an adult here. You get exactly the same say as the rest of us, but also – and we haven't talked about this up until now – have the same responsibilities. Membership of the group is optional, but I think we should all expect each other to contribute and behave in a way that is acceptable. That means that if any of us, and I include myself and you in this Shane, either don't work for the group or step outside what the others think is acceptable, the others could vote to expel that person."

Jack looked round at faces which were, without exception, registering shock at his words.

"I know it sounds extreme, and I am sure that it won't come to it, but I think it's worth talking about how it all works. There's no law here now and so we have to have rules and it's as well to state them formally. This is only my suggestion, if any of you, and that means you as well, Shane, want to put forward something else then now is the time."

There was a long silence while they all thought about this. It was Melissa who eventually spoke up.

"I agree with Jack. We have to work together and we have to behave acceptably. As judged by the others. We should all commit to that, and so this is me saying I do."

Tim was next. "It's a good suggestion. Me too."

"OK, I can live with that. Me too," was Shane's agreement, as he raised his gaze and looked Jack in the eye.

"I'm in. Me too," Xanthe said simply.

"Does this mean that I could be sent away if I, y'know, don't behave?" Emily asked in a small voice.

"No Emily, it doesn't," Xanthe answered her immediately. "We expect you to help, but you wouldn't be sent away. You don't have to worry about that. You're staying with us now." And Xanthe pulled the little girl over towards her and gave her a hug which was only partially resisted.

"Then it's agreed," Jack finished. "Enough of the heavy conversation. Time for another cup of tea before a trip to the airport, I think."

"Wait," Shane jumped in, unexpectedly. "There's something else I want to talk about first." He paused and looked round the group, who were watching him like an unexploded bomb. Jack certainly had no idea what Shane was going to say but wasn't sure he liked the slightly defiant jut to Shane's chin before he started talking. "You guys are all making plans to head off to England but nobody has talked about what God would want us to do. He brought this plague and killed everybody and He also made us survive. We should talk about what His Plan is and what He wants us to do."

This statement was met with a profound silence. Jack didn't really know how to answer this and, judging by the lack of response, the others too were at a loss. Eventually it was Xanthe who mustered a question rather than any kind of answer.

"When you talked about God's Plan to your Mum and Dad, what did they say?"

"Well, Mum never said much about God," the boy replied. "She said that she couldn't see what He wanted clearly and so listened to others. Dad could hear more clearly. He always knew what the right thing to do was. Like if me or Ben, my brother, did something wrong then Dad always knew what the right punishment was. Not just that. Other things too." The boy suddenly paused and looked around.

"You do believe in God, don't you?" This was almost more of a statement than a question, but once again was met with a silence. This time it was Tim who spoke up.

"I have to admit that I don't. I'm an atheist and I always have been." Shane stared at Tim.

"Were you brought up an atheist?" Shane asked the young man. Jack felt he could detect a note of pity in Shane's voice as he asked this question.

"Not really," Tim answered slowly. "My Mum and Dad used to go to church and take me and my two sisters with them. They always claimed that they believed in God, but I'm not sure that they really did, I think they were just a bit afraid of coming out and admitting that they didn't believe it. But none of it ever made any sense to me. It all just seemed like wishful thinking, I suppose. I can see lots of reasons why men would have invented God, and I can't see any evidence that they didn't."

"How can you say that? Look around you at everything He has made. How do you explain it?" Jack could see that Tim was already wondering how sensible it was to engage the teenager in a religious debate, but he could not see how to help them out of a conversation that was becoming sticky.

"I'm afraid I believe in science, Shane," Tim spoke gently. "I believe in things I can see evidence for and so far none of that points to intelligent design, in my mind at any rate."

"But science doesn't explain everything. Scientists don't know what created the Big Bang." Jack wondered if the rest of the group found it as spooky as him that Tim was having a debate on the Creator with the ghost of Shane's father.

"You're right, Shane. Scientists can't explain lots of things. Including the Big Bang. But two hundred years ago there were a lot more unexplained phenomena that we have since understood and none of them turned out to be the direct work of God, although nearly all of them were attributed to him originally. History has been full of scientists discovering the real explanation for something, only to be burned at the stake for heresy. And then a few years later the church have to update their doctrine to include the new knowledge."

"But what created the Big Bang if it wasn't God?" Shane too now looked like he wanted out of this conversation but felt like backing down would be unacceptable.

"I don't know," Tim answered simply. "We haven't found that out yet. It may turn out that it was a sentient being, or perhaps some crazy natural phenomenon. Who knows? I'm not totally ruling out the existence of a God, but I am ruling out the existence of a God who cares about me as an individual. Or even about this whole planet. The universe is just too big. But there's something else I'd like to say," Tim continued in the same measured tone he had used throughout this exchange, "and it's this. I'm not going to try and convince you that God doesn't exist. I'm just telling you what I believe. I envy your belief and I have no intention of taking it away from you. I'd like to believe in God, but wanting to believe doesn't help me to actually do it." Shane was silent after Tim had finished speaking, absorbing what the older man had said. Eventually he looked round at the others.

"What about you guys? What do you believe?"

"I don't really believe, although I don't really *not* believe, if you know what I mean. I'm, an agnostic I suppose." Melissa answered first, her face sympathetic.

"I'm like that too, I think," Xanthe sounded uncertain. "An agnostic as well." Shane turned last to Jack, who took his time answering.

"I think my beliefs are close to Tim's," the older man eventually answered. "But it's good that we've had this discussion, Shane. I'm glad you brought it up. If we're going to go travelling the world and meeting who knows who, then a group that has a varied point of view is valuable. I think the fact that you are a believer makes it all the more important that you come with us. If God has a Plan then we need someone with us who can help us all understand it."

Shane looked serious for a few moments, his mouth pursed in thought before he nodded once in agreement, stood up and exited the room on his crutches, leaving the remaining five exchanging looks.

"These all look a little on the large side," Tim commented as they walked along the terminal building past the deserted gates that looked out on a variety of jet-airliners.

"Yes, they do indeed," Jack agreed, thinking how great a bicycle, or even a set of roller-skates or a skateboard, would be on the massive expanse of empty polished floor that they were negotiating. It was just the two of them investigating the silent, cavernous airport. Jack was reflecting how much larger it all looked when totally empty of the usual air-travel throng.

"It was a very tidy plague," Tim suddenly announced.

"What do you mean?"

"Well, I mean that everybody got sick quite slowly and so had time to go home to get over what they thought was a bad cold or flu. And then quite quickly they got too sick to do anything and so died at home. It means that everywhere we go there aren't corpses or anything. And because it all happened at exactly the same time there wasn't an evacuation, with traffic snarl-ups and food riots and all that stuff. Things that are messy. Instead we went from everybody being alive and business as usual to everybody being dead with minimum fuss."

"I suppose that's one way to look at it," Jack commented drily.

"Just saying…" Tim suddenly cut off as they both stopped walking. Adrenaline squirted into Jack's system as he froze. They had just rounded a corner in the airside section of the airport and two men were walking towards them.

"Jesus, that gave me a fright," Tim commented, as they started walking again and their reflections in the large mirror did the same thing.

"Me too." Jack exhaled loudly. He had thought that they were all getting used to creepy, deserted places, but his fright at his own reflection showed that the vast, echoing terminal building had taken creepy to another level.

"I don't think any of these are really what we're looking for," Jack continued as his heart rate approached normal, "but let's check one out anyway." They picked the smallest of the planes they could see parked at a jet-way. They had to break open the door that would let them board, although this took only a few moments. Jack was becoming extremely adept at opening doors using the small pry bar, which he carried as part of the cut down break-in kit on his back. Walking down the too-hot jet-way was a surreal experience for Jack who had been a regular air traveller in his previous life. The door to the aircraft was open, which was good because Jack didn't think the little kit in his rucksack was the equal to a door made by Boeing.

Even before they entered they knew they'd made a mistake with their choice of aircraft, since there was a certain smell, which they both recognised, growing stronger as they approached. Sure enough the front row in the small aircraft was occupied by a corpse in a hi-viz jacket who hadn't quite conformed to the rules of Tim's tidy plague.

"Let's find another plane," was all Jack said and without discussion they retreated to do just that.

Three gates along was an identical aircraft to the occupied one and luckily this one was vacant. It was a small as airliners go, with two jets mounted on the tail. The main cabin was only four seats wide, three in the little first class section, and Jack judged that the whole plane could hold less that a hundred passengers. Plenty of room for six of them then. The safety card in a seat pocket declared it to be a CRJ900 (00), for what that was worth.

The flight deck was the usual bewildering array of knobs, dials and switches, interspersed with screens that were all dark. Jack plumped himself down in the pilot's chair and Tim took the right-hand seat.

"So, do you think you could fly this?" he asked.

"Well, I'm not sure," Jack replied as he examined the various labels on controls and instruments in front of him. "The way I see it we have a number of different challenges associated with flying something like this."

"You mean other than taking off and, more importantly, landing?"

"Yes. There's the flying part. Taking off, landing, getting the thing to fly where you want to go at the height and speed that you want. That part is probably the least complex, although it's also the part that really has to be done right. The landing in particular is probably the single most tricky part of the whole operation. Not complicated per-se, but tricky and mistakes will, um, get punished."

"That's one advantage of boats," Tim pointed out. "Docking the things doesn't tend to be so life-and-death."

"That's true, which is why planes are good and bad. They go really fast, which means you get where you want to go quickly, but crashes are a bit higher energy."

"So what else?"

"Well," Jack continued. "The next obvious challenge is getting the thing ready to fly. You've got to fuel it up and have some idea of how far it will take you so you can plan your flight and know where you are going to land. There'll be fuel here at the airport but we've got to work out how to pump it into the plane. Should be feasible, I would think. And then there's the navigation."

"Wouldn't you just use GPS?"

"Yes, you would. I'm sure it has GPS fitted, and we could take a spare or two with us."

"Would a hand-held GPS work in the plane? When it's flying? Wouldn't it, you know, interfere with the plane systems? Isn't that why they tell you to turn phones off?"

"A hand-held GPS is receive only, so no, it wouldn't."

"So, three things. Flying, refuelling and navigating," Tim summarised. His voice and sentences were always precise and Jack was impressed with Tim's ordered mind. He was not, Jack judged, an out-of-the-box thinker, but he thought in a structured way that made him effective at completing tasks he set out to execute.

"There's the whole weather thing, which I think you might consider part of navigation," Jack had given this topic quite a bit of thought as he and Xanthe had trundled around the Australian countryside. "About the weather there's really not much you can do. Only fly on days when it appears to be OK, but of course things can change when you fly thousands of miles. Other than that, all you can do is avoid big clouds that might be too turbulent and be ready to land if it seems to be deteriorating.

"But there's one more thing which I think might be a challenge."

"What's that," Jack could see that Tim was paying attention. In fact he seemed so focused Jack was wondering if the younger man might hunt down a pen and paper and take notes.

"Well, it's the running of the aircraft," Jack gestured at the banks of instruments around them. Not many of these are concerned with actual flying. Most of them control things like internal temperatures and pressures. They turn on various heaters and coolers. There's the radios, of course, and also fuel pumps and things like that. Many of them won't be that critical, but some will be. It doesn't matter if the cabin gets a bit hot, or cold, but it does matter if you run out of fuel because you didn't open a valve on the second fuel tank. Or if ice builds up on the wings so the plane can't fly."

"And do you think we can work all that stuff out? I can help."

"We might be able to, Tim. I think we might. But it occurs to me that this might not be the best kind of plane to do it on. Maybe a smaller one might be easier."

"You mean like a little propeller plane?"

"Well, probably not. A propeller plane is likely to have less range, and if we're going to fly we don't want to make too many hops. I was thinking maybe a private jet might be the best compromise."

"Shall we go and look for one?"

"Sure. But while we're here let's see if we can start the engines on this thing shall we?"

Twenty Three

"So what did you boys find then?" Xanthe asked, putting two cups of black tea in front of them, collecting her own and sitting down next to Jack at the kitchen table. Melissa and Emily were also in the room, although Shane was absent, either in his room or somewhere else in the big house.

"I think we found a plane that might work for us," Jack ventured cautiously. He could definitely sense an edge to Xanthe's question.

"It's a private jet," Tim jumped in. "It's really nice inside. It even has a bedroom. Pretty cool." Melissa smiled at Tim who grinned back. "We started the engines on it. We did the same on one of the big ones at the airport." Xanthe looked rather less impressed than Melissa.

"We also tried out the radios to see if we could raise anyone," Tim continued, "but we didn't hear anything. We didn't know what channel to try, but scanning through we didn't find anything. The radio can do a hundred and eighty different frequencies and so we tried transmitting on the ones it had pre-set, but got nothing."

"And do you think you can fly it? Land it?" she asked Jack, her grey eyes earnest.

"I think so, but there's quite a bit of preparation to do. I need to spend some time working out all of its systems and then maybe a couple of test flights. On my own."

"Jesus, Jack, is this a good idea? I mean the first time you're going to land this you have to get it right. There's no margin for error."

"I know that. Although it's not quite true that I can't practice. Tim and I picked up that on the way home," Jack pointed to large cardboard box that he'd deposited on the kitchen table. "It's a laptop with a joystick, pedals and several flight simulator packages. It's obviously not exactly the same but it will give me a chance to practice and work out the procedures that I can use when I actually fly."

"Are you sure? Those things are just games, aren't they?"

"Well, yes and no. They are getting pretty detailed these days and are definitely better than nothing. If I can't reliably land a plane similar to the one we're using on a simulator, then I won't even go for a test flight. If I can land it on the simulator every time, then I think I might consider a test flight."

Xanthe looked less than impressed, but didn't pursue the subject further.

Jack was sitting in one of the large and comfortable rooms downstairs, with the noise of the generator audible through the open window. He was setting up the simulator equipment that he had looted, when Emily came sidling into the room.

"Hi Emily. How are things?" Jack asked, noting the troubled look on the little girl's face.

"OK," was all she answered. Jack continued setting up the equipment. She clearly wanted to talk but there was no point in hurrying her, he was best waiting until she was ready to talk.

He had the laptop plugged in, booted up and loading software by the time she broke the silence.

"This plane you and Tim found. How big is it?" she said, abruptly.

"Well, it's not as big as a big passenger plane. But it's bigger than a little propeller plane."

"Is it bigger than a car?"

"Yes," Jack replied slowly. "Quite a bit bigger." A suspicion of where she was going with this was starting to form.

"Is it bigger than the motorhome?"

"Yes. It's a bit bigger than that."

"So will William be able to fit in it?" Emily blurted, confirming Jack's suspicion.

"I'm afraid not, Emily," Jack said as gently as he could. He knew from experience of children that it was important to be clear here. Ambiguity would not help the situation so he shouldn't use killer words like 'probably' or 'maybe'. "I'm afraid it's too small for him to fit in, and even if he could he would find it very frightening."

"Well, in that case I'm not coming," Emily stated calmly. If she had stamped her foot and wailed then Jack would have found it less alarming, but Emily was not trying to change his mind, she was just stating what she intended to do. "I'll stay here with William and you can go and see if your family are alive and, then come back here. You can bring them with you if they're alive."

"Emily," he turned to her, fully focusing his attention, "you can't stay here. We can make sure William is alright, but I'm afraid there is no way you can stay here with him."

Emily was silent for a few seconds and a big tear leaked onto one cheek.

"I thought you would say that, but you don't understand. William is the only part of my family that's still alive. I can't leave him behind. Me and him are the only two left and we have to stick together." She was trying hard to hold it together but her angular little face was starting to crumple, and so Jack gathered her slight frame into his arms where she let the sobs go. It was quite some time before she recovered enough to show her face, leaving a certain amount of snot on his shoulder as well as depositing some on her own sleeve. It was sufficient time for Jack to give the matter some thought, and so he made a statement that he hoped he would not live to regret.

"OK, I'll think about how we can take William with us. I can't make any promises, but I'll think about it. I understand how important family are. We're a family now as well, us survivors, and so we have to stick together no matter what."

Emily gave him a long look but didn't say anything, just wiped her nose again, nodded once in that rather disconcertingly adult way she had, and left the room.

Jack spent the evening playing on the simulator, trying to remember everything that he had ever learnt about flying. The simulator was great and a big part of what he needed to do was try the various different aircraft and ascertain what the pros and cons of each one was. He had to run the generator again to recharge the laptop, and by the time Xanthe came to get him for supper his head was aching and his thoughts buzzing.

She stood behind him put her hand on his shoulder as she watched him landing the plane he was currently testing.

"OK Ace? Supper's ready" He was acutely aware of how close her smooth cheek was to the side of his face as she bent down to peer at the screen, but he managed to stop this distraction from getting the better of him and successfully landed the virtual plane on the virtual runway.

"Very good," she murmured, "What kind of plane was that?"

He switched the view to an outside shot of the aircraft. "A Boeing 767."

"I thought we were taking a little private jet? Doesn't it have those?" she gestured at the screen.

"It does. Let's go and have supper. I'll tell you later."

It was actually well after supper and after Emily had gone to bed that Jack recounted the conversation he had had with the nine year old. Uncharacteristically, it was Shane who spoke up.

"So you're suggesting, despite the fact the none of us are pilots, that we take a jumbo so we can fly a ten-year-old girl's horse to England?"

"I suppose I am, yes. It does sound a bit crazy but I think there are reasons why it's the right thing to do."

"It does sound crazy, but hey, what the hell, right?" The teenager had a slightly feral grin on his face. "Emily's lucky to still have her horse. This whole situation is shit," he looked around challengingly, "but I don't see any point in playing it safe. If God had meant us to die then we'd have died with everybody else. We're meant to live and, so I'm up for it." Melissa and Tim both looked faintly shocked at this, but Jack re-assessed his opinion of the surly boy. Shane had clearly been in the grip of a depression and did not appear to have recovered well from his experiences in Adelaide, but this looked like it might engage his interest in the world again. Although Jack did feel that Shane's reasoning was flawed. God seemed to have no qualms about saving people from one death only to supply a different one soon after, he had noticed. Conversely it was fairly impressive that Shane was showing some empathy, not generally a teenaged trait, for Emily's position.

"What are the advantages?" Tim asked. "Surely it's going to be easier to land a small plane?"

"Well, yes and no," Jack replied. "A big plane travels much faster, which does mean your approach speed is higher. You have to get yourself well set up in advance. But the big plane is also more stable, less twitchy than the little one and it has all the pilot aids, which definitely help.

"But the real advantage," Jack continued, "is the range. The big planes can go much further in one hop, and so we wouldn't have to stop so often. They're also, well, bigger and that means we could easily take William with us."

"How would we get him into the plane?" Melissa asked.

"We'll have to go and check it out, but I'm thinking there has to be equipment for loading stuff on to planes at the airport. You know, loading luggage and food and things. We should go and look tomorrow."

"And do you think William would go along with your scheme?" Xanthe asked, one eyebrow raised.

"He does seem to do what Emily wants, I've noticed. But it occurred to me that perhaps you could give him something that would help keep him calm. Not knock him out, since we need him to walk on, but you know, make him a bit mellow."

Xanthe looked thoughtful at this suggestion. "I probably could, actually. There'll be Ketamine at the hospital, but I think I might want to experiment a bit on William to get the dosage right."

Shane was grinning again. "I can just picture it. Us, flying along in a jumbo, with horse standing in the aisle. Not too many people have done *that*."

"Actually, I was thinking we'd probably have to make a kind of stable for him. More like a horse box, maybe. So he's enclosed like in the horse box out there," Jack waved, "so he can't fall over. We could just remove some of the seats. We certainly won't need them all."

Over the next few days the group became infected with purpose as Jack's plan to fly them to England, horse and all, started to gather momentum. Jack and Xanthe continued their morning runs together, and Jack was gratified to see that he was finding keeping up with Xanthe a little easier each day, although there was still plenty of sweat by the time they got back to Saltview.

They all spent quite a bit of time out at the airport learning as much as they could about the resources they would need. Tim, Melissa and

Shane worked together on the ground equipment they would need. They had found a fleet of refuelling tankers and worked out how to pump fuel into the big plane that Jack had selected, although at his request they didn't fill it up since he didn't want to do the test flight with a full plane. The trio also experimented with other ground vehicles that they might need, although played might be a better term. Why Shane and Tim needed to tear around the airport in the articulated buses used to move passengers wasn't clear to Jack, but he enjoyed their fun. They also gathered and tested the big lifting platforms they had found, which would be perfect for getting William into the aircraft, if the pony was amenable.

"So why did you smash the window on that bus?" he did ask Tim one evening.

"I've always wanted to test one of those little red hammers," the young man replied. "You know, the ones that say 'In Emergency Break Glass'. It turns out it's not so easy to do."

Jack concentrated on the aircraft itself and often Xanthe, with Emily never far away, would join him. He worked his way through the various checklists that were in the cockpit, trying to fathom as many of the entries as possible. 'Parking Brake: On' was easy enough but 'MFD: EICAS' was not so obvious and there were many such entries. There was a printed manual, which provided some answers, but there were some items that Jack just had to score off the list as things he did not understand. He had to hope that none of these were essential items.

He started the engines on the big plane and Shane, using the purpose built tractor, pushed them off the stand. Jack, with Xanthe sitting beside him, then spent an hour taxiing around the tarmac and eventually re-parked the Boeing back near the same gate. He couldn't get it right next to the jetway, which was powerless to move, but Shane turned up driving a set of stairs that let them off the plane.

In the evenings, Jack spent his time in front of the simulator while the others kept the generator fuelled and running. He practised endless landings, trying to be methodical about the process. He had once heard the phrase 'the secret of a good landing was a good approach', and so he worked on getting well set up and executing his pre-landing checklist as early as possible.

Xanthe sat in on some of his simulator work, just sitting at his shoulder, watching and asking the occasional question. This made Jack feel uncomfortable as he tried a few different strategies that didn't result in a good landing, but after a few days almost all the landings were going by the numbers. On the evening of the third day Xanthe had watched three or four landings before she spoke up.

"Jack, are you going to need a co-pilot for this flight? Is it even possible to land a jumbo on your own?"

"I think it is possible, yes. My plan is to take off and fly around in a rectangle and approach from a good distance out. I've been experimenting with speeds and things and I think I can do it."

"But would it help to have someone else there? Another pair of hands and eyes, even if that person doesn't know what they are doing?"

"Well, maybe, but I don't think it's a good idea. It probably wouldn't make any difference. The bottom line is, I don't want to take anybody else on my test flight. For obvious reasons."

"Yes," Xanthe pressed on, "I understand why you don't want someone along, but if it would help at all I think you should have someone with you. It's not good for any of us if you crash."

"I can't ask anybody to come. It wouldn't be right."

"You don't have to ask. I'm offering."

Jack turned to Xanthe. "I don't want to be mean, Xanthe, because that is a brave and kind offer. But you are absolutely *not* coming with me. I have to do that first flight on my own and after that I will fly you all to Hong Kong and beyond. But the test flight happens with just me."

"But you said yourself it might help to have someone else in the cockpit."

"I did, and it might help, although it also might not. There is an appreciable risk attached, there's no point in denying it."

"I'm not frightened," Xanthe insisted. "Well, maybe a bit, but I'm prepared to take the risk. If I can help make the whole venture safer then I want to do that. You've got a family to think about. There's no reason why you should take all the risk, and you're no good to Jane if you're smeared all over the runway in Sydney." This hung between them for a few seconds. After a few seconds Jack sighed.

"Two reasons why you're not coming, Xanthe," his voice sounded tired, even to him. He didn't need this argument. He was quite frightened enough already. "The first reason you can't is that it's kind of me driving this. I'm the one who needs to get home and I'm the one saying I can land this plane. But the second reason is the big one. Emily. She needs you now, Xanthe. You have to look after her. Tim, Melissa and Shane are great, but they're not the people to look after Emily, but you are. If it wasn't for her you could come with me, but, as it stands, it just doesn't make sense."

Xanthe was silent for a long time after this statement, looking out of the window into the far distance. Eventually she said, "OK. I agree," and she left the room without another word or a glance in his direction.

Jack spent one more day after that getting ready for his test flight. He spent more time in the aircraft, taxiing round the large airport and twice doing half a take-off, followed by a reverse thrust and braking manoeuvre before taxiing round to repeat. He felt he was as ready as he could be. Although the controls in the real plane were different, they were sufficiently similar to the virtual ones that he could manage the transition, and he had reduced the landing checklist to one he felt he could handle during the approach.

He taxied the airliner back to the terminal, parked it and then waved to Shane who, as designated chauffeur, was messing around with a baggage handling tractor and its train of trucks. Shane pulled up next to the stairs, crutched over to them athletically and then started the engine on the mobile stairway, driving them across to the door that Jack had opened high up above. Jack stepped on to the stairs, which were already set to the right height, holding on tightly while Shane immediately backed away from the plane and drove across to the waiting BMW that they had arrived in.

"So, you all ready?" Shane asked as he started up the BMW and drove at speed across the airport tarmac towards the gate in the perimeter fence they had 'opened' using one of the tanker lorries.

"I think so," Jack replied cautiously. "I'm going to do the test flight tomorrow, I think."

"Wow. Are you scared?" Shane asked as he manoeuvred the car on the main road and set off for Saltview.

"Well. A bit nervous I suppose. But I think it will be OK. Are you nervous about getting into a plane that I am flying?"

"Nah. If you can land the thing here then you should be able to do it in Hong Kong. We're not going to die on a plane crash. It's not His plan." This was all said with a good deal of confidence and so Jack couldn't really tell if Shane was nervous and wanting to hide it or if he genuinely was without fear.

That evening at supper Jack found it hard to join in the general chatter. His statement to Shane that he was 'a bit nervous' was enough of an understatement to be considered an outright lie. He tried to behave normally but quite a few times his attention wandered and they must surely have noticed his lack of chit-chat.

On the converse side he noticed that the rest of the group were extremely solicitous towards him, fetching and carrying his food and drink, making sure he had what he needed, although no mention of the test flight was made. Xanthe too had little to say for herself, and hardly said a word to Jack during the course of the meal. She did give a fairly terse report on a test dosage she had given William that day. It had resulted in seemingly little effect, although Emily insisted that he was 'more dopey that usual.' Xanthe said she would try again tomorrow with a slightly increased dose, and see how he was after that.

"It won't hurt him, will it? You know giving him more the day after?" Emily wanted to know.

"I think he'll be fine," Xanthe answered seriously. "Ketamine is a tranquiliser that was developed for horses, although we use it on people now as well."

"And people use it on themselves," commented Tim.

"Yes. Well anyway, I think he'll be fine. We just need to make sure he's calm when we put him on the plane so he doesn't hurt himself," the nurse answered, her blonde hair falling forward and blocking Jack's view of her face as she spoke.

The others chatted happily enough and in particular Jack noticed that Melissa, who had been so quiet on that first evening in the Gardens, was starting to come out of herself more. She had a razor sharp sense of humour, which she used on both Tim and Shane on occasions during the meal. Shane wasn't quite sure how to respond to this but Tim seemed to enjoy it, and responded with banter of his own. In fact, Jack noticed, there was not only banter but quite a bit of unnecessary touching going on between those two. Things definitely brewing, he decided, if they were not already brewed.

Jack sat on his bed and rubbed his face, the stubble rasping under his fingers. He had had a single beer in the hope that it would allow him to sleep, but now that he was upstairs on his own he wasn't so confident that it would work. There was no denying it, he was frightened, but also he wanted to go ahead with the flight, and so knew he was not going to pull out. He was as ready as he could be and now whatever was going to happen would happen.

He had been keeping his anxiety at bay through activity, but it was now getting harder and harder to banish worries about home from his mind. Although he was scared about the test flight, he had to admit to himself that he was at least as frightened to think that he could be back in England in a few days and who knew what he would find there.

He stripped down to his boxer shorts, climbed into bed and blew out the candle he had brought up with him. Moonlight filtered around the closed curtains but Jack had never felt less like sleeping. He went through the planned flight in his mind again. The take-off, the pattern he would fly, the checklist on approach and the landing itself.

He was approaching the runway for the umpteenth time in his mental simulator when he heard his door open and close again quietly. He didn't move and heard stealthy footsteps cross the room before a warm body climbed carefully into bed and cuddled up behind him.

"Thought you might want some company," Xanthe whispered in his ear. Jack froze, immobilised by a fear that was sharp and inexplicable. Afterwards he realised he was simply fear of his own reaction as he felt Xanthe's breasts pressing against his back through the thin fabric of whatever she was wearing.

She kissed the back of his neck and then took hold of his shoulder gently and tugged at it, to turn him to face her, but Jack was still frozen solid. She tugged a little harder and he reached up and took her hand in his, still holding his body immobile.

"Company is nice. But no, um, hanky-panky." This was greeted by a long silence during which she too was frozen in position before she rolled on to her back, breaking that hot contact he had been so aware of.

"Hanky-panky? Jesus, Jack. Do they still say that in England?" Jack didn't know what to say to that and so he said nothing. When Xanthe spoke again, a harder edge was creeping into her voice.

"I thought you might be worried about tomorrow. You know, scared, and might appreciate not being on your own tonight."

"I am scared. And some company would be nice. But it's just that…" he trailed off, not sure how to finish this sentence. When it became obvious that he wasn't going to complete it Xanthe spoke again, her voice flat and uninflected.

"Obviously not that scared. Sorry to keep you awake, Jack." And with that she got out of bed and left the room, unseen in the darkness.

Jack lay for some time after that thinking about what had happened. He certainly didn't want to fall out with Xanthe and he would be lying to himself he denied the fact that he was attracted to her.

They could be in England in a matter of days and so doing something now that he later regretted would seem like madness. Would Jane understand such a lapse? Not a question to which he wanted to find out the answer.

He was also finding it hard to banish a sneaking suspicion that was growing in his mind about Xanthe. It was, he told himself, entirely unfair and he had no evidence that her thought processes were so calculating. But ever since the Ben episode he was finding it hard not to think of Xanthe as an 'Alpha Male' kind of girl. He couldn't shake the suspicion that her interest in him was more down to his status in the group than any real affection or attraction.

Despite her protests and apologies, even she did not claim that she had made any kind of effort to find out what had happened to Jack as he staggered, bleeding, around the city.

Maybe he was being too analytical here. Perhaps the separation of male status and female attraction was a bit like trying to separate male attraction from female curves. Jack was worldly enough to know that attraction was a complex subject, and much of it was wired at a level below the conscious, and so it was probably harsh to judge Xanthe on such criteria.

Jack fell asleep while mulling over the conundrum rich people must face when working out if they are just liked for their money.

The next morning he was not woken by Xanthe coming in to get him up for their daily run, despite it being passed the hour when she usually did just that. He got up and dressed in his running gear, but found Xanthe had already left; the door to her room standing open but no sign of the woman herself.

He didn't encounter her as he jogged round their usual route, but she was sitting in the kitchen, obviously cooling off after a run on her own, when he returned, soaked in his post-run sweat. She was looking, he couldn't deny, fantastic in a form fitting running vest and lycra shorts, her tanned calves tapering down to her delicate ankles and bare feet which sat on the stone floor next to her recently removed trainers and socks.

She nodded to him when he entered the kitchen, but there was no trace of a smile. She rose, picked up a glass of water and her trainers and left the room, heading upstairs, without a word being exchanged.

Jack had, of course, heard the cliché about a 'woman scorned' but this was the first time in his life he was the recipient. All he could do was hope that she could move on.

Twenty Four

"I've got a question," Tim announced. "When we get to Hong Kong how are we going to get out of the plane? If there is nobody there to drive some steps up so we can get out, that is." They were all six of them packed into the cockpit of the plane as Jack went through his last minute preparations. The five non-flyers had been quiet in general and Tim's question had obviously come from a careful think through of that first flight.

"I asked him the same question," Shane answered on Jack's behalf, "and do you know what he said?"

"What?" Emily chipped in.

"The emergency escape slide! I can't wait," Shane did sound keen. "I'm sure I can manage that even with this leg."

"Actually I think we should examine your leg later today," Xanthe suggested. "If it still needs more time I can change the cast but if it looks OK we might take the cast off." Jack was grateful that she was acting normally around the rest of the group, although he did wonder if the others had noticed that no words were exchanged between the two of them.

"OK, everybody. I think I'm just about ready," Jack cut in. "Time for you guys to make a like a tree."

"What does that mean?" Emily wanted to know.

"He means leave," Melissa answered her gently.

"So before you go, a couple of things," Jack continued. "Firstly, I am going to take off and fly in a big circle, well, rectangle actually, which will bring me back here. I have no intention of trying to land the first time around, OK? The first time will be a bit longer to give me a chance to get used to it and try the radios while I'm in the sky."

"Do you think you will be able to talk to someone?" Emily's eyes were wide.

"No, I don't think so. But I'll give it a go just in case. Then I'll bring the plane in as if I am going to land, wheels out and everything, but when I'm approaching the runway I will put the power back on and go round again. I'm going to do that at least twice before I actually land. Maybe four or five times."

"Why?" Tim wanted to know.

"Well there's a saying I once heard that the secret to a good landing is a good approach, and so I want to practice the approach a couple of times. Also I have a couple of choices on how I use the GPS and I want to try them both out before I actually try and do a landing."

"Won't you run out petrol?" asked Emily.

"I don't think so," Jack tried to smile encouragingly, but wasn't sure he'd pulled it off. "I've got fuel for a couple of hours flying and each circuit should only take ten or fifteen minutes. So I can go around at least eight times before that becomes an issue. So don't panic if you see me going round a few times, this flight is meant to be about practice. OK?" There were general nods.

"The other thing to be aware of is that it is quite possible that I'll make a messy landing but be OK."

"What do you mean?" this from Melissa.

"I mean it might be that I bang it down very hard on the runway, or even miss the runway entirely, and that the undercarriage collapses and I go skidding off the end of the runway shedding sparks and stuff. And although that's not what I am planning, it's not the end of world. The plane itself doesn't really matter, it's disposable, and we're not committed to a long flight. Once I'm back on the ground we can talk about whether we want to go ahead with the big flight. Everybody OK with that?" Again there was general assent, although Jack could see in a few faces that they had also worked out that if he didn't make it to that discussion then it would be a short one.

"Right. Time to get lost, you lot. I'll see you in a while." And soon after that Jack was in the air, flying solo in the enormous aircraft.

The first lap went pretty well, with Jack relying almost entirely on the autopilot, which behaved as he hoped it would. His attempt to talk to someone on the radios was more token than realistic and he felt slightly foolish as he announced his presence to an unresponsive world on the frequencies the plane's radios were set to.

He used the GPS to home in on the waypoint he had set on the end of the runway and controlled his rate of descent using the autopilot again, continuously monitoring his altitude and distance from the waypoint. He had written down distances and heights at his approach speed and he felt that this method was not too bad, although he ended up a bit higher than he should be in the last section. As he approached the runway he dialled the speed and altitude back up, which caused the big plane to roar and climb away from the runway again.

"So far so good," he practically shouted to himself, as a burst of exhilaration coursed through him.

The second lap he mostly flew manually, and this was altogether trickier, and resulted in a much more erratic approach. The same distances and altitudes applied but he found it hard to follow a steady path down to the runway, with many corrections of both direction and height. The plane itself was not too difficult to control, although it did seem much more sensitive than he would have expected for such a massive vehicle. As he came in towards the runway he was definitely too high and too far to the left and his efforts to correct did not get him on track. Once again he asked the autopilot to take him up and away and it obliged. So he had learned that manual flying was going to need some more practice, but that the autopilot behaved much as it did in the simulator.

He flew the third lap back on the autopilot and was looking good as he turned onto the approach, although even more nervous now that knew he was genuinely trying to land the beast. He made sure his height didn't creep over the planned glide slope, which was a challenge with no beacon or marking lights, but he felt the approach was going as well as he could hope.

About five hundred meters out he switched to manual and aimed the plane at the end of the runway, but once again he found himself too far left. Again he tried to correct but this resulted in a yaw, which he found hard to damp. With the sweat beading on his forehead and stinging his eyes he once again aborted and climbed away from the runway.

He tried to calm himself. One failure didn't mean he couldn't do it. Round he went again and on to the approach, trying to replicate the last flight path, which had been fine until he'd taken manual control. Again at five hundred meters he switched across to manual and consciously squeezed a little to the right, trying to hold the descent rate steady as he hurtled towards the end of the runway and the ground.

He was on target. "Steady," he cautioned himself. "Steady." The runway was coming up fast and he was going to hit it, which was, of course, the plan. When he was sure that he couldn't fall short, he throttled back and started to pull back on the yoke, looking to flare for a smooth landing, but he had misjudged how far above the ground he was and the wheels hit the ground too soon and too hard.

The huge plane bounced back into the sky and Jack fought to hold it steady as it peaked and descended again. He knew that major input in any direction would be mistake, and so he let it return to earth with another jarring impact, but this time it stayed on the runway and the nose wheel came down with another thump.

The autobrakes were already engaged and so Jack throttled up reverse thrust, going to full power and steering with the rudder pedals, as the jet rumbled down the runway towards the lights and markers that he would run over if he ran out of tarmac. Although commercial pilots tended to disengage reverse thrust quite quickly, Jack had no such intention. He kept the throttles at maximum until the plane was practically stationary, before cutting the reverse thrust. The plane, still with brakes full on, lurched to a standstill with several hundred meters of runway to spare.

He sat back and let out the enormous breath that he had been holding. "Jesus. Right. One more time."

It took him another half hour to taxi round and take off and land one more time, and this time he landed on the first approach and brought the plane to a halt, well before the end of the runway. The second landing was rather better than the first, although by professional standards it was still pretty jarring. It did not involve a bounce back into the air and, all in all, Jack was pretty pleased with it. He had demonstrated that he could land this monster and the relief was so intense he found himself whooping and cheering as he taxied back to the terminal where the others waited.

When he brought the machine to halt, Shane already had the motorised stairs moving. By the time Jack had reached the rear door and got it open, the others were already at the top and knocking on the window. He got a big hug from Tim, which surprised him, and general shoulder slapping and congratulations from the others, who were all smiles. Xanthe's smile looked strained and didn't really interact with her eyes much. She stood at the back of the group on the top of the steps without comment, but Jack's relief was so enormous that he couldn't keep a big grin off his face.

Since these people were considering getting into a plane that he was flying, he did his best to hide the shake in his hands as the adrenaline reaction set in.

Jack's successful landing had re-energised the group's efforts to get ready to go. After general agreement round the Saltview kitchen table that they would indeed fly off on their airborne adventure, they set about getting ready.

That evening Xanthe did not come padding into his room, and there was no doubt that that was for the best. Home had just come a massive step closer.

A big piece of getting ready was preparing William's accommodation on the airliner, and for Xanthe to make sure that she was happy with the drugs she was planning to give the pony.

On that first day, exactly one month since Jack had woken in his hotel to a dead world, Tim took charge of the work to build William a flight stable, with help from Melissa, while Jack refuelled the plane assisted by Shane.

They had set the departure date for two days hence, and selected Hong Kong as the first destination. Once the plane was refuelled, needing two tanker trucks to completely fill it up, Shane drove Jack back to Saltview. Jack spent the rest of the day doing several simulator runs of the exact route, using the time acceleration feature of the simulation software. He planned alternate landing places and noted the exact coordinates of airfields they could divert to en route if, for any reason, they needed to land early. Xanthe took Shane to the hospital to inspect his leg and, if necessary change his cast. They had just left when Tim and Melissa burst into the room Jack was using as his virtual cockpit.

"Jack, something has happened and it's not good news," Tim announced.

"What's up?"

Tim held up a TomTom GPS unit. "The satellites have gone off-line. None of the GPS units can get a lock on any satellite."

"What? Are you sure?" This was obviously a stupid question, but Jack was still processing Tim's statement and its implications.

"Absolutely," Melissa replied. "We've tried four different units and none of them can get a satellite. We were trying to find a shop where we could get foam to line William's box with and couldn't work out why the GPS wasn't telling us where to go. Now we know why. What do you think has happened?"

Jack didn't answer, but instead took the GPS unit from Tim's hand and walked out of the door and into the garden, the other two following in his wake. Even as he walked he was trying to make sense of what they had told him, what it meant and what he could do about it. He came to a halt in the middle of the garden, the pressure beginning to building up in his chest.

He stared at the GPS unit, which of course was reporting no satellites, and Tim and Melissa looked on in silence. The pressure continued to build, forcing a tear out of one eye, until it was simply too great. Without a word he handed the now-useless piece of electronics to Tim, slumped on to the floor, put his face in his hands, and cried.

It was several minutes later before he had recovered enough to resume the conversation. Tim and Melissa had sat with him and he was now wiping his nose on a tissue which Melissa had offered without comment.

Once he was mostly wiped he gave them a twisted, apologetic smile.

Their faces reflected their understanding and Tim even squeezed his shoulder.

"What do you think has happened?" Melissa eventually asked.

"I have no idea." His voice was wobbly, but firmed up as he spoke. "Maybe the satellites haven't received a signal from their Mum and Dad in the American military. Maybe the American military are still talking to them and have told them not to share with us civilians. I don't think there's any way of knowing." There was a long pause as the trio looked at each other. Eventually Jack broke the silence.

"Well, if that's the case, we're not flying anywhere. I don't think I can fly that plane without the GPS."

"Are you sure?" Tim wanted to know. "People used to fly planes before GPS was around. It must be possible."

"So you think we absolutely can't fly if there's no GPS?" Xanthe asked Jack. She had said hardly a word to him over the last few days but was quizzing him pretty vigorously on *this* subject.

They were sitting around the kitchen table once again, having an impromptu meeting to discuss this latest development. Shane was absent-mindedly rubbing his newly-exposed leg, which looked very skinny and white next to its counterpart, but Xanthe had declared it 'OK for walking'. Tim and Melissa, who had already had this conversation with Jack, both sat back, poses mirrored, with crossed arms and crossed legs. Emily sat in the end chair watching the adults in silence as she waited for a decision to emerge. No doubt she was evaluating every option for its impact on her beloved pony.

"Well, Tim and I had this conversation earlier. Obviously people did fly before GPS so it is *possible*. I'm not an expert in this but I think a lot of pre-GPS flying was done using ground beacons to navigate, which are clearly defunct now. I think they particularly used them to home in on airports. The other thing they used were Inertial Navigators, which airliners used to have. They were a kind of poor man's GPS, but without the satellites. Not very accurate, but good enough to get you in the vicinity of the airport and from there you could use the beacon."

"So you think we might not find the airport and run out of fuel?"

"I think there's a chance of that, yes. To some degree we could navigate by looking out of the window and tracking where we are, but then there might be cloud, and there are not many notable features across the middle of Australia, so it would be easy to get off course. And even if we did find the airport, there's another issue."

"What's that?" Xanthe was still the one getting up to speed.

"I use the GPS to help fly the plane on the approach. If I was an expert pilot I probably wouldn't need it, but I use it to keep the heading straight and to tell me how far from the runway I am. I did try a manual approach yesterday and it didn't go very well. So even if we found the airport, I think the actual landing is much more dodgy without GPS."

"So the summary is that you think it's too dangerous?"

"I'm afraid so, yes. And believe me, I don't want it to be. You know that I am keen to fly, but having done the test flight I just don't think I can do it without GPS. I'm sorry."

"It's not your fault the GPS has failed," Xanthe didn't soften this statement of fact with a smile. "A pity it couldn't have lasted another week."

"Yes, although maybe lucky that it didn't last a day or two more. We wouldn't want it fail when we were in the sky."

"That's true. So what now?" Melissa asked the question.

"We originally said either air or sea, so I suppose we're now down to sea," Tim stated the obvious.

"I thought the option was to drive to Darwin and take some kind of boat to Singapore from there?" Mellissa's usually smooth face was frowning.

"Yes, we did say that," Jack agreed. "But I think we should check out boats here, so we know what we're going to do when we get to Darwin. Tim's the only one of us who has any sailing experience, so maybe he and I should go and look at some boats today so we can start planning.

The pressure was still with Jack, the homesickness only just kept at bay, but he knew that activity was the only way he could stay functional.

The broad esplanade around Darling harbour still looked strange without people, even after more than a month of nothing but deserted streets. The various shops and restaurants looked blankly down on Tim and Jack, as they strolled towards the small marina set down at the tip of the long inlet. The sun was fierce and both men wore wide brimmed hats to keep it at bay. They'd brought the dogs, which were running around sniffing everything they could find.

Jack had walked this exact piece of paving on the first night in Australia. A mid-level manager from McArthur's customer had taken the three of them, Rick, Cynthia and Jack, out for a meal. Jack remembered how Rick and he had clearly been surplus to requirements in the man's mind, although he struggled to remember the customer's name now. Andy? Dave? Something like that, he thought.

It wasn't a large marina but they'd come here just because Jack knew where it was and, without the GPS, navigation was a little trickier now. He eyed the boats, which reeked of money, as they approached.

"So do you have an idea of the kind of boat we need?" Jack asked the young man.

"I think I do. But you must bear in mind that I am not a real expert. I have done some sailing, but not as skipper on bigger boats."

Jack smiled at Tim's precise tones as he qualified his expertise. "Tim, as far as we can tell you are the best sailor in Australia at the moment.

Things that we don't know we will just have to work out, one way or another. We don't need to do it right. We just need something that works."

"Well, yes. Agreed." Tim nodded his acceptance of Jack's comment. "But have you ever heard the phrase 'Worse things happen at sea'?"

"I have. I always assumed that it referred to the old days in the British navy when it was ruled by rum, buggery and the lash, and men had to drink their own urine and eat their shipmates and so on."

"Well, yes. I think that's true. It does. But maybe in some ways we're back there."

"OK. If it comes to that, you're all welcome to eat me," Jack clapped Tim on his skinny shoulder, suddenly feeling a wave of kinship with the young Australian. "But let's see if we can avoid that, shall we? So what are we looking for?"

It turned out that there weren't many craft that met Tim's criteria in the little harbour.

"We need a sailing boat, a yacht, that's at least forty five feet long, maybe a bit bigger. And ideally is well kitted out with the kind of gadgets you need for long passages"

"Why not one of these motorboats?" Jack asked, walking up the gangplank of an enormous, sleek machine and standing on the wide deck at the rear, arms outstretched. "This thing looks pretty serious and must go faster than any sailing boat?"

"Well, yes. It will go a lot faster, Tim agreed, joining Jack. "But there are two issues. The first is range. I don't think a thing like this can go thousands of miles without re-fuelling. In fact I think it might struggle for a thousand.

"That's the first issue. The other is that I don't think these things are good when the sea gets rough. I don't have first hand experience of this, but my uncle always said that these things were dangerous when it was blowing. A sailing boat has a deep keel but one of these doesn't have that, which makes them unstable in big waves and wind."

"Are we expecting rough weather?"

"Since we can't get forecasts I think we need to be ready for anything," Tim answered, a touch primly.

"Makes sense. So there are some sailing boats over there. What gadgets are we looking for?"

"That's where my knowledge runs out," Tim admitted as they strolled down the pontoon towards the yachts. "I think the most important thing would be a decent solar panel so that it can charge the batteries without running the engine. Most big boats have things like self-steerers these days. A reasonably simple set of sails would also be good. I'd suggest a mast-furling mainsail would be better than slab reefing."

"Whatever that means," Jack muttered. They ambled past a number of yachts before Tim stopped at one.

"This is the kind of thing, I think." To Jack's untutored eye it didn't look much different to the ones they had already passed, although maybe a little bigger. It did sport a sizable solar panel on the deck, which might have been one thing that Tim liked about it. It also had a variety of ropes and deck-mounted fittings whose purpose was wholly opaque to Jack.

"Yes, this is the kind of thing." Tim hopped up into the cockpit and turned back to Jack. "Have you got the break-in kit?" Jack didn't answer, just unslung the heavy little rucksack and passed it up to Tim, before climbing over the rail himself and inspecting the large cockpit with its twin wheels and various nautical gadgets.

"We're going to struggle to get William onto this thing, Tim." Tim sheared the lock off the hatch using the bolt cutters, before passing the rucksack back to Jack.

"I don't think we can take William. I know it's tough on Emily but I don't see that we have any choice. Yachts and horses don't go together and I think taking William would be both cruel to him, because we'd have to tie him up, and also dangerous for us all. I know that's really tough on Emily, but I think it's our only option. We can either wait here indefinitely for someone to rescue us or we can go and see what's happening in the rest of the world and leave William behind."

"How fast does one of these things go, Tim?"

"Top speed is probably close to ten, but I should think we will be averaging five or six, at a guess. I've never done a really long ocean passage before."

"Knots. As in nautical miles an hour?"

"Yes. Of course."

"So that means," Jack was thinking out loud, "the two thousand miles to Darwin would take us, let's see, about four hundred hours. So that's a bit over two weeks. Which means I think you are right. I don't think we could take William on this thing." Jack spoke this last sentence rather absent-mindedly as he looked into the distance.

"So I think you, or Xanthe, need to sit down with Emily and explain to her that we can't take William. She trusts you guys," Tim said. Then asked, "What are you looking at?"

"Well," Jack said slowly, "if we took a bigger boat we might not need to explain that to Emily. What about if we took one of those?" He pointed north.

Tim followed his pointing finger. "D'you mean one of the tour boats? They will have the same problem as that big gin palace we looked at just now. They won't have enough range to get us across to Singapore."

"No beyond those, the big white one."

"Those are all tour boats and I don't think that any one of them will have the range, as I said."

"Beyond all the tour boats. The great big white one."

"You mean the cruise ship?"

"Yes, I do." There was a long pause in the conversation as they both stood in the sun and looked at the huge white ship tied up at the north end of Darling Harbour.

"You can't be serious, Jack. None of us have ever skippered anything bigger than a dinghy and you want to try and sail a cruise ship to Singapore?"

"Would it have the range?" Jack asked.

"I should think easily. But we can't possibly get it out of the harbour and crew it."

"I'm sure you're right. But will you do me a favour and indulge me? Let's just go and have a little look, shall we?"

The first problem after they had boarded the *Pacific Sun* was just finding their way to the bridge of the enormous vessel. There were signs, but they were for the benefit of passengers and not the crew, who were obviously expected to know their way to the bridge. The ship was a warren of passages and steep stairs, but eventually Jack and Tim found their way to the huge bridge and were confronted with the most fantastic view of the Sydney Harbour Bridge out of the massive windows.

They were also confronted with a rotting corpse in uniform, although whether or not it was the Captain, choosing to die on the bridge of his ship, they could not tell.

At the side of the bridge was a kind of balcony, which gave a clear view of the entire flank of the vessel and so between them Jack and Tim dragged the corpse outside and tipped it over the rail. It was a long drop and it made quite a splash, although neither man stayed to watch it bobbing in the ocean.

They turned their attention to the myriad of controls, dials and screens that festooned the bridge. The screens were dark and the dials all sat at zero.

"Do you think we can start the engines?" Jack asked Tim.

"I don't know," came the reply. "But a ship like this will run on shore power when it's tied up, I would think. But I'm guessing it has some kind of power generator separate from the main engines. The first challenge would be to see if we can start that. If there's not enough juice left in the batteries to start the generator then I think this ship is staying right where it is."

Tim spent another fifteen minutes switching switches and reading labels and pressing buttons before he was rewarded. A very slight, but noticeable, tremor ran through the deck under their feet and there was a chorus of beeps as the equipment around them sprang to life. Lights also came on in the ceiling, screens showed start up messages and dials flicked to their correct reading.

Tim looked around grinning. "Looks like there was enough power. Maybe there are solar panels to keep them topped up or maybe they just held enough."

"Well done, Tim. That's fantastic. I suppose that this ship is now officially the comfiest place in Australia. Do you think we could start the main engines?"

"I should think so, now we've got power. Let's just run the generator for a few minutes and let everything settle down before we try." Ten minutes later they repeated their success with the main engines. As Tim pressed the main engine start, a large button under a transparent plastic cover, the lights on the bridge dimmed. This lasted a few seconds before a distinct vibration throbbed through the deck. The engines were as much felt as heard, although Jack rushed out on the balcony and could see smoke rising from one of the huge funnels behind the bridge.

"Well done, again. So that's the engines ready to drive?"

"I think so, yes. I'll give a little nudge forward to test before we shut them down." Tim was grinning from ear to ear.

Twenty Five

"Jesus, Jack. What is it with you and size? First you want to take the biggest plane at the airport and now you want to take the biggest boat. Are you trying to compensate for something?" Thankfully Xanthe smiled as she asked this question, taking some of the sting out of it, although it still made Jack squirm a little bit.

"Well. Firstly it was not the largest plane in the airport. There were a couple that were a bit bigger," Jack tried a smile in return. "The one I chose was just big enough to satisfy my ambitions. And secondly, I am worried about your comfort and I think that this ship will just about be comfortable enough for you guys." There was a bit of laughter at this, from Melissa and Tim at any rate.

"On a more serious note," Jack continued, "there are quite a few things we still need to answer about this ship. Although Tim started the engines, and we know it has fuel for a good long voyage, we don't know if we could refuel it if and when we want to. We also don't know that we can get it out of the harbour, and there are some serious safety concerns."

"Such as?" Melissa asked.

"The main issue is what happens if it stops working," Tim took over.

He'd been sharing his thoughts with Jack on the way home and so Jack let him speak. "On a big ship like that there are probably thousands of maintenance jobs. Most of them won't be disastrous if they are ignored, but some might be. That means that there is a distinct possibility that even if we get the ship out of the harbour, at some point on the voyage it will stop working."

"Leaving us adrift at sea," Xanthe pointed out.

"Exactly," Tim continued. So the only way we can really be safe is to make sure we have a way to get to shore if and when it conks out."

"How long do you think it might run for?" Shane asked.

"There's no way of knowing," Tim replied. "Could be an hour. Could be a day. Could be months or even years. Since we don't know what we don't know there's no way to tell."

"So how will we get to shore 'if and when' that happens?" Xanthe prodded.

"Jack had some thoughts on that. Jack?"

"Yes. Two things occur to me. Firstly the thing is bristling with lifeboats. Tim and I stuck our heads into one and they are enormous, with seats for loads of people. Maybe a hundred. So the first job is to find out the range of one of those and then, if necessary, fit an extra fuel tank to one to make it enough. Then once we have a big enough range we just need to make sure that we never get further from land than the super-lifeboat can travel."

"That sounds like it will take weeks. And didn't we say we would drive to Darwin and get a boat from there?"

"We did, but perhaps the *Pacific Sun* is too good an opportunity to pass up. It'll take us weeks to sail from Darwin to Singapore anyway, but a cruise ship can go a lot faster, so total journey time is probably quite a bit less.

"It's fully filled with fuel and seems ready to go. It could get us to Darwin in a week and then be ready to motor on from there. We need to be ready in case it doesn't keep running, but we hope that it will. Getting it ready will take a little while, but we'd have to get a boat ready in Darwin anyway." Jack looked around the group and could see nods of agreement and so carried on.

"And we've a few other things to do as well as get a lifeboat ready."

"Like what?" Shane asked.

"I think there are three main tasks," Jack answered. "The first is the one I've just described – getting a lifeboat ready for the eventuality that the ship gives up on us."

"Will William be able to fit on the lifeboat?" Emily broke her silence.

"They are easily big enough for William," Jack answered. "So we just need to remove some seats so there is space for him."

"How would we persuade him to get into a lifeboat?" Tim asked.

"If we need to knock him out with Ketamine and drag him then we'll do that." Jack gave Emily a smile and she allowed a small smile in return. "In fact the deck where the lifeboats are is pretty huge and would make a good place for William to live while we're on board.

"So task number one: Lifeboats. Task number two: provisioning the ship. We need to make sure that we've plenty of food for all of us for a good long time."

"And for William," Xanthe pointed out.

"And for William, which brings me on to task number three. The inside of the ship is not really designed for horses so we're going to have to find a way to get William on board. The only method I can think of – and I'm open to other suggestions – is a crane."

"So. Lifeboats, food, William," Xanthe summarised. "Anything else?" There was a touch of sarcasm, or perhaps scepticism in Xanthe's voice, but she didn't sound like she'd totally made up her mind.

"There's one more. Navigation." Tim announced. The young man hadn't mentioned this on the way home and so after a pause Jack prompted him.

"Go on, Tim."

"Well, navigation is primarily the art of working out where you are," Tim continued, sounding like he was giving a university lecture. "Obviously people mostly use GPS these days but without that there are three methods we can use to find out where we are at sea. The first is taking bearings on known points, like islands or churches or things like that, which you can then draw on a chart to find out your location. The second is dead reckoning, where you extrapolate from a known position based on course and distance travelled. I'm reasonably familiar with these two methods, but the problem is that they only work when you're quite near shore, so you can see features, and DR becomes inaccurate pretty quickly as errors build up."

"So what's the third method?" Melissa was trying to encourage Tim to get to the point without sounding too impatient.

"The third method is what they always used to use, of course, but it's notoriously difficult to do. It's astro-navigation. Using the stars and planets to work out your position on the ocean. The problem is that I have never done any and I have no idea how to do it. In a big ship, like that cruise liner, we will need to stay far off shore, which means that fixes will be hard to take. And that means that I think one of us needs to learn the basics of astro so we can work out where we are. We do have the advantage that we have accurate clocks, so that should help."

"When you say, 'one of us', you mean you, right?" Jack said this with a smile on his face, but Tim knew that this was a serious question.

"I'll do it if you like. I'd have to find a book or two, and some equipment, but I'm sure I can do that."

"If you want to take it on then I think you should make it your number one priority. The rest of us will work on the other three things."

"OK. It's a deal," Tim agreed.

"There's one thing that occurs to me that you haven't mentioned," Xanthe said slowly. The group looked at her in the candlelight and waited for her to carry on. "Where are we going to sleep on this ship?" Jack and Tim looked at each other. Tim looked confused and Jack too had no inkling where Xanthe might be going with this.

"This ship can sleep thousands," Tim answered cautiously. "We thought we would just take some cabins. We didn't look but I bet there are some really nice ones we could use."

"But you didn't look in them?"

"Well. No. We didn't. We started the engines and had a brief look at the lifeboats. Then we came back here."

"So what about the cabin's current occupants? Is another job clearing the bodies out of the cabins and cleaning them up so we can use them?" There was a silence after this. That didn't sound like fun.

"You're right. That may need doing. I'll check out the situation tomorrow and, if necessary, I'll clear some cabins out," Jack volunteered.

"I've got to say, I'm not totally convinced," Xanthe admitted. "But let's all go down to the ship tomorrow and take a look."

The next morning after breakfast, during which Jack noted that Xanthe appeared to at least be talking to him again, the six humans, leaving dogs, horses and chickens behind, set off for Darling Harbour, and it didn't take long to establish that they were in luck. The *Pacific Sun* had obviously not been on a cruise at the time of the plague since all of the passenger cabins were empty. The crew cabins had occupants and they found a couple of corpses in the engine room, but the fact that the ship was not packed with dead passengers was a massive bonus. The generator was still running and it seemed like luxury to be able to switch on lights and not have to carry lamps into the windowless depths of the ship. The tour took a while as they tramped through a seemingly endless succession of cavernous restaurants and lengthy corridors.

Exploring the upper part of the ship they found an even bigger bonus. On the deck above the bridge and lifeboats was a row of suites that were absurdly luxurious. Each had two huge double beds, a sparkling bathroom and balcony high above the sea.

It was hard not to be impressed and the six survivors, who had stuck together on their tour of the ship, all flopped down on various beds and chairs.

"OK. This does it for me. I'm convinced," Xanthe declared. I think I'm prepared to tough it out in one of these rooms. And anybody who says we should do anything else is just plain crazy. This is how we are going to travel."

That week the group worked hard. Melissa came up with the suggestion that they could lower a lifeboat directly onto the dock. This allowed them to both fit it out and use it to hoist William up into the ship, and so that was what they did. They unbolted most of the seats out of the lifeboat and then Shane and Jack loaded and unloaded a truckload of straw and hay, under Emily's instructions. They used some of the bales to cradle the lifeboat as it lay on the dock and, in turn, used the lifeboat to haul loads up into the ship. They stacked bales on what they referred to as William's deck, although the passenger signs referred to it as the 'Lido Deck'. There certainly were a lot of straw and straw for one smallish horse and they didn't get it all moved.

"Let's do the rest tomorrow," Jack announced after the second load. Shane looked relieved by this and, like Jack, removed his gloves and sat on a nearby bale.

"It sure seems like a lot to eat, even for a horse. Does he really need all of this?" The teenager waved his hand vaguely.

"He only eats the hay. The straw is for his comfort."

"Huh," was all Shane managed in reply.

"And anyway, we did the calculation and this is what we need to be sure of not running out any time soon. Let's go and get a drink and then head out to Saltview and get William."

Although it had taken three days they were now ready to move William himself and Jack was amazed at how smoothly this operation went. They had a wide and strong board, which Jack had braced with some scaffolding poles, to use as a ramp and William, with only a small shot of Ketamine ("To make him feel good," Xanthe said), seemed happy enough to be led up into the lifeboat by Emily. He was slightly more reluctant to go down the ramp at the other end, but with a bit of coaxing and some scolding from Emily, he ventured down on the deck itself, and that was that.

One more trip to Saltview brought the full quota of chickens and a diversion to a pet shop allowed them to load a pallet of sacks marked 'Layer's Pellets' into the horsebox with the chickens. These were all transferred into the lifeboat and hoisted to the deck to join William. The two dogs accompanied this whole operation and while Shane, Jack and Emily worked on animals and their provisions, Xanthe and Melissa had been working on human provisions, although this had involved more time doing an inventory of the ship's contents than collecting more loot.

Emily had turned the ship's pizzeria into a stable, by spreading some straw on the wooden floor and breaking a bale of hay apart and William seemed more than content with his new lodging. What he would think of it all once they were at sea was hard to tell, but they would have to wait and see what happened. The chickens wandered around the deck pecking at things they thought might be food until Jack, Xanthe and Emily rounded them up and shut them in with William for the night.

After that there didn't seem any reason to be staying at Saltview any longer, so the six of them packed up their various possessions and move permanently to the suites on the *Pacific Sun*. That first evening they heated up a big meal of various tinned food, accompanied by fresh bread and couple of bottles of wine and sat at a table on the deck, eating and watching the sun set.

"So how long will it take us to get to Singapore?" Melissa asked.

"I think around eight or nine days," Tim answered immediately. "It depends on what the most fuel-efficient speed is, but I'm guessing around fifteen knots, which means we can cover the two thousand miles to Darwin in five and half days. Assuming we go all day and all night."

"So will we have to work shifts? They call them watches in the navy, don't they?" Xanthe asked, stroking Rufus, who she had lifted on to her lap.

"Yes, we will. Although we can slow right down, if the person on watch is uncomfortable. I'm thinking that we will come nearer shore maybe once a day, if we can, to try and get a sighting on something and confirm where we are. But most of the time we can be far out to sea and so there's nothing to hit. That's why the range on the lifeboat is important."

"How's the navigation work going?" Jack asked, since he'd hardly seen Tim over the last few days.

"Not bad, I think. The instruments on this thing are pretty sophisticated, even without GPS, so a combination of visual fixes and dead reckoning is going to be better than I first thought. But we need the astro-navigation as a back up, so I'm still working on it."

"Is it hard?"

"It's as much art as science. Getting a good reading takes practice, but I've done quite a few sightings. Getting latitude is reasonably easy, but I haven't got as far as getting a longitude fix yet. I've got a book from the library that I am working through, and I've got a sextant from a boat at the big marina. I had to look in loads of yachts before I found one that had a sextant though. Took me ages."

"What's a sextant?" Emily asked, the question that was clearly behind Shane's frown as well.

"It's a device for measuring how far above the horizon an object is. Like a star, or the sun. It's pretty cool, actually. I'll show you tomorrow. I've got to re-iterate that all this work could turn out to be a waste of time. Getting this thing out of here without touching the bottom is going to be tricky. If I run it aground then we'll be back at square one."

"If you go slowly couldn't you just rub up against the bottom a bit and be OK?" Melissa commented.

"Not really. The ship's so heavy that even a low speed contact is likely to hole it. I obviously will go slowly, but just bear in mind that this is not going to be easy and might end in tears. Or at least salt water. We should be ready to abandon ship until we're well clear of the coast. Normally big ships have skilled captains, specialist pilots for the harbour and a tug or two to help pull it around, and even then they sometimes go aground. Like that Italian ship that sunk. We don't have any of those things, so it's hard to be confident."

"Do you think it's even possible? Should we even be trying it?" Jack asked, slightly alarmed by Tim's negative tone.

"Oh, yes, it's possible. If we needed to reverse out then I think we might be struggling, but because we can drive out forwards we can edge out gently and I think it could be done. Maybe. I think it's a bit like your test flight in the Boeing. The theory says it's possible but we won't know for sure until we try. I should mention as well that Melissa has been working out the radios." He smiled across at her and she returned his grin, with none of the self consciousness that had dominated her demeanour a few weeks previously.

"I'm guessing you haven't spoken to anyone or you might have mentioned it," Xanthe commented drily.

"No, I haven't. Tim thinks that the VHS doesn't have the range and that the ship uses satellites for long-range communication. I've tried that as well but haven't been able to raise anyone yet. I'll keep trying. It's pretty complicated." She shrugged a self-deprecating shrug.

"How is the lifeboat work going?" Tim interjected.

"Now that we've got William aboard," Jack gestured towards the pony, tied to the rail by Emily since he had been keen to join their meal. William looked back at them hopefully. "The next task is to improve the range. Shane's got an important job on that front."

"Yeah. Tomorrow I'm going to lower one of the other lifeboats into the sea and drive it around until I've used enough fuel to estimate the range." Shane sounded surprisingly keen on a job which Jack thought was going to be quite boring. But then again, the teenager did like to drive things, Jack had noticed. "Then we will know how much we need to put in. Jack says the target is a hundred miles, but we'll have to see how possible that is. Right, Jack?"

"That's right. The boats run on normal diesel as best as I can judge, so we need to work out how much extra we're going to need. I don't know whether it will be a few jerry cans or something more."

The group continued to talk and as darkness fell the ship shrank from an enormous building, so large and solid it was hard to believe it was floating, to an island of lights that was totally alone in the vast Australian night. By the time it was properly dark Emily was yawning and the meal was over. Xanthe took Emily up to her room, while the other four cleared away the meal and released William, shutting him back in his stable for the night.

Jack headed to his room but stopped short of actually undressing. He was caught in indecision, but, after a few moments pacing, he plucked up his courage and went back out into the corridor. Without giving himself a chance to change his mind he knocked on the door of Xanthe's suite.

She answered, wearing a white towelling robe, and raised an eyebrow.

"It's a nice evening," he started a little nervously. "I wonder if you'd like to join me for a drink? A nightcap."

Xanthe eyed him suspiciously before asking, a little harshly, "Hanky panky?"

Jack pursed his lips and shook his head. After a couple more seconds Xanthe took a deep breath, almost more of a sigh before saying. "OK. What the fuck. Come in here. There's drinks in the fridge." She stepped back and allowed him to pass, gesturing at the fridge. He headed straight over there.

"What would you like?"

"I think I'll go for a gin and tonic," she answered, opening the sliding glass doors to the balcony and stepping out. Jack found himself wondering what, if anything, she was wearing under that robe, although he did his best to squash the thought. He made the drinks, G and T for her and whisky for him and took them out to where she stood on the dark balcony. She accepted her drink with a nod but continued to stare out into the darkness. He leant on the rail next to her and for a few minutes they both just sipped their drinks.

"Xanthe. I'm sorry about the other night," Jack eventually broke the silence, but Xanthe didn't answer immediately. When she did it was in that detached voice that he'd heard quite a bit of in the last few days.

"No, Jack. It's me who should be sorry. You did the right thing."

Jack didn't know how to respond to that and so the silence resumed while he worked out what he wanted to say.

"The thing is I don't want to fall out with you. I really care about you. It's just that..."

"Sex is out of the question?" Xanthe interrupted.

"Look. I know that it is likely that my family is dead," just saying these words was painful but Jack knew he needed to start preparing himself. "But until I know for sure, one way or the other I have to focus on that. You must understand." Xanthe glanced across at him, met his eyes for a few moments before looking out into the night again. When she spoke the hard voice was gone and she sounded more like her old self.

"Look Jack. I'm sorry about the other night. I shouldn't have done what I did."

"You've nothing to be sorry about," Jack answered, but she gave a small and slightly ironic laugh.

"Well I am sorry. And embarrassed as well, I suppose. But I'll get over it."

"Friends?" Jack proffered his glass and smiled at her and, after slight hesitation she clinked her glass against his and gave him a slightly twisted smile in return.

"Friends. Of course." And they both took a drink and leant back on the rail.

After a few more minutes of silence, rather more companionable than the first, Xanthe held up her glass.

"It's funny how things have changed, isn't it?"

"Maybe not that funny. How do you mean?"

"Well. The things we had to worry about before are all gone. And now we have a completely new set of things. Like this drink, or this room, for that matter. This would all have been out of my league back when we had to pay for it."

"Mine too."

"But now we own the whole bloody ship and all we have to worry about is driving it and staying alive. There used to be other people to worry about that stuff. And all we had to worry about was paying for it all."

"I know. It's hard to adjust to the new rules, even now." Jack took a sip of his own drink.

"The stars haven't changed," she commented.

"No. They won't get the news for some time yet." Xanthe glanced over at him and he smiled back.

"When you say it like that I suppose it puts it all in perspective," she said, thoughtfully. "You're a funny one, Jack Stevens. A lot of stuff seems to be going on in that head of yours. Which is lucky for me and the others."

"Maybe not so lucky. We don't know how all of this is going to turn out."

Xanthe was silent for a few seconds, gaze focused out into the night. Eventually she asked, "What was your job title? Back before it happened."

Jack was rather wrong-footed by this change in direction. "My job title? Senior Systems Analyst. Sounds stupid now doesn't it? It's only been a month but it all seems so long ago."

"Yes it does seem long ago. Me pointing that shotgun at you on the road when we met seems like another life. Although in some ways you've been promoted pretty rapidly."

"What do you mean?"

"Well, just over a month ago you were a Senior Systems Analyst and now you're President of Australia. Or maybe King or Emperor would be a more fitting title." She was smiling gently as she said it, her face lit softly by the cabin lights.

"Much as I've always wanted to be an Emperor, I'm afraid I'm going to have to disagree with you. I'm not in charge of anything."

"Of course you are," she said shortly. "If you're not leading this expedition, then who is? And don't say Tim or me, because we are both looking to you."

"That's kind, although like I say, I don't really agree. Would you like your Emperor to get you another gin and tonic?"

"There's an offer a girl doesn't get every day. Sure."

When Jack re-joined her with the fresh drinks, Xanthe accepted hers and then said, "And so now that you're the ultimate authority, you get to decide how things should be."

"I think," Jack said thoughtfully, "that we're all still having trouble adjusting to the way things are. Ben was quickest to realise how much had changed. Have you thought how weird it will be if we find other people and go back to normal life, or something like it? I don't know if I could do that."

"I could, although it won't be like it was before. Even if some places have been affected less by the plague, or even not at all, nowhere will be the same. There'll always be before and after, for everybody."

"That's true," Jack agreed, and they lapsed into silence again for another few minutes.

"They might still be alive, you know. Jane and your daughters."

"I know that, but I have to be careful not to hope too much."

"I understand. Still. You're doing everything you can to get back to them. You can't do more than that."

"Actually I could. I could have gone and got a plane and set off on day two or three, instead of waiting a month. I'd be back by now."

"Maybe. Or maybe you'd be dead." She gave him a serious look. "If it was me I'd want you come home as quickly as you could, but I'd want you to keep yourself safe. And anyway, what about the rest of us? Like it or not we're in this together." And, of course, Jack knew that to be true.

Twenty Six

The next day was the twentieth of December, five days before Christmas. It started well for Jack but was to take a turn for the worse later on.

He was woken by Xanthe knocking, before putting her head around the unlocked door and asking him if he was coming for a run. He told her that he was and scrambled into his running kit, to join her for a resumption of their morning routine.

They got off the ship and ran around the point under the harbour bridge and got as far as the Opera House before turning back. Little was said on the run but Jack was happy they had managed to put the incident of the other night behind them. He was confident that he had done the right thing, although there was small part of his mind which asked him what would happen if they did find the other side of the world deserted. However much he disliked that calculating part of his nature, the question was out there and would remain so until he walked into his house in Fleet. One way or the other.

On the return journey they had the brief shock of seeing a pedestrian on the pavement but very quickly identified the mystery person as Melissa, who told them she had taken to walking in the mornings.

The girl gave them both a big smile and it was hard not to feel slightly buoyed up by the new-found confidence she was displaying.

Back on board the *Pacific Sun* they both went for a luxurious shower before arriving refreshed and ready for the day at the restaurant where they had been eating their meals.

Nobody else was present (apart from the two dogs) as Jack and Xanthe helped themselves to breakfast, but while they were eating, sitting outside in the morning sun, Shane appeared, looking a bit bleary eyed. Jack had to wonder what the teenager had been up to that had obviously kept him up a long time after they had all said goodnight, but decided against quizzing him about it. If Shane was to carry adult responsibilities then he also had the right to spend his evenings as he chose. No doubt there were plenty of DVDs on this ship and Jack's best guess was that Shane had found some of them and was enjoying the fact that they had twenty four hour electricity on board.

"Morning, Sunshine," Xanthe greeted Shane as he flopped into a chair at the table and surveyed his breakfast options. These amounted to bread, baked yesterday by Melissa, with various choices of spread, and a pot of coffee. He looked like the short walk from his suite had exhausted him.

"Morning," he grunted, glancing up at Xanthe, then at Jack and then back at Xanthe. Was it obvious that Xanthe and Jack were back on speaking terms? Had it been obvious that they hadn't been? Jack doubted that Shane was overly sensitive to vibes in the atmosphere around him.

"Coffee? I just made it," Jack offered Shane, who grunted and nodded. "So are you looking forward to driving a lifeboat around for a few hours?"

"We've all got to do our bit," Shane replied, but softened it with half a smile.

331

At that point a small skinny girl led a pony around the corner and joined them.

"We're going to need a wheel barrow," Emily announced. "Otherwise we're all going to be treading in a lot of horse shit." All three at the table couldn't help laughing at the matter of fact adult tone that came out of Emily's mouth. She looked slightly offended by this.

"Well, we will. William isn't house trained. Or boat trained, and it's hard to muck out his stable without a wheelbarrow. It'll need to be small one because I'm not that strong."

"That sounds like a plan," Xanthe answered, trying to get back to a straight face. Why don't you and me go and look for one? Maybe Melissa will come to. We can do a girl's outing."

"And here comes the aforementioned girl," Jack commented, as Tim and Melissa joined the group.

"At last. Everybody have a nice lie in?" Tim grinned round at the group. "We've been up on the bridge. Melissa and I were up early. I've been working on the navigation equipment since then. I think I'm getting the hang of it."

"Nice walk, Melissa?" Xanthe asked.

"Yes, it was. Weird to think that soon we'll be confined to the ship though."

"It is indeed," the nurse agreed.

They cleared breakfast and Tim headed back to his domain, the bridge. The three girls left on a wheelbarrow mission, with some evasive comments from Xanthe that they needed to "pick up some other stuff." Jack didn't enquire any further.

That left Shane and Jack to get on with lowering a lifeboat into the water to find out what kind of range they had. This operation was fairly straightforward, with clear printed instructions on how to work the hoists from which the lifeboat dangled, and also their prior experience of lowering 'William's boat' onto the dock.

"You get in and I'll just lower you down," Jack suggested.

"OK," Shane agreed and hopped on to the swinging lifeboat. A few seconds later he was descending towards the glinting ocean.

Once the boat was floating far below the deck on which Jack stood, Shane tried the engine, which fired up first time, and then unhooked the hoists so he was floating free.

"Can you hear me?" Jack shouted down, over the muted thudding of the diesel.

"Yup," came back up from below.

"Drive around for as long as it takes to burn enough fuel. Until you think you can tell how long it will last and how far it will go. It's ten forty-five now," Jack held up his watch and tapped it. "I'll time it but you watch the miles on the log as well. OK?"

Shane gave a thumbs-up.

"And when you're done, tie up on a dock down there," Jack pointed down into Darling Harbour where the tour boats were tied up, but where there were quite a few vacant pontoons. This got another thumbs-up from Shane, showing he'd understood.

"OK. One last thing. Don't drive too fast. Not flat out. It uses too much fuel. Just go at a speed that seems comfortable for the boat. OK? I'll be here so I'll see you later."

One last thumbs-up and then Shane ducked inside the covered lifeboat and gunned the engine. The blocky craft moved away from the side of the *Pacific Sun*, picking up speed, with its wake spreading wide across the harbour behind it. Jack watched for a few minutes as the boat curved across the harbour, before he descended through the ship and out onto the dock.

He judged that it would take two more loads to get all the bales up on the ship and so he worked steadily, pacing himself. It was hot and he sweated freely, soaking his T-shirt but he pressed on. After a while he retrieved a deliciously cool bottle of water from inside the ship and worked on in the heat. He could hear the diesel engine of the lifeboat swelling and fading as Shane moved about the harbour. Occasionally Jack could even see the boat as it went under the Sydney Harbour Bridge, but mostly it was hidden by the bulk of the *Pacific Sun*. Both dogs were with him, but had found a shady spot to lie and watch his efforts.

By the time Jack had stacked the bales in the lifeboat, hoisted it up and then unloaded onto the stack that was growing on the deck, he was tired. He went round to the other side of the ship and leant on the rail, sipping water. It was after midday and Jack still had another load to do, albeit a smaller one. The sun reflected fiercely off the sea below, but Jack spent a minute squinting into the light to see if he could see Shane. There was no sign of the little lifeboat and neither could Jack hear its diesel engine. *Had he already tied up at a pontoon?* Jack wondered. Anyway, it was too hot to stand in the sun, so he retreated into the shade for the rest of his short break. He took a ten-minute rest and gave Rufus and Alf a drink before lowering the lifeboat, dogs and all, back on the dock and getting back to work.

The second load was smaller than the first, and so it was only about three-quarters of an hour before Jack was once again standing on William's deck looking out over the ocean. It was still hot, and there was still no sign of Shane.

"Bloody idiot," Jack muttered under his breath as he scanned the north shoreline for a moving dot. He could see nothing stirring, other than the sea and the birds, and so he stomped up to the bridge to see if Tim had seen where Shane had got to.

"Umm, no," Tim admitted. "I saw him earlier on but I've been working on these charts and haven't been looking." Tim indicated the table he was sitting at which was strewn with paper charts.

"Mmm, I hope all is well. D'you want some lunch?"

"Sure. Let me finish up here and I'll be down in five minutes."

"Aye, aye, skipper."

By the time Tim and Jack had finished lunch there was still no sign of either Shane or the three girls. The two men went back up to the bridge and scanned the section of Sydney Harbour they could see from that vantage point using binoculars, but there was no sign of the missing lifeboat.

"He left here at quarter to eleven. That's nearly three hours ago. I have to admit that I'm starting to worry a little bit. Maybe he ran out of fuel or something. I should have told him to stay in sight. I just assumed he would."

"Do you think we should go and look for him? We could use one of those big RIBs that they used for tours of the harbour." Tim pointed back behind the ship, although there was no view that way from the bridge.

"What's a RIB? One of those speedboats?"

"Yes. The speedboats."

"OK. Let's leave a message for the girls and do that."

They shut the dogs back in the restaurant thinking that they wouldn't enjoy a speedboat ride, wrote out a message and taped it to the rail of the gangplank. It was then five-minute walk down to the tour boats. These were of all shapes and sizes, but among them were a couple of large speedboats with rows of seats for many passengers and two enormous outboards on the back of both. Unfortunately when they hopped on board Tim and Jack found they needed keys to start the things up and since the keys were probably hidden in the tour sales booth, Jack had to jog back to the *Pacific Sun* to retrieve his break-in kit. That done, with more sweat soaking through his T-shirt, they decided it would be quicker to just break into one of the smaller cruiser boats that were lined up on the wharf.

They chose one and its padlocked wheelhouse offered little resistance to the experienced looters. It was a catamaran; about fifty feet long, and looked sleek and fast to Jack's eyes.

"You get us untied while I get the engines started," Tim suggested and Jack complied, freeing ropes that didn't seem vital for keeping the craft against the dock until he was down to one at each end. As he was doing this the boat's engines rumbled into life and Tim stuck his head out of the window of the wheelhouse.

"OK. You can cast off when you're ready."

Jack once again obeyed and in moments Tim was backing the big catamaran out of its berth and they were on their way. Jack climbed the companionway and joined Tim as they picked up speed.

"Wow. This is fast." Tim sounded a little nervous as well as impressed.

"That's good. Which way shall we go?"

"Let's try down here first. I definitely saw Shane go this way earlier. Although I also saw him come out again." Tim pointed to a wide opening that was becoming visible on their left, even though the main body of Sydney Harbour and the famous bridge were some way ahead of them. The inlet branched and they took the larger of the two options, which branched again. And again.

Tim and Jack searched for two hours before returning briefly to the *Pacific Sun*. They hoped to find Shane asking them where they'd been, but of the teenager there was no sign. The three girls were back, but had also seen no sign of Shane and so after a brief discussion and a cold drink they took some bottled water and set off again into the labyrinth that Sydney Harbour was turning out to be.

They searched until dusk but found no sign of Shane or the lifeboat. They motored at speed through an endless series of bays and inlets, scanning the shoreline for the lifeboat and, although they both had several false alarms, each time they approached the craft it turned out to be another boat, which just resembled the one they were looking for.

As the light faded over the water and the heat of the day was replaced with a chill wind, driven by the forward speed of the catamaran, Tim and Jack made their way back to the cruise ship. Their hope that somehow Shane had found his way back was crushed as they were greeted by a shake of Xanthe's head.

"So. Let's go through the possibilities and then we can make a plan of attack for tomorrow." The entire remaining group were standing on the bridge of the *Pacific Sun*, from where they had a great view of the dark harbour. Xanthe sounded worried but purposeful.

"First option is that he went ashore for some reason, and either tied up or just left the lifeboat," Tim replied.

"And although we don't know why," Jack added in, "the reasons break down into those that will involve him coming back here and those that don't. It's possible that, for whatever reason, he has decided not to come with us on our, um, cruise."

"He'd tell us before he left, wouldn't he?" Melissa sounded unsure.

"He might or he might not," Xanthe was matter-of-fact. "We have to face the fact that none of us know him very well and so it's hard to guess. I know that teenagers will do almost anything to avoid an embarrassing scene, so he might have decided he just couldn't face the debate and would rather just quietly slip away. What do you think, Jack?"

"I have no idea. Yes, I suppose we don't know him very well, so he might have left without telling us. He could certainly be moody. Sometimes quite hyper and other times, well, I suppose sullen is the word. And, of course, there's the whole religion thing." He paused, slightly embarrassed by lumping such a big topic into such a dismissive sentence. He tried again. "Although he's not raised it much, he was obviously a bit shocked that we were all, you know, unbelievers – if that's the right word."

"That's true," Xanthe frowned. "And because of that it's possible that he decided to slip away but may change his mind when his mood changes. How did he seem when you last saw him, Jack?"

"Pretty cheerful, actually. Seemed very positive and helpful. Keen to get on, I thought."

"OK. So the other possibility is that Shane has got himself into some kind of difficulty, and he wants to come back but for some reason he can't." Xanthe looked around, eyebrow raised to invite comment.

"And if we apply triage to that option, then it's probably the option where he's in difficulty and needs our help that we need to think about," Jack pointed out.

"What do you mean?" asked Melissa.

"What's triage?" Emily was also curious.

"It's a nursing term," Xanthe answered for Jack. "It's how you prioritise which patients to deal with first. Patients who might die without help come top, but patients who will get better on their own or ones who will die whatever you do, come later."

"Do you think Shane might be dead?" the little girl asked.

"We don't know, Emily," Xanthe's voice was gentle. "I'm sure he's fine, but Jack's suggesting that we work on the assumption that Shane needs our help, and I think that's a good suggestion."

"The most likely issue is probably mechanical," Tim ventured. "The lifeboat might have conked out and he's just drifting, maybe too far away to swim to shore."

"Agreed. It's also possible that he's not well and so either put the boat ashore or left it drifting," was Jack's suggestion.

"Either way we have to search for the lifeboat. Let's look at the charts and divide up where we are going to look. Then we can get an early night and start at first light in the morning."

The evening meal was a subdued affair and they all made for an early bed, with no social chit-chat or setting the world to rights.

Jack was woken early by the beeping of his alarm and he rolled out of bed with a slight feeling of foreboding over-shadowing his mood. Soon after that all five humans and both dogs were assembled on the bridge once again.

Melissa had brought a loaf of bread and some jam and they all helped themselves while Tim went through what they were planning in terms of search. It was a simple plan, dividing Sydney Harbour into two halves with the Harbour Bridge as the dividing line. They would split up and systematically tour the myriad of bays and inlets that comprised the harbour, gathering back at the *Pacific Sun* at midday for food and fuel.

"Shouldn't I stay here?" Emily suggested, munching her bread and jam. "That way if Shane comes back they'll be someone to, you know, say what's going on."

Jack and Xanthe exchanged a look that made it clear they shared an opinion on this suggestion. Xanthe answered, "I don't think so, Emily. I think you should come with Jack and me. We'll leave a message for Shane so if he comes back he knows to stay here."

They shut up the dogs, who would not be a help on this venture, and made their way down through the ship, piling into two cars that were parked on the dock. These scooted them down to the waterfront. Jack then snapped the padlock off the door of the sales booth and, sure enough, there was a key safe to which he also applied his break-in tools.

The first of the big RIBs didn't start as the batteries appeared to be flat, but the second did and so Jack, Xanthe and Emily boarded the big catamaran, while Tim and Melissa took the RIB. The two groups headed off, the RIB passing under the bridge to search the east harbour while the other three took the west half.

They searched seemingly endless bays and channels that morning. Scanning the shoreline and examining thousands of moored boats, but of Shane and the lifeboat there was no sign. The sun beat down on them and Xanthe insisted on regular smearings of suncream on both Jack and Emily, despite the fact that they were sheltered in the wheelhouse of the catamaran. They returned to the dock at midday and Tim and Melissa's RIB was already tied up at the pontoon, with the young pair's disconsolate body language clearly showing what they had found without words being necessary. They spent an hour refuelling the two craft by pumping directly out of the tanks of two of their vehicles and then they were on their way again.

The afternoon was the same. Jack had no idea that Sydney harbour was such an extensive waterway. The crenulations seemed endless, although he marked the chart as they went, and by three in the afternoon he could see that they would finish searching it all before the light failed.

In fact they scanned the last bay and its quota of moored pleasure boats at about five o'clock and were back at the *Pacific Sun* less than thirty minutes later. The RIB was, once again, already tied up with, Tim and Melissa visible sitting in the Mitsubishi ute. Tim climbed out as they approached and came down to the pontoon to help tie up the catamaran.

"We found the lifeboat," he called across the water as Xanthe was preparing to throw a rope across the gap. The call was clearly audible to Jack through the open door of the wheelhouse. Xanthe called back, although Jack didn't catch what she said.

"No. No sign. Nothing," Tim answered her.

Once the catamaran was loosely tied to the dock Jack shut down the engine and joined Tim, Xanthe and Emily where they stood on the dock, lit by the sinking sun.

"You found the lifeboat?"

"Yes. But no sign of Shane."

"Where was it?"

"Round the corner in Spring Cove, near Manly. I can show you on the chart. It was just floating a couple of hundred yards from the shore. I went on board but couldn't start the engine. It looked like the fuel tank was totally empty."

"Jesus. Right, let's head back to the *Pacific Sun* and get something to eat. We can talk there about what to do."

Twenty Seven

"So there's two scenarios I can see." Xanthe spoke from where she was sprawled on a chair, as they sat around a table on William's deck. "Either Shane went ashore voluntarily and just abandoned the lifeboat."

"Leaving the engine running," interjected Jack.

"Leaving the engine running," she agreed. "And if he went ashore on purpose he is either planning to come back or he isn't. And there's not really much we can do. The other possibility is that he was forced to abandon the lifeboat."

"Or abandoned it by mistake," Jack pointed out. "He could have either fallen off or maybe gone ashore for some reason, but perhaps didn't tie the boat up properly and it drifted off."

"Agreed," Xanthe nodded. "And if any of those are the case we have to assume that he will want to re-join us and just hasn't got back yet."

"That's assuming he is, well, capable of re-joining," Tim said. They all digested those words for a few seconds.

"Tim, do you think the lifeboat would have drifted far if Shane abandoned it yesterday? Or would it just float around in the same area?"

"There's quite a bit of tide that slops around the harbour, and that on its own could move the boat quite a way. And that's without the wind and any drive from the engine, which, as you say, must have been running and might have been driving."

"So it could have been miles away when Shane got off? However that happened. In which case there doesn't seem a lot of point in searching further. Either he's going to come back here or he isn't."

"Well, there might be," Melissa disagreed. "We could go round that part of the harbour one more time. We know now we're not looking for the lifeboat. Just for Shane."

"It's a good point, Melissa. Let's do that tomorrow. We should also wait here for a couple of days in case he changes his mind."

"OK. It's agreed," Xanthe announced.

Later that evening, after another supper full of silences, Jack and Xanthe found themselves the last two people awake, not counting William who they could just see watching them through the window of his stable.

"I suppose it's yet another way that life has changed now. The not knowing." Xanthe started.

"What do you mean?"

"Well, if Shane had gone missing in normal life, there would be search parties and all of that malarkey. We would know what had happened. If he had died then his body would be found and if he tried to vanish then we would find out where he had gone."

"Not necessarily. People went missing before. The police have filing cabinets full of them."

"Not that many people. And you know what I mean," she gave his shoulder a gentle punch to emphasize her point. "People did go missing, but not many. Especially children, because so many resources were available to find them. The only time children went missing was when a stranger took them, and we can be pretty confident that that didn't happen to Shane. But now it's just us and we're going to have to settle for the fact that we just don't know."

Jack was silent and they both thought about it.

"It's sad, and scary. But it's also just plain annoying. And frustrating," she finished off. "It is *so* annoying that we just don't know."

"It is that," Jack agreed. "But we're just going to have to accept it and move on. Unless he turns up tomorrow, of course."

They lowered another lifeboat and Tim and Melissa carried out the experiment that Shane was conducting, combining it with another search of the eastern half of the harbour. But the only result was a prediction of the range of the lifeboat, which was about sixty nautical miles.

In the meantime, Jack sourced a horsebox full of large plastic jerry cans and filled twenty of them with diesel since, as best as he could tell, the lifeboats ran on the same fuel as diesel trucks. These twenty he then strapped securely into William's lifeboat and hoisted into place on the side of the *Pacific Sun*. This should give that lifeboat close to a hundred and fifty miles range, although it would take fifteen hours to cover that distance, by Jack's calculations.

With the search lifeboat returned and all preparations done there was then nothing to do but wait. At dinner that evening they agreed they would wait two more full days, making it four since Shane disappeared. They debated over the number, but in the end decided that four days was probably long enough.

The days passed slowly, with all preparations now complete for the journey. Tim spent most of his time on the bridge, fiddling with the various systems up there. A few times Jack felt the deck throb under his feet as Tim fired up the engines, and a couple of times there was distinct movement as he engaged a drive system briefly. Melissa spent most of her time with Tim, which left Jack, Emily, Xanthe and, of course, William, Rufus and Alf kicking their heels, paws and hooves on William's deck.

Emily had a brief panic over William's supplies, prompting a trip out to a riding school to retrieve more hay and some salt licks. But other than that there was little to do, and the three lazed, reading books about a vanished world. At Tim's request, Jack also started reading the manuals that Tim had found down in the engine room, in an effort to learn about any vital maintenance tasks that might be needed.

Jack debated filling the large swimming pool, which was the central feature of William's deck, with water from the *Pacific Sun*'s vast tanks, but in the end decided that it was just too wasteful. He certainly didn't want to live to regret it, and so instead filled the smaller round pool near the stern on that same deck. He and Xanthe also went into town and found some rechargeable radio handsets. They were all spending more time than they liked wandering around the *Pacific Sun* trying to find each other and so the handsets were charged and handed out and a channel picked. All five agreed to wear their radios all the time so they could be found. The little group passed the time with a swim as they waited, hoping that Shane would return.

But he did not and on the evening of the second day of waiting they discussed their plans one more time.

"So do we just leave him?" It was Melissa who asked the question.

"If he's chosen not to come with us then he might still change his mind," Xanthe pointed out, her brow furrowed. "But equally he might not. We could wait weeks and for nothing."

"We have no deadline," was Jack's comment. "We could wait." He said this but the waiting was really preying on his nerves. While he was working the internal pressure was held at bay but with enforced laziness it came back with a vengeance. He wanted to be fair to Shane, but he also wanted to leave. To get home.

"That's true," Tim agreed. "But equally we've given him four days and there's no sign. If he doesn't want to leave with us then there's no point in waiting."

"And being realistic, if he didn't choose to abandon the lifeboat then he's probably not turning up now. I know that sound harsh but I think it's true." This from Xanthe.

"We can debate it all night. Shall we vote?" Tim looked round at the others.

"We can't ask Emily to do that," Xanthe put her hand on the little girl's shoulder as she sat silently, eyes wide and face serious.

"I agree, which means we have an even number. I suggest if we are evenly split that we wait another day. We should have a clear majority to leave." This was Melissa's suggestion.

"OK. I'm afraid I vote we go tomorrow," Tim answered straight away. His thin face looked round at them one by one. "I know it's seems mean, but I don't think Shane is coming back, I'm afraid. If I did I would vote the other way."

"I'm not going to vote. I can't decide," Melissa looked pained by the process, shooting Tim an apologetic look.

"I also vote we leave," Xanthe was next. "I agree with Tim. I don't think Shane is coming back."

"Which means I don't need to vote," Jack was relieved. "There's a clear majority to go tomorrow, so we're leaving to see what we can find out there."

"But if you did have to vote, which way would you go?" Xanthe looked him in the eye and there was a silence as he thought about not answering.

"I vote to leave tomorrow as well. I'm with you two." It was decided.

The morning of the departure was all activity again after two days of quiet. If five people alone on a massive cruise ship could be called activity. Emily was tasked with loading William into his lifeboat, along with the dogs, and keeping them happy, so that this wouldn't have to be done after the ship had started sinking in the event Tim's manoeuvring wasn't a success.

Jack and Xanthe were the cast off crew. All five went through the plan one more time on the bridge.

They stood clustered around the chart table feeling nervous. Jack noted how close together Tim and Melissa stood as Tim directed the meeting. He was fairly sure that Melissa and Tim shared a cabin, but nothing had been said. Jack was happy for the young couple, who both seemed so much more confident then that night in the Botanicals when they had first met.

"Right. We've got forty-five minutes until high tide," Tim was all business. "I want to leave a bit before high tide so that we can manoeuvre out under the bridge while the water is slack."

"Let's go through it one more time. The main challenge is to avoid the shallow area here," he pointed at the large-scale paper chart of the harbour, "and also this spit here. We need to get the ship turned between these two as quickly as we can since we'll have no serious steerage way. But first you two cast off all ropes and cables except a single bow and stern rope."

"Should we try and bring the ropes on to the ship?" Jack asked. "We might need them later if we want to dock again, and we're obviously not going to be able to keep the bow or stern ropes."

"No, I don't think so," the young man answered. "I don't think we would ever try and dock this thing. That'd be worse than trying to land a jumbo. When we want to go ashore we will anchor and go in a lifeboat."

"OK. You're the skipper," Xanthe gave him an encouraging smile, and he nodded in acknowledgment.

"So when I give the word on the radio…"

"Why don't you sound the hooter?" Emily asked.

"I don't think…" he trailed off and was silent for a moment.

"Actually that's a good idea," he grinned, looking younger than ever. "When I sound the hooter you cast off the bow rope and run straight back to the stern rope. OK?"

"Got it," Jack turned to Emily. "When you hear the hooter you need to make sure you are with William in the lifeboat to keep him calm. OK? It's your job to look after William, Rufus and Alf as we do this."

"Aye, aye, skipper," Emily saluted.

"I'm not the skipper. I think I'm the second mate," Jack smiled. "One last suggestion, Tim. If we do hit something, or you think we're definitely going to, then use the hooter to signal abandon ship."

"OK. Three blasts on the hooter means abandon ship. If you hear that then head straight to William's lifeboat. Agreed?"

The ship's hooter sounded a long blast, shockingly loud in the quiet morning air. Xanthe turned to Jack and raised an eyebrow.

"Here we go," she said. "Do your thing." It took Jack two pulls on the starter rope of the chainsaw he was holding to get it running. He waved Xanthe clear as he stepped up to the enormous rope where it fed through the rail and revved the saw to full speed.

The fibres sprang apart as he touched the blade to the top of the rope and Jack applied a bit more pressure, keeping his head clear of the line of the blade. He was worried that there might be metal strands within the structure of the rope, but the saw continued to cut swiftly through. The final section ripped apart without assistance as the tension that the *Pacific Sun*'s hidden winches had applied snapped the remaining fibres, springing the mighty rope back across the deck. Jack killed the chainsaw engine, leaving sudden silence.

"Bow rope's gone," Xanthe spoke into her handset. Despite the cable being clear Jack could feel no movement in the deck below his feet.

"Acknowledged," came Melissa's voice.

As Jack and Xanthe started to jog towards the stern a rumbling started below their feet. They both peered over the rail and saw green water boiling in the widening gap between the white hull and dock. The bow-thruster was obviously working, pushing the nose of the giant vessel clear of the concrete.

Tim didn't give the bow-thruster long and by the time Jack and Xanthe arrived at the stern rope it was already silent. Even from here Jack could see that the ship was angling out from the dock.

"We're at the stern rope. Let us know when you want us to cut it," Xanthe spoke into the radio.

"Tim says now," crackled the reply.

"OK. Here we go." The chainsaw fired on the first pull and Jack made short work of the stern rope, after checking that both he and Xanthe would be clear of any backlash. This turned out to be an unnecessary precaution as there seemed to be little tension on their final link with the Australian mainland. The rope fell away and Jack killed the chainsaw and put it down on the deck.

"The stern rope's away," Xanthe announced.

"OK. Thanks," Melissa replied, with nerves or excitement clear in her voice.

"Shall we go up to the bridge and watch Tim at work?" Jack asked Xanthe.

"I suppose so," she answered, although had a slightly wistful look on her face as she looked at the widening gap between the *Pacific Sun* and Australia. As she turned, giving him another of those slightly twisted smiles, a deep throbbing built up under the deck as, for the first time, the main engines started to push the huge craft forward.

By the time the two of them were on the bridge, the *Pacific Sun* was well clear of the dock and seemingly inching forward.

"We're making three knots and I think that's enough," Tim told them as he cut the throttles. "She's already responding a little to the helm and as soon as the bow is clear of the spit I'll begin bringing her head round with the bow-thruster."

The ship continued to inch forward, with Jack and Xanthe watching from the balcony that stuck out of the right-hand side of the bridge. It afforded a superb view as they came up towards the Sydney Harbour Bridge.

As they drew level with it, the rumble of the bow-thruster started again and this time stayed on for quite a few minutes as the ship pivoted slowly around to face the gap under the bridge.

"How's it going?" Jack asked as Tim, who had been flitting around the bridge, rushed out to scan from their vantage point for a moment.

"OK. I think. We're still in the middle of the channel. Which is the main thing," was all Tim answered before scurrying back inside.

Once she was lined up with the bridge the main engine throb started again, even stronger than before, as Tim gave it full power. Slowly and surely the *Pacific Sun* began to gather forward momentum. Xanthe leaned on the railing, peering up at the famous bridge as they passed underneath, its ancient steel devoid of the hum of traffic. Jack too peered up but rather than any kind of feeling of loss he felt only excitement and relief. They were at last on their way.

"Did you know it's Christmas Eve today?" he asked her.

"Really? No I didn't. Why didn't you say?"

"It seemed wrong to get excited about Christmas with all this," he gestured to indicate Sydney, its empty skyscrapers rising behind the Opera House as it slid slowly past them.

"Well we should have a special meal tomorrow. Christmas Day."

Tim stepped out on to the balcony again, with Melissa in his wake.

"How are we doing, Captain?" Xanthe asked him.

"Pretty good, actually. You know that was easier than I expected. We're doing ten knots now and I'm just using the self-steerer to maintain course. We'll maintain this speed until we're clear of the Heads, I think."

Jack clapped Tim on the shoulder. "Well done, Tim. That's awesome." The two shook hands as Tim's smile turned a little embarrassed.

"I think I was lucky."

"Rubbish. Good preparation and then accurate execution. Perfect."

"And the log is showing the ship's range with the current fuel load as well," Tim commented slightly absent-mindedly as he stared ahead, his pose still showing his excitement and concentration.

"What does it say?" Jack was genuinely curious.

"It's saying over three thousand miles and counting up. I think once we're up to speed we'll probably have over five thousand. If the engines keep running that long."

"Well, so far so good," Xanthe murmured.

"How much chance of going aground from here?" Melissa asked.

"Not much, actually. There's plenty of room and no need to worry about hitting any other boats."

Melissa lifted the radio to her lips. "Emily. We're clear now. You can come up to the bridge."

"I'm coming," Emily chirruped in reply.

And so the whole group assembled on the wing of the bridge of the mighty ship and watched the Sydney skyline slip behind them. Tim made frequent trips inside to make course adjustments, but other than that they stood together saying little.

Jack thought back over the last month and all that had happened as he watched Australia slip away. So much had happened it was hard to imagine he was the same man who had arrived on these shores. In fact, he reflected, he most certainly wasn't the same man. They had all changed beyond recognition, been forced into a new and more self-reliant mode of life that would never have occurred to any of them before the plague.

He looked around at his companions, each gazing out as the shore slid past.

Melissa, so timid when they had first met, but now blossoming and into a confident and resourceful woman, whose intelligence and common sense were becoming increasingly evident. And she was brave, there was no doubting that. He would never forget what she had done for him. Her decisive action meant that he owed her his life, quite literally.

Her companion Tim, also seemed utterly changed. From a young man who enjoyed an academic discussion, to one who could make a plan and bring it to reality. Like Melissa, a surprising confidence was underneath his shy exterior and his ability to make decisions and get things done was becoming impressive. Jack only needed to look about at the vast ship that Tim had successfully piloted out of Sydney Harbour to see the evidence of that.

Jack also found himself wondering if Tim and Melissa were happier now than they had been before the epidemic. They had both lost family members, but they had found each other. Maybe that, along with the opportunity to act without criticism, had actually improved their lives. He was sure that neither would admit to it, but looking at them now he was pretty sure they were enjoying being wrapped up in their adventure. The satisfaction that Tim was gaining from captaining the *Pacific Sun*, and the pride that Melissa showed in his performance, shone out from both their faces.

Emily was standing next to Xanthe, who had arm around the little girl. There was no doubt that out of all of them Emily had had the toughest ride, and was still recovering from her emotional wounds. She was growing to trust them, especially Xanthe, but it would be quite a while before they saw her genuinely smile and laugh without the spectre of her loss lurking behind her wide eyes. Jack felt enormously protective of her, and was self-aware enough to know that she was, in part, a proxy for his own daughters on the other side of the world.

The missing presence in the group was palpable to Jack as he considered his companions. Were they also thinking of the absence that stood among them? They would never know now what had happened to Shane and, frustrating though it was, they would all have to come to terms with it. Although Jack had not spoken the thought aloud, he felt that in all likelihood Shane had died that day. However there would never be confirmation of this theory and so he just had to let it go.

The last in the group was Xanthe. Diminutive, assured, sensible, practical. Beautiful. Complicated. She stood, hugging Emily to her in the sun as the breeze picked up and ruffled their hair, and he wondered what the future held for them. He still had mixed feelings about the nurse but there was no doubt that she was right. They were in this together. It was a long way from here to England, but they would tackle that journey as a team.

The wind was rising further as the ship picked up more speed and Jack leant against the railing. He peered down at the blue green sea below as it foamed past the white hull and then looked back up at his companions. He didn't know what was going on in the heads around him but he watched with strong emotions as the little group stared back at the North and South Heads falling astern. *The little family* Jack thought to himself. *We're a family now. Five humans, two dogs, fifteen chickens and a horse.* He had no idea what they would find on this voyage but they were on course to find it.

Reader,

Now that you've finished, I hope you enjoyed this tale. I certainly enjoyed writing it.

If you have any comments then please feel free to send them to me at:

areturnticket@gmail.com

Tom Duke

Made in the USA
Lexington, KY
13 November 2013